WHITE MARS

ALSO BY BRIAN ALDISS

*The Twinkling of an Eye: Or, My
Life as an Englishman* (1998)

Common Clay: 20-Odd Stories (1995)

The Detached Retina (1995)

At the Caligula Hotel (1995)

Somewhere East of Life (1994)

A Tupolev Too Far (1993)

Remembrance Day (1993)

Dracula Unbound (1991)

Forgotten Life (1989)

A Romance of the Equator (1989)

The Year Before Yesterday (1987)

Trillion Year Spree (with David
Wingrove) (1986)

Seasons in Flight (1986)

Helliconia Winter (1985)

Helliconia Summer (1983)

Helliconia Spring (1982)

An Island Called Moreau (1981)

Life in the West (1980)

A Rude Awakening (1978)

Enemies of the System (1978)

Brothers of the Head (1977)

Last Orders (1977)

The Malacia Tapestry (1977)

The Eighty-Minute Hour (1974)

Frankenstein Unbound (1973)

A Soldier Erect (1971)

Neanderthal Planet (1970)

The Hand-Reared Boy (1970)

The Moment of Eclipse (1970)

The Shape of Further Things (1970)

Barefoot in the Head (1969)

Report on Probability A (1969)

Cryptozoic (1968)

Who Can Replace a Man? (1966)

Cities and Stones (1966)

Earthworks (1965)

The Dark-Light Years (1964)

Greybeard (1964)

The Long Afternoon of Earth (1962)

The Primal Urge (1961)

Galaxies Like Grains of Sand (1960)

Starship (1959)

No Time Like Tomorrow (1959)

*Space, Time and Nathaniel
(Presciences)* (1957)

The Brightfount Diaries (1955)

ALSO BY ROGER PENROSE

The Large, the Small and the Human Mind (1997)

Shadows of the Mind (1994)

The Emperor's New Mind (1989)

WHITE MARS

Or, The Mind Set Free
A 21st-Century Utopia

BRIAN W. ALDISS

in collaboration with

ROGER PENROSE

St. Martin's Press ♏ New York

Library of Congress Cataloging-in-Publication Data

Aldiss, Brian Wilson.
    White Mars, or, The mind set free : a 21st century utopia / Brian
W. Aldiss in collaboration with Roger Penrose.—1st U.S. ed.
        p.   cm.
    ISBN 0-312-25473-3
    1. Twenty-first century—Fiction. 2. Mars (Planet)—Fiction.
3. Utopias—Fiction. I. Title: Mind set free. II. Penrose, Roger.
III. Title.

PR6051.L3W47   2000
823'.914—dc21   99-462291

First published in Great Britain by Little, Brown and Company

First U.S. Edition: April 2000

10 9 8 7 6 5 4 3 2 1

Dedicated to the Warden and Fellows
of
Green College, Oxford

This people is 500 miles from Utopia eastward
                    Sir Thomas More, *Utopia*

We are getting to the end of visioning
The impossible within this universe,
Such as that better whiles may follow worse,
And that our race may mend by reasoning
          Thomas Hardy, *We Are Getting To The End*

Contents

Memoir by Moreton Dennett, Secretary to Leo Anstruther,
Concerning the Events of 23 June AD 2041

On this day, Leo Anstruther decided he would walk to the
jetport because he believed in being unpredictable. I went
with him, carrying his notecase. Two bodyguards walked
behind us, following at a short distance.

We wound our way down narrow back streets. Anstruther
walked with his hands clasped behind his back, seemingly
deep in thought. This was a part of his island he rarely
visited; it held few charms for him. It was poverty alley. The
narrow houses had been sub-divided in many cases, so that
their occupants had overflowed into the streets to pursue their
livelihoods. Vulcanisers, toy-makers, shoemakers, kite-sellers,
junk-dealers, chandlers, fishermen and sellers of foodstuffs –
all obstructed the freeway with their various businesses.

I knew Anstruther had a concealed contempt for these
unfortunates. These people, no matter how hard they
worked, would never improve their lot. They had no vision.
He often said it. Anstruther was the man of vision.

He paused abruptly in a crowded square, looking about
him at the shabby tenements on all sides.

'It's not just the poor who help the poor, as the absurd
saying has it,' he said, addressing me although he looked
elsewhere, 'but the poor who exploit the poor. They rent
out their sordid rooms at extortionate rates to other families, inflicting misery on their own families for the sake of
a few extra shekels.'

I agreed. 'It's not a perfect world.' It was my job to
agree.

Among the dreary muddle of commerce, a bright stall

stood out. An elderly man dressed in jeans and a khaki shirt stood behind a small table on which were stacked jars of preserved fruit, together with mangoes, blackcurrants, pineapples and cherries, as well as a handful of fresh vegetables.

'All home-grown and pure, señor. Buy and try!' cried the old man as Anstruther paused.

Observing Anstruther's scepticism, he quoted a special low price per jar for his jams.

'We eat only factory food,' I told him. He ignored me and continued to address Anstruther.

'See my garden, master, how pure and sweet it is.' The old man gestured to the wrought-iron gate at his back. 'Here's where my produce comes from. From the earth itself, not from a factory.'

Anstruther glanced at the phone-watch on his wrist.

'Garden!' he said with contempt. Then he laughed. 'Why not? Come on, Moreton.' He liked to be unpredictable. He gestured to the bodyguards to stay alert by the stall. On a sudden decision, he pushed through the gate and entered the old fellow's garden. He slammed the gate behind us. It would give the security men something to think about.

An elderly woman was sitting on an upturned tub, sorting peppers into a pot. A sweet-smelling jasmine on an overhead trellis shaded her from direct sunlight. She looked up in startlement, then gave Anstruther and me a pleasant smile.

'Buenos dias, masters. You've come to look about our little paradise, of that I'm certain. Don't be shy, now.'

As she spoke, she rose, straightened her back and approached us. Beneath the wrinkles she had a pleasant round face, and though fragile with age stood alertly upright. She wiped her hands on an old beige apron tied about her waist and gave us something like a bow.

'Paradise, you say! It's a narrow paradise you have here, woman.' Anstruther was looking down its length, which was circumscribed by tile-topped walls.

'Narrow but long, and enough for the likes of Andy

2

and me, master. We have what we require, and do not covet more.'

Anstruther gave his short bark of laughter. 'Why not covet more, woman? You'd live better with more.'

'We should not live better by coveting more, merely more discontentedly, sir.'

She proceeded to show her visitors the garden. The enclosing walls became concealed behind climbers and vines.

Their way led with seeming randomness among flowering bushes and little shady arbours under blossom trees. The paths were narrow, so that they brushed by red and green peppers, a manioc patch and clumps of lavender and rosemary, which gave off pleasant scents as they were touched. Vegetables grew higgledy-piggledy with other plants. The hubbub of the streets was subdued by a murmur that came from bees blundering among flowers and the twitter of birds overhead.

The woman's commentary was sporadic. 'I can't abide seeing bare earth. This bit of ground here I planted with comfrey as a child, and you see how it's flourished ever since. It's good for the purity of the blood.'

Anstruther flicked away a bee that flew too near his face. 'All this must cost you something in fertiliser, woman.'

She smiled up at him. 'No, no, señor. We're too poor for that kind of unwise outlay. Human water and human waste products are all the fertilising we require in our little property.'

'You're not on proper drainage? Are you on the Ambient?'

'What's that, the Ambient?'

'Universal electronic communication system. You've never heard of it? The American bio-electronic net?'

'We are too hard-up for such a thing, sir, you must understand. Nor do we require it for our kind of modest living. Would it add to our contentment? Not a jot. What the rest of the world does is no business of ours.' She searched his face for some kind of approval. He in his turn

3

studied her old worn countenance, brown and wrinkled, from which brown eyes stared.

'You say you're content?' He spoke incredulously, as though the idea was new to him.

She gave no answer, continuing to gaze at him with an expression between contempt and curiosity, as if Anstruther had arrived from another planet.

Resenting her probing regard, he turned and commenced to walk back the way we had come.

'You aren't accustomed to gardens, I perceive, señor.' There was pride in her voice. 'Do you shut yourself in rooms, then? We don't ask for much. For us, ours is a little paradise, don't you see? The soil's so rich in worms, that's the secret. We're almost self-sufficient here, Andy and me. We don't ask for much.'

He said, half joking, 'But you enjoy moralising. As we all do.'

'I only tell you the truth, sir, since you invited yourself in here.'

'I was curious to see how you people lived,' he told her. 'Today, I'm off to discuss the future of the planet Mars – which you've probably never heard of.'

She had heard of Mars. She considered it uninteresting, since there was no life there.

'No worms, eh, my good woman? Couldn't you do something better with your life than growing vegetables in your own excreta?'

She followed us up the winding path, brushing away a tendril of honeysuckle from her face, amused and explaining, 'It's healthy, my good sir, you see. They call it recycling. I've lived in this garden nigh on seventy years and I want nothing else. This little plot was my mother's idea. She said, "Cultivate your garden. Don't disturb the work of the worms. Be content with your lot." And that's what Andy and I have done. We don't wish for Mars. The vegetables and fruits we sell keep us going well enough. We're vegetarian, you see. You two gentlemen aren't from the council, are you?'

4

Something in the tone of her voice stung Anstruther.

'No. Certainly not. So you've simply done what your mother told you all the years of your life! Did you never have any ideas of your own? What does your husband make of you being stuck here for seventy years, just grubbing in the soil?'

'Andy is my brother, master, if you refer to him. And we've been perfectly happy and harmed no one. Nor been impolite to anyone . . .'

We had regained the tiny paved area by the gate. We could smell the fragrance of the thyme, growing in the cracks between the paving stones, crushed underfoot. The two looked at each other in mutual distrust. Anstruther was a tall, solidly built man, who dominated the fragile little woman before him.

He saw she was angry. I feared he might destroy all her contentment with an expression of his irritation at her narrow-mindedness. He held the words back.

'Well, it's a pretty garden you have,' he said. 'Very pretty. I'm glad to have seen it.'

She was pleased by the compliment. 'Perhaps there might be gardens like this on Mars one day,' she suggested, with a certain slyness.

'Not very likely.'

'Perhaps you would like some beans to take away with you?'

'I carry no money.'

'No, no, I mean as a gift. They might improve your temperament after all that factory food you eat.'

'Don't be disgusting. Eat your beans yourself.'

He turned and gestured to me to open the gate. His two security men were waiting for him outside.

Anstruther's jet took us to the UN building. Members of the United Nationalities rarely met in person. They conferred over the Ambient, and only on special occasions were they bodily present; this was such an occasion, when the future of the planet Mars was to be decided. For this reason, the United Nationalities building was small, and not particularly imposing, although in fact it was larger than it needed to be, to satisfy the egos of its members.

On my Ambient I called Legalassist on the third level and gained entry to their department while Anstruther fraternised with other delegates below.

A Euripides screened me various files on EUPACUS, the international consortium whose component nations – the European Union, the Pacific Rim nations, and the United States – all had a claim on Mars.

Flicking to a file on the legal history of Antarctica, I saw that a similar situation had once existed there. Twelve nations had all laid claim to a slice of the White Continent. In December 1959 representatives of these nations had drawn up an Antarctic Treaty, which came into effect in June 1961. The treaty represented a remarkable step forward for reason and international cooperation. Territorial disputes were suspended, all military activities banned, and the Antarctic became a Continent for Science.

I took print-outs of relevant details. They might prove useful in the forthcoming debate. What the twentieth century had managed, we could certainly better, and on a grander scale, in our century.

In the ground-floor reception rooms, I found my boss consorting with Korean, Japanese, Chinese and Malay diplomats, all members of interested Pacrim countries. Anstruther was improving his shining image. A great amount of smiling by activating the zygomatic muscle went on, as is customary during such encounters.

When the session gong sounded, I accompanied Anstruther into the Great Hall, where we took our assigned places. Once I was seated at a desk in the row behind him, I passed him the Legalassist prints. Unpredictable as ever, he barely glanced at them.

'Today's the time for oratory, not facts,' he said. His voice was remote. He was psyching himself up for the debate.

When all delegates were assembled and quiet prevailed

6

in the hall, the General Secretary made his announcement: 'This is the General Assembly of the United Nationalities, meeting on 23 June 2041, to determine the future status of Planet Mars.'

The first speaker was called.

Svetlana Yulichieva of Russia was eloquent. She said that the manned landing on Mars marked a new page, if not a new volume, in the history of mankind. All nationalities rejoiced in the success of the Mars mission, despite the tragic loss of their captain. The way of the future was now clear. More landings must be financed, and preparations be made to terraform Mars, so that it could be properly colonised and used as a base for further exploration of the outer solar system. She suggested that Mars come under UN jurisdiction.

The Latvian delegate was eloquent. He agreed with Yulichieva's sentiments and said that the space-going nations must be congratulated on the enterprise they had shown. The loss of Captain Tracy was regretted, but must not be allowed to impede further progress. Was not, he asked rhetorically, the opening-up of a new world part of a human dream, the dream of going forth to conquer space, as envisioned in many fictions, book and film, in which mankind went forward boldly, overcoming everything hostile which stood in its way, occupying planet after planet? The beginning of the eventual encompassing of the galaxy had begun. The terraforming of Mars must assume top priority.

The Argentinian delegate, Maria Porua, begged to disagree. She spoke at length of the hideous costs of an enterprise such as terraforming, the success of which was not guaranteed. Recent disappointments, such as the failure of the hypercollider on the Moon – the brainchild of a Nobel Prize winner – must act as a caution. There were terrestrial problems enough, on which the enormous investments required for any extraterrestrial adventure could more profitably be spent.

Tobias Bengtson, the delegate for Sweden, scorned the last speaker's response to a magnificent leap into an expanding future. He reminded the assembly of the words of Konstantin Tsiolkovsky, the great Russian aeronautical engineer, who had said that Earth was the cradle of mankind, but that mankind could not remain for ever in the cradle. 'This great nineteenth-century visionary woke up the human race to its destiny in space. The dream has grown more real, more accurate, more pressing, as the years have progressed. A glorious prospect must not be allowed to slip away. A few deaths, a little expense, along the way must not deflect the nationalities from achieving our destiny, the conquest of all solar space, from the planet Mercury right out to the heliopause. Only then will the dreams of our forefathers – and our mothers – be fulfilled.'

Other speakers rose, many arguing that terraforming was a necessity. Why go to Mars if not to create more living space? Some warned that Mars would become a United States dependency, others that a ruling was required, otherwise competing nations would use Mars not as living space, but as a battlefield.

'I am going to talk practicalities,' said a delegate from the Netherlands. 'I have listened to a lot of airy-fairy talk here today. The reality is that we have now acquired this entire little planet of waste land. What are we to do with it? It's no good for anything.' He thumped the desk for emphasis. 'Who'd want to live there? You can't grow anything on it. But we can dump our dangerous nuclear waste on Mars. It would be safe there. You can build a mountain of waste by one of the poles – it might even make the place look a bit more interesting.'

It was Leo Anstruther's turn to speak. The antagonism generated against the previous delegate's speech gave him the opportunity to put his argument forward. He walked deliberately to the rostrum, where he scrutinised the assembly before speaking.

'Do you have to act out the dreams of your mothers and fathers?' he asked. 'If we had always done so, would we not still be sitting in a jungle in the middle of Africa, going in fear of the tribe in the next tree? EUPACUS – and not

8

simply NASA – has achieved a great feat of organisation and engineering, for which we sincerely congratulate them. But this arrival of a crew of men and women on the Red Planet must have nothing to do with conquest. Nor should we turn the place into a rubbish dump. Have we lost our reverence for the universe about us?'

My boss went on to say that he had nothing but contempt for people who merely sat at home. But going forward did not mean merely proliferation; proliferation was already bringing ruin to Earth. Everyone had to be clear that to repeat our errors on other planets was not progress. It more closely resembled rabbits overrunning a valuable field of wheat. Now was our chance to prove that we had progressed in Realms of Reason, as well as in Terms of Technology.

What, after all, he asked, were these dreams of conquest that mankind was supposed to approve? Were they not violent and xenophobic? We had not to permit ourselves to live a fiction about other fictions. To attempt to fulfil them was to take a downward path at the very moment an upward path opened before us, to crown our century.

The old ethos of the nineteenth and twentieth centuries had been crude and bloody, and had brought about untold misery. It had to be abandoned, and here was a God-given chance to abandon it. He disapproved of that too readily used metaphor that said 'a new page in history had been turned'. Now was the time to throw away that old history book, and to begin anew as a putative interplanetary race. Delegates had to consider dispassionately whether to embark on a new mode of existence, or to repeat the often bloody mistakes of yesterday. 'All environments are sacrosanct,' Anstruther declared. 'The planet Mars is a sacrosanct environment and must be treated as such. It has not existed untouched for millions of years only to be reduced to one of Earth's tawdry suburbs today. My strong recommendation is that Mars be preserved, as the Antarctic has been preserved for many years, as a place of wonder and meditation, a symbol of our future guardianship of the entire solar system – a planet for science, a White Mars.'

The General Secretary declared a break for lunch.

The German delegate, Thomas Gunther, came up to Anstruther, glass in hand. He nodded cordially to us both.

'You have a fine style of rhetoric, Leo,' he said. 'I am on your side against the mad terraformers, although I don't quite manage to think of Mars as in any way sacred, as you imply. After all, it is just a dead world – not a single old temple there. Not even an old grave, or a few bones.'

'No worms either, Thomas, I'm led to believe.'

'According to latest reports, there's no life on it of any kind, and maybe never has been. "Martians" are just one of those myths we have lumbered ourselves with. We need no more silly nonsense of that kind.'

He smiled teasingly at Anstruther, as if challenging him to disagree. When Anstruther made no answer, Gunther developed his line of argument. The safe arrival of men on the Red Planet could be traced back to the German astronomer, Johannes Kepler, who – in the midst of the madness of the Thirty Years War – formulated the laws of planetary motion. Kepler was one of those men who, rather like Anstruther, defied the assumptions of others.

To declare for the first time that the orbit of a planet was an ellipse, with the sun situated at one focus, was a brave statement with far-reaching consequences. Similarly, what was decided on this day, in the hall of the UN, would have far-reaching consequences, for good or ill. Brave statements were required once more.

Gunther said his strong prompting was not to vex the delegates with talk of the sanctity of Mars. Since much – everything, indeed – was owed to science, then the planet must be kept for science. Sow in the minds of delegates the doubt whether the long elaborate processes of terraforming could succeed. Terraforming so far existed only in laboratory experiments. It was originally an idea

10

cooked up by a science fiction writer. It would be foolhardy to try it out on a whole planet – particularly the one planet easily accessible to mankind.

'You could quote,' Gunther said, 'the words of a Frenchman, Henri de Chatelier, who in 1888 spoke of the principle of opposition in any natural system to further change. Mars itself would resist terraforming if any organisation was rash enough to try it.'

He advised Anstruther to stick with the slogan 'White Mars'. The simple common mind, which he deplored as much as Anstruther, would wish something to be done with Mars. Very well. Then what should be done was to dedicate the planet to science and allow only scientists on its surface – its admittedly unprepossessing surface. People should not be allowed to do their worst there, building their hideous office blocks and car parks and fast-food stalls. They must be stopped, as they had been prevented from invading the Antarctic. He and Anstruther must fight together to preserve Mars for science. He believed there was a delegate from California who thought as they did.

After all, he concluded, there were experiments that could be conducted only on that world.

'What experiments do you mean?' Anstruther enquired.

At this, Gunther hesitated. 'You will think me self-interested when I speak. That is not the case. I seize on my example because it comes readily to mind. Perhaps we might go out on a balcony, since there are those near us anxious to overhear what we say. Take a samosa with you. I assure you they are delicious.'

'My secretary always accompanies me, Thomas.'

'As you like.' He threw me a suspicious glance.

The two men went out on the nearest balcony, and I followed them. The balcony overlooked beautiful Lake Louise, the pellucid waters of which seemed to lend colour to the sky.

'No doubt you know what I mean by "the Omega Smudge"?' Gunther said. 'It's the elusive final ghost of a particle. When it's known – all's known! As I presume you are aware, I am the president of a bank that, together with the Korean Investment Corporation, financed a search for the Gamma Smudge on Luna, following the postulate of the Chin Lim Chung-Dreiser Hawkwood formulation.' He bit into his samosa and talked round a mouthful.

'It was thought that the lunar vacuum would provide ideal conditions for research. Unfortunately, the fools were already busy up there, erecting their hotels and supermarkets and buggy parks and drilling for this and that. As you know, they have now almost finished construction on a subway designed to carry busybodies back and forth to their nasty little offices and eateries.

'At great expense, we built our ring – our superconducting search ring. Useless!'

'You did not find your smudge, I hear.'

'It is not to be found on the Moon. The drilling and the subway vibration have driven it off. Certainly experts argue about whether that was so – but experts will argue about anything. It has still to be discovered.' Gunther went on to explain that the high-energy detection of the Beta Smudge nearly two decades ago had merely disclosed a further something, a mess of resonances – another smudge. Gunther's bank was prepared to fund a different sort of research, to pin down a hidden symmetry monopole.

'And if you find it?' Anstruther asked, not concealing his scepticism.

'Then the world is changed ... And I'll have changed it!' Gunther puffed out his chest and clenched his hands. 'Leo, the Americans and the Russians have tried to find this particle, and others, without success. It has an almost mystical importance. This elusive little gizmo so far remains little more than an hypothesis, but it is believed to be responsible for assigning mass to all other kinds of particle in the universe. Can you imagine its importance?'

'We're talking about a destroyer of worlds?'

Gunther gestured dismissively. 'In the wrong hands, yes, I suppose so. But in the right hands this elusive smudge will provide ultimate power, power to travel right across the galaxy at speeds exceeding the speed of light.'

Anstruther snorted to show he regarded such talk as ridiculous.

'Well, that's all hypothetical and I'm no expert,' said Gunther, defensively, and went on, laying emphasis on his words. 'I am not yet ruined and I wish for this quest to be continued. It can be continued only on Mars. I know I can raise the money. We can find the Omega Smudge there, and transcend Einstein's equations – if we fight today to keep Mars free of the terraformers.'

Anstruther gave me a glance, as if to show that he was aware of Gunther's bluster. All he asked, coolly, was, 'What in practical terms do you have against terraforming?'

'Our search needs silence – absence of vibration. Mars is the only silent place left in the habitable universe, my friend!'

When the bell rang for the afternoon session, the delegates trooped back to their places in a more sober mood than previously. The delegate for Nicaragua gave voice to a general uncertainty.

'We are required to pronounce judgement on the future of Mars. But can "judgement" possibly be a proper description for what will conclude our discussions? Are we not just seeking to relieve ourselves of a situation of moral complexity? How can we judge wisely on what is almost entirely an unknown? Let us therefore decide that Mars is sacrosanct, if only for a while. I suggest that it comes under UN jurisdiction, and that the UN forbids any reckless developments on that planet – at least until we have made doubly sure that no life exists there.'

Thomas Gunther rose to support this plea.

'Mars must come under UN jurisdiction, as the delegate from Nicaragua says. Any other decision would be a disgrace. The story of colonisation must not be repeated, with its dismal chapters of land devastation and exploitation of workers. Anyone who ventures to Mars must be assured that his rights are guaranteed right here. By maintaining the Red Planet for science, we shall give the world notice that the days of land-grabbing are finally over.

'We want a White Mars.

'This is not an economic decision but a moral one. Some delegates will remember the bitter arguments that raged when we were deciding to move the international dateline from the Pacific to the middle of the Atlantic. That was a development dictated purely by financial interests, for mere convenience of trade between the Republic of California and their partners of the Pacrim. We must now make a more serious decision, in which financial interest plays no part.

'If we are to explore the entire solar system and beyond, then this first step along the way must be marked by favourable omens and wise decisions. We must proceed with due humility and caution, forgetting the damaging fantasies of yesterday.

'I beg you to set aside a whole folklore of interplanetary conquest and to vote for the preservation of Mars – White Mars, as Mr Leo Anstruther has called it. By so doing, we shall speak for knowledge, for wisdom, as opposed to avarice.' Gunther nodded in a friendly way to Anstruther as he strode from the podium.

Other speakers went to the podium to have their say, but now, increasingly, the emphasis was on how and why the Red Planet should be governed.

The sun was setting over the great milky lake beyond the conference hall when the final vote was taken. The General Secretary announced that the UN Department for the Preservation of Mars would be set up, and the White Mars Treaty executed.

Taking Thomas Gunther aside, the Secretary asked casually if Anstruther should be appointed head of the department.

'I would strongly advise against it,' Gunther said. 'The man is too unpredictable.'

2

My eyes had not been trained to see such a panorama. I was disoriented, like my entire physical body depended on my sight. Closing my eyes, I became aware of another source of strangeness. I was standing on solid ground, but I had lost pounds in weight.

Bracing myself, I tried to take account of our surroundings. Beyond the suited figures of my friends lay a world of solitude, infinite and tumbled, with nothing on which the gaze could rest. My mind, checking for something familiar, ran through a number of fantasy landscapes, from Dis to Barsoom, without relief. Grim? Oh yes, it was grim – but marvellously complex, built like a diabolical artist's construct. I was looking at something wonderfully unknown, indigestible, hitherto inaccessible. And I was among the first to take it all in!

And suddenly I found myself flushing. Like a blow to the heart came the thought: But I am of a species more extraordinary than anything else there ever was.

One day all this desolation would be turned into a fertile world much like Earth.

We broke from our trance. Our first task was to unload the body of Captain Tracy from our vehicle and place it in its body bag on the Martian surface. Although he was in his late thirties, Guy Tracy had seemed to be the fittest among us, but the acceleration and later deceleration had brought on the heart attack that killed him before we landed.

This death in Mars's orbit had seemed like a bad omen for the mission, but, as we laid his body down among

15

the rocks of the regolith, a glassy effect flared into the sky as if in welcome. Low, almost beyond the visible, it was, we figured later, an aurora. Charged particles from the sun were interacting with molecules of the thin atmosphere trapped in Mars's slight magnetic field. The ghostly phenomenon seemed to flutter almost at shoulder level. It faded and was gone as we stepped back from the body bag. For a planet receiving sunlight equivalent to only some 40 per cent of Earth's generous ration, the little illumination show was encouraging.

Calls from base broke into our solemn thoughts. We were reluctant to talk back to Earth. They challenged us to say what had gone wrong.

'You have to be here to understand. You have to have made the journey. You have to experience Mars in its majesty to know that to try to alter – to terraform – this ancient place would be wrong. A terrible mistake. Not just for Mars. For us. For all mankind.'

There was a long pained argument. It takes forty minutes for a signal to traverse the distance between Earth and Mars and back – and between experiences. Night came on, sweeping over the plain. The stars glittered overhead.

We waited. We tried to explain.

Base ordered us to continue with our duties.

We said – everything was recorded – 'It is our duty to tell you that humanity's arrival on another planet marks a turning point in our history. We should not alter this planet. We must try to alter ourselves.'

Forty minutes passed. We waited uneasily.

'What do you mean by this talk? Why are you going moral on us?'

After some discussion, we replied, 'There has to be a better way forward.'

After forty minutes, a different voice from base. 'What in hell are you going on about up there? Have you all gone crazy?'

'We said you wouldn't understand.' And we closed the link and went to our bunks. Not a sound disturbed our sleep.

Our salaries, like our training, came from the EUPACUS combine. I knew and trusted their engineering skills. Of their intentions I was less sure. To win the Mars tender, the consortium had agreed merely to run all travel arrangements for ten years and to organise expeditions. I was well aware that they intended to begin the long process of terraforming by the back door, so to speak. Their hidden intentions were to turn Mars into saleable real estate; profitability depended on it. So I was told.

EUPACUS was contracted to run all ground operations on Mars, and could prevent unwanted curiosity there. Their investors would be eager to get their money back with interest, without being too concerned with how it was done. I woke with a firm determination to defy the stockholders.

Like everyone else, our crew had seen and been seduced by computer-generated pictures of EUPACUS-format Mars. Domes and greenhouses were laid out in neat array. Factories were set up for the task of extracting oxygen from the Martian rock. Nuclear suns blazed in the blue sky. In no time, bronzed men in T-shirts stepped forth among green fields, or climbed into bubble cars and drove furiously among Martian mountains already turning green.

Standing amid that magnificent desolation, the salesman's dream fizzled out like a punctured balloon.

We had landed almost on the equator, in the south-western corner of Amazonis Planitia, to the west of the high Tharsis Shield. Our parent ship acted as communication relay satellite, so that we could travel and keep in touch with one another. Highly necessary on a world where the horizon – supposing the terrain to be flat, which it mostly was not – was only 25 miles away. In its areosynchronous orbit, travelling 17,065 kilometres above ground, the ship appeared stationary to us, a reassuring sight when so much was strange.

But before we began our surveying we had to erect our geodesic dome to support a one-millimetre-thick dome fabric. We had been weakened by the months of flight, despite in-board exercise. This weakness turned the building of the dome into a major task, impeded as we were by our space-suits. Night was upon us before we were half finished. We had to retreat back into the module, to wait for morning.

When morning came, out we went again, determined not to let the structure beat us. We needed the dome. It would afford protection against the deepest cold and dust storms. We could exercise here and offload into it some of the machinery that made life in the module maddeningly cramped. Of course, as yet we had no means of filling it with breathable air at a tolerable pressure, even after we made it airtight. Since the dome had to go up, up it eventually went. When the last girders were bolted together and the last tie of the plastic lining secured – why, we needed no more exercise . . .

Our brief was to explore a few kilometres of the planet. Its enormous land area was as great in extent as Earth's, if not quite as various. It had plains, escarpments, riverbeds, vast canyons greater than anything terrestrial and extinct volcanoes – none of them traversed by human beings. We activated the TV cameras, and climbed aboard the two methane-powered buggies, to head eastward.

The intensity of that experience will always remain with me. While folks back home might see nothing on their screens but a kind of broken desert, that journey for us carried a strong emotional charge. It was as if we had travelled back in time, to a period before life had begun in the universe. Everything lay waiting, still, latent, piercing. None of us spoke. We were experiencing a different version of reality – a reality somehow menacing but calming. It was like being under the thunderous eye of God.

As we climbed, the regolith became less rocky. We might have been traversing the palm of an old man's withered hand. On either side were dried gulleys, forming intricate veins, and small impact craters, evidence of the bombard-ment of this world from space. We stopped periodically, taking up samples of rock and soil and storing them in an outer compartment for examination later, always marking the micro-environment from which they came. Since the

18

ground temperature was sixty degrees below, we had little expectation of finding even a micro-organism.

Our progress became slower as the slope became steeper. We were now within sight of the flanks of the massive Tharsis Shield. August, lugubrious, it dominated the way ahead. It would be the subject of a later and better equipped exploration. Once we had caught sight of the graceful dome of Olympus Mons – a volcano long extinct – we turned the vehicles about and went back to base.

For the first kilometre of the return journey, the dust we had disturbed still hung in the thin atmosphere.

The laboratory was in my charge. By sundown, I had begun to test the first rock samples. The gas chromatograph mass spectrometer gave no indication of life. Part disappointed, part relieved, I went to join the others in the canteen for supper.

We were a strangely silent group. We knew something memorable had happened in the history of mankind and wanted to digest the meaning of the occasion. Drilling equipment had been set up in the dome before our excursion. A computer beeping summoned us to judge results. Water had been discovered 1.2 kilometres below ground level. Upon analysis, it was found to be relatively pure and inert. No traces of micro-organisms.

We rejoiced. With a water supply, living on Mars was now practicable. But the way lay open for terraforming.

Cang Hai's Account

3

Should the citizens of the United States, for example, be answerable solely to Martian law when on Mars? Eventual answer: Yes. Mars is not a colony, but an independent world.

This was the sensible legal decision that became the foundation stone for the Deed of Independence that governs our lives on Mars and will stand as exemplar for all the other worlds we inhabit in times to come.

One of the greatest achievements of the last century was the establishing of preliminary planetary surveys. Less acknowledged was a system of workable international law.

From the start, weapons were prohibited here. Smoking is necessarily prohibited, not only as a pollutant but as a needless consumer of oxygen. Only low-grade alcohols are allowed. Habit-forming drugs are unknown. An independent judicial system was soon established. Certain categories of science are encouraged. We owe everything to science.

Under these laws and the laws of nature, we have built our community.

When I think back to this early time just now, I find consolation there. My daughter, Alpha Jefferies – now Alpha Jefferies Greenway – left Mars last year to live on a planet she had never known. I fear for her on that alien globe, although she now has a contract-husband to protect her.

She told me once, when we were still in communication, that Earth is the world of life. My image of it is as a world of death – of starvation, genocides, murders, and many horrors from which our world here does not suffer.

My arguments with my dear lost daughter have caused me to look again at those first years on Mars, when there was an excitement about being on a strange world and we were not entirely free of Earth-generated myths regarding ancient life on Mars, of finding old land-locked canals leading nowhere, or great lost palaces in the deserts, or the tombs of the last Lords of Syrtis! Well, that's all juvenile romanticism, part of the fecundity of human imagination, which sought to populate an empty world. And that is what still thrills me – this great empty world in which we live!

I will introduce myself. I am the adopted daughter of the great Tom Jefferies. I first knew life in the crowded city of Chengdu in China, where I was trained as a teacher of handicapped children. After five years of teaching in the Number Three Disability School, I felt a longing to try another planet. I applied for work on a UN work scheme and was accepted.

For my community service, I served for a year as kennel-maid at a dog-breeding station in Manchuria, where life was extremely hard. I passed the behavioural tests to become a fully fledged YEA. After all the preliminaries, including the two-week MIC – or Martian Inculcation Course – I was permitted to board the EUPACUS ship to Mars, together with two friends, on an ORT, an Opposition Return Trip.

What excitement! What dread!

Although I had anticipated that Mars itself would be bleak, I had not imagined life in the domes, which, by the time I arrived, was unexpectedly colourful. As a reminder of the semi-Oriental composition of Marvelos, the travel bureau subsidiary of EUPACUS which freighted everyone to Mars and back, brilliant lanterns were hung among the simple apartment blocks. Tank-walls of living fish stood everywhere. Flowering trees (originating from

21

Prunus autumnalis subhirtella) were planted along avenues. And what I liked best were the genetically adapted macaws and parrots that cast a scatter of colour as they flew free, and sang with sweet voices instead of croaking.

Apart from this pleasant sound, the domes were reasonably quiet, since the small jojo ('jump-on-jump-off') electric buses taking people about made little noise.

As I grew to know the settlement better, I found this colourful sector was just the 'tourist spot'. Beyond it lay the rather grimmer Permanents Sector, austere and undecorated, lying behind P. Lowell Street.

All this was enclosed, of course, under domes and spicules. Outside lay an airless planet of rumpled rock. My spine tingled just to look out at it.

Not that this view was featureless. To the west lay the rumpled extent of Amazonis Planitia, on the eastern edge of which we were situated. The domes had been built squarely on the 155th latitude, 18 degrees north of the equator. The site was sheltered from ferocious winds, which had built the yardangs to westward.

Our shelter loomed to the east of us, to the immense bulk of Olympus Mons, the cliff-like edges of whose skirts were only some 295 kilometres away. Its seamed slopes were lit every evening by the dull sun.

The Pavonis Observatory began immediately to give brilliant results. Studies of the gas giants became transformed almost into a new branch of astrophysics. Research into earlier temporalities and proto-temporalities was enlarging an understanding of the birth of the universe. Probes launched from the Martian surface had brought back iron-hard samples of ammonia-methane mix from Pluto containing impurities suggesting that the distant planet had its origins beyond the solar system.

A meteorite watch station became operative.

Thomas Gunther's Omega Smudge detector was being established when I made my first trip outside. The tube was under construction. I heard it said that clever lawyers were bending the proscriptions on doing science under Martian law in order to permit a larger ring to be built if needed.

However that was, the research unit, established half a kilometre from the domes (Areopolis as it now is), came under the control of the authoritarian particle physicist, Dreiser Hawkwood.

Because of its later significance, I must report a conversation that took place some time in those early days. It was recorded, as were most discussions in the first years, and now resides in the Martian Archive. Maybe similar conversations took place elsewhere. They assumed importance in the light of later discoveries.

Four scientists in the Pavonis Observatory, perched high on the Tharsis Shield, were talking. The deepest voice was identifiable as that of Dreiser Hawkwood himself. He was a bulky man with an unfashionable moustache and a gloomy expression.

'When we were driving up here,' a woman said, 'I kept thinking I saw white objects like tongues slicking away underground, fast as an oyster goes down a gullet. Tell me I was dreaming.'

'We've established there is no life on Mars. So you were dreaming,' said a colleague.

'Then I was dreaming too,' said another. 'I also saw those white things sticking up, disappearing as we approached. It seemed so unlikely I didn't care to say anything.'

'Could they be worms?'

'What, without topsoil?' Dreiser Hawkwood asked. His deep voice is easily identifiable. He laughed, and his colleagues laughed obediently with him. 'We shall find a natural geological explanation for them in time. They may be a form of stalagmite.'

The fourth member of the group did not contribute to this conversation. He was sitting somewhat distant from his friends, staring out of the canteen window at Olympus Mons, only a few kilometres away.

23

'Must get together an expedition to look at that weird volcano,' he said. 'The largest feature on the planet and we make little of it.'

Olympus Mons was about 550 kilometres across. It rose to 25 kilometres above the Mars datum, in consequence of which it could be seen from Earth even in the days of terrestrial telescopes. It rated as one of the most remarkable objects in the solar system.

Despite the interest of the scientists, increased demand for oxygen and water severely limited exploration work. Fuel for vehicular exploration consumed more oxygen. It was to be some while before Olympus Mons was investigated – or really entered our consciousness to any extent.

I'm not accustomed to being an historian. Why have I set myself this task? Because I was there on that occasion when Tom Jefferies stood up and declared, 'I'm going to kick down a rotten door. I'm going to let light in on human society. I'm going to make us live what we dream of being – great and wise people, cicumspect, daring, inventive, loving, just. People we deserve to be. All we have to dare to do is throw away the old and difficult and embrace what's new and difficult and wonderful!'

I'm getting ahead of myself, so I'd better describe how it was in the early days on the Red Planet.

I want to set down all the difficulties and limitations we, the first people on an alien planet, experienced – and all our hopes.

EUPACUS got us there, EUPACUS set up all the dimensions of travel. Whatever went wrong later, you have to admit they never lost a ship, or a life, in transit on the YEA and DOP shippings.

You certainly stayed close to nature on Mars, or the Eternal Verities, as a friend of mine called them. Oxygen and water supplies were fairly constant preoccupations.

Water was rationed to 3.5 kilograms per person per day. Communal laundering drank up another 3 kilograms per head per day. Everyone enjoyed a fair share of the supply; in consequence there were few serious complaints. Spartan though this rationing may sound, it compared quite favourably with the water situation on Earth. There, with its slowly rising population, industrial demands on fresh water had increased to the point where all water everywhere was metered and as expensive as engine fuels of medium grade. This effectively limited the economically stressed half of the terrestrial population to something less than the Martian allocation.

The need to conserve everything led to our system of communal meals. We all sat down together at table in two shifts, and were leisurely about our frugal meals, eking out food with conversation. Sometimes one of the company would read to us during the evening meal – but that came later.

At first I was shy about sitting among all those strange faces, amid the hubbub. Some of the people there I would later get to be friends with (not Mary Fangold, though), such as Hal Kissorian, Youssef Choihosla, Belle Rivers, funny Crispin Barcunda – oh, and many others.

But by luck I chanced to sit next to a pretty bright-faced YEA person. Her shock of curly dark brown locks was quite unlike my own straight black hair. She overcame my shyness, and obviously treated the whole business of being on a strange planet as a wonderful adventure. Her name was Kathi Skadmorr.

'I've been so lucky,' she told me. 'I just came from a poor family in Hobart, the capital city of Tasmania. I was one of five children.'

This shocked me. It was not permitted to have five children where I came from.

She said, 'I served my year at Darwin, working for IWR, International Water Resources. I learned much about the strange properties of water, how the solid state is lighter than the liquid state, how with capillary action it seems to defy gravity, how it conducts light . . .' She broke off and laughed. 'It's boring for you to hear all this.'

'No, not at all. I'm just amazed you wanted to talk to me.'

She looked at me long and carefully. 'We all have important roles to play here. The world has narrowed down. I'm sure your role will be important. You must make it so. I intend to make mine so.'

'But you're so pretty.'

'I'm not going to let that stop me.' And she gave a captivating chuckle.

As almost everyone of that first Martian population agreed, to survive on Mars close cooperation was a necessity. The individual ego had to submit to the needs of the whole body of people.

Continual television reports from Mars brought to the attention of the Downstairs world (as we came to call Earth) the fairness of Martian governance and our egalitarian society. It contrasted markedly with terrestrial injustice and inequality.

I don't want to talk about my own troubles, but I had been rather upset by the voyage from Earth, so much so that I had been referred to a psychurgist, a woman called Helen Panorios.

Helen had a dim little cabin on one of the outer spicules where she saw patients. She was a heavily built lady with dyed purple hair. I never saw her wearing anything other than an enfolding black overall-suit. A mild woman she was, who did seem genuinely interested in my problems.

As I explained to her, the six-month journey in cryosleep had terrified me. I had been detached from my life and seemed unable to reconnect with my ego. It was something to do with my personality.

'Some people hate the experience; some enjoy it as a kind of spiritual adventure. It can be seen as a sort of death, but it is a death from which you reawaken – sometimes with a new insight into yourself.' That's what she kept telling me. Basically she was saying that most people accepted cryosleep as a new experience. Just coming to Mars, being on Mars, was a new experience.

I had come to hate the very name EUPACUS. The thought of undergoing that same annihilation getting home again to Earth scared me rigid. There had to be a better way of making that journey across millions of miles of space – or *matrix* as the new more correct term had it. Interstellar matrix teemed with radiations and particles, so that to naked experience 'space' had come to have a Victorian ring about it.

Travel between Earth and Mars was on the increase, or at least it had been before the disaster. Marvelos was hard pressed to meet the demand. Space vehicles were manufactured in terrestrial orbit under licence. Practically every industrialised nation of Earth was involved in their manufacture, if only in making pillows for the coffin-cots. The space vehicles, each with elaborate back-up facilities, were billion-dollar items. Shareholders were reluctant to invest in more rapid development. Takeovers and mergers of companies were happening all the time under the EUPACUS roof.

Helen talked me through the entire process of a voyage.

The consortium's ferry ships carried us passengers up from Earth to the interplanetaries, which parked in orbit about Earth and Luna. I was queasy from the start, even with a g-snort in me. I'm really not a good traveller. Then we passed into the interplanetary passenger ships, popularly known as 'fridge wagons'. You never forget the curious smell in a fridge wagon. I believe they start right away with some sort of airborne anaesthetic circulating.

'I didn't care for the way the compartments were so like refrigerated coffins,' I told Helen. Even before the wagon released from orbit, you were going rapidly into that dark nowhere of cryosleep as bodily functions slowed. That was terror for me . . .

'You were primed beforehand, Cang Hai, dear,' said Helen. 'You know well the economics of that journey back at that stage of development. Taking passengers in

27

cryosleep obviates the need for the ships to carry food and water. Little air is needed. Fuel and expense are saved. Otherwise, well, no trip . . .'

I relived the rush upwards from Earth. For most people, the spirit of adventure overcame any feelings of sickness, though not for me. Two hundred and fifty-six kilometres up, the barrel shape of the fridge wagon loomed, riding in its orbit. It had looked small, then it was enormous. Its registration number was painted large on its hull.

You have to admit it was a neat manoeuvre, considering the speed at which both bodies were travelling. With hardly a jar, they locked. I did then dare, before entering the wagon, to take a last look out at the Earth we were leaving. Fridge waggons have no ports.

I had to cry a little. Helen tenderly placed a hand on my shoulder, like the mother I never had, saying nothing. I was leaving behind my Other, back in Chengdu. Nobody would understand that.

Once in that strange-smelling interior, dense with low murmurs of various machines, we were guided to a small apartment, a locker room really. There one undressed with a neuter android in attendance, stowed away one's few belongings, and took a radiation shower. It was like preparing for a gas chamber. Advised by the android, you now had to lock your bare feet into wall-grooves and clasp the rungs in the curving wall above head level. The compartment now swung and travelled to a vacant coffin-cell. Music played. The aria 'Above my feet the roses speak . . .' from Delaport's opera *Supertoys*.

Then you were somehow motionless and monitors uncoiled like snakes. Tiny feeds attached themselves to your body. Before the wagon left orbit, your body temperature was approaching that of frozen meat. You might as well have been dead. You were dead.

I did a bit of screaming in front of Helen Panorios. Gradually I seemed to get better.

We worked through the disorientation of rousing back

to life in Mars orbit, speeding above all that varied tumble of rock and desert and old broken land.

'You certainly have to welcome new experience to get that far!' I said at one point.

When disaster struck, those who welcomed new experience were certainly well prepared for anything. Which was an important factor in influencing what happened to us all.

Helen rather liked to lecture me. She called it 'establishing a context'. Marvelos organised two types of visit to Mars, one when Earth and Mars were in conjunction, (called the CRT, the Conjunction Return Trip), one when they were in opposition (called the ORT, the Opposition Return trip).

Outward bound both trips took half a year. It was inevitable that those trips had to be passed in cryosleep.

Perhaps it's worth reminding people that by 'year' I always mean Earth year. Earth imposed its year on Mars thinking much as the Christian calendar had been imposed over most of Earth's nations, whether Christian or not. We will come to the rest of the Martian calendar and our clocks later.

The difficulty lay in the provision of return journeys. Helen grew quite excited about this. She showed me slides. While the return leg of an ORT took an uncomfortable year, the CRT took only half a year, no longer than the trip outwards. The snag was that the ORT required a stay of only thirty days on Mars, which was generally regarded as a pretty ideal time period, whereas the CRT entailed a stay of over a year and a half.

I was booked for an ORT, and found I couldn't face the mere thought of it. Helen had booked on a CRT. Her time away from Earth was going to be eighteen times longer than mine. Although I remained in touch with my Other in Chengdu, I could not have faced such a long stretch away. Now I found I could not face the long year in cryosleep.

Of course everyone who came to Mars had made these decisions. Despite such obstacles, the number of applications for flights increased month by month, as those returning reported on what for most was the great emotional experience of their lifetime.

The UN and EUPACUS between them agreed on the legal limits of those permitted to visit Mars. Their probity had to be proved. So it had fallen out that those who came to Mars arrived either as YEAs or as DOPs.

The arrangements for a Mars visit were long and complex. As EUPACUS grew, it became more and more bureaucratic, even obfuscatory. But the rule was quickly established that only these two categories of persons ever came to Mars, and then only under certain conditions. (This excluded the cadre needed for Martian services.)

The main category of person was a Young Enlightened Adult (YEA). This was my category, and Kathi Skadmorr's. Provision was also made for – the Taiwanese established this term – Distinguished Older Persons (DOPs). Tom Jefferies was a DOP.

Once these visitors reached Mars – I'm talking now about how it was back in the 2060s – she or he had to undergo a week's revival and acclimatisation (the unpopular R&A routine). Maybe they also saw a psychurgist. R&A took place in the Reception House, as it was then called, a combined hospital and nursing home run by Mary Fangold, with whom I did not get along. This was in Amazonis. Later other RHs were set up elsewhere.

'In the hospital,' Helen reminded me, 'you were given physiotherapy in order to counteract any possible bone and tissue loss and to assist in the recovery of full health. Why did you not accept the offer of psychurgy there and then?'

This was when I had to admit to her that I was different.

'How different?'

'Just – different.' I did not wish to be explicit, which was perhaps a mistake.

If you were unversed in history, you might wonder that anyone endured all these demanding travel conditions. The fact is that, given the chance to travel, people will endure almost any amount of discomfort and danger to get to a new place. Such has been the case throughout the history of mankind.

Also you must remember that an epoch was drawing to a close on Earth. There was no longer the promise of material abundance that once had prevailed. Not through exploration, conquest, or technological development. The human race had proved itself a cloud of locusts, refusing to curb their procreative and acquisitive habits. They had sucked most of the goodness from the globe and its waters. The easier days of the twentieth century, with individual surface travel readily available, were finished.

So for the young, us YEAs, harsh Martian conditions were seen as a challenge and an invitation. The experience of being on Mars, of identifying with it, was seen as worth all the time spent in community work and matrix travel.

But somehow, with me . . . well, it was different. I guess I just took longer to adjust. It was something to do with my personality.

We have the testimony of an early Mars visitor, Maria Gaia Augusta (age twenty-three) on video. Her report says: 'Oh, the experience must not be missed. I have ambitions to be a travel writer. I spent my YEA community service in the outback of Australia, seeding and tending new forest areas, and was glad to have a change.

'At the back of my mind was a decision to gather material on Mars for knocking copy. I mean, Mars was to me like just a shadowy stone in the sky. I couldn't see the attraction – apart from curiosity. But when I got there – well, it was another world, quite another world. Another life, if you like.

'You know what the surface of Mars is? Loneliness made solid, rock solid.

'Course, there were restrictions, but they were part of the

deal. I loved all the fancy-shaped domes they're setting up in Amazonis Planitia. In the desert, in fact. They put you in the mood of some Arabian Nights fantasy. You get to thinking, "Well, look at the frugal life the Arabs used to lead. I can do that." And you do.

'I did the compulsory aerobic classes during my R&A period after we had landed, and got to enjoy them. I had been a bit overweight. Aerobics is weird in lighter gravity. Fun. I met a very sweet guy in the classes, Renato, a San Franciscan. We got along fine.

'We enjoyed sex in that light gravity and maybe invented a few positions not in the Kama Sutra. Mars is going to be left behind in a few years' time, when we settle the moons of Jupiter. Sex will really be something out there, in real low gravity! Meantime, Mars is the best thing we got in that respect.

'Me and Renato got on the list for a four-body expedition beyond the domes. Four-bodies were then the standard package. I know it's different now. Two-bodies were considered too dangerous, in case one body got ill or something. Not that there are all that many illnesses on Mars, but you never know.

'We didn't go madly far, just to the Margarite Sinus, towards the equator, because of fuel restrictions, but that was enough. Of course, every little four-body had to have a scientific component – the buggy was like a small lab, complete with cameras and electrolysis equipment and I don't know what-all. Radio, of course, to keep us oriented, and listen out for dust storms. We were exploring the canyons in Margarite and we came on a great wall of rock, rubbed smooth by the wind. Me and Renato were seized with a mad idea. We slipped into suits – you have to wear suits – atmosphere there was about 10 millibars, compared to 1,000 millibars back on Earth. Any case, you couldn't breathe it. We got these paints from the buggy store, climbed outside and began to decorate the rock surface. The other couple joined in. There we were, actually alone on the open surface. Wild!

'And we painted a lovely luminous Mars dragon, flying up to the stars. We worked till nightfall, just using red, green and gold colours. To finish off, we had to turn on the buggy headlights. There was a sort of – well, I almost said religious feeling about what we were doing. It was like we were aborigines, making a sacred kind of hieroglyph.

'When we got back to base, we showed photos of the dragon around and nearly started a panic. Some people thought it was the work of autochthonous Martians! Quite impossible, of course, but some folk are incurably superstitious.

'No, I lapped up my time on Mars. It was a life apart. A formative experience. I longed to be out there alone, or alone with Renato, but that wasn't considered safe until my last month there. Just to be out in the desert at night, in a breathertent, it's beyond description. You're alone in the cosmos. The stars come down and practically touch you. You just feel they should come right in and penetrate your flesh . . .

'It's contradictory. You're entirely isolated – you could be the only person who ever lived, ever – and yet you are an intense part of everything. You know you're – what's the word? – well, somehow you're an integral part of the universe. You are its consciousness.

'Like being the seeing eye of this incalculably vast thingme out there . . .

'I say it's contradictory. What I mean is the perception feels contradictory, because you've never experienced it before. You'll never forget it, either. It's a tattoo on your soul, sort of . . .

'Oh, sure, there were things I missed out there. Things I did without but didn't miss, and things I missed. What things? Oh, I missed trees. I missed trees quite badly at first.

'But my life has changed since I was there. I can never go again but I'll never ever forget it. I try to live a better life because of it.

That's no joke in the muddle we're in here, downstairs on Earth.'

END TAPE.

*   *   *

The 'fancy-shaped domes' to which Maria Gaia Augusta refers are the linked spicules, constructed from a small number of repetitive sections, which formed the basis of what was eventually to become Mars City or Areopolis. The monotony of this structure was relieved by conjoined tetrahedral structures, rather similar to those erected in the north of Siberia a few years previously.

From orbit, this sprawling structure, white-painted against the tawny Martian regolith, made a striking pattern.

4

Broken Deals, Broken Legs

Looking back, I see how silly I was in my early days
– silly and shy. I worked in the biogas chamber unit,
and practically took refuge there. Everyone else seemed
so clever. Kathi was clever. Why did she seek out my
company?

Her interest at this time was in politics, about which
she talked endlessly. Placements within the YEA and DOP
brackets were systematically arranged through the Mars
Department, under Secretary Thomas Gunther. Kathi had
a particular dislike of Gunther, saying he was radically
corrupt.

Whether that was true or not – many people praised
Gunther – there was always bad feeling over the placements. Who was accepted or not as a YEA was open to
local manipulation. I thought the system worked pretty
well, enabling as many people as possible to visit the
Red Planet. The United States insisted that matrix travel
(the term 'space travel' had become old-fashioned) was a
democratic right.

Kathi's main complaint concerned the whole business
of selection as a YEA. To qualify within the 16–28 years
age bracket we had to undergo a rigorous Genetic and
Superficial Health Test as well as a GIQ Exam. The
General Intelligence was supposedly free from cultural
and sexual bias and intended to establish the emotional
stability of the examinee. Kathi was one-eighth Aborigine, and swore this was held against her at the Sydney
board.

'I came up against a filthy little man who gave me the

final interview. Do you know what he said? Only my granting him sexual favours would get me through! Can you imagine?'

I hardly dared ask what she had done.

She tossed her hair back. 'What the hell do you think? I wasn't going to let him stop me. I let him screw me. Next day my boyfriend broke both his stinking legs in his back yard . . .'

By far the greatest percentage of YEAs had no means by which to cover the exorbitant costs of interplanetary travel. Nor was financial payment allowed – although Kathi said this too could be arranged if you were one of the Megarich. Funding poured through the UN Matrix Tax to EUPACUS. Gunther was pocketing a 'whole river' of this money, according to Kathi. I had seen pix of Gunther and thought he looked nice.

Having passed their exams, the young educated adults were allocated to stations in which to spend a year of community service. Some got lucky, some lived like slaves, as I did. Some laboured on newly established fish farms in Scapa Flow, or the anchovy nurseries off the west coast of South America. Some served in the great new bird ranges of the taiga, or in satellite manufactories, 2,000 miles above Earth. Some were sent to Luna to work on the underground systems as technicians. Kathi was lucky and went to Darwin and the Water Resources.

'And sitting there like a fat pig in a strawberry bed was Herby Cootsmith, a Megarich, squatting on his investments, gradually buying up all Darwin,' Kathi said.

As a group, the YEAs were mistrustful of the socioeconomic systems from which they emerged. They hated the disparity between the poor, with their harsh conditions and short lives, and the Megarich, whose existences were projected to extend over two centuries. Life for the Megarich, Kathi declared, misquoting Hobbes, was 'nasty, brutish, and long'.

It was estimated that 500 people owned 89 per cent of the world's wealth. Most of them belonged in the

Megarich category, being able to pay for the antithanatotic treatments.

After your year's community service, you had to pass the various behavioural tests. Then you were qualified for the Mars trip.

'How did you manage?' Kathi asked.

I hesitated, then thought I might as well tell her. 'A rich protector came forward with a bribe.'

Kathi Skadmorr gave a harsh cackle. 'So we're both here under false pretences! And I wonder how many others – YEAs and DOPs?! Don't you just long for a decent society, without lies and corruptions?'

It came as a surprise to me to discover that Tom Jefferies and his wife Antonia – both of them DOPs – had also used a bribe to get to Mars. That I shall have to tell about in a minute, and to describe Antonia's death.

Antonia died so many years ago. Yet I can still conjure up her fine, well-bred face. And I wonder how different history would have been if she had not died.

The DOPs were reckoned to have served their communities; otherwise, they would hardly be Distinguished. As Older Persons, they did not have to undergo the GIQ examination. However, the Gen & S Health test was particularly rigorous, at least in theory, in order to avoid illness en route, that long, spiralling, burdensome route to the neighbouring planet. In some cases, behavioural tests were also applied.

DOP passages were generally paid for by some form of government grant from their own communities. In the eighteenth century, Dr Johnson told Boswell that he wished to see the Great Wall of China: 'You would do what would be of importance in raising your children to eminence ... They would be at all times regarded as the children of a man who had gone to view the Wall of China. I am serious, sir.' To have visited Mars brought a similar mark of distinction – conferred, it was felt, on whole communities as well as on the man or woman who had gone to Mars and returned home to them.

One of the excitements of being on Mars was that one occasionally met a famous DOP, not necessarily a scientist, perhaps a sculptor such as Benazir Bahudur, a literary figure such as John Homer Bateson, or a philosopher such as Thomas Jefferies. Or my special friend, Kathi Skadmoor.

I first saw Tom Jefferies from afar, looking sorrowful and remote, but I held the popular misconception that all philosophers looked like that. He was an elegant man, sparse of hair, with a pleasing open face. He was in his late forties. A vibrancy about him I found very attractive.

So I was immediately drawn to him, as were many others. While I was drawn, I did not dare speak to him. Would I have spoken, had I known how our paths would intertwine? Perhaps it is an impossible question – but we were destined to face plenty of those . . .

Many scientists went to Mars under the DOP rubric, among them the celebrated computer mathematician, Arnold Poulsen, and the particle physicist I have already mentioned, Dreiser Hawkwood. A percentage of those who had travelled on the conjunction flight became acclimatised to Mars and, because the work and lighter gravity there were congenial to them, stayed on. It should be added that many YEAs stayed on for similar reasons – or simply because they could not face another period of cryogenic sleep for the return journey.

From 2059 onwards, as interplanetary travel became almost a norm, every Martian visitor was compelled by law to bring with him a quota of liquid hydrogen (much as earlier generations of air travellers had carried duty-free bottles of alcohol about with them!). The hydrogen was used in reactions to yield methane for refuelling purposes.

Another factor powered the movement in the direction of Mars. Competition to exist in modest comfort on the home planet grew ever more intense. To gratify its desire for profit and then more profit, capitalism had required economies of abundance, plus economies of scarcity into whose markets its entrepreneurs could inflitrate. Now, under this guiding but predatory spirit, there existed only the voracious developed world and a few bankrupt states, mainly in Africa and Central Asia. Increased industrialisation, bringing with it global overheating and expensive fresh water, made life increasingly difficult and corrupted the competence of democracies. Prisons filled. Stomachs went empty.

While there were many who deplored this state of affairs, they were as powerless to alter it as to stop an express train.

Now a number of them had an alternative.

The Martian community developed its own ethos. Being itself poor in most things, it proclaimed an espousal of the poor, downtrodden and unintelligent. More practically, it fostered a welcoming of the estrangement that Mars brought, a passion for science, a care for the idea of community.

Most Martians had discarded their gods along with the terrestrial worship of money. They were thus able to develop a religious sense of life, unwarped by any paternalistic reverences. Always at their elbows was the universe with its cold equations; living just above the subsistence level, the Martians sought to understand those equations. It was hoped that the tracing of the Smudge would resolve many problems, philosophical as well as scientific.

We lived under stringent laws on Mars, laws to which every visitor was immediately introduced. The underground water source would not last for ever. While it did last, a proportion of it underwent the electrolysis process to supply us with necessary oxygen to breathe. Buffer gases were more difficult to come by, although argon and nitrogen were filched from the thin atmosphere. The pressure in the domes was maintained at 5.5 psi.

It will be appreciated that these vital arrangements absorbed much electricity. Technicians were always alert for ways of extending our resources. To begin with they relied on heat-exchange pumps as generators, and photo-voltaic cells.

I have to tell myself that I am a serious person, interested in serious matters. I will not speak of my increasing affection for Kathi Skadmorr, who after all is a marginal person like me, or my admiration for Tom Jefferies, who is a central person unlike me. Instead, I will talk about worms.

In one Amazonis laboratory was a precious Martian possession – 'the farm', a wit called it. Dreiser Hawkwood had introduced it; his side interest was biochemistry. The farm was contained in a box two metres square and a metre and a half deep. In it was rich top soil from the Calcutta Botanical Gardens, expensively imported by courtesy of Thomas Gunther and his EUPACUS associates. In the box grew a small weigela and a sambucus. Below, in the soil, were worms of the perichaeta species, working away and throwing up their castings.

The metabolism of the worms had been accelerated. Their digestion and ejection of soil was rapid. They worked at dragging down the leaves fallen from the plants, thus enriching the soil with vegetable and microbial life. The enriched soil was to be set in a bed inside one of the domes to provide the first 'natural'-grown vegetables. The tilth would eventually cover acres of specially prepared regolith, breaking it down under greenhouse domes into arable land.

From this modest beginning in the farm, great things were to come. It is doubtful if Mars would ever have become more than marginally habitable without that lowly and despised creature, the earthworm, which Charles Darwin regarded so highly, not dreaming that it would one day transform an alien planet as it had transformed Earth itself.

This new agricultural revolution, intended to supplement

the food grown in chemical vats, was assisted by work carried out high above the Martian crust.

Mars has two small satellites that chase across the sky, Swift and Laputa. Early astronomers had bestowed on these two small bodies the unbecoming names of Phobos and Diemos. Swift unwearyingly rises and sets twice in a Martian day. Landings have been made on both satellites. On Swift have been found metallic fragments, presumably the remains of an unsuccessful twentieth-century Russian mission.

Working from a small base on Swift, a series of large PIRs – polymer inflatable reflectors – was set in orbit about Mars to reflect much needed sunlight to the surface. The PIRs are cheap, and easily destroyed by space debris, but equally easily replaced.

The PIRs can be seen in daylight or at night, when they shine brightly unless undergoing occasional eclipse.

It will be deduced from these developments that, despite all the protests, Mars was slowly and inevitably being drawn nearer to terraforming.

Despite all the regulations, the pressure to live brought this change about.

The observatory built on Tharsis Shield near Olympus Mons continued to yield results. The meteorite watch station became operative. The new branch of astrophysics studying the gas giants was officially named jovionics. The telescopes of the observatory tracked many asteroids. Dedication to research was a feature of the scientific atmosphere on Mars. There was little to distract the scientists, as the asteroid-watchers sought to prove the small bodies were the remains of a planet that, before being torn apart by forces of gravity, occupied an orbit between Mars and Jupiter.

Studies of magneto-gravitic irregularities revealed a remarkably high gravity reading for the region near Olympus Mons. I discovered that Kathi was interested in this. No such anomaly existed on Earth, she claimed. She was reading many scientific papers on her Ambient, and told me she believed there was a connection between magneto-gravitic influences and consciousness, so that at present she was looking for a dimensionless quality, but I did not understand her.

When I questioned this connection she believed in, she explained patiently that there were electric and magnetic fields. Whereas electric charges were the direct sources of electric fields, as far as was known there were no equivalent magnetic charges – that is to say, no magnetic monopoles. The influence of hidden-symmetry monopoles on consciousness was subtle and elusive – or appeared to be so as yet. The sophistry underlying the apparently simple laws of the physical universe, the exceptional qualities of many elementary particles, might lead one to suspect the universe of possessing a teleological character.

She was continuing the explanation when I had to admit I could follow her no further.

With a sympathetic smile, Kathi nodded her head and said, 'Who can?!'

She became inquisitive about my beloved Other in Chengdu. Feeling sorry I had mentioned her, I was not very forthcoming. Later, I saw she was interested in the question of consciousness; the existence of my Other, so simple to me, seemed to raise complex questions in her mind.

There seemed little for biochemists and xenobiologists to do once it was agreed that Mars held no life and that its early life forms – archebacteria and so forth – had perished many millions of years before mankind appeared on Earth.

The heliopause, with its strange turbulences, was studied. While Mars was regarded as a completely dead world, indications of life on Ganymede, one of the moons of Jupiter already mentioned, were observed by new instruments.

But I am getting ahead of our history again. Things were well enough for the Martian-terrestrial relationship, until the disaster occurred that changed the situation, entirely and for ever.

5

Corruption, Cash, and Crash

You need to remember how complex and ill judged terrestrial affairs were up to this period.

Among the harsh pleasures of Mars were many negative ones. I was particularly glad to escape the constant surveillance to which we had been subject. On Earth crime rates were such that every city, every road, every apartment house and condominium and almost every room in those buildings was watched day and night by the glass eyes of security cameras. The sellers of masks profited accordingly, and crime thrived. Oppression and blackmail prospered even more.

The mansion of Thomas Gunther was well equipped with surveillance devices, including those of the latest type. The camgun for instance, would fire yards of adhesive at any visitor to the building whose characteristics were not held in its computer.

Not all forms of crime yielded to inspection. Fraud and corruption could take place in broad daylight, with smiles to outface any camera. Smiles had been worn like masks in the upper echelons of the EUPACUS consortium.

The collapse of the entire enterprise began with a seemingly small event in 2066. A senior clerk in the tall ivory-white tower in Seoul that was the main EUPACUS building was caught embezzling.

The clerk was sacked. No charges were brought against him. He was found dead in his apartment two days later. Possibly it was suicide, possibly murder. But an electronic message was released, triggered by the stoppage of the clerk's electronic heart, to be received at the North American Supreme Court of Justice. It led the court to uncover a massive misappropriation of funds by EUPACUS directors. In comparison the clerk's misdemeanours were nugatory.

A cabal of senior executives was involved. Five arrests were immediately made, although all managed mysteriously to escape custody and were not recaptured.

Investigators visiting a vice-chairman's residence on Niihau Island, in the Hawaiian chain, were met by gunfire. A two-day battle ensued. In the bombed-out ruin of the palace were found disks incriminating directors of the consortium: tax evasion on a massive scale, bribing of lawyers, intimidation of staff and, in one instance, a case of murder. The affairs of EUPACUS were put on hold.

EUPACUS offices were closed, sealed off for judicial investigation. All flights were halted, all ships grounded. Mars was effectively cut off. Suddenly the distance between the two planets seemed enormous.

Our feelings were mixed. Along with alarm went a sort of pleasure that we had been severed from the contemptible affairs of Earth for a while.

We did not understand at first how long that while was to be. Earth's finances were entangled with the vast EUPACUS enterprise. One by one, banks and then whole economies went bust.

Japan's Minister of Exterior Finance, Kasada Kasole, committed suicide. Four hundred billion yen of bad debts were revealed, hidden outside the complex framework of EUPACUS accounts. The debts stemmed from tobashi trading; that is, moving a client's losses to other companies so that they do not have to be reported. Chiefly involved was the Korean banking system, which had invested heavily in its own right in EUPACUS.

An equities analyst said that the Korean *won*, closely linked to the Japanese economic system, was now standing against the US dollar at 'about a million and falling'.

Recession set in, from which the EU was particularly

slow to recover, as its individual members were forced, one by one, to close shop.

All round the globe were companies and manufacturies that had relied on or invested in EUPACUS business. Many were already in debt because of delayed payments. The closure of EUPACUS Securities led to a collapse of the world banking system.

Shares fell to just over one quarter of their 2047 peak. Property values followed, leaving the PABS – Pacrim Accountancy and Banking System – with substantial bad debts and asset write-offs. The IFF was unable to muster a credible rescue package.

The deflationary impact was already being felt in North America. The situation, said one US official, was deteriorating dramatically as Asian speculators were selling off their huge holdings of US financial assets in order to try and meet their obligations nearer home. 'The US home market is going into meltdown,' an official said.

Only a month after this remark, the world's economy was in meltdown.

We sat on our remote planet and watched these proceedings with a horrified fascination. Bad went to worse, and worse to worse again. There came the day when terrestrial television went dead. And we were truly alone.

A fish stinks from the head. I'm told it's an old Turkish proverb. Despite the rigorous checks that had been set up by the UN, bad conditions and poor pay had made workers in the Marvelos Health Registration Department just as open to bribery as those at the top of the vast organisation.

So it was that Antonia Jefferies and her husband Tom were able to pass the Gen & S Health Test and travel to Mars on a CRT trip just under four years before EUPACUS collapsed, and the world economy with it.

Antonia suffered from a cancer of the pancreas, on which she had refused to have nanosurgery; it was a long while before I discovered why. Nevertheless, the gallant woman was determined to set foot on the Red Planet before she became too ill to travel. Her interest was in the Smudge experiment, which she saw as an extreme example of the interlinkage between science and human life, for good or bad.

She was a historian. Her boovideo, *The Kepler Effect*, had been a bestseller. Tom Jefferies had moved from employment as a theoretical physicist specialising in monopole research to what he called Practical Philosophy. His new profession brought him fame and the soubriquet the 'Rich Man's Tom Paine'.

Tom was in his early fifties. His wife was forty-eight. They had no children. He had married Antonia only after the cancer, then in her pancreas, had been diagnosed. The diagnosis had been in 2052.

Roused from cryosleep, disembarking from their ship, the Jefferies went to the R&A Clinic. Her cancer had not slept on the voyage. The diagnosis by Mary Fangold revealed that she was very ill. Tom told me later that Fangold was 'an angel', but was not able to provide a cure.

At Antonia's request, Tom drove her in a buggy to the Tharsis Shield. They sat at nightfall with remoteness all about them – in Tom's words, 'with that singing quality which absolute isolation has' – as Earth rose above the horizon, a distant star. There Antonia died, lying and gasping out her life in her husband's arms.

'Thank you for everything,' she said. Those were her last words.

He buried his face on her shoulder. 'You are my everything, my darling wife.'

Tom Jefferies had to return to base when his oxygen was running low. A memorial service was held before Antonia's body was slipped into one of the biogas chambers. I saw her go. At that service, Tom vowed he would never leave the planet where his wife had died. He would dedicate himself instead to the stability of the Martian community.

In fact, he all but gave up his research work in order to serve the community. Tom Jefferies came to the fore when EUPACUS collapsed and connections between Earth and Mars failed. It is amazing what the will of one man can achieve.

I can see this must include some personal history, as well as the story of the development of Mars. I arrived on the same fridge wagon as did the Jefferies, and came to know both Tom and Antonia slightly in the R&A Hospital. Kathi was helping out as a nurse and invited me in. Antonia's ivory-white face was so fine, so intelligent, it was impossible not to want to be near her. Tom was quite a large man, but elegant, as I have said.

What is more difficult to tell is what set him apart from everyone else. His manner was less severe than well controlled. He showed great determination for the cause in which he believed, yet softened it with humour, which sprang from an innate modesty. He was not above self-mockery. In his speech, he adopted the manner of a plain man, yet what he said was often unexpected. Under the calm surface, he was quite a complex person.

To give an example. At one time I happened to sit near to him at a communal meal, when I overheard a scrap of his conversation. This was shortly after his wife had died. Ben Borrow, his neighbour at table, had said something about 'soul' – I know not in what context. He butted in on what Tom was saying about the dimension and temporality of the universe being compatible with a human scale, remarking with a tinge of scorn, 'I want to talk about your soul, Tom, and all you'll talk about is the damned universe.'

To which Tom said, 'But we can train ourselves to listen to two tunes at once, Ben.'

Challenged to explain what exactly he meant, Tom gave as an example the view of Earth as seen from Mars. It was merely a dim star, often lost against the background of stars. It was clear to us that Earth was not the centre of the universe as was supposed for many centuries.

'But this is not to say that mankind is a meaningless accident,' he said. 'Indeed, our existence seems to depend on a number of strange cosmic coincidences involving the exothermic nuclear reactions that generate the heavier elements. Those elements are eventually utilised to build living things. As you know, we are all constructed from such elements – dead star matter.' He looked about him to see that we understood what he was saying. 'This is proof of our intimate relationship with the cosmos itself.

'Of course, this creative process takes time. About ten billion years, in fact. Since we're in an expanding universe, it follows that its size is a function of its age. So why is the observable universe fifteen billion light years in extent? Because it is fifteen billion years old.

'It seems unlikely, bearing these facts in mind, that life could have evolved elsewhere much earlier than it did on Earth. There are no Elder Gods.

'So why have we come into existence? Possibly because we are an integral part of the design plan of the universe. Not accidental. Not irrelevant!

'Each one of us is insignificant in him or her self. But as a species . . . Well, perhaps we should reconsider what a universe is, what it means. Without itself being conscious, it may need a consciousness fully to exist.

'By coming to Mars, we may be enacting the first minute step of a vast process. Whether we are up to seeing the process through, well . . .'

'Quite, quite,' agreed Ben, hastily. 'Mmm. Well . . . Let's see . . .'

That was one of the things which set the wonderful Tom Jefferies apart. He could always hear two opposed tunes playing and make harmony from them, possibly because he had trained himself to think of unimaginably distant futures.

Of course I attended Antonia's memorial service. I was full of grief – hers was the first death on Mars, and a man wrote an elegy on it.

At the time of the EUPACUS collapse, when we found we were stuck on the Red Planet, all hell broke loose. There was rioting, and I was witness to one incident that Tom quelled with a quick answer.

An idiot was trying to incite violence, shouting out that they must destroy the domes. 'We've been lied to. Our lives have been stolen. What they call civilisation is just a sham, a stinking sham. There's no truth – it's all a lie. Burn the place down and have done, it's all a big lie. Everything's a lie!'

Tom stood up, saying loudly, 'But if that were true, then it would be a lie.'

Silence. Then strained laughter. The crowd stood about uneasily. The orator disappeared. The domes were not destroyed.

It must be admitted, I was in despair; I was really scared of being stuck on Mars for any length of time. I took a buggy from the buggy rank without authorisation and made off into the steeps of Tharsis to hide myself away, to commune with myself, to adjust. Although I spoke with my Other, she was a nothing, a green weed floating under water. When night was coming on, I parked myself on the edge of a gully and watched darkness gather, comforted in a way by its remorseless advance, as death had advanced on Antonia.

Whatever you do, I thought to myself, the darkness is always encroaching.

A wind rose. A dust storm brewed up from nowhere. Sudden gusts slammed against my vehicle. It seemed to stagger. Then it was falling over and over, down the gully. I struck my head on a support and became unconscious, although curiously aware all the while.

In that trance-like state, the person with whom I was closest came to stand by me. She sat in a room with a wide window overlooking the Pearl River and unbound her piled dark hair. This she shook out in a dark shower, to show that she knew of my ill fortune and grieved for me.

In her hands she held a silver carp, the meaning of

which I did not understand. The carp swam from her grasp, through the pure air.

When my senses returned I was confusedly aware of a pain and a light. The pain came from my right leg – or was it coming from the pinpoint of light glaring at me over a shoulder of Tharsis? Waves of pain prevented me from thinking coherently.

Eventually I managed to drag myself up. Then I realised that the light I had seen was Saturn, shining low over the rock. The buggy lay on its side against a cliff. By good fortune, it had not cracked open during the drop, or I would have died from lack of oxygen while senseless.

Yet I might as well have been dead. My trip having been unauthorised, I had no radio with which to summon help. Nor had I a suit in which to attempt to extricate myself. Could I have climbed into a suit? That was doubtful with my ruined leg. I could do nothing but crouch there, waiting to die.

But the Martians look after their own. They had instituted a search once the buggy had been reported missing. When the dust storm died, they were out in strength.

I became hazily aware of a noise overhead. A man was scraping the dust away from a side window and looking down at me. I could not recognise his face, and fainted away.

When I roused, I was in a hospital bed, in the Reception House, coming round from anaesthesia. A handsome but stern woman bent over me. Gently brushing my forehead with her hand, she said, 'You see, it was irrational to take out an unauthorised buggy, wasn't it?' Those were the first words Mary Fangold ever said to me.

Only later did I find that my shattered right leg had been removed and a synthetic limb grown in its place.

Now I understood the meaning of the silver carp that my dear friend had shown me in a dream. It swam away from her to indicate that one could live well without legs.

Tom Jefferies came to visit me every day. It was he who had discovered me, trapped in my stolen buggy.

Perhaps he felt he had been given my life to compensate for the loss of Antonia's. I loved him platonically. It was like a fairy tale. I clung to him. I could not let him out of my sight; he was to me the father and mother I had never had.

When I was out of hospital, I besought him and besought him, as a man of destiny, to let me love him and look after him. So I became his adopted daughter, Cang Hai Jefferies.

And all this time – little though I realised it – Tom was planning a constitution for utopia, and holding discussions with people every day.

Testimony of Tom Jefferies

6

A Non-Zero Future!

Stranded on Mars! Although I wished only to mourn the death of Antonia, some force within me insisted that I should turn to the future and face the challenge of existence on a Mars isolated for an indefinite period.

This necessity became more urgent when we were confronted by a wave of suicides. There were those whose spirit was not strong enough to face this challenge. Whereas I saw it as an opportunity. Perhaps it was curiosity that drove me on.

Taking command, I ordered that there should be only one memorial service for all suicides, which numbered thirty-one, the majority of them single men in their thirties. I viewed the act of despair with some contempt and saw to it that the memorial service was kept short. At its conclusion the corpses were consigned to the biogas chambers below ground.

'Now we are free to build our future constructively,' I declared. 'Our future lies in operating as a unit. If we fail to cooperate – zero future!'

The strange airless landscapes beyond our domes had only a remote relationship with our existences; our task was to make good what was inside, not outside, the domes. And since I had taken command – though not without opposition – a grand plan developed slowly in my mind: a plan to transform our society, and hence humanity itself.

I called people together. I wanted to address them direct and not through the Ambient.

'I'm going to kick down a rotten door. I'm going to let light in on human society. I need your help to do it.' That's what I said. 'I'm going to make us live as we dream of being – great and wise people, circumspect, daring, inventive, loving, just. The people we deserve to be.

'All we have to do is dare to throw away the old and difficult crooked ways and leap towards the new and difficult and wonderful!'

I was determined that the collapse of EUPACUS and our subsequent isolation on Mars – for however long that might be – should not be viewed negatively. After the considerable sacrifices everyone had made to reach the Red Planet, we had to struggle to exist, to prove something. With the death of my beloved wife, I decided I would never leave Mars, but remain here all my days, finally to mingle my spirit with hers.

Ambient was already in place. Working with other technicians, we extended it so that everyone had a station. I now sent out a nine-point questionnaire, enquiring into which features of terrestrial life we who were temporarily stranded on Mars were most pleased to escape. I asked for a philosophical approach to the question; such factors as bad housing, uncertain climatic conditions, etc., were to be taken for granted.

Instead of isolating myself with any period of mourning, I set about analysing the responses I received. Remarkably, 91 per cent of the domes' inhabitants answered my questionnaire.

Enlisting the assistance of able organisers, I announced that there would be a meeting to discuss the ways in which we might govern ourselves happily, in justice and truth. All Martian citizens were invited to attend.

At this momentous meeting, a great crowd assembled in our grandest meeting-place, Hindenburg Hall. I took the chair, with the distinguished scientist, Dreiser Hawkwood, at my right hand.

'There is only one way in which we can survive the

crisis of isolation,' I said. 'We must cooperate as never before. We do not know how long we will have to stay on Mars with our limited resources. It will be sensible to anticipate a long stay before world finances and the pieces of EUPACUS are put together again. We must make the best of this opportunity to work together as a species.

'Do not let us regard ourselves as victims. We are proud representatives of the human race who have been granted an unique chance to enter into an unprecedented degree of cooperation. We shall make ourselves and our society anew – to turn a new page in human history, as befits the new circumstances in which we find ourselves.'

Dreiser Hawkwood rose. 'On behalf of the scientific community, I welcome Tom Jefferies's approach. We must work as a unit, setting aside nationality and self-interest. Without attributing intention to what looks like blind chance, we may be given this opportunity to put ourselves to a test, to see what miracles unity can work.

'The humble lichen you see on boulders or stonework back home can flourish in the most inhospitable environments. Lichen is a symbiosis between an alga and a fungus. We might regard that as an inspiring example of cooperation. On this boulder, on which we are temporarily stranded, we will also survive.

'Remember that our survival is necessary for more than personal reasons, important though those are. We scientists are here to press forward with the Smudge Project, in which much finance and effort has been invested. A positive result will influence the way in which we comprehend our universe. For a successful outcome, here too we need unity and what we used to call good old team work . . .'

Heartened by Hawkwood's support, I went on to say, 'In our misfortune we can see great good fortune. We are in a position to try something new, revolutionary. We have here a population equivalent to that of ancient Athens in numbers – and in intellect about equal – and in knowledge much greater. We are therefore ideally placed to establish a small republic for ourselves, banning those elements of existence we dislike, as far as that is possible, and enshrining the good in a constitution upon which all can agree. That way we can flourish. Otherwise, we fall into chaos. Chaos or new order? Let's talk about it.'

As I spoke, I heard murmurs of dissent from the audience. Among the visiting YEAs were many who cared nothing for the Smudge Project and regarded Hawkwood as a career man.

A Jamaican TV star, by name Vance Alysha, one of the YEAs, spoke for many when he rose and said, 'This Smudge Project is typical of the way science has become the tool of the rich. It's all abstract nowadays. There was a time when scientific, or let's say technological, advance brought the poor many advantages. It made life easier – you know, motorbikes, motor cars, refrigerators, radio, of course, and the television. All that was practical, and benefited the poor all over the world. Now it's all abstract, and increases the gulf between rich and poor – certainly in the Caribbean, where I come from. Life becomes harder all the time for our people.'

There were murmurs of approval from the hall. Dreiser asked, 'Is it an abstraction that such ills as cancer and Alzheimer's disease are now curable? We cannot predict exactly what the Smudge will bring, but certainly we would not be here on Mars without investment in the research.'

At this point a young dark-eyed woman stood up and said, in clear tones, 'Some may view our being stranded here as a misfortune. They should think again. I would like to point out that our being here, living in the first community away from Earth and Luna, comes as the end result of many kinds of science and knowledge accumulated throughout the centuries – science both abstract and practical.

'We're fooling ourselves if we don't grasp this opportunity to learn new things.'

As she sat down, Hawkwood leaned forward and asked her what sort of things she imagined we should learn.

She stood up again. 'Consciousness. Our faulty consciousness. How does it come about? Is it affected perhaps by magneto-gravitic forces? In the lighter gravity of Mars, will our consciousness improve, enlarge? I don't know.' She gave an apologetic laugh. 'You're the scientist, Dr Hawkwood, not I.' She sat down, looking abashed at having spoken out.

'May I ask your name?' This from Hawkwood.

'Yes. My name is Kathi Skadmorr and I come from Hobart in Tasmania. I worked in Water Resources in Darwin for my community year.'

He nodded and gave me a significant look.

Assembled in the Hindenburg Hall were almost all the men, women, and children on the planet. Since there were insufficient chairs to seat everyone, boxes and benches were drawn up. When everyone was as comfortable as could be, the discussion proper began.

It was interrupted almost at once by a commotion from the rear door, and female cries for us to wait a minute.

In came three overalled women from Communications, bringing with them lights and video cameras.

The leader, Suung Saybin, showed herself to be a perceptive woman. She had thought of something that had not occurred to the rest of us. 'Allow us to set up our equipment,' she said. 'This may prove an historic occasion, which must be recorded for others to study.'

The scene was lit, she gave the sign, we began our discussion.

Almost immediately a group of six masked men charged the platform. Both Dreiser and I were roughly siezed.

One of the masked men shouted, 'We don't need discussion. These men are criminals! This dome remains EUPACUS territory. They have no right to speak. We are in charge here until EUPACUS returns—'

But they were mistaken in naming EUPACUS so boldly. It had turned into a hated name, the name of failure, the label for those who had isolated us. Half the hall

56

rose en masse and marched forward. Had any of the masked intruders been armed – but guns were forbidden on Mars – there would have been shooting at this point. Instead, a fight ensued, in which the intruders were easily overpowered and Dreiser and I released.

How were the masked men to be punished? All proved to be EUPACUS technicians in charge of landing operations, refuelling or repairs. They were not popular. I sent for six pairs of handcuffs, and had them cuffed around metal pillars for six hours, with their masks removed.

'Is that all their punishment?' asked one of my rescuers.

'Absolutely. They will not reoffend. They suddenly lost their authority. They are only disoriented by the new situation, as we are. Now everyone can have a look at them. That will be shame enough.'

One of my attackers shouted that I was a fascist.

'You are the fascist,' I said. 'You wanted to rule by force. I want to use persuasion – to bring about a just and decent society here, not a mob.'

He challenged me to define just and decent.

I told him I would not define what the words meant just then, particularly since I had never experienced a just and decent society. Nevertheless, I hoped that we would work together to form a society based on those principles. We all knew what just and decent meant in practice, even if we did not define them with precision. And I hoped that in a few months we would recognise them as prevailing in Mars City.

The man listened closely to this, pausing before he spoke.

'My name, sir, is Stephens, Beaumont Stephens, known as "Beau". I will assist your endeavours if you will free me from these handcuffs.'

I told him that he must serve his punishment. Then he would be welcome to help me.

Our forum found a powerful supporter in Mary Fangold, the woman who ran the Reception House. She was a neat, rather severe-looking woman in her late thirties, of

Mediterranean cast, with dark hair cut short, and striking dark blue eyes. I had developed a strong liking for her through her kindness to Antonia in the latter's last days.

'If we are to survive here as a society, then everyone must be given a chance to be part of that society.' Her voice, while far from shrill, held a ring of conviction. I was to find that indeed she was a woman with a strong will. 'On Earth, as we all know, millions of people are thrown on the scrap heap. They're unemployed, degraded, rendered useless, while the rich and Megarich employ androids. These wasteful creatures are the new enemies of the poor – as well as being inefficient.

'It's no good talking about a just society. First of all, we must ensure that everyone works, and is kept busy at a job that suits her or his intellect.'

'What job is that?' someone shouted.

Mary Fangold replied coolly, 'My Reception House must become our hospital. I need enlarged premises, more wards, more equipment of all kinds. Come and see me tomorrow.'

While I had anticipated that many of us would harbour negative responses, even feeling suicidal, about being stranded on Mars, I had not expected so many clearly stated objections to everyday existence on Earth. These the forum wished to discuss first of all, as bugbears to be disposed of.

These bugbears came roughly under five heads, we finally decided. The first four were Mistaken Historicism, Transcendics, Market Domination and Popular Subscription, all of which made existence more difficult than it need be for the multitudinous occupants of our green mother planet. Fifthly, there was the older problem of the rich and the poor, the Haves and Have Nots, a problem of heightened intensity since a long-living Megarich class had developed.

When it came my turn to sum up the debate, which continued for some days, I had this to say (I'm checking here with the records):

'Some issues on Earth are much discussed, or at least make the headlines. They consist in the main of crime, education, abortion, sex, climate, and maybe a few other issues of more local interest. These issues could be fairly easily dealt with, if the will were there.

'For instance, education could be improved if the teaching profession were paid more and better respected. That would happen if children and their futures were the subject of more active general concern. And, if that were the case, then crime rates would fall, since it is the disappointed and angry child who becomes the adult lawbreaker. And so on.

'Unfortunately, a dumbing-down of culture has precluded the general consideration of five issues about which you have expressed unhappiness. They are far less easy to deal with, being more nebulous. Perhaps they are difficult to discern in the general hubbub of competing voices and anxieties. The six thousand of us assembled here must seize on the time and chance we have been given to consider and, if possible, to eliminate these issues.

'I will take these issues, which do not mirror our needs for a decent society and are impediments to such a society, one by one, although they are interrelated.

'Mistaken Historicism is a clumsy label for the problems of squaring a global culture with varied local traditions. The problems spring perhaps from conflating human history with evolutionary development. We are prone to conceive of deep cultural differences as merely an episode on the way to a universal consensus – a developmental phase, let's say, to an homogenous civilisation. Our expectation is that these various local traditions will die out and the global population become homogenised. This idea is patronising, and will not hold water much longer, as the days of Euro-Caucasian hegemony draw to a close.

'For example, we cannot expect the quarter of the terrestrial population that speaks a Chinese language to convert to English instead. Nor can we expect those whose faith is in Mohammed to turn into churchgoers of the Methodist persuasion. The Chinese and the Muslims may fly by airplanes manufactured in the United States for at least a few decades longer: that does not alter their inward beliefs in the superiority of their own traditions one whit.

'We observe the tenacity of tradition even within the European Union. A Swede may spend all his working life in Trieste, designing parts for the fridge wagons; he may speak fluent Italian and enjoy the local pasta; he may holiday on the beaches of Rimini. But, when it comes time to retire, he returns to Sweden, buys a bungalow in the archipelago, and behaves as if he had never left home. He soon forgets how to speak Italian.

'Our traditional roots are valuable to us. We may argue whether or not they should be, but the fact remains that they are. Nor are the arguments against them always valid.

'For instance, such roots are supposedly the cause of war. True, certainly they have been in the past. There were the Crusades, the Opium Wars against China, and so on and so forth. But modern wars, when they happen, are most frequently not between different civilisations but are waged among the same civilisations, as were the terrible wars in Europe between 1914 and 1918 and 1939 and 1945.

'The mistaken assumption that cultural differences are going to disappear and a single civilisation will prevail, perhaps in the manner of Mr H.G. Wells's Modern Utopia, has precluded constructive intellectual thought on ways to ease friction between cultures which are, in fact, permanent and rather obdurate features of the world in which we have to live. The sorry tale of the conflict between Israel and Palestine is a recent example of the ill effects of Mistaken Historicism.

'If we could drop our Mistaken Historicism, we might establish more effective international buffers for intercultural relationships.'

At this point there was an important intervention by a small sharp-featured man with scanty white hair. He rose and introduced himself as Charles Bondi, a worker on the

Smudge Project, whom we already knew was one of the prime movers of the scientific project.

'While I take your point about linguistic differences and religious differences and so forth,' he said, in a pleasant husky voice, 'these are all global items we have learned to put up with, and to some extent overcome. I believe it might be claimed that cultural differences are dying out, at least where it matters, in public relations. Certainly there is evidence of a fairly general wish to help them die out, or else we would have no revived United Nationalities.

'You could argue, indeed, that Mistaken Historicism was mistaken but is no longer. Don't we see a convergence in prevailing attitudes of materialism, for instance, in East and West – and all points in between? What we want is a new idea, something that overrides cultural difference. I believe that the revelations that the detection of a Smudge phenomenon will grant us could be that transforming idea.'

'We'll discuss that question when a Smudge has been identified,' I said.

'Smudge interception is vastly more likely than utopia,' Bondi said, sharply. I thought it wiser not to answer, and continued with my list.

'We come next to Transcendics. I use the term rather loosely, not in the Kantian sense, but to mean the transcendence of humanity over everything else on the globe. Perhaps anthropocentrism would be a better word. Despite the growth of geophysiology, people by and large value things only as they are useful for human purposes. The rhinoceros, to take an obvious example, was hunted to extinction within the last forty years, simply because its horn was valued as an aphrodisiac. This splendid creature was killed off for an erroneous notion.

'But more widely we still use our seas as cesspits and our globe as a doormat. We take and take and consume and consume. We have a belief that we are able to adapt to any adverse change, and can survive and triumph, in spite of all the diseases that rage among us – in many cases diseases we have provoked through our ruination of the balance of nature. For instance when that vegetarian grazing animal, the cow, was fed meat and offal, bovine spongiform encephalitis infected herds and spread to the perpetrators of the crime.

'The myth of man's superiority over all other forms of life is, I'm bound to say, propagated by the Judaic and Christian religions. The truth is that the globe would thrive without human beings. If our kind was wiped from the earth, it would heal over in no time and it would be as if we had never been . . .'

At this point, reflection on the miseries we had created for ourselves on the beautiful terrestrial globe overcame me. I cried aloud in protest at my own words, knowing in my heart that, though we must make the best of our opportunities on Mars, Mars would never be the lovely place that Earth was, or had been.

Perhaps I should interrupt my narrative here to say that the hall in which we held our public discussions was dominated by a blow-up of one of the most extraordinary photographs of the Technological Age. Towering over us in black and white was a shot taken in 1937 of an enormous firework display. When the Nazi airship the *Hindenburg* was about to attach itself to a mooring mast, having flown across the Atlantic to the United States, its hydrogen tanks exploded and the great zeppelin burst into flame.

That beautiful, terrifying picture, of the gigantic structure sinking to the ground, may seem like the wrong signal to those who had crossed a far greater distance of space than had the ill-fated airship. Yet it held inspiration. It showed the fallibility of man's technological schemes and reminded us of evil nationalist aspirations while remaining a grand Promethean image. We spoke under this magnificent Janus-faced symbol.

But, for a moment, I was unable to speak.

*   *   *

Seeing my distress, Hal Kissorian, a statisticial demographer and one of the stranded YEAs, spoke up cheerfully.

'We all have complaints against our mother planet, Tom, much though we love it. But we have to learn things anew, to suit our new circumstances here. Do not be afraid to speak out.

'Let me offer you and all of us some comfort. I have been looking into the computer records, and have discovered that only fifteen per cent of us Martians here assembled are the first-borns in their families. The great majority of us are later-born sons and daughters.'

There was some laughter at the apparent irrelevance of this finding.

Kissorian himself laughed so that his unruly hair flopped over his brow. He was a cheerful, rather wanton-looking, young fellow. 'We laugh. We are being traditional. Yet the fact is that over a great range of scientific discoveries and social upheavals which have changed mankind's view of itself, the effects of familial birth order have played their part.'

At calls for examples, Kissorian instanced Copernicus, William Harvey, discoverer of the circulation of the blood, William Godwin with *An Enquiry Concerning Political Justice*, Florence Nightingale, 'The Lady with the Lamp', the great Charles Darwin, Alfred Wallace, Marx, Lenin, Dreiser Hawkwood, and many others, all later-born progeny.

A DOP I recognised as John Homer Bateson, the retired principal of an American university, agreed. 'Francis Bacon, Lord Verulam, makes more or less the same point,' he said, leaning forward and clutching the chair back in front of him with a skeletal hand, 'in one of his essays or counsels. He says that, among children, the eldest are respected and the youngest become wantons. That's the term he uses – wantons! But in between are offspring who are pretty well neglected, and they prove themselves to be the best of the bunch.'

This observation was delivered with such majesty that it incurred a number of boos.

Whereupon the retired principal remarked that dumbing-down had already settled itself on Mars.

'Anything can be proved by statistics,' someone called to Kissorian.

'My claim will demonstrate its validity here by our general contrary traits and our wish to change the world,' Kissorian replied, unperturbed.

'Our wish is to unite and change this small world,' I rejoined, and went on with my catalogue of the five partially concealed causes of global unhappiness.

'Our preconceived concept of mankind as master of all things prevents us from establishing sound institutions – institutions that might serve to provide worldwide restraints against the sort of depredations of which we have talked. Were it not for our anthropocentrism, we would long ago have established a law, observed by all, against the pollution of the oceans, the desecration of the land, and the destruction of the ozone layer.

'The myth that we can do anything with anything we like causes much misery, from the upsetting of climates onwards. As you all know, had we acted under that mistaken belief, Mars would now be flooded with CFC gases in an attempt to terraform it, had it not been for a good man as General Secretary of the UN and his few far-sighted supporters.

'Transcendics I regard as embodying something destructive in the character of mankind. For instance, the lust to obliterate old things, from buildings to traditions, which make for stability and contentment. Terraforming is just one instance of that intention. Yet new things have no rich meaning for us unless they can be seen to develop from the old. Existence should be a continuity.

'While I am no believer, I see the role of the Church – and its architecture – in communities as a stabilising, unifying factor. Yet from within the Church itself has emerged a retranslation of Bible and prayer into so-called plain language – a dumbing-down that destroys the old sense of mystery, reverence and tradition. We need those elements. Their loss brings a further challenge to family life.'

'Forget family life!' came a voice.

'Yeah, let's forget oxygen,' came a speedy rejoinder from my new supporter, Beau Stephens.

For some minutes an argument raged about the value of family life. I said nothing; I did not entirely know where I stood on the question; mine had been a strange upbringing. I held what I considered an old-fashioned view: that at the centre of 'family life' was the woman who must bring forth a new generation, and both she and her children needed such protection as a male could give. Undoubtedly, the time would come when the womb was superseded. Then, I supposed, family life would fade away, would become a thing of the past.

After a while, I called for order and returned to my list of discontents.

'Let's move on to the third stumbling block to contentment, Market Domination – another little item we have escaped here on Mars. We have all felt, since we came here, the relief of having no traffic with money. It feels strange at first, doesn't it?

'Money, finance, has come increasingly to dominate every facet of life on Earth, particularly the lives of those people who have least, who are at the bottom of a wasps' nest of economics. How can we claim that all men are equal when on every level inequalities exist?

'It became a shibboleth in the twentieth century that maximum economic growth would resolve human problems. Earning power outweighed social need, as the quest for greater profit failed to count the cost in civilised living.

'One way in which this happened was in the dismantling of welfare provisions, such as health care, pensions, child benefit, unemployment allowances.'

Mary Fangold interrupted. She stood tall and proud.

'Tom, I have been thankful to live on Mars, having to watch terrestrial affairs go from bad to worse. Perhaps the people there don't notice the decline. The dismantling of welfare provisions of which you speak has deepened a well of worldwide poverty. One result is an increase in many infectious diseases.

'We all know smallpox returned with the pandemic of about ten years ago. Cholera is rampant in the Pacrim countries. Many contagious diseases once thought all but vanished early in the century have returned. Fortunately those diseases do not reach Mars.'

'Sit down then!' someone shouted.

Mary looked towards the interruption. 'Bad manners evidently have travelled. I am making a reasonable point and will not be deflected.

'I would like everyone here to realise how fortunate we are. The encouraging medical statistics put out by terrestrial authorities are often drawn from the Megarich class, who of course have their own private hospitals, and whose orderly records make them easy subjects for study.

'There is at present a serious outbreak of multiple drug resistance, notably of VRE, or vancomycin-resistant-enterococci, particularly in the ICUs in public hospitals. This is caused in part by the overemployment of antibiotics, while the synthesis of new and effective antibiotics has been falling off. Many thousands of people are dying as a result. Hundreds of thousands. Intensive Care Units are breaking down everywhere on Earth.

'A cordon sanitaire exists between Earth and Mars. Because of the long journey time, anyone who happens to be carrying VRE or any virus or infective disease – not, alas, cancer, or any malfunctioning cellular illness' – here she glanced sympathetically at me – 'will have recovered from the disease or have died from it. People do die in their cryogenic caskets en route, you know. Perhaps that statement surprises you. We try to keep it quiet.

'So all you YEAs and DOPs, do not wish the journey to take a shorter time. We are fairly safe from terrestrial disease. And that, to my mind, counts for more on the plus side than these dreary negatives we are listening to.'

For her speech Fangold was applauded. She gave me a glance, half apology, half smile, as she sat down.

I could only agree about the dreary negatives, and called a break for lunch.

As usual, we all sat at long communal tables. We were served with vegetable soup, so-called, followed by a synthetic salami stew, accompanied by bread and margarine.

Discussion ran up and down the table. Several voices were raised in anger. Aktau Badawi asked me what I was going to say about Market Domination. 'Is this about multinationals?'

'Not really. We all know about the biggest of the lot, EUPACUS, which has stranded us here.

'Downstairs, on Earth, work became an overriding imperative for those in whom poverty and unemployment had not become ingrained. The family mealtime, often rather better than what we are getting now, where families talked and argued and laughed and ate in a mannerly way together, fell victim to the work ethic at an early stage. Fast food was often eaten while preparing to leave for work, at work, or in the streets. There was no mingling of the generations, such as we have here in Amazonis Planitia, no conversation. At least we have that,' I said, pushing my plate aside.

'If jobs were not available locally, then the worker must go elsewhere. In the United States of America, this was no great hardship; it was already a pretty rootless society, and the various states made provision for people to move from one state to another. Elsewhere, the hunt for jobs can mean exile – sometimes years of exile.'

Aktau Badawi said, in his halting English, 'My family is from Iran. My father has a big family. He has no employ. His brother – his own brother – was his enemy. He travels far to get a job in the Humifridge plant in Trieste, on a distant sea, where they make some units for the fridge

67

wagons. After a two-year, we never hear from him. Never again. So I must care for my brothers.

'I am like Kissorian has said, second brother. I go north. I work in Denmark. Is many thousand kilometres from my dear home. I see that Denmark is a decent country, with many fair laws. But I live in one room. What can I do? For I send all my monies to home.

'Then I do not hear from them. Maybe they all get killed. I cannot tell, despite I write the authorities. My heart breaks. Also my temper. So I rather do the community year in Uganda in Africa. Then I come here, to Mars. Here I hope for fairness. And maybe a girl to love me.'

He hung his head, embarrassed to have spoken so openly. May Porter, a technician from the observatory, sitting next to him, patted his arm.

'Labour markets require high mobility, no doubt of that,' she said. 'Careers can count very low in human values.'

'Human values?!' exclaimed Badawi. 'I don't know its meaning until I listen today to the discussions. I wish for human values very much.'

'Another thing,' said Suung Saybin. 'Food warehouses dominate cities because, once a machinery of supply is established, it is hard to stop. Small shops are forced out by competition. Their closure leads to social disorder and the malfunction of cities. The bigger the city, the worse this effect.'

A little Dravidian whose name I never learned broke in here, saying, 'There is always the excuse given by pharmaceutical manufacturers. They profit greatly from the sale of fertilisers and pesticides that further decimate wildlife, including the birds. My country now has no birds. These horrible companies claim that improved crop yields are necessary. This is one of their lies. World food production is more than sufficient to feed a second planet! There are 1.5 billion hungry people in the world of today, many of them personally known to me. Their problem is not so much the lack of food as lack of the income with which to purchase food already available elsewhere.'

Dick Harrison agreed. 'Don't by this imagine we're talking only of starving India, or of Central Asia, forever unable to grow its own food. The most technologically advanced state, the United States, has forty million people on the breadline – forty million, in the world's largest producer of food! I should know. I came from New Jersey to Mars to get a good meal . . .'

After the laughter died, I continued.

'The all consuming machinery of greater and greater production entails deregulation of worker safety laws and health provisions. In our lifetimes we have seen economic competition increasing between states. They must grow monstrous to survive, as trees grow to eclipse a neighbour with their shade. So bad capitalist states drive out good, as we see in South America. Greater profits, greater general discomfort.'

At this point, I was unwilling to continue, but my audience waited in silence and expectancy.

'Come on, let's hear the worst,' Willa Mendanadum, the slender young mentatropist from Java, called down the table.

'Okay. The three concealed discomforts we have mentioned occasion much of the unhappiness suffered by terrestrial populations. They form the undercurrents behind the headlines. Where remedies are applied only to the headline troubles – capital punishment for murder, private insurance for accident, abortion for unwanted babies – they do little good. They merely increase the burdens of life.

'Why are they not thrown out and deeper causes attended to?

'The answer lies in Popular Subscription, our fourth impediment.'

'Now we're getting to it,' said Willa. Someone hushed her.

'What it means, Popular Subscription?' asked Aktau Badawi.

'We are conditioned to subscribe to the myths of the age. We hardly question the adage that fine feathers make fine birds, or that young offenders should be shut up in prisons for a number of years until they are confirmed in misery and anger. When witch-hunts were the thing, we believed in witches or, if we did not believe, we did not like to speak out, for fear of making ourselves silly or unpopular.

'That fear is real enough, as we see in the instances of rare individuals who dare to speak out against unscrupulous practices in giant pharmaceutical companies or national airlines. Their lives are rapidly made impossible.

'It is Popular Subscription that permits the three other mistaken conceptions we've mentioned to beggar our lives.'

'This is no new perception, by the way, Tom,' came the supercilious voice of John Homer Bateson. 'The learned Samuel Johnson remarked long ago that the greatest part of mankind had no other reason for their opinions than that they were in fashion.'

I nodded in his direction. 'The fifth of our bugbears is, simply, the prevalence of Haves and Have Nots – of the gulf between rich and poor. It has always existed on Earth. Perhaps it always will exist there. Now we have the new long-lived Megarich class, living behind its golden barricades.

'But here – why, on Mars we start anew! We're all in the same boat. We have no money. We're all dirt poor and must live at subsistence level. Rejoice that we have escaped from a deep-rooted evil – as deeply rooted as the diseases of which Mary Fangold has spoken.

'We six thousand Crusoes are cut adrift from these miseries – and other miseries you can probably think of. Our lives have been drastically simplified. We can simplify them still further by maintaining a forum here, wherein we shall endeavour to extirpate these errors of perception from our society.

'With a little team work, we can and we will build a perfect and just society. The scientists will do their work. As for the rest of us – why, we have nothing better to do!'

7

Needless to say, my summing up of mankind's problems did not go undisputed.

At one juncture I was challenged to say what was the point of my lengthy disquisition. I responded, 'We are listing some of the preconceptions of which we must rid our minds. There are others to come. While we are here – while we have the chance – I want us to change, change for our own sweet sakes. We have been slaves to the past. We must become people of the long future. We must set the human mind free. Only then can we achieve the greatest things.'

'Such as what?' a YEA called.

'Once you have set your mind free, I will tell you!'

Willa Mendanadum ignored this vital point. She summed up the opposition.

'These hidden stumbling blocks to mankind's happiness are interesting in their way, but are academic to our present discussion. If we wish to find a means to govern ourselves here, happily and justly, then we must forget about what they are up to on Earth.

'Besides, there are worse and more immediate impediments to our happiness than the ones you mention. If you take my own country, Indonesia, as an example, there you can see a general rule in operation, that big decisions are always made by well-fed people. The well-fed control the ill-fed, and it is in their interest to keep it that way.'

Amid general laughter, as we acknowledged the force of this truism, someone intervened to say, 'Then we can make fair decisions here, because we are all ill-fed.'

Another important statement was made by May Porter, who said, 'I like the word justice. I dislike the word happiness, always have done. It has a namby-pamby taste in my mouth. It was unfortunate that the American Declaration of Independence included that phrase about the pursuit of happiness being an inalienable right. It has led to a Disneyfied culture that evades the serious meaning – the gravitas, if you like – of existence. We should not speak of maximising happiness, but rather of minimising suffering. I seem to recall from my college days that Aristotle spoke of happiness as being only in accordance with excellence.

'It makes sense to strive for excellence. That is an attainable goal, bringing its own contentment. To strive for happiness leads to promiscuity, fast food, and misery.'

Laughter and general clapping greeted this statement.

As a break from all this debate, which I was not alone in finding exhausting, I did the morning rounds with Arnold Poulsen, the domes' chief computer technician, after the day's communal t'ai chi session.

Poulsen was one of the early arrivals on Mars. I regarded him with interest. He was of ectomorphic build, with a slight stoop. A flowing mop of pale yellowish hair was swept back from a high brow. Although his face was lined, he seemed neither young nor old. He spoke in a high tenor. His gestures were slow, rather vague; or perhaps they might be construed as thoughtful. I found myself impressed by him.

We walked among the machines. Poulsen casually checked readings here and there. These machines maintained atmospheric pressure within the domes, and monitored air content, signalling if CO_2 or moisture levels climbed unacceptably high.

'They are perfectly reliable, my computers. They perform miracles of analysis in microseconds which would otherwise take us years – possibly centuries,' Poulsen said. 'Yet they don't know they're on Mars!'

'If you tell them – what then?'

He gave a high-pitched snort. 'They would be about as emotionally moved as the sands of Mars . . . These machines can compute but not create. They have no imagination. Nor have we yet created a program for imagination,' he added thoughtfully. 'It is because of their lack of imagination that we are able completely to rely on them.'

They could arrive swiftly at the solution of any problem set for them, but had no notion what to do with the solution. They never argued among themselves. They were perfectly happy, conforming to Aristotle's ancient dictum, as quoted by May Porter, that happiness was activity in accordance with excellence – whereas I felt myself that morning to be baffled and cloudy.

Should I not have allowed myself to mourn in solitude the death of my beloved Antonia, rather than embark on the substitute activity of instigating a suitable Martian way of life?

Against one wall of the computer room stood three androids. The computers would activate them when necessary. They were sent out every morning to polish the surfaces of the photovoltaic plates on which we relied for electricity. They had completed their task for the morning to stand there like butlers, mindlessly awaiting fresh orders.

I remarked on them to Poulsen. 'Androids? A waste of energy and materials,' he said. 'We had to discover how to create a mechanical that could walk with reasonable grace on two legs – thus emulating one of mankind's earliest achievements! – but once we've done it . . .'

Pausing, he stood confronting one of the figures. 'You see, Tom, they give off no CPS, no CPS. Like the dead . . . Do you realise how greatly we humans depend on each other's signals of life? It emanates from our basic consciousness. A sort of mental nutrition, you might say.'

73

I shook my head. 'Sorry, Arnold, you've lost me. What is a CPS?'

Poulsen looked at me suspiciously, to see if I was joking. 'Well, you give one off. So do I. CPS is Clear Physical Signal. We can now pick up CPSs on what we call a savvyometer. Try it on these androids: zilch!'

When I asked him what the androids were here for, he told me they had been intended to maintain the integrity of the air-tight structures in which we lived. 'But I will not trust them. In theory they're on lease from EUPACUS. You see, Tom, they're biotech androids, with integrated organic and inorganic components. I ordered BIA Mark XI – the Euripedes. The EUPACUS agent swindled us and sent these Euclids, Mark VIII, obsolete rubbish. I wouldn't entrust our lives to a mindless thing, would you?'

The androids regarded us with their pleasant sexless faces.

Turning to one of the androids, Poulsen asked it, 'Where are you, Bravo?'

The android replied without hesitation, 'I am on the planet Mars, mean distance from the Sun, 1.523691 AUs.'

'I see. And how do you feel about being on Mars as opposed to Earth?'

The android answered, 'The mean distance of Mars from the Sun is 1.523691 AUs. Earth's mean distance is 1 AU.'

'Feel. I said feel. Do you think life's dangerous on Mars?'

'Dangerous things are life-threatening. Plagues, for instance. Or an earthquake. An earthquake can be very dangerous. There are no earthquakes on Mars. So Mars lacks danger.'

'Sleep mode,' Poulsen ordered, snapping his fingers. As we turned away, he said, 'You see what I mean? These androids have halitosis instead of CPS. They create hydroxils. I rate certain plants higher than these androids – plants mop up airborne hydroxil radicals and protect us from sick-building syndrome . . .'

When I asked which plants he recommended, Poulsen

74

said that it was necessary to maintain a clean atmospheric environment. Ozone emissions from electronic systems mixed with the chemicals humans gave off to form what he called 'sass' – sick air soups. Mary Fangold's hospital was handling too many cases of sore throats and irritated eyes for comfort. Selected plants were the things to swallow up the harmful sass.

'What can we do to ease the problem?' I asked.

Poulsen replied that he was getting suitable plants into the domes. A consciousness-raising exercise would be the rechristening of streets and alleys with plant names. K.S. Robinson Avenue could become Poinsettia, and K. Tsiolkovski Place Philodendron.

'Come on,' I said. 'Who could pronounce Philodendron?'

We both chuckled.

Using my Ambient, I spoke to the YEA from Hobart, Kathi Skadmorr. Her manner was defensive. She looked straight at me and said, 'I happened to be viewing Professor Hawkwood's *Living Without Knowing It.*'

'I'm sorry to have interrupted you. What do you make of his theory of the coming of consciousness?'

Without replying to my question, she said, 'I love learning – particularly hard unquestionable science. Only it is difficult to know what is actually unquestionable. I have so much to take in.'

'There are good technical vids about Mars. I can give you references.'

'So where is the dateline on Mars? Has that been established?'

'We have yet to place it. The question is not important yet.'

'It will be, though. If God wills it.'

I gave a laugh. 'God hasn't got much to do with it.'

I thought I detected contempt in her voice when she replied, 'I was speaking loosely. I suppose I meant some higher consciousness, which might well seem like a god to us, mightn't it?'

'Okay, but what higher consciousness? Where? We have no proof of any such thing.'

'Proof!' she echoed contemptuously. 'Of course you can't feel it if you close your mind to it. We're awash here with electromagnetic radiation, but you don't sense it. We're also awash with each other's CPS signals, isn't that so? Maybe consciousness, a greater consciousness – supposing that here on Mars – oh, forget it. Why are you logging me?'

The question somehow embarrassed me. I said, 'I was interested in the way you spoke up in our debates. I wondered if I could help in any way?'

'I know you have been of great help to Cang Hai. But thanks, Dr Jefferies, I must help myself, and stop myself being so ignorant.'

Before she switched off, a ghost of a sweet smile appeared on her face.

A mystery woman, I said to myself, feeling vexed. Mysterious and spikey.

At one time, a woman called Elsa Lamont, a slip of a person with dyed-blonde hair cut short, came to my office, accompanied by a sullen-looking man I recognised as Dick Harrison. I had marked him out as a possible trouble-maker, although on this occasion he was civil enough.

Lamont came to the point immediately. She said that my talk of terrestrial discomforts had ignored consumerism. It was well known that consumerism was responsible for much greed and injustice. She had worked for a big advertising agency with world-wide affiliations, and had been responsible for a successful campaign to sell the public Sunlite Roofs, at one time very fashionable, though scarcely necessary.

She explained that their TV commercials had been aimed at everyone, although only 20 per cent of viewers could afford such a distinctive luxury item. However the remaining 80 per cent, knowing they could never afford such a roof, respected and envied the 20 per cent, while the 20 per cent understood this very well and felt their status increased by the clever commercial.

Behind Lamont lay a period of art training. She woke one morning realising she disliked the nature of her advertising job, which was to make people feel greedy or ashamed, so she left the agency and worked to become a YEA and visit an ad-free world. Now she asked, would not people on Mars miss commercials, which had become almost an art form?

We talked this over. She argued that we needed commercials to dramatise the concept of unity. She had been trained as an orthogonist at art school, and using orthogonal projection she could create figures on the walkways that would appear to be erect – amusing figures, dancing, walking, holding hands.

At this point she introduced Dick Harrison, saying that he had studied art and would assist her.

It seemed to me that the idea had possibilities. If anyone volunteered to do anything, it was sensible to let them try. She was given Bova Boulevard to experiment on. Soon she and Harrison had covered the street with amusing Chirico-like figures, without faces, dancing, jumping, cheering. From a distance, they did seem to stand up from the horizontal.

It was clever. But no pedestrian could bring themselves to walk on the figures, which meant the boulevard was virtually closed. It was clever, but it was a failure.

However I liked Elsa Lamont's energy and ideas, and later appointed her to be secretary of Adminex.

Dick Harrison's future was less distinguished.

In the space we used for our debating hall, many people were already assembled, discussing, arguing or laughing among themselves.

The subject that arose from the chatter and had to be formally addressed was how we should govern ourselves. Beau Stephens, who had long been released from his pillar together with his associates, suggested that he should be in command. His argument was that he remained a EUPACUS official and, when EUPACUS returned in strength, he would have to hand over affairs in an orderly and accountable manner.

Amid boos, his bid was turned down.

An argument broke out. The YEA faction did much shouting. Finally the tall bearded Muslim with whom I had already spoken, Aktau Badawi, rose to speak. He was born in the holy city of Qom, as he reminded us. It seemed that already his English was improving. Later I found that he was taking lessons from a fellow Muslim, Youssef Choihosla.

Badawi said that shouting was never to be trusted. In the Muslim faith there was a saying: 'Do not walk on the Earth in insolence'. By and large, the Muslim nations rejected the present way of getting to any other planet; he was here only because he had been elected as a DOP. But he would not walk on Mars in insolence. He was content to be governed, if he could be governed wisely, by people who did not shout. But, he asked, how could they be governed if there was no money? If there was no money, then no taxes could be raised. Hence there could be no government.

A thoughtful silence fell. This point had not been made before.

I said that we needed an ad hoc government. It need only rule for a transitional period, until our new way of life was established. It would quietly wither away when everyone had 'got the message'.

What did I mean by that? I was asked.

'All must understand that our limitations hold within them great possibilities for constructive life modes. We are operating in a radically new psychological calculus.'

Rather to my surprise, this was accepted. Then came the question of what the government should be called. After a number of suggestions, some ribald, we settled for 'Administration Executive', or Adminex for short.

We talked about the question of incentives. Not everyone

could be expected to work for good will alone. Something had to replace money by way of incentive.

Not on that momentous day but later, when Adminex held its first meeting, we drew up a rough schedule. Men and women could not be idle. To flavour the pot, incentives were necessary, at least at first. The degree of participation in work for the common good would be rewarded by so many square yards of floor living space. Status could be enhanced. Plants had scarcity value, and would serve as rewards for minor effort.

A common Teaching Experience should be established. We had already seen how separation from the mother planet downstairs had engendered a general wish to stand back and consider the trajectory of one's own life. Personal life could itself be improved – which was surely one of the aims of a just and decent society.

Benazir Bahudur, the sculptor and teacher, spoke up shyly. 'Excuse me, but for our own protection we must establish clear prescriptions. Such as the rules governing water consumption. Increase of personal water consumption must not be on offer as a reward for anything; it would lead only to quarrels and corruption.

'All the same, my suggestion is that we women require a larger water ration than men because of our periods. Men and women are not the same, whatever is claimed. Washing is sometimes a priority with us.

'With none of the terrestrial laws in effect, and no money in circulation, education could play a greater role, provided education was itself overhauled. It must include current information. For instance, how much water exactly remains on this terrible planet.'

As I was to learn later, this vital question of water resources was already being investigated by the science unit. Involved in these investigations was our lady from Hobart, Kathi Skadmorr. I had noted Dreiser Hawkwood's interest in her. He too had spoken to her by Ambient, and received a better reception than I had done.

Dreiser had offered to coach her in science – in what

he was now calling 'Martian science'. When he questioned her about her work with International Water Resources, Kathi had told him she had been employed at one time in Sarawak. I later turned up the record and heard her voice.

'My bosses sent me to Sarawak, where work was being done on the caves in Mulu National Park.'

'What are these caves?' Dreiser asked.

'You don't know them? Shame on you. They are vast. Great chains of interconnected caves. Over 150 kilometres have been explored. The Malaysians who own that part of the world are piping water to Japan.'

'What was your role in the project?'

'I was considered expendable. I did the dangerous bit. I did the scuba work, swimming down hitherto unexplored submerged passageways. With faulty equipment. Little they cared.'

Dreiser gave a snort. 'You do see yourself as a victim, don't you, Ms Skadmorr?'

She replied sharply. 'I'm Kathi. That's how I'm called. You must have some knowledge of the mysterious workings of the authoritarian mind.

'Anyhow, the fact is that I loved that work. The caves formed a wonderful hidden environment, extensive, beautiful, cathedrals in rock, with the water – sometimes still, sometimes racing – as their bloodstream. It was like being inside the Earth's brain. So you'd expect it to be dangerous. What's your interest in all this, anyhow?'

He said, 'I want to help you. Come and live in the science unit.'

'I've had male help before. It always carries a price tag.' She raised her hands to her face to cover a naughty grin.

'Not this time, Kathi. There's no money here, so no price tags. I'll send a vehicle for you.'

'If I come to your unit, I want to walk. I need to feel the presence of Mars.'

The first I knew of all this was when Kathi paid me a personal visit. Her claws were not in evidence. She needed my support. She was eager to see science in action and wished to go to the science unit but also to remain a member of the domes and retain her cabin with us.

She had far more eyelashes, above and below her eyes, than most women. I agreed to her request without even consulting the other members of Adminex.

'Wouldn't it be simpler for you to remain in the science unit?'

'I have friends here, believe it or not.'

She went. Although I do not wish to get ahead of my narrative, it makes sense to set down here what happened when Kathi came under Dreiser's wing.

Our overhead satellite had revealed what looked like entrances to caves in the vast stretches of the Valles Marineris, a kind of Rift Valley. This formidable feature stretches across the Martian equator for a total of some 34,500 square kilometres, almost a quarter of the surface of Mars, so that one sector can be in daylight while the rest is in night. For this reason, ferocious winds scour the valley.

Marineris is like no physical feature on Earth. It is 100 kilometres wide in places and up to 7 kilometres deep. Mists roll down its length at daybreak. It is not a good place to be.

This enormous rift was probably caused by graben events, when the relatively brittle crust fractured. Analysis shows that lakes had once existed along the base of Marineris.

So Hawkwood decided that what seemed like cave entrances would be worth inspecting. He hoped to find reservoirs of underground water. This was in the third month of 2064. However, when assembling his expedition, he found he could muster only one speleologist, a nervous young low-temperature physicist called Chad Chester. To Dreiser's way of thinking, Kathi Skadmorr was much the more foolhardy of the two.

Two buggies containing six people as well as equipment and supplies made the difficult journey overland. Dreiser had insisted on being present. He could strike up no conversation with the Hobart woman, who had retreated into an all-embracing silence.

Kathi stared unspeaking at the Marscape. She had known not dissimilar landscapes back home, long ago. Her intuition was that the very antiquity of these empty vistas had rendered them sacred, as she told me later. She experienced a longing to jump out and paint religious symbols on the boulders they passed.

At last they gained the comparatively smooth floor of the great rift valley. Its high wall towered above them. Of the cliff on the far side they could see nothing; it was lost in distance.

They made slow progress against a strong wind and, when they came to the first three caves, found them blind. The fourth they were able to enter further. Kathi and Chester wore scuba gear. Chester had allowed Kathi to go ahead. Her headlamp showed that the passage was going to narrow rapidly. Suddenly, the floor beneath her caved in and she fell. She disappeared from sight of the others. They cried with alarm before advancing cautiously on the hole.

Kathi was sprawling 2 metres below. 'I'm okay,' she said. 'It was a false floor. Things get more interesting here. Come on down, Chad.'

She stood up and went ahead without waiting for the others.

The rock in her path was tumbled and treacherous. She climbed down with the roof overhead narrowing, until she was moving within a chimney and in danger of snagging her suit. She called up to the rest of the expedition not to follow, else she would have been struck by falling rock.

At last she reached the end of the chimney. Slipping amid scree, she was able to stand again – to find herself in a large cave, which she described over the radio as the size of a cottage – 'contemptible by the dimensions of caves in the Mulu Park area'.

The floor of the cave contained a small pool of ice.

The rest of the team cheered when they heard of this.

Skirting the ice, Kathi explored the cave and reached a narrow cleft at the far end. Squeezing through it, she entered a small dark hole. She was forced to crawl on hands and knees to cross it, where she found a kind of natural staircase, leading down. This she reported to Dreiser.

'Take care, damn it,' he said.

The staircase widened. She squeezed past a boulder and found herself in a larger cavern, in cross-section resembling a half-open clam. The roof was scalloped elaborately, as if by hand, the ancient product of swirling water. And the floor of this cavern held a pool of water, unfrozen. She lobbed a small rock into it. Ripples flowed to the sides in perfect circles.

Her heart was beating fast. She knew she was the first person ever to see extensive water in its free state on the Red Planet.

She waded into it. The ripples stirred by her entry caused light patterns to play on the roof above.

The water came up to her breasts and no further. She plunged and swam below the surface. Her light revealed a dark plug hole on the stony bed. She swam vertically down it, to find herself in a chimney with smooth sides. As it narrowed, she had to push against the sides rather than swim. The fit became tighter and tighter. She could not turn to go back. Her light failed.

The team were calling her on the radio. She did not reply. She could hear her own labouring breath. She squeezed forward with great effort, her arms stretched out in front of her.

The tube seemed to go on for ever as she moved, head down. She thought there was a dim light ahead, or else her sight was failing.

She found herself shooting from the tube like a cork from a bottle. She was floundering upward in a milky sea. Her head emerged into the open. Breathing heavily, she managed to haul herself on to a dry ledge. She was in some sort of a natural underground reservoir. The ceiling

was only 2 feet above her. She thought, 'What if it rains?'
But that thought came from back in Sarawak, where even
a distant shower of rain might cause water levels to rise
dramatically and drown an unwary speleologist. On Mars
there was no danger of rain.

As her pulse steadied, she stared across the phosphorescent pool, whose depth she estimated to be at least 12
metres. Kathi knew that humble classes of aquatic animals
emitted light without heat. But was there not also a mere
chemical phosphorescence? Had she stumbled on the first
traces of Martian life? She could not tell. But lying on the
shelf of rock, unsure of how she would ever emerge again
to the surface, she told herself that she was detecting a
Martian consciousness. She looked about in the dimness:
there was nothing, only the solemn slap of water against
rock, reflected and magnified by the low roof overhead.
Was she not in the very throat of the monster?

She lay completely still, switching off her radio to listen,
there, at least a kilometre beneath the suface of the planet.
If it had a heart, she was now a part of it.

The situation was somewhat to her liking.

When she switched on her radio, the babble of humanity
came to her. They were going to rescue her. Chad was
possibly in an adjacent chamber. She was to stay put. Was
she okay?

Without deigning to answer that, she reported that the
temperature reading was 2 degrees above zero Celsius and
that she had taken a water sample. She still had a reserve
of 3.6 hours of air. Sure, she would stay where she was.
And she would keep the radio on.

She lay on the ledge, perfectly relaxed. After a while she
swam in the phosphorescent reservoir. At one corner, water
fell from the roof in a slow drip, every drop measuring out
a minute.

Raising herself in the water, her fingers detected a crevice
in the rock overhead. Hauling herself up, she found she
could thrust her arm into a niche. With this leverage
she could also wedge a foot in the niche, and so cling,

dripping, above the water. By slow exploration, she was able to ease herself into the rock. She cursed the lack of light, and cursed her failed headlight. Inch by painful inch, she dragged herself through the broken rock fissures. She was in total darkness, apart from an occasional glint of falling water drops. She struck her head on rock.

The one way forward was to twist over on her back and propel herself by hands and feet. She worked like that for ten minutes, sweating inside her suit. Then she was able to get on to her hands and knees.

Gingerly she stood up. Hands stretched before her, she took a step forward. Something crackled beneath the flippers of her suit. She felt and brought up a fragment of ice. In so doing, she clipped her headlamp against rock. Feeling forward, she came on sharp rock everywhere. She stood in the darkness, nonplussed. When she stretched her arms out sideways, she touched rock on either side. As far as she could determine, she was trapped in a narrow fissure. In the pitch dark, the fallen rocks were too dangerous to negotiate. So she stood there, unable to move.

At length, with what seemed to her like unutterable slyness, the dimmest of lights began to glow. Slowly the illumination brightened. Coming from a distant point, it showed Kathi that she was indeed standing in the merest crack between two rough shoulders of rock. The floor of this crack was littered with debris. She recognised a vadose passage, formed by a flow of water cutting into the rock.

She summoned up all her courage. With her awe came a cold excitement. She was convinced that she had intruded into a lofty consciousness and that some part of it – whether physical or mental – was now approaching her. Her upbringing had accustomed her to sacred places. Now she must face the wrath or at best the curiosity of something, some ancient unknown thing. She felt her lower jaw tremble as the light increased. There was nowhere she could run to.

The light became a dazzle.

'Oh, there you are! Why did you rush off like that?' said

Chad Chester, in an annoyed voice. 'You could have been in deep shit.'

She was back in the buggy, sipping hot coffdrink. Dreiser put an arm protectively about her shoulders. 'You gave us all quite a scare.'

'Why wasn't your lousy headlamp maintained? You're as bad as the slavedrivers in Sarawak.'

'At least we have established the existence of subterranean water, thanks to you,' he said comfortably.

8

Meanwhile our humdrum lives in the domes were continuing, but I at least was filled with optimism regarding our plans, which ripened day by day.

Adminex circulated our findings on the Ambient and published them on impounded EUPACUS printers. We emphasised that people must be clear on what was acceptable. We invited suggestions for guiding principles.

We suggested a common meeting for discussion in Hindenburg every morning, which anyone might attend.

We placed a high priority on tolerance and the cultivation of empathy.

We concluded by saying, What Cannot be Avoided Must Be Endured.

I received a message back on my Ambient link, saying, 'Be practical, will you? We need more toilets, boss. What cannot be endured must be avoided.' I recognised Beau Stephens's voice.

In those days, I became too busy to think about myself. There was much to organise. Yet some things organised themselves. Among them, sport and music.

I was jo-joing back from the new hospital wing when I saw the freshly invented game of skyball being played in the sports arena. I stopped to watch. Aktau Badawi was with me.

Skyball was a team game played with two balls the size of footballs. One ball, painted blue, was half filled with helium so that, when kicked into the air, its descent was slow. Play could continue only when the blue ball was in

87

the air. Grouping and positioning went on while it was descending. The blue ball could not be handled, unlike the other ball, which was brown.

'Thankfully, we are too old to play, Tom,' said Aktau.

A young man turned from the watching crowd and offered to explain the subtleties of the game to us.

We laughingly said we did not wish to know. We would never play.

'Nor would I,' the man said, 'but I in fact invented the blue ball in honour of our lighter gravity. My name is Guenz Kanli, and I wish to speak to you about another innovation I have in mind.'

He fell in with us and we walked back to my office.

Guenz Kanli had a curious physiognomy. The flesh of his face seemed not to fit well over his skull, which came to a peak at the rear. This strange-looking man came from Kazakstan in Central Asia. He was a YEA who, at twenty years of age, had fallen in love with the desolation of the Martian landscape. His eyes were bloodshot, his cheeks so mottled with tiny veins they resembled an indecipherable map.

He lived at the top of one of our spicules, which gave him a good outlook on the Martian surface. He described it in eloquent terms.

'It's all so variable. The wispy clouds take strange forms. You could watch them all day. There are fogs, and I have seen tiny snow falls – or maybe frost it was. The desert can be white or grey or almost black, or brown, or even bright orange in the sun.

'Then there are many kinds of dust storm, from little dust devils to massive storms like avalanches.

'None of this can we touch. It's like a form of music to me. You teach people to look inward on themselves, Tom Jefferies. Maybe looking outward is good too.

'We need more of a special music. It exists already, part sad, part joyful.

'If I may, I will take you to hear the wonderful Beza this evening.'

*　　*　　*

Guenz Kanli was enthusiastic to a remarkable degree, which was perhaps what commended him to me in the first place. I dreaded that a mood of irreversible depression would descend on us if the ships did not soon return.

That evening, we went to hear Beza play.

I was seized with Guenz's idea, although I never entirely saw the connection, as he did, between Beza's gipsy music and the Martian landscape.

There was always music playing somewhere in the domes – classical, jazz, popular, or something in between. But, from that evening on, one of our favourite musicians was Beza, an old Romanian gypsy. I persuaded the leading YEAs to listen – Kissorian, May Porter, Suung Saybin, and others. They were taken by it, and from then on Beza was in fashion.

Beza had been elected as DOP – rather against his wish, we gathered – by a remote community in the Transylvanian highlands.

To see Beza during the day, sitting miserable and round-shouldered at the Mars Bar or a café table, wearing his floppy off-white tunic, you would wonder what such a poor old fellow was doing on Mars. But when he took up his violin and began to play – *bashavav*, to play the fiddle – his real stature became apparent.

His dark eyes gleamed through his lank grey hair, his stance was that of a youngster, and the music he played – well, I can only say that it was magic, and so compelling that men ceased their conversation with women to listen. Guenz sometimes took up his fiddle too and played counterpoint.

With the fiddle at his chin and his bow dancing, Beza could play all night. His music was drawn from a deep well of the past, like wine flowing from centuries of slavery and wandering, rising from the pit of the brain, from the fibres of the body. These tunes were what is meant when music is said to be the first of all human arts.

A time dawned when Guenz's theory that this was the

true music of Mars became real to me. I wondered how it had come into being before Mars had ever been thought of as a place for habitation.

After I had listened to Beza I would lie in bed, wide awake, trying to recreate his music in my head. It always eluded me. A slow sad *lassu*, with its notes long drawn out, would be followed by a sprightly *friss*, light and airy as a stroll along an avenue, which then broke into the wild exhilaration of the *czardas*. Then, quite suddenly, sorrow again, driving into the heart.

I must admit I learned these foreign terms from Guenz, or from Beza himself. But Beza was a silent man. His fiddle spoke for him.

Beza's music was so popular that it became subject to plagiarism. In a small classical quintet was an ambitious Nigerian, Dayo Obantuji. He played the violin adequately, and the quintet was a success, perhaps because Dayo was something of a show-off. He liked to leap to his feet to play solos and generally appear energetic.

The quintet became less popular while Beza's music was still the rage.

Dayo was also a composer. He introduced a piece, a rather elegant sonata in B flat major, which he christened 'The Musician'.

After 'The Musician' had been played several times, Guenz became suspicious. He made a public denunciation of the fact that much of the sonata, transposed into another key and with altered tempo, was based on a piece that Beza played.

Dayo strongly denied the accusation.

When Beza was brought into an improvised court as a witness in this case of plagarism, he would only laugh and say, 'Let the boy take this theme. It is not mine. It hangs in the air. Let him play with it – he can only make it worse.'

There the matter was dropped. But 'The Musician' was not played again.

Instead Dayo came to me and complained that he was the victim of racism. Why had this unfair charge been brought, if not because he was black? I pointed out that although Beza was himself of a minority – indeed a minority of one – he was almost the most popular man in Mars City. I said I felt strongly that racism had no place on the planet. We were all Martians now. Dayo must be mistaken.

Angrily, Dayo asserted that I was denying what was obvious. He had been disgraced by the accusation. His name had not been properly cleared. He was the victim of injustice.

A long argument ensued. Finally Guenz was brought in. He also denied prejudice. He had found an echo of Beza's music in Dayo's piece. It was hardly surprising, but there it was. However, he had been convinced that the similarity was accidental, so powerful was Beza's influence. He was content to believe that Dayo's name had been cleared. And he apologised graciously, if rather playfully, for having made the charge in the first place.

Dayo again asserted he had been victimised. He burst into angry tears.

'Oh dear, the blue ball is in the air again,' said Guenz.

Then Dayo changed tack. He admitted that he had stolen the theme from Beza's music, having been unable to get it out of his head.

'I admit it. I'm guilty as hell. You lot are guilty too. Okay, you show no racial prejudice against Beza and the Orientals, but you are prejudiced against us blacks. You secretly don't believe we're good for anything, though you'll never admit it. I'm quite a good musician, but still I'm a black musician, not just a musician. Isn't that the case?

'My compositions were not appreciated. Not until I took that Romanian tune and transcribed it. Didn't Brahms do the same sort of thing? What's wrong with it? I altered it, made it my own, didn't I? But just because I was black, you picked on me.'

'Perhaps the mistake was,' said Guenz, mildly, 'not to

label the piece "Romanian Rhapsody" – to acknowledge the borrowing. Then you'd have been praised for your cleverness.'

But Dayo insisted that he would merely have been accused of stealing.

'I meant no harm. I only wished to raise my status. But if you're black you're always in trouble, whichever way you turn.'

He went off in dejection.

Tom and Guenz looked at each other in dismay.

Then Guenz broke into a laugh. 'It's you whites who are to blame for everything, including getting us here,' he said.

'My instinct is to legislate. But what could legislation do in a case like this? How might one word it? Can I ask you, Guenz, do you feel yourself racially discriminated against, as a Central Asian?'

'It has sometimes proved to be an advantage, because it had some slight novelty value. That's worn off. There was a time when people were suspicious of my foreignness, but that is in-built, a survival trait. I was equally suspicious of you whites. Still am, to a degree.'

They discussed whether they had any extra in-built discrimination against the Nigerian, Dayo. Had they expected him to 'get away' with something? Had the dismal past history of white victimisation of blacks anything to do with it? Was there a superstitious mistrust of 'black' as a colour, as there might be of lefthandedness?

These were questions they could not answer. They had to conclude it might be the case. Certainly, they would be wary if a traditional green Martian appeared in their midst.

They could only hope that such atavistic responses would die away as rational men of all colours mixed.

We could only hope that the colour question would fade away, united as we were by a common concern regarding survival and in perfecting our society. However, the matter was to arise again later, and in a more serious case.

92

During this period, I consulted with many people, delegating duties where it was possible to do so. Many people also came to my office to deliver advice or complaint. One of these visitors was a rather lacklustre-looking young YEA scientist. He announced himself as Chad Chester.

'Maybe you know my name as the guy who went down into the water caves off Marineris with Kathi Skadmorr. I guess I didn't make a great showing compared with her.'

'Not many of us do. What can I do for you?'

Chad explained that he had listened to my lecture on the five obstacles to contentment on Earth. He noted that at one point I had referred to the slogan, 'All men are equal'. He was sure this saying embodied a mistaken assumption; he never thought of himself as equal to Kathi, for example. That experience in the caves had led him to put down his thoughts on paper. He felt that 'All men are equal' should not be used in any utopian declaration we might make, for reasons he had tried to argue.

When he had gone I set Chad's paper aside. I looked at it two days later.

His argument was that the very saying was self-denying, since it mentioned only men and not women. It was meaningless to pretend that men and women were equal; they were certainly similar in many ways, but the divergence between them made the question of being equal (except possibly in law) irrelevant. Furthermore, the diversity of the genetic code meant a different inheritance of capacities even within a family.

'All men are equal' held an implication that all could compete equally; that also was untrue. A musician may have no capacity for business. A nuclear physicist may be unable to build a bridge. And so forth, for several pages.

He suggested that a better slogan would be, 'All men and women must be allowed equal opportunities to fulfil their lives.'

I liked the idea, although it had not the economy, the

snap, of the original it replaced. I wondered about 'All dudes are different.'

Any such sloganeering boiled down to one thing. It was important to have maximum latitude to express ourselves within the necessarily confining rules of our new society. Someone mentioned the dragon that earlier YEAs had painted on the rock face; they emphasised the way in which it had caused alarm, being unexpected. Yet creativity must continue to produce the unexpected or the community would perish. Although latitude was needed, it was generally accepted that our society had to operate within prescribed rules.

Creativity we needed, but not stupidity and ignorance.

We had begun to discuss education when a slightly built and handsome young woman with dark hair came forward. She poured out from the pockets of her overalls on to a central table a number of gleaming objects, various in shape.

'Before you speak of any orderly society, you'd better be aware,' she said, 'that Mars is already occupied by a higher form of life. They carved these beautiful objects and then, evidently dissatisfied with them, cast them away.'

The room was in an uproar. Everyone was eager to examine the exquisite shapes, seemingly made of glass. Some appeared to be roughly shaped translucent models of small elephants, snails, labias and phalluses, puppy dogs, hippopotami, boulders, coproliths, and hedgehogs. All were bright and pleasant to the touch.

The faces of those who picked up the objects were full of alarm. Always at the back of our minds had been the suspicion that the yet almost unexplored planet might somehow, against all reason, harbour life.

The young woman allowed the drama of the situation she had created to sink in before saying, loudly, 'I'm an areologist. I've been working alone in the uplands for a week. Don't worry! These are pieces of rock crystal, chemical formula SiO_2. They're just translucent quartz, created by nature.'

A howl mingled with dismay and approbation rose.

The young woman said with a laugh, 'Oh, I thought I'd just give you a scare while you were making up all these rules to live by.'

I persuaded her to sit by me while the crowd reassembled. She was lively and restless. Her name was Sharon Singh, she told me. She was half-English, half-Indian, and had spent much of her young life in the terrestrial tropics.

'You can't find Mars particularly congenial,' I remarked.

She gave a wriggle. 'Oh, it's an adventure. Unlike you, I do not intend to live here for ever. Besides, there are many idle and eager men here who enjoy a little romance. That's one of the real meanings of life, isn't it? Mine is a romantic nature . . .' She flashed a smile at me, then regarded me more seriously. 'What are you thinking?'

I could not tell her, saying instead, 'I was thinking that we can sell these pretty rock crystal objects for souvenirs when matrix traffic resumes.'

Sharon Singh uttered a rather scornful laugh, momentarily showing her pretty white teeth. 'Some things are not for sale!' She gave her wriggle again.

That night, I could not sleep. The smile, those dark eyes fringed by dense lashes, the carelessness, the wriggle – they filled my mind. All my serious contemplations were gone, together with my resolves. I thought – well, I thought that I would follow Sharon Singh to Earth, and gladly, if need be. That I would give anything for a night with her in my arms.

In order to sublimate my desire for Sharon Singh, I made a point of talking personally to as many men and women as possible, sounding out their opinions and gathering an impression of their feelings towards our situation and the practicalities of living decently.

My quantcomp rang as I was going down K.S. Robinson. A woman's voice requested an appointment. In another half-hour, I found myself confronting Willa Mendanadum and her large companion, Vera White. I saw them in my small office. With Vera in her large flowing lilac robes, the room was pretty full.

Willa had a commanding voice, Vera a tiny one.

'As you will no doubt be aware, Vera and I are mentatropists,' said Willa. 'While we support your wish to form a utopian society, we have to tell you that such is an impossibility.'

'How so?' I asked, not best pleased by her haughty manner.

'Because of the contradictory nature of mankind in general and individuals in particular. We think we desire order and calm, but the autonomous nervous system requires some disorder and excitement.'

'Is it not exciting enough just to be on Mars?'

She said sternly, 'Why, certainly not. We don't even have the catharsis of S&V movies to watch.'

Seeing my slight puzzlement, Vera said in her high voice, 'Sex and Violence, Mr Jefferies, Sex and Violence.' She spread "violence" out into its three component syllables.

'So you consider utopia a hopeless project?'

'Unless . . .'

'Unless?' Vera White drew herself up to her full girth. 'A full course of mentatropy for all personnel.'

'Including all the scientists,' added Willa in her deepest tone.

They departed in full sail when I thanked them for their offer and said Adminex would consider it.

Kissorian came in and exclaimed that I looked taken aback. 'I've just met some mentatropists,' I said.

He laughed. 'Oh, the Willa-Vera Composite!' And so they became known.

We did not forget – at least in those early days – that we constituted a mere pimple on the face of Mars, that grim and dusty planet that remained there, uncompromising, aloof. Despite the reinforcements of modern science, our position was best described as precarious.

The static nature of the world on which we found ourselves weighed heavily on many minds, especially those of delicate sensibility. The surface of Mars had remained stable, immovable, dead, throughout eons of its history. Compared with its restless neighbour from which we had come, Mars's tectonic history was one of locked immobility. It was a world without oceans or mountain chains, its most prominent feature being the Tharsis Shield, that peculiar gravitic anomaly, together with the unique feature of Olympus Mons.

Emerging from the hectic affairs of the third planet, many people viewed this long continued stillness with horror. For them it was as if they had become locked into one of the tombs in Egypt's Valley of the Kings. This obsessive form of isolation became known as areophobia.

A group of young psychurgists was called before Adminex to deal with the worst afflicted cases. Some of them had earlier reproached me for the thirty-one suicides, saying their services, had they been called into action, would have saved the precious lives. I found among them an enormous respect for the Willa-Vera Composite; clearly the mentatropy duo were not the figures of fun I had taken them for. Psychurgy itself had developed from a combination of the old psychotherapy and more recent genome research; whereas mentatropy, embodying a new understanding of the brain and consciousness, was a much more hands-on approach to mental problems.

The psychurgists reported that sufferers from areophobia endured a conflict of ideas: with a fear of total isolation went a terror that something living but alien would make its sudden appearance. It was a new version of the stress of the unknown, which disappeared after counselling – and, of course, after a reassurance that Mars was a dead world, without the possibility of life.

For this fear of alien beings I felt that Mr H.G. Wells and his followers were much to blame. The point I attempted to make was that Mars's role in human thought had been benevolent and scientific – in a word, rational.

To this end, I persuaded Charles Bondi to give an address. Although he regarded my attempts to regulate society as a waste of time, he responded readily enough to deliver an exposition of Mars's place in humanity's progressive thought.

His speech concluded: 'The great Johannes Kepler's study of the orbital motions of the body on which we find ourselves yielded the three laws of planetary motion. Space travel has come to be based on Kepler's laws. The name of Kepler will always remain honoured for those brilliant calculations, as well as for his wish to reduce to sense what had previously been muddle.

'If we are to remain long enough on Mars, our eccentric friend here, Thomas Jefferies, will try to perform a feat equivalent in sociological terms to Kepler's, reducing to regulation what has always been a tangle of conflicting patterns of behaviour from which, to my mind, creativity has sprung.'

Bondi could not resist that final dig at me.

Yes, ours was an ambitious task. I saw, as he did not, that it could be accomplished because we were a small population, and one which, as it happened, had been self-selected for its social awareness.

During one debate the Ukrainian Muslim YEA named Youssef Choihosla rose and declared that we were all wasting our time. He said that whatever rules of conduct we drew up, even those to which we had readily given universal consent, we would break; such was the nature of mankind.

He was continuing in this vein when a woman of distinguished appearance spoke up to ask him cuttingly if he considered we should have no rules?

Choihosla paused. And if we were to have rules, pursued the woman, pressing home her advantage and looking increasingly majestic, was it not wise to discover what the best rules were and then try to abide by them?

The Ukrainian became defensive. He had spent his year of community service, he claimed, working in an asylum for the mentally deranged in Sarajevo. He had experienced terrible things there. He believed as a result that what Carl Jung called 'the shadow' would always manifest itself. It was therefore useless to hope to establish even a mockery of a utopia. You could not pump morality into a system to which it was not indigenous. (A year or two later, interestingly, he would put forward a much more positive viewpoint.)

Several voices attempted to answer him. The woman who had previously spoken quelled them with her clear firm tones. Her name was Belle Rivers. She was the headmistress in charge of the cadre children, semi-permanently stationed on Mars.

'Why is there a need for laws, you ask? Are laws not present in all societies, to guard against human "shadows"? As scientific people, we are aware that the human body is a museum of its phylogenetic history. Our psyches too are immensely old; their roots lie in times before we could claim the name of human. Only our individual minds belong to ontology, and they are transient. It is the creatures – our archetypes, Jung calls them – that reside in the unconscious, like your shadow, which act as prompts to the behaviour of the human species.

'The archetypes live in an inner world, where the pulse of time throbs at a drowsy pace, scarcely heeding the birth and death of individuals. Their nature is strange: when they broke into the conscious minds of your patients in Sarajevo, they undoubtedly would have precipitated psychosis. Your psychurgists will tell you as much.

'But we moderns know these things. The archetypes have been familiar to us for more than a century. Instead of fearing them, of trying to repress them, we should come to terms with them. That means coming to terms with ourselves.

'I believe that we must draw up our rules firmly and without fear, in acknowledgement of our conscious wishes. I also regard it as healthy that we acknowledge our unconscious wishes.

'I therefore propose that every seventh day be given

over to bacchanalia, when ordinary rules of conduct are suspended.'

My glance went at once to the bench where Sharon Singh lounged. She was gazing serenely at the roof, the long fingers of one hand tapping gently on the rail of her seat. She was calm while much shouting and calls for order continued round her.

An old unkempt man rose to speak. He had once been Governor of the Seychelles; his name was Crispin Barcunda. We had spoken often. I enjoyed his quiet sense of humour. When he laughed a gold tooth sparkled briefly like a secret signal.

'This charming lady puts forward a perfectly workable idea,' he said, attempting to smooth down his mop of white hair. 'Why not have the odd bacchanalia now and again? No one on Earth need know. We're private, here on Mars, aren't we?'

This suggestion was put forward in a droll manner so that people laughed. Crispin continued more seriously. 'It is curious, is it not, that before we have established our laws, there should be what sounds like rather a popular proposal to abolish them every seventh day? However welcome the throwing off of restraints, dangers follow from it . . . Is the day after one of these bacchanalias to be declared a mopping-up day? A bandaging-of-broken-heads day? A day of broken vows and tears and quarrels?'

Immediately, people were standing up and shouting. A cry of 'Don't try to legislate our sex lives' was widely taken up.

Crispin Barcunda appeared unmoved. When the noise died slightly, he spoke again.

'Since we are getting out of hand, I will attempt to read to you, to calm you all down.'

While he was speaking, Barcunda produced from the pocket of his overalls a worn leather-bound book.

As he opened it, he said, 'I brought this book with me on the journey here, in case I woke up when we were only three months out from Earth and needed something to read. It is written by a man I greatly admire, Alfred Russell Wallace, one of those later-borns our friend Hal Kissorian mentioned in his remarkable contribution the other day.

'Wallace's book, by the way, is called *The Malay Archipelago*. I believe it has something valuable to offer us on Mars.'

Barcunda proceeded to read: '"I have lived with communities of savages in South America and in the East, who have no laws or law courts but the public opinion of the village freely expressed. Each man scrupulously respects the rights of his fellow, and any infraction of those rights rarely or never takes place. In such a community, all are nearly equal. There are none of those wide distinctions, of education and ignorance, wealth and poverty, master and servant, which are the product of our civilisation; there is none of that wide-spread division of labour, which, while it increases wealth, produces also conflicting interests; there is not that severe competition and struggle for existence, or for wealth, which the dense population of civilized countries inevitably creates.

'"All incitements to great crimes are thus wanting, and petty ones are repressed, partly by the influence of public opinion, but chiefly by that natural sense of justice and of his neighbour's right which seems to be, in some degree, inherent in every race of man."'

Snapping the book shut, Barcunda said, 'Mr Chairman, my vote is that we have but one law: Thou shalt not compete!'

A YEA immediately shouted, 'That's all very well for you DOPs. We young men have to compete – there aren't enough women for all of us!'

Again I looked towards Sharon Singh.

She was examining her nails, as if remote from intellectual discussion.

After the session closed, I talked with Barcunda. We had a coffdrink together. His pleasant personality came across very clearly. I said that it was unfortunate we were not in as favourable a position as Wallace's savages.

He replied that our situations were surprisingly similar, sunshine deficiency apart.

Our work was not labour, our food was adequate, and we had few possessions.

And we had a benefit the savages of Wallace's East could not lay claim to, which was the novelty of our situation: we were in a learning experience, isolated millions of miles from Earth.

'It is vitally important that we retain our good sense and good humour, and draw up an agenda for a just life quickly. We cannot secure total agreement, because the pleasure of some people is to disagree. What we require is a majority vote – and our agenda must not be seen to be drawn up merely by DOPs. That would give the young bucks among the YEAs an opportunity to challenge authority. They can't go out into the jungle to wrestle with lions and gorillas to prove their manhood: they'd wrestle with us instead.'

He gestured and pulled a savage face face to demonstrate his point.

'You can't say I'm a very dictatorial chairman.'

'I can't. But maybe they can. Take a day off, Tom. Hand over the chair to a young trouble-maker. Kissorian might be a good candidate, besides having such a fun name.'

'Kissorian goes by favour, eh?'

Looking at me poker-faced, Crispin said that he wanted legislation to improve the Martian brand of ersatz coffee. 'Tom, joking apart, we are so fortunate as to have the bad luck to be stuck on Mars! We both see the survival of humanity on a planet on which we were not born as an extraordinary, a revolutionary, step.

'I must say I listened to your five bugbears with some impatience. I wanted you to get to the bugbear we have clearly escaped from: the entire systematic portrayal of sexuality and violence as desirable and of overwhelming importance. We no longer have these things pouring like running water from our television and Ambient screens. I fancy that deprived of this saccharine/strychnine drip, we can only improve morally.'

102

At the next meeting of Adminex (as always, televised for intercom and Ambient), we discussed this aspect of life: the constant projection of violence and sexual licence on media that imitated life. Both Kissorian and Barcunda were coopted on to the team. It was agreed – in some cases with reluctance – that most of us had been indoctrinated by the constant representation of personal assult and promiscuity on various screens, so as to accept such matters as an important part of life, or at least as a more dominant component of our subconscious minds than we were willing to admit to. In Barcunda's elegant formulation: 'If a man has an itch, he will scratch it, even when talking philosophy.'

Without pictorial representations of a gun and sex culture, there seemed a good chance that society might become less aggressive.

But Kissorian disagreed. 'Sex is one thing, and violence quite another. Barcunda compounds them into one toxic dose by talking of the saccharine/strychnine drip. I agree that it's really no loss that we do not have these activities depicted on TV here, but, believe me, we need sex. What else do we have? Everything else is in short supply. We certainly need sex. You speak as if there were something unnatural about it.'

Barcunda protested that he was not against sex, only constant and unnecessary depictions of its various activities.

'It's a private thing,' he said, leaning across the table. 'Showing it on the screen transforms a private thing into a public, a political, act. And so it muddies the deep waters of the spirit.'

Kissorian looked down his nose. 'You DOPs had better realise that for the amount of screwing that goes on you'd think we were on Venus.'

Kathi Skadmorr's activities as a speleologist had made her the hero of the hour. It was suggested at the end of the meeting that I should coopt her on to the Adminex, if only to make that body more popular. I agreed, but was not eager to have another confrontation with her on Ambient.

We continued our discussion of Crispin Barcunda's saccharine/strychnine drip privately. One of the fundamental questions was whether love and sexuality would become more enjoyable if they retreated into being private things? Without constant representation visually in the media, would not a certain precious intimacy be restored to the act? But how to bring this thing about without censorship: that is, to influence public opinion so that ordinary persons who wished to do so could rid themselves of the poisonous drip, as they had in previous ages rid themselves of the enjoyments of cock-fighting, slavery and tobacco-smoking?

Crispin said, 'You want to advance towards the betterment of mankind? Maybe it can be done, maybe not! But let's have a try, Tom. After all, it gives our lives here an objective. Betterment means a break with the past – chop, like that! – not just a continuation of it, as would have been the case had the terraformers and realtors had their way. Maybe we can do it. But I'd be against any suspicion that sexuality and eroticism was not in itself one of mankind's blessings. The older I get, and the more difficult sex gets, the more I become convinced it holds the meaning of any valued life.'

I could but agree. 'We must try to influence minds. It is important – and not just for our little outpost here. We're not going to be isolated for ever. Once EUPACUS or its successors have been reassembled, once the world economy has picked up, ships are going to be operating again.

'By that time, we must have our mini-utopia up and running. Just to be a shining example to Earth, to which most of us wish to return.'

'Then maybe on Earth, as in good old Wallace's island community, the ideal might be reached, where each man scrupulously regards the rights of his fellow man.' As he spoke, Crispin gazed earnestly and short-sightedly into my eyes. 'Like not shooting him or fucking his wife.'

He was a good man. Talking with him, I was convinced we could become a better, happier, humanity – without the pathetic need of saccharine/strychnine drips.

'Now you'd better go and coopt Skadmorr,' he said. 'She'll lower the average age of Adminex by a few years!'

I was up early next morning. Runners and the semi-flighted were already about in the streets, exercising. Although we had yet to solve the question of the Martian date line, we had solved the problem of dividing up the days and weeks. Mars's axial rotation makes its day only sixty-nine minutes longer than Earth's day. In the time of EUPACUS, an extra 'hour' of sixty-nine minutes had been inserted to follow the hour of two in the morning. This was the 'X' hour. The other hours conformed to the terrestrial twenty-four.

The innovation of the 'X' hour meant that at first terrestrial watches had to be adjusted every day, until an ingenious young technician, Bill Abramson, made his reputation by inserting what he called 'the "X" trigger,' which suspended the momentum of watches and clocks for sixty-nine minutes every night, after which they continued working normally as before.

Since an hour is basically the way we measure our progress through the day, there were few complaints at this somewhat ad hoc arrangement. But it did mean that human activity restarted fairly early in the day.

Taking in the scene around me, I could only appreciate the change from the city on Earth I had left, with its gigantic byzantine structures housing thousands of people, walled in like bees in their cells with Ambient connections supplying many of their needs, the façades of these structures awash with pornographic images once sun had set. Below those great ragged skylines, below the coiling avenues, lived the impromptus, subsisting on the city's grime, anaesthetised by the free porntrips overhead.

But here, under our low ceilings, was a more hygienic world, where coloured plastic ducts were running in parallel or diverging overhead, with jazzy patterns in rubber tiles below our feet and stylised lighting. Birds flew and called among the plant clusters at every intersection. It was at once more abstract and more human in scale than terrestrial cities. I recalled an exhibition I had attended in my home city hall of the paintings of an old twentieth-century artist, Hubert Rogers. Those visions of the future that had so inspired me as a young man were here realised. I recalled them with pleasure as I hopped on a jo-jo bus.

So it was just before six o'clock that I called on Mary Fangold at the hospital for a coffee. I liked to talk over events with this reasonable and attractive woman – and incidentally to visit my adopted daughter, whose implanted leg was now almost completely regenerated.

The first person I encountered was Kathi Skadmorr. She was striding out of the gym with a towel round her neck, looking the picture of health.

'Hi! I was watching your discussion of the prevalence of violent and sexual material. I thought you were talking sense for once.' She spoke in a friendly way, regarding me through those dark, lash-frilled eyes of hers. 'What we usually do in private should remain private. Ain't that what you were saying? It's pretty simple really.'

'Bringing about the change is a problem, though. That's not simple.'

'How about telling people to keep it quiet?'

'It's better to get people's consent rather than just telling them.'

'You could tell them, then get their consent. Remember the old saying, Tom: Once you get folk by the balls, their hearts and minds will follow.' She giggled.

'So what are you doing here, so early in the morning?'

'I came over from the science unit to see Cang Hai. Then I did an hour's work-out. Are you visiting your daughter?'

'Um, yes. Yes, I am.'

She then asked me what I made of Cang Hai's Other,

her mental friend in Chengdu. I had to admit I had really not considered it. Her Other did not impinge on my life.

'Nor apparently does your daughter,' she said with a return to her earlier asperity. 'She really loves you, you know that? I believe she has an unusual kind of consciousness, as I have. Her Other may be a kind of detached reflection of her own psyche. Or it may be a little encapsulated psyche within her own psyche, like a – a kind of cyst within her soul. I'm studying it.'

At this juncture, Mary appeared. She was direct as usual and told us to enter her office for coffee and a talk. 'But it had better be a brief talk. Say twenty minutes at most. I have a lot to do today.'

As we sat down, I asked Kathi if her unusual kind of consciousness was also a 'cyst within her soul'. I used her phrase.

'My consciousness embraces an external. It embraces Mars. It's all to do with the life force. I'm a mystic, believe it or not. I've been down into the gullet, or maybe the vagina, of this planet, into its bladder. I have nothing but contempt for those thirty or however many it was who committed suicide here. They were prats. Good that they died! We don't want people like that. We want people who are able to live beyond their own narrow lives.'

'They were all victims, cut off from their families,' Mary Fangold said.

'They didn't do their families much good by killing themselves, did they?'

She crossed her long legs and sipped at the mug of coffdrink Mary had brought. Almost to herself, she said, 'I thirst for what Tom proposed – the mind set free!'

Mary and I started to talk together, but Kathi cut us short, speaking eagerly. 'You should get rid of all this flaunting of sex, as you say. Sex is just a recreation, after all, sometimes good, sometimes not so good. Nothing to be obsessed about. Once you get it out of the way you can fill everyone's minds with real valuable things, mental occupations. Without TV or the other distractions, we can be educated in science in all its branches. We must learn more, all of us. It's urgent. "Civilisation is a race between education and catastrophe" – you remember that saying? Education throughout life. Wouldn't that be wonderful?'

Somehow I did not take that opportunity to invite her to join Adminex. I felt she might be too disruptive. However Kissorian asked her a few weeks later. Kathi turned down the offer, saying she was not a committee person. That we could well believe.

Kissorian had a piece of gossip too. He said Kathi was having a love affair – 'frequently in the sack', was his way of putting it – with Beau Stephens. We thought about that. Beau at this time showed little ambition, and was working on the jo-jos.

I realise that I have made little mention in this record of Cang Hai, who had attached herself to me. Certainly she is devoted, and it is hard not to return affection when it is offered without condition. She became increasingly useful to me, and was no fool.

Of course she was no substitute for Antonia.

Cang Hai's Account

9

Improving the Individual

In hospital I learned to walk with my artificial leg. At first it had no feeling; cartilage growth was slow. Now the nerves were growing back and connecting, giving a not unpleasant fizzy sensation. When I was allowed out of hospital for an hour at a time, I took a stroll through the domes, feeling my muscle tone rapidly return.

Attempts had been made to brighten the atmosphere of our enforced home while I had been out of action. The jo-jo buses were being repainted in bright colours; some were decorated with fantastic figures, such as the 'Mars dragon'.

Glass division walls were tanks containing living fish, gliding like sunlit spaceships in their narrow prisons. The flowering trees recently planted along the main avenues were doing well. More Astroturf had been planted. Between the trees flitted macaws and parrots, bright of plumage, genetically adapted to sing sweetly.

I liked the birds, knowing they had been cloned.

Inspired by these improvements, I tried to brighten Tom's spartan quarters.

When I was fit enough to rejoin my fellows, I found more confidence in myself, perhaps as a result of my friendship with Kathi.

So a year passed, and still we remained isolated on Mars.

Our society was composed as follows. There were

412 non-visitors or cadre (all those who were conducting scientific experiments, technicians, 'carers', managers, and others employed permanently on Mars before the EUPACUS crash), together with their children. This number comprised 196 women, 170 men and 46 children, ranging in age from a few months to fifteen years old, plus 62 babies under six months. Of the 2,025 DOPs, 1,405 were men and 620 women, and of the 3,420 YEAs, 2,071 were men and 1,349 women. A visiting inspection team consisted of 9 medics (5 women and 4 men) and 30 flight technicians (28 men and 2 women).

Thus the total population of Mars in AD 2064 was 5,958.

To which it must be added that two carers, two DOP women and 361 of the YEA women (about one-quarter of them) were pregnant. The population of the planet was, in other words, due to increase by about 6 per cent within the next six months.

This caused some alarm and much discussion. Blame went flying about, mainly from the DOPs, although as a group they were not entirely blameless. A pharmacist came forward to admit that the pharmacy, which was housed in the R&A hospital, had run out of anti-conception pills, having been unprepared for the EUPACUS crash and the cessation of regular supplies of pharmaceuticals.

After this revelation some DOPs suggested that young people use restraint in their sexual lives. The suggestion was not well received, not least because many couples had discovered that sex held an additional piquancy and that an act of intercourse could be sustained for longer, in the lighter Martian gravity. Nevertheless worries were expressed concerning the extra demands on water and oxygen supplies that the babies would exert.

I tried to commune with my shaded half in Chengdu. My message was: 'Once more, the spectre of overpopulation is raising its head – on an almost empty planet!' It was puzzling to receive in return an image of a barren moorland covered in what seemed to be a layer of snow.

As I tried to peer at this snow cover, it resolved itself into a great white flock of geese. The geese bestirred themselves and took to the air. They flew round and round in tight formation, their wings making a noise like the beating of a leather gong. The ground had disappeared beneath them.

It was all beautiful enough, but not particularly helpful.

Tom and I took a walk one evening, and were discussing the population question. A strip of sidewalk along the street was covered with an Astroturf that mimicked growth and was periodically trimmed. This was Spider Plant Alley, renamed after the plants that mopped up hydroxyls, much as Poulsen had said. Throughout the domes, plants were pervading the place.

I particularly liked Spider Plant at the evening hour. It was then that the quantcomp that controlled our ambient atmospheric conditions turned lighting low and cut temperatures by 5 degrees for the night. A slight breeze rustled the plants – a tender natural sound, even if controlled by human agency.

As I hung on Tom's arm, I asked him when he was going to regulate primary sexual behaviour.

He replied that anyone who attempted such regulation would meet with disaster, that sexuality was a vital and pervasive part of our corporeal existence. While other facets of that existence were denied us on Mars, it was only to be expected that sexual activity should intensify.

'You also have to understand, dear daughter, that sexual pleasure is good in itself – a harmless and life-enhancing pleasure.' He looked down at me with a half-smile. 'Why else has it excited so many elders to control it throughout the ages? Of course, beyond the sexual act lie potential ethical problems. With those we can perhaps deal. I mean – well, the consequences of the sexual act, babies, diseases and all those rash promises to love for ever when lust is like fire to the straw i' the blood, as Hamlet says.'

We walked on before I added, 'Or, of course, whether both parties give their consent to the merging of their bodies.'

I thought of how I was always reluctant to give that consent. Had I, by becoming Tom's adopted daughter, somehow managed to avoid giving that consent yet again? I did not know myself. Though I lived in an info-rich environment, my inner motivations remained unknown to me.

'You are justifying sex simply because it's enjoyable?' I asked.

'No, no. Sex justifies itself simply because it's enjoyable. Sometimes it can even seem like an end in itself.'

Silence fell between us, until Tom said – I thought with some reluctance – 'My father spent all his inherited wealth on a medical clinic in a foreign land. I was brought up there. When I was repatriated at the age of fifteen, both my parents were dead. I was utterly estranged, and put under the nominal care of my Aunt Letitia.' He stopped, so that we stood there in the semi-dark. I held his hand.

'I fell in love with my cousin, Diana – "Diana, huntress chaste and fair", the poet says. Luckily, this Diana was fair and unchaste. I was cold, withdrawn – traumatised, I suppose. Diana was a little older than I, eager to experience the joys of sexual union. I cannot express the rapture of that first kiss, when our lips met. That kiss was my courageous act, my reaching out to another person.'

'Is that what it needs? Courage?'

He ignored me. 'Within hours we were naked together, exploring each others' bodies, and then making love – under the sun, under the moon, even, once, in the rain. The delirium of innocent joy I felt . . . Ah, her eyes, her hair, her thighs, her perfume – how they possessed me! . . . I'm sorry, Cang, this must be distasteful to you. I'll just say that beyond all sensual pleasure lies a sense of a new and undiscovered life.

'No, I'm a dry old stick now, but I'd be a monster if I tried to deny such pleasures to our fellow denizens . . .'

I was feeling cold and suggested we went inside.

'People still think you're some kind of a dictator,' I said, with more spite in my tone than I had intended.

Tom replied that he imagined he was rather a laughing stock. Idealists were always a butt for humour. Fortunately,

he had no ambition, only hope. Enough hope, he said,
lightly, to fill a zeppelin. He repeated, enough hope . . .
Yet in his mouth that last word held a dying fall.
That night, when alone, I wept. I could not stop.

I wept mostly for myself, but also for humanity, so
possessed by their reproductive organs. Our Martian population was slave to unwritten ancient law, multiplying as
it saw fit. That pleasure of which my Tom spoke always
came with responsibilities.

At least the R&A hospital could prepare for an outburst
of maternity, its original duties being in abeyance. There
were no new intakes of visitors to be acclimatised. One
ward was converted into a new maternity unit, all brightly
lit and antiseptic, in which births could be conducted with
conveyer-belt efficiency.

Everywhere, there was industry. Existing buildings were
converted to new uses. The synthesising kitchens were
extended. Factories were established for the synthesis of
cloth for clothing. All talents were seized upon for diverse
works. During the day the noise of hammering and drilling
was to be heard. We would endeavour to be comfortable,
however temporary our stay.

There was music in the domes. Not all terrestrial music
was to our taste, and composers like Beza were sought to
compose Martian music – whatever that might be!

The more far-sighted of us looked ahead to a more
distant future. Among these was Tom. Whether or not he
really had hope, he and his committee pressed ahead with
his plans to involve everyone in everyone else's welfare.
They engrossed him; sometimes I felt he had no personal life.

He declared that it was a matter of expedience that the
education of young children should be given priority. There
I was able to assist him to some extent.

Several committees were elected to formulate with others
their hopes and endeavours for a better society. They held

colloquia, which began in itinerant fashion, the more appealing ones becoming permanent features of our life. Sometimes they were met with impatience or hostility, although it was generally conceded that conditions in the domes might get rapidly worse unless they were rapidly improved. Improvement was something we strove for.

Emerson's remark long ago that people preened themselves on improvements in society, yet no one individual improved, lay at the basis of many endeavours. The mutuality required for a just society implied that we must hope to improve the individual, to fortify him; otherwise any improvements would merely enhance the status of the powerful and lower that of the less powerful, and we would be back with the suppressions so prevalent on Earth.

Somewhere in the individual life must lie the salvation of whole societies, or else all was lost.

Hard as I tried, I found it difficult to study. If only I could learn more, I told myself, Tom would love me more. Many a time, I would simply sit in a café and listen to the music that filled the place. Kathi Skadmorr and I had many conversations. For her, learning seemed easy. She worked with Dreiser Hawkwood and found him, she said, a little overpowering. I thought privately that anyone Kathi found overpowering was worth a great deal of respect.

She had become absorbed in studying Olympus Mons. At times, the great volcanic cone seemed to fill her thought. She had submitted a carefully reasoned paper to Dreiser on the Ambient, suggesting a name change. Olympus was a 'fuddy-duddy' name. She had found a better name for it when talking with an Ecuadorian scientist, Georges Souto. He had told her of an extinct volcano in Ecuador, the top of which, he said, because of the oblate spheroidal nature of Earth, was the point furthest from the centre of the Earth. In fact, it was 2,150 metres further from that centre than Everest, commonly assumed to be the highest point on Earth.

The sophistry of this argument greatly amused Kathi. When she learned that this defunct volcano was named Chimborazo, meaning the 'Watchtower of the Universe', she campaigned for Olympus Mons to be renamed Chimborazo. The campaign was a failure at first, and Dreiser, she said, was annoyed with her for talking nonsense.

Shortly after this, she studied satellite photographs of the Tharsis Shield, and observed – so she claimed – tumbled and churned regolith on the far side of Olympus, as if something had been burrowing there. When she pointed this out to Dreiser, he told her not to waste his time, or she would be sent back to the domes.

Many of the pressures extant on Earth – or Downstairs, as had become the fashionable term for our mother planet – had been relieved by our exile Upstairs. The intense pressure of commercialism had been lifted. So had many of the provocations of racism; here, we were all in the same boat, rather than in many jostling boats.

In particular, money, the gangrene of the political system, had been removed from play, although admittedly a sort of credit scheme existed, whereby payments were postponed until we were hypothetically returned Downstairs.

After a year or so, this credit scheme had taken sick and died, primarily because we found we could manage without it, and secondarily because we ceased to believe in it.

It was deemed futile to approach any individual with ambitious schemes if he or she was miserable. Many people missed or worried about their families Downstairs. Once our communication cards ran out, there was no renewing them, and the terrestrial telecom station was closed down – another feature of the EUPACUS fiasco. Counselling was provided, and the psychurgical group was kept busy. Also effective in healing was the community spirit that had arisen, and a renewed sense of adventure. We lived in a new place, within a new context, the 'different psychological calculus'.

One of our colloquia became engaged in the art of making new music: primarily a capella singing, which we raised to high standards. We had brought in home-made and revolutionary musical instruments. The 'Martian Meritorio' was established in time as our great success. But I still remember with affection our solo voices raised in song – in specially written song.

> No bird flies in the abyss
>   Its bright plumage failing
> No eye lights in the dark
>   Its sight unavailing
> The air carries no spark
>   Only this –
>   Only this
> Where sunlight lies ailing –
> Our human hopes sailing
>   In humankind's ark

The improvement of the individual was pursued in such sessions as body-mind-posture, conducted at first by Ben Borrow, a disciple of the energetic Belle Rivers. Borrow was a little undersized man, full of energy, as easily roused to anger as to raucous laughter. He drove and inspired his attendees to believe, as he did, that the secret of a good life lurked in how one stood, sat and walked in the light gravity.

Perhaps because the bleak surroundings led our thoughts that way, our Art of Imagination colloquium was always successful. Swift and Laputa, those two satellites, first dreamed of by an Irish dean, that chased regularly above our heads, were used to connect the reality of our lives with the greater reality of which we were a transitory part.

A way of knowing ourselves was to relate our lived

experience with the flow of language, thought and concepts surrounding us, by which the mundane could be reimagined. 'Know thyself' was an exortation requiring, above all, imagination. In this department, the Willa-Vera Composite, one so whippetlike, the other so much like a doughnut, proved invaluable.

Hard work along these lines produced some extraordinary artistries, not least the four-panel continuous loop video abstract entitled 'Dawning Diagram' which, with its mystery and majesty, affected all who watched it. Human things writhed into shape from the molecular, rose, ran, flowered in bursts of what could have been sun, could have been rain, might have been basalt, died, bathed in reproductive dawns. In another quarter of the screen an old Tiresias read in a vellum-bound volume, tirelessly turning the same page.

Everything happened simultaneously, in an instant of time.

The aim of the Art of Imagination colloquium was to revive in adults that innocent imagination lost with childhood (although children also enjoyed the programme and gave much to it).

'I know the Sun isn't necessarily square. I just like it better that way.' This remark by an eight-year-old, as comment on his strange painting, *Me and My Universe*, was later embodied in a large multimedia canvas hung at the entrance of the Art of Imagination Department (previously Immigration).

There were those who attended this colloquium who were initially unable to seize on the fact that they were alive and on Mars. So obnubilated were their imaginations they could not grasp the wonder of reality. They needed a metaphorical sense to be restored to them. In many cases, it was restored.

Then they rejoiced and congratulated themselves that they were Upstairs.

To our regret, the scientists in the main kept to their own

quarters, a short distance from the domes. It was not that they were aloof. They claimed to be too busy with research.

I accompanied Tom to the station when he went to talk privately with Dreiser Hawkwood. A woman who announced herself as Dreiser's personal assistant asked us to wait in a small anteroom. We could hear Dreiser growling in his office. Tom was impatient until we were admitted to his presence by this same assistant.

Dreiser Hawkwood was a darkly semi-handsome man, with the look of one who has bitten deep into the apple of the Tree of Knowledge. Indeed, I thought, noticing that his teeth protruded slightly under his moustache, he might have snagged them on its core. He was much preoccupied with the fact that the paper substitute was running out.

'Predictions are for amusement only,' he said. 'When computers came into general use, there was a prediction that paper would be a thing of the past. Far from it. High-tech weaponry systems, for instance, require plenty of documentation. US Navy cruisers used to go to sea loaded with twenty-eight tonnes of manuals. Enough to sink a battleship!'

He jerked his head towards the overloaded bookshelves behind him, from which manuals threatened to spill.

Tom asked him what he was working on.

'Poulsen and I are trying to rejig the programme that controls all our internal weather. It's wasteful of energy and we could use the computer power for better things.'

He continued with a technical exposition of how the current programme might be revised, which I did not follow. The two men talked for some while. The scientists were still expecting to find a HIGMO.

Regarding the science quarters rather as an outpost, I was astonished to see how well the room we were in was furnished, with real chairs rather than the collapsible ones used in the domes. Symphonic music played at a low level; I thought I recognised Penderecki. On the walls were star charts, an animated reproduction of a late-period Kandinsky and a cut-away diagram of an American-made MP500 sub-machine gun.

The personal assistant had her own desk in one corner of the room. She was blonde and in her thirties, wearing a green dress rather than our fairly standard coveralls.

At the sight of that dress I was overcome with jealousy. I recognised it as made from cloth of the old kind, which wore out, and so was expensive, almost exclusive. The rest of us wore costumes fabricated from Now (the acronym of Non-Ovine Wool), which never wore out. Now clothes fitted our bodies, being made of a semi-sentient synthetic that renewed itself, given a brush occasionally with fluid. Now clothes were cheap. But that dress . . .

When she caught my gaze, the personal assistant flashed a smile. She moved restlessly about the room, shifting paper and mugs, while I sat mutely by Tom's side.

Tom said, 'Dreiser, I came over to ask for your presence and support at our debates. But I have something more serious to talk about. What are these white strips that rise from the regolith and slick back into it? Are they living things?' He referred to the tongues (as I thought of them) we had encountered on our way over to the unit. 'Or is this a system you have installed?'

'You think they are living?' asked Dreiser, looking hard at Tom.

'What else, if they are not a part of your systems?'

'I thought you had established that there was no life on Mars.'

'You know the situation. We've found no life. But these strips aren't a mere geological manifestation.'

Hawkwood said nothing. He looked at me as if willing me to speak. I said nothing.

He pushed his chair back, rose, and went over to a locker on the far side of the room. Tom studiously looked at the ceiling. I noticed Dreiser pat the bottom of his assistant as he passed her. She gave a smug little smile.

119

He returned with a hologram of some of the tongues, which Tom studied.

'This tells me very little,' he said. 'Are they a life form, or part of one, or what?'

Dreiser merely shrugged.

Tom said that he had never expected to find life on Mars, or anywhere else; the path of evolution from mere chemicals to intelligence required too many special conditions.

'My student, Skadmorr, seems to believe we're being haunted by a disembodied consciousness or something similar,' Dreiser remarked. 'Aborigine people know about such matters, don't they?'

'Kathi's not an Aborigine,' I said.

Tom took what he regarded as an optimistic view, that the development of cosmic awareness in humankind marked an unrepeatable evolutionary pattern; humankind was the sole repository of higher consciousness in the galaxy. Our future destiny was to go out and disperse, to become the eye and mind of the universe. Why not? The universe was strange enough for such things to happen.

Dreiser remained taciturn and stroked his moustache.

'Hence my hopes of building a just society here,' said Tom. 'We have to improve our behaviour before we go out into the stars.'

'Well, we don't quite know what we've got here,' replied Hawkwood, after a pause, seemingly ignoring Tom's remark. He thumped the hologram. 'With regard to this phenomenon, at least it appears not to be hostile.'

'It? You mean they?'

'No, I mean it. The strips work as a team. I wish to god we were better armed. Oxyacetelyne welders are about our most formidable weapon . . .'

As we started the drive back to the domes, Tom said, 'Uncommunicative bastard.' He became unusually silent. He broke that silence to say, 'We'd better keep quiet about these strips until the scientists find out more about them. We don't want to alarm people unnecessarily.'

He gave me a grim and searching look.

'Why are scientists so secretive?' I asked.

He shook his head without replying.

10

Some malcontents rejected everything offered them in the way of enlightenment, so impatient were they to return to Earth. They formed an action group, led by two brothers of mixed nationality, Abel and Jarvis Feneloni. Abel was the more powerful of the two, a brawny games player who had done his community service in an engineering department on Luna. Jarvis fancied himself as an amateur politician. Their family had lived on an Hawaiian island, where Jarvis had been one of a vulcanism team.

Expeditions outside the domes to the surface of Mars were strictly limited, in order to conserve oxygen and water. The Fenelonis, however, had a plan. One noontime, they, and four other men, broke the rules and rode out in a commandeered buggy. With them they took cylinders of hydrogen from a locked store.

A certain amount of hardware littered the area of Amazonis near the domes. Among the litter stood a small EUPACUS ferry, the 'Clarke Connector', abandoned when the giant international confederation had collapsed.

The action group set about refuelling the ferry. In a nearby heated prefab shed stood a Zubrin Reactor, still in working order despite the taxing variations in Martian temperatures. It soon began operating at 400° Celsius. Atmospheric carbon dioxide plus the stolen hydrogen began to generate methane and oxygen. The RWGS reaction kicked in. Carbon dioxide and hydrogen, plus catalyst, yielded carbon monoxide and water, this part of the operation being maintained by the excess energy of the operation. The water was immediately electrolysed to produce more oxygen, which would burn the methane in a rocket engine.

The group connected hoses from the Zubrin to the ferry. The refuelling process began.

As the group of six men sheltered in the buggy, waiting for the tanks to fill, an argument broke out between the Feneloni brothers, in which the other men became involved. Each man had a pack of food with him. The plan was that when they reached the interplanetary vessel orbiting overhead, all except Abel would climb into cryogenic lockers and sleep out the journey home. Abel would fly the craft for a week, lock it into an elliptical course for Earth, allow the automatics to take over, and then go cryogenic himself. He would be the first to awaken when the craft was a week's flight away from Earth, and would take over from the guidance systems.

Abel had shown great confidence during the planning stage, carrying the others with him. Now his younger brother asked, hesitantly, if Abel had taken into account the fact that methane had a lower propellant force than conventional fuel.

'We'll compute that once we're aboard the fridge wagon,' Abel said. 'You're not getting chicken, are you?'

'That's not an answer, Abel,' said one of the other men, Dick Harrison. 'You've set yourself up as the man with the answers regarding the flight home. So why not answer your brother straight?'

'Don't start bitching, Dick. We've got to be up in that fridge wagon before they come and get us. The on-board computer will do the necessary calculations.' He drummed his fingers on the dash, sighing heavily.

They sat there, glaring at each other, in the faint shadow of the ferry.

'You're getting jumpy, not me,' said Jarvis.

'Shut your face, kid.'

'I'll ask you another elementary question,' said Dick. 'Are Mars and Earth at present in opposition or conjunction? Best time to do the trip is when they're in conjunction, isn't it?'

'Will you please shut the fuck up and prepare to board the ferry?'

'You mean you don't bloody know?' Jarvis said. 'You told us the timing had to be right, and you don't bloody know?'

A quarrel developed. Abel invited his brother to stay bottled up on Mars if he was so jittery. Jarvis said he would not trust his brother to navigate a fridge wagon if he could not answer a simple question.

'You're a titox – always were!' Abel roared. 'Always were! Get out and stay out! We don't need you.'

Without another word, Jarvis climbed from the buggy and stood there helplessly, breathing heavily in his atmosphere suit. After a minute, Dick Harrison climbed down and joined him.

'It's all going wrong,' was all he said. The two men stood there. They watched as Abel and the others left the buggy and went towards the now refuelled ferry. As the men climbed aboard, Jarvis ran over and thrust his food pack into his brother's hands.

'You'll need this, Abel. Good luck! My love to our family!'

His brother scowled. 'You rotten little titox,' was all he said. He swung the pack on to his free shoulder and disappeared into the ferry. The hatch closed behind him.

Jarvis Feneloni and Dick Harrison climbed into the shelter of the buggy. They waited until the ferry lifted off into the drab skies before starting the engine and heading back to the domes. Neither of them said a word.

Abel Feneloni's exploit and the departure of the fridge wagon from its parking orbit caused a stir for a day or two. Jarvis put the best gloss he could on the escape, claiming that his brother would present their case to the UN, and rescue for all of them would soon be at hand.

Time went by. Nothing more was heard of the rocket. No one knew if it reached Earth. The matter was eventually forgotten. As patients in hospital become so involved in the activities of their ward that they wish to hear no news of

124

the outside world, so the new Martians were preoccupied with their own affairs. If that's a fair parallel!

Lotteries for this and that took place all the time. I was fortunate enough to win a trip out to the science unit. Ten of us travelled out in a buggybus. The sun was comparatively bright, and the PIRs shone like a diamond necklace in the throat of the sky.

Talk died away as we headed northwards and the settlement of domes was lost below the near horizon. We drove along a dried gulch that served as a road. There was something about the unyielding rock, something about the absence of the most meagre sign of any living thing, that was awesome. Nothing stirred, except the dust we churned up as we passed. It was slow to settle, as if it too was under a spell.

This broken place lay defenceless under its thin atmosphere. It was cold and fragile, open to bombardment by meteors and any other space debris. All about us, fragments of primordial exploded stars lay strewn.

'Mars resembles a tomb, a museum,' said the woman I was travelling next to. 'With every day that passes, I long to get back to Earth, don't you?'

'Perhaps.' I didn't want to disappoint her. But I realised I had almost forgotten what living on Earth was like. I did remember what a struggle it had been.

I thought again, as I looked out of my window, that even this progerial areoscape held – in Tom's startling phrase – that 'divine aspect of things' which was like a secret little melody, perhaps heard differently by everyone susceptible to it.

I managed to terrify myself by wondering what it would be like to be deaf to that little tune. How bearable would Mars be then?

I was grateful to him for naming, and so bringing to my conscious mind, that powerful mediator of all experience. All the same, I disliked the drab pink of the low-ceilinged sky.

The tall antennae and the high-perching solar panels of the Smudge laboratory and offices showed ahead. It was only a five-minute drive from Mars City (as we sometimes laughingly called our congregation of domes). We drew nearer. The people in the front seats of the bus started to point excitedly.

At first I thought paper had been strewn near the unit. It crossed my mind that these white tongues were plants – something perhaps like the first snowdrops of a new spring. Then I remembered that Tom and I had seen these inexplicable things on our visit to Dreiser Hawkwood. As we drew close to them they slicked out of sight and disappeared into the parched crusts of regolith.

'Life? It must be a form of life . . .' So the buzz went round.

A garage door opened in the side of the building. We drove in. The door closed and atmosphere hissed into the place. When a gong chimed, it was safe to leave the buggy. The air tasted chill and metallic.

We passed into a small reception hall, where we were briefly greeted by Arnold Poulsen. As chief computer technician, Poulsen was an important man, answerable only to Hawkwood and seldom appearing in public. I studied him, since Tom had spoken highly of him. He stood before us in a wispy way, uttering conventional words of greeting, looking pleasant enough, but forgetting to smile. Then he disappeared with evident relief, his social moment finished.

We were served a coffdrink while one of the particle physicists, a Scandinavian called Jon Thorgeson, youthful but with a deeply lined face, spoke to us. He was more communicative than Poulsen, whom he vaguely resembled, being ectomorphic and seemingly of no particular age.

Did he recognise me from my previous visit? Certainly he came over and said hello to me in the friendliest way.

Thorgeson briefed us on what we were going to see. In fact, he admitted, we could see very little. The science institution comprised two sorts of people. One was a somewhat monastic unit, where male and female scientists thought about what they were doing or what they might do, free from pressures to produce – in particular the pressure to produce 'Big Science'. The other unit comprised people actually doing the science. This latter unit was still adjusting the equipment that, it was hoped, might eventually detect Rosewall's postulated Omega Smudge.

As we were being shown around, Thorgeson explained that their researches were aimed at tackling the mystery of mass in the universe. Rosewall had made an impressive case for the existence of something called a HIGMO, a hidden-symmetry gravitational monopole. The team was running a pilot project at present, on a relatively small ring, since the density of HIGMOs in the universe remained as yet unknown. The ring lay at the rear of the science unit, under a protective shield, we were told.

One of the crowd asked the obvious question of why all this equipment and this team of scientists were shipped to Mars at such enormous expense.

Thorgeson looked offended. 'It was Rosewell's perception that you needed no expensive super-collider, just a large ring-shaped tube filled with appropriate superfluid. Whenever a HIGMO passes through this ring, its passage will be detected as a kind of glitch appearing in the superfluid. Any sort of violent activity outside the tube would ruin the experiment.'

I found myself asking how HIGMOs could manage to pass through the ring. He seemed to look hard at me before answering, so that I felt silly.

'Young lady, HIGMOs can pass clean through Mars without disturbing a thing, or anyone being any the worse for it.'

Someone else asked, 'Why not build this ring on the Moon?'

'The Moon – we're too late for that! Tourist activities, mining activity, the new transcore subway . . . The whole satellite shakes like a vibrator in a wasps' nest.'

Turning his gaze on me, he asked, 'You understand this?'

I nodded. 'That's why you're out here. No wasps' nests.'

'Full marks.' He came and shook my hand, which made me very uncomfortable. 'That's why we're out here. It's fruitless to pursue the Smudge on Earth or on Luna. Far too much racket. The Omega Smudge is a shy beast.' He chuckled.

'And if you capture this Smudge, what then?' asked one of the group, Helen Panorios, the YEA woman with dyed purple hair and dark complexion.

'It holds the key to many things. In particular, it will tell us just how the microverse relates to the macroverse, giving us the precise parameters for the dividing line between the small-scale quantum world of atoms and fundamental particles, and the larger-scale classical world of specks of dust upwards to galaxies and so on. I take the view of current 'hard science' that these parameters should also tell us how the exterior universe relates to human consciousness. The detailed properties of the universe seem to be deeply related to the very existence of conscious observers – observers maybe like humans, maybe a more effective species which will supersede us. If so, then consciousness is not accidental, but integral. At last we'll have a clear understanding of all existence.'

'So you hope,' ventured a sceptical voice.

'So we hope. When the ships come back and we can obtain more material, we expect to build a superfluid ring right around the planet. Then we'll see.'

'Now we see through a glass darkly . . .' said Helen, admiringly.

'We don't quote the Bible much here but, yes, more or less.'

A man who had already asked a question enquired rather sneeringly, 'What exactly is this key between the large and small you mention? Isn't human consciousness just a manifestation of the action of the quantputers in our heads?'

'That may well be true in principle, but we can't proceed without knowing some important physical parameters more exactly, most particularly what's labelled the HIGMO q-factor, whose value is completely unknown at present – let's call it "the missing-link of physics".'

'So what what happens when you find it? Will the universe come to an end?'

Jon Thorgeson laughed to the extent of exciting the deep lines in his cheeks. He said that life for the majority of people might go on as usual. But even if the universe did end – well, he said, to make a wild guess, the probability was that there were plenty of other universes growing, as he put it, on the same stem. Mathematics indicated as much.

He came to a halt in the middle of a corridor, and our group halted with him and gathered round as he talked.

'As you know, stars keep going by exothermic fusion of hydrogen into helium-4. When the core hydrogen is almost used up, gravitational contraction starts. The consequent rise in temperature permits the burning of helium. In our universe, nucleosynthesis of all the heavier elements is achieved by this continued process of fuel exhaustion, leading to contraction, leading to higher central temperatures, leading to a new source of fuel for the sustaining nuclear energy.

'But in our universe there are what in lay terms we may call strange anomalies in this process. For instance, unless nucleosynthesis proceeded resonantly, the yield of carbon would be negligible. By a further anomaly, it happens that the carbon produced is not consumed in a further reaction. So we live in a universe with plentiful carbon and, as you know, carbon is a basic element for our kind of life.

'I wouldn't like my boss to hear me saying this, but – who knows? – in a neighbouring universe, these strange anomalies may not occur. It might be entirely life-free, without observers. Or maybe life takes another course and is, say, silicon-based. Such possibilities will become clearer if we can get the tabs on our Smudge.'

One of our group asked if it would be possible for us to enter another universe, or for something from another universe to enter ours.

The lines on Thorgeson's face deepened in amusement. 'There we venture into the realms of science fiction. I can't comment on that.'

At the end of our tour, I managed to speak to Thorgeson face to face. I told him that many of the people in the domes, particularly the YEAs, were interested in science but did not understand what the particle physicists were working at. Indeed, the scientific team were regarded as being rather secretive.

Lowering his voice, he said that there was dissension in the scientific ranks. The issues were complex. Many men and women on the team did not see the Omega Smudge as worth pursuing, and favoured more practical concerns, such as establishing a really efficient comet- and meteor-surveillance system. On the other hand . . . Here he paused.

When I prompted him to continue, he said that practical goals were for people without vision – clever people, but those without vision.

'Was Kepler being practical when, in the middle of a war, he sat down and computed the orbits of planets? Certainly not. Yet those planetary laws of his have eventually brought us here. That's pure science. The Smudge is pure science. I'm not very pure myself' – said with a sly laughing glance at me – 'but I support pure science.'

Since I understood those sly glances, I asked him boldly if he would visit the domes and lecture us on the subject?

'Want to come and have a drink with me and talk it over?'

'I have to keep with my group. Sorry.'

'Too bad. You're an attractive lady. Korean, are you? We're a bit short of adjuncts to living over here. Monastic is what we are.'

'Then leave your monastery and lecture us on particle physics.'

'You might find it rather dull,' he said. Then he smiled. 'It's a good idea. I'll see what I can do. I'll be in touch.'

At that stage, I did not realise how prophetic those words were.

We were waiting in the reception area for our buggybus to finish recharging. I started talking to the technician on duty, and asked her about the small white tongues we had seen outside the building.

'Oh, the Watchers? I can show you them on the monitors, if you like.'

I went behind her desk to take a look at the surveillance system. It clearly showed the white tongues, unmoving outside.

The technician flicked from screen to screen. The tongues surrounded the establishment. Behind them, Olympus Mons could be seen distantly, dominating its region.

'You get a clearer idea of them when I switch over to infrared,' said the technician, so doing.

I exclaimed in alarm. The tongues were no longer tongues. They reminded me, much more formidably, of gravestones I had seen in an old churchyard, tall and unmoving. They formed almost a solid wall about the establishment. It seemed they were covered in a kind of oily, scaly skin of a dull green colour. I asked if they were going to break in.

'They're quite harmless. They don't interfere. We think they're observing. They don't get in anyone's way.'

As we looked, a maintenance engineer came into view on the screens, suited up and shouldering welding equipment. As if to confirm the duty technician's words, the Watchers flicked back into the regolith and were gone, offering him no impediment. He moved out of view and the tongues at once returned.

I could not help feeling cold fear running through my body.

'So there is life on Mars,' I said.

'But not necessarily Martian life,' the technician said. 'Sit down for a minute, pet. You look terribly pale. I'm only joking. There's no life on Mars. We all know that.'

But jokes frequently hold bitter kernels of truth. Knowledge of the Watchers spread and caused alarm. But custom dulls the edge of many things. Whether alive or not, they made no hostile moves. We became used to their presence and finally ignored them.

After my return from Thorgeson and company, I told Kathi over the Ambient how impressed I was by Thorgeson's intellect. She asked what he had said.

I tried to explain that he had claimed the consciousness of humanity, or of a species that might supersede us, was – what had he said? – an integral function of the universe.

She laughed scornfully. 'Who do you think he got that idea from?' she asked.

After a silence, she said, 'If we cannot behave in a better and more utopian way, then we deserve to be superseded, don't you think?'

I changed the subject and spoke about the tongues surrounding the science unit.

'Don't worry,' she said lightly. 'We shall find out their function in good time. Do you know about quantum state-reduction? No? I'm reading up about it now. It's the collapse of the wave function, such as Schrödinger's cat – you know all about Schrödinger's cat, Cang Hai?'

'Of course I've heard of it.'

'Well then, the collapse of the wave function resolves the problem of that poor hypothetical quantum-superposed moggie. It becomes either a dead cat or a live cat, instead of being in a quantum superposition of both a dead and an alive cat.'

'I see . . . Is that better or worse for the cat?'

She scowled at me. 'Don't try to be funny, dear. Such

quantum superpositions occur in the electron displacements in a quantcomp. The definitive experiments conducted by Heitelman early this century made it clear that state-reduction actually takes place when it is the internal gravitational influences that become significant. You see where this leads us?'

I shook my head. 'I'm afraid I don't, Kathi.'

'I'm working on it, babe!' With a cheery wave of its hand her image faded from view.

Sitting there vexed, I tried to understand what she was saying. The gravitational link puzzled me. On inspiration, I decided to Ambient Jon Thorgeson in the science unit.

An unfamiliar face came up in the globe. 'Hi! I'm Jimmy Gonzales Dust, Jon's buddy. We're training for the marathon and he's busy on the running machine. Can I help? He's spoken to me about you. He thinks you're cute.'

'Oh . . . Does he? Do you know anything about the – what do you call it? The gravitational . . . no . . . The magneto-gravitic anomaly? Have you any information about it?'

He looked hard at me. 'We call it the M-gravitic anomaly.' He asked me why I was worrying. I said I didn't really know. I was trying to learn some science.

Jimmy hesitated. 'Keep this to yourself if I give you a shot from the upsat. There's been a slight shift in the anomaly.'

The photograph he released came through the slot.

I stared at it. It was an aerial view of the Tharsis Shield from 60 miles up. The outline of Olympus Mons – or Chimborazo, to use Kathi's name – could clearly be seen. Across the shot someone had scrawled with marker pen G – WSW + 0.13°.

Why and how, I asked myself, should the anomaly have shifted? Why in that direction – in effect towards Arizonis Planitia and our position?

As I stared at the photo, I noticed furrowed regolith to the east of the skirts of Olympus. Kathi had pointed this furrowing out to me earlier. Now it seemed the furrowing was rather more extensive. I could not understand what it meant. In the end, I returned to my studies, not very pleased with myself. Cute? Me?!

The domes had become a great hive of talk. There were silent sessions by way of compensation. Sports periods were relatively quiet. Other colloquia concentrated on silence, and were conducted by the wooden tongue of a pair of clappers. Silence, meditation, walking in circles, sitting, all reinforced at once a sense of communality and individuality. Those who concentrated on these buddhistic exercises reported lowered cholesterol levels and a greater intensity of life.

Much later, these colloquia became the basis of Amazonis University.

Fornication evenings were a popular success. Masked partners met each other for karezza and oral arts under skilled tutors. Lying together without movement, they practiced inhalation, visual saturation and maryanning. Breath control as a technique for increasing pleasure was emphasised.

Breath control formed the entire subject of another colloquium. In a low-lit studio, practitioners sat in the lotus position and controlled ingoing and outgoing breaths while concentrating on the *hara*. Mounting concentrations of carbon dioxide in the blood led to periods of timeless 'awayness' which, when achieved, were always regarded as of momentous value, leading to a fuller understanding of self.

This opening up of consciousness without the use of harmful drugs became highly regarded in our society, so that the breathing colloquium had to be supplemented by classes in pranayama. At first, pranayama was seen as exotic and 'non-Western', but, with the growing awareness that we were in fact no longer Western, pranayama became regarded as a Martian discipline.

Whether or not this concentration on the breath, entering

134

by the nose, leaving by the mouth, was to be accounted for by our awareness that every molecule of oxygen had to be engineered, this discipline, in which over 55 per cent of our adults soon persevered, exerted a considerable calming effect, so that to the remoter regions of the mind the prospect of a tranquil and happy life no longer seemed unfamiliar.

'A better life needs no distraction . . .'

In all the colloquia, which rapidly established themselves, the relationship between teacher and taught was less sharp than usual. No one had a professional reputation to uphold; it was not unknown for a teacher to exclaim to a bright pupil, 'Look, you know more about this than I – please take my place, I'll take yours.'

Old hierarchies were dissolving: even as Tom had predicted, the human mind was becoming free.

At all this great activity I looked in amazement. To repair the damage done to my body I studied pranayama, becoming more aware of Eastern influence in our society. I wondered if this was really the case, or did I, with my Eastern inheritance, merely wish it to be so?

I asked this question of Tom. Perhaps we had grown closer over the past year. Tom said, 'I cannot answer your question today. Let's try tomorrow.'

On the morrow, when we met with Belle Rivers again for another discussion of what education should consist, he looked amused and said, 'Has your question been answered overnight?'

Playing along with this zen approach, I replied, 'No religion has a monopoly on wisdom.'

At this he yawned and pretended to be bored. He said he believed, though without sure foundation, that there had been a time when the West, the little West which then called itself Christendom, had been a home of mysticism. Come the Renaissance, people forgot constant prayer, loving instead the riches and excitements of the world about them. They had given themselves up to the worldly things and even neglected to love, first others, then themselves. Now it was possible that in our reduced circumstances we might learn to love ourselves again with a renewed mysticism.

'And love God?' I asked.

'God is the great cul de sac in the sky.'

'Only to those with spiritual myopia,' Belle said, with a trace of irritation.

I couldn't resist teasing Tom – a tease in which there was some flattery – telling him he was the new mystic, come to guide us.

'Don't get that notion in your head, my dear Cang Hai, or try to put it in mine. I cannot guide since I don't know where we are going.'

But he offered me, chuckling, a story of a holy man who finally gave up calling on Allah because Allah never spoke in return, never said to the man, 'Here am I.' Whereupon a prophet appeared to the holy man in a vision, hot foot from Allah. What the prophet reported Allah as saying was this: 'Was it not I who summoned thee to my service? Was it not I who engaged thee with my name? Was not thy call of "Allah!" my "Here am I"?'

I said I was pleased that Tom had a mystical as well as a practical side, to which he answered that he clung to a fragment of mysticism, hoping to be practical. That practicality might permit our grandchildren to espouse the contentment of real mysticism.

I thought about this for a long time. It seemed to me that he denied belief in God, and yet clung to a shred of it.

Tom admitted it might be so, since we were all full of contradictions. But whether or not there was a god outside, there was a god within us; in consequence he believed in the power of solitary prayer, as a clarifier, a magnifying glass, for the mind.

'At least, so I believe today,' he said teasingly. 'My dear Cang Hai, we all have two hemispheres to our brains. Can we not carry two different tunes at the same time? Do you not wish to be silent in order to listen to them?'

While we were talking in this abstract fashion, our

friends were making love and more children were being conceived. Too many would threaten the precarious balance of our existence. To find Tom planning for two generations ahead made me impatient.

'We must deal with our immediate difficulties first, not add to them. This random procreation threatens our very existence. Why do you not issue a caution against unbridled sexuality?'

'For several good reasons, Cang Hai,' he said. 'The foremost of which is that any such caution would be useless. Besides, if I, a DOP, issued it, it would be widely – and maybe rightly – regarded as an edict flung across the generation gap.'

I laughed – 'Don't be afraid of that. You are older, you know better! Don't you?' – for I saw his hesitation.

'No, to be honest I don't know better. Sexual temptation does not necessarily fade with age. It's merely that the ease with which one can give in to it disappears!' He laughed. 'You see, our generations have become too preoccupied with sexuality. You know what Barcunda said.

'Our relationships with natural things withered and died in the streets. We no longer tend our gardens – or sleep under the stars, unless we are down-and-outs. We think stale city thoughts, removed from nature. All we have to relate to is each other. That's unnatural; we should be responding to agencies outside ourselves. The quest for ever more sexual satisfaction runs against true contentment. Against love, joy and peace, and the ability to help others.'

'Ah, those "agencies outside ourselves" . . . Yes . . .'

We sat silently for a while.

At last I said, 'It is sometimes difficult for us to speak our minds. Perhaps it's because I have reverence for you that I agree with what you say. Yet not only that . . . I have not found great pleasure in sex, with either men or women. Is that something lacking in me? I seem to have no – warmth? I love, but only platonically, I'm ashamed to admit.'

Tom put his large hand on mine.

'You need feel no shame. We are brought up in a culture where those who seek solitude or chastity are made to think of themselves as unwell – fit subjects for new sciences like psychurgy and mentascopism – almost beyond the pale of society. It was not always so and it will not be so again. Once, men who sought solitude were revered. These matters are not necessarily genetic but a question of upbringing.'

After a pause, he said, 'And your upbringing, Cang Hai. Where are you in Kissorian's scheme of things – a later-born, I'd guess?'

'No, Tom, dear. I am a dupe.' Looking searchingly at him, I was surprised he did not immediately understand.

'A dupe?'

'A clone, to use the old-fashioned term. I know there's a prejudice against dupes, but since our difference doesn't show externally we are not persecuted. My counterpart lives in China, in Chengdu. We are sometimes in psychic touch with one another. But I do not believe that case affects my attitude to sexuality. As a matter of fact, I spend much time in communication with those archetypes of which you say someone spoke in the debate. I believe I am in touch with myself, though I'm vexed by mysterious inner promptings. Those promptings brought me to Mars – and to you.'

'I am grateful, then, for those inner promptings,' he said, giving me a grave smile. 'So you are that rare creature, not born of direct sexual union . . .'

I told him I knew of at least a dozen other dupes with us on Mars.

With a sudden intuition, Tom asked if Kathi was also a dupe. I said it was not so; was he interested in her?

He chose to ignore this. Dropping his gaze, he said, 'My destiny seems to be as an organiser. I'm doomed to be a talker, while in my heart of hearts, that remote place, I believe silence to be a greater thing.'

'But not the silence, surely, that has prevailed on Mars for centuries?'

His face took on a ponderous expression I had observed previously. He stared down at the floor. 'That's true. That's a dead silence. We shall have to cure it in the end . . . Life has to be the enemy of such tomb-like silence.'

Smiling apologetically, he dismissed me.

I regretted not telling him that Kathi did not find Mars's silence a dead silence; she claimed that it could be heard if only we attuned ourselves to it. But she and I had no authority. After all, Tom was a famous and successful man, and who was I? Although I relished his attention, and his kindly looks, he had said nothing about his personal history since the evening on Spider Plant when he had spoken of his first love. Did he regret confiding in me? Could I bear any more of the same?

This is not intended to be a record of my personal feelings. Yet I must admit here that I often thought about that fortunate girl who, Tom had told me, was the youthful Tom's first lover. I could imagine everything about her.

Even while I practised my breathing exercises – even then, I found myself thinking of her. And of young Tom. And of the two of them, locked together with rain bathing their naked bodies.

This is not really a record of history. I never told anyone this before. But unexpectedly I started thinking that Tom Jefferies did not care for me at all. I felt so bad. I secretly thought I was beautiful and my body was lovely, even if he never noticed, even if no one noticed. Except Jon, who thought I was cute.

Kathi Skadmorr came over from the science unit with some discs of an old jazz man called Sydney Bechet and some laboratory-distilled alcohol. She was spending the night with her lover, Beau Stephens, and invited me to drink with them.

After some drinks, I asked Beau if he thought I was pretty.

'In an Oriental way,' he said.

I told him that was a stupid remark and meant nothing.

'Of course you're pretty, darling,' said Kathi. Suddenly, she jumped up, put her arms round me, and kissed me on the mouth.

It went to my head like the drink. A track then playing was a number called 'I Only Have Eyes For You'. I had never heard it before. It was good. I began to peel off my Nows and dance. Just for the fun of it. And my new leg looked fine and worked beautifully.

When I was down to my bra and panties it occurred to me not to go further. But the two of them were cheering and looking excited, so off they came. My breasts were so nice and firm – I was proud of them. I flung my clothes at Beau. What did he do? He caught my panties and buried his face in them. Kathi just laughed.

With the track ending, I suddenly felt ashamed. I had shown so much crotch. I ran into the bathroom and hid. Kathi came to soothe me down. I was crying. She sang softly, 'I don't know if we're in a garden, Or in a crowded rendezvous.' And I felt awful next morning.

I never told anyone about this before.

'We must take the most tender care,' Tom said, when the Adminex was discussing education, 'of our youngsters, so that they do not think of themselves negatively as exiles from earth. Education must mean equipping a child to live in wisdom and contentment – contentment with itself first of all. We need a new word for a new thing, a word that means awareness, understanding . . .'

'There's the Chinese word juewu. It implies awareness, comprehension,' I suggested.

'Juewu, juewu . . .' He tried it on his tongue. 'It has something of a jewel about it, whereas education smells of dusty classrooms. I can almost hear children going to their first playschool at the age of three, chirruping jewey-woo jewey-woo . . .'

The word was adopted by the group.

We then fell to discussing what activities those early chirrupers should engage in.

Sharon Singh was certain that young children most enjoyed music and verse with strong rhymes; rhythm, clapping, she said, was the beginning of counting, counting of mathematics, and mathematics of science.

Mary Fangold remarked that in the discussions in Plato's *Republic* some time is spent wondering which metrical feet are best to express meanness or madness or evil, and which ones grace. The speakers conclude that music engenders a love of beauty.

I ventured to say that 'beauty' had become a rather suspect, or at least a specialised, word.

Tom agreed that it had accumulated some embarrassments; yet we still understood that it had something to do with rightness and truth. It was hard to define except by parallels; certainly the right music at the right time was a benison. Better even than the art of speaking with grace, was employing a rich vocabulary – which was rarely the mark of an empty head.

And with the music had to go activity, dancing and such like. This was a way in which juewu helped to unite mind and body.

But we agreed that, while good teaching was important, it could be achieved only by good teachers. As yet no method had been established for guaranteeing good teachers, beyond the simple expedient of training and paying well, though not lavishly.

'But once the system is established,' Tom said, 'then our well-taught children will make the best teachers. Patience, love and empathy are more valuable than knowledge.'

The next stage was the regularisation of educational curricula for various ages.

We wanted our first generation of Martian children to understand the unity and interconnectedness of all life on Earth.

We also wished them to understand themselves better

than any generations had done before. Phylogeny was a required subject, for only from this could grow knowledge of one's self.

Ambient and computer skills were already being taught, together with history, geophysiology, music, painting, world literature, mathematics. There would be personality sessions, wherein children could discuss any problems brewing; difficult situations could be dealt with swiftly and compassionately.

Tom appeared pleased with the work. Almost as an afterthought he suggested that the entire scheme should be shown to Belle Rivers, who had spoken on the subject of archetypes during our debates and was in charge of teaching cadre children.

Belle Rivers was slender and elegant, with a certain grandeur to her. She carried her head slightly to one side, as if listening to something the rest of us were unable to hear. She was about forty years old, perhaps more.

Tom opened the conversation by apologising for altering her curriculum. Altered circumstances demanded it. He said that he hoped the revised syllabus, a copy of which we had printed out, would please her.

Without responding, Rivers read through the syllabus. She set it down on a desk, saying, 'I see you do not wish religion to be taught.'

'That is correct.'

'We have had to train our children for future careers. Nevertheless we always take care to include world religions in our curriculum. Do you not believe that God prevails as much on Mars as on Earth?'

'Or as little. We cannot leave it to any god to remedy in future those things he or she has failed to remedy in the past. We must attempt a remedy ourselves.'

'That's rather arrogant, isn't it?' She appeared less offended than contemptuous.

'I trust not. We are merely amused by ancient Greek tales of gods and goddesses interfering directly in the affairs of humanity. Such beliefs are outdated. We must try to laugh at any belief that imaginary, omnipotent gods will remedy our deficiencies. We must try to do such things for ourselves, if that is possible.'

'Oh? And if it proves impossible?'

'We do not know it will be impossible until we have tried, Belle.'

'That may be true. But why not enlist God in your enterprise? I seem to recall that the great utopian, Sir Thomas More, made certain that the children of his utopia were brought up in the faith and given full religious instruction.'

'The sixteenth century thought differently about such matters. More was a good man living in a circumscribed world. We must go by the advanced thought of our own time. All utopias have their sell-by dates, you know.'

'And your utopia has dropped any sense of the divine aspect of things.'

Tom offered a chair to Belle Rivers and invited her to be seated. His manner became apologetic. He said he realised that he had made a mistake in having Adminex draw up a new syllabus without consulting her in the first place. It must seem to her that he had usurped her powers, although that had been far from his intention. He had been too hasty; there was much still needing attention.

However, she would notice that her ideas had been taken into consideration. Phylogeny was on the timetable for even small children, wherein the make-up of human consciousness and her understanding concerning archetypes could be considered.

She gazed frowningly into a corner of the room.

Tom shuffled somewhat before asking Belle Rivers not to believe that he was without sympathy for her religious instincts. He was himself all too conscious of the divine aspect of things. Did not everyone who was not utterly bowed down by misfortune or illness, he asked, have a sense of a kind of holiness to life?

Staring hard at Belle, he became lyrical and so, I thought, possibly insincere.

As we moved through our lives, he continued, was there not a vein of enchantment in events, in awakening, in sleeping, in our dreams and in the power of thought? That elusive element, which the best artists, writers, musicians, scientists – even ordinary persons in ordinary jobs – experienced, that special lovely thing of which it was difficult to speak, but which gave life its magic. It might perhaps be simply the ticking of the biological clock, the joy in being alive. Whatever it was, that firefly thing, it was something of which the poet Marlowe spoke:

> One thought, one grace, one wonder, at the least
> Which into words no virtue can digest.

Listening to this speech, Belle Rivers clasped her hands on the desk in front of her and appeared to study them.

Religion, at least the Christian religion, Tom said, changed over time, abandoning the ill-tempered and savage Jehovah of the Old Testament for a more responsive faith in redemption – though it still based itself on such impossibilities as virgin birth, the resurrection of the dead and eternal life – impossibilities designed to impress the ignorant of Christ's unscientific age.

When the Omega Smudge would be detected, we should see a genuine miracle – once we understood what had been detected. (Yet would I ever understand this area of science? I made a resolve to learn still more . . .)

By going two steps forward and one step back, continued Tom, humankind since the days of Jesus Christ had scraped together some knowledge of the world, the universe and themselves. The situation now, in the late middle of the twenty-first century, was that God got in the way of understanding. God was dark matter, an impediment rather than an aid to our proper sense of the divine aspect of things. We had been forced to leave many good things behind on Earth; God should be left behind too.

The world was more wonderful without him.

Belle Rivers, continuing to regard her hands, said merely, 'It cannot be more wonderful without him, since he created it.'

Until this juncture Mary Fangold had remained silent, watching Tom and Belle with a faint smile on her lips. Tom said afterwards that Mary, the apostle of reason, knew we had fallen into human error by excluding the hard-working Belle from most of our educational plans. She felt her position to be undermined. Mary spoke up.

'The prospectus is only at the planning stage, Belle. We rely on you to continue teaching, just as the children rely on you. We wonder if you would care to include a subject such as we might call, say, Becoming Individual, in your time-table, whereby religion would form a part of it, together with archetypal behaviour and the interrelationship of conscious and sub-conscious.'

Belle regarded her suspiciously. 'That does not sound like my idea of religion.'

'Then let's say religion and reason . . .'

After a moment's silence, Belle smiled and said, 'Do not think I am trying to be difficult. Basically, your entire plan for improved learning cannot flourish without one additional factor.'

She waited for us to ask her what that factor might be. Then she explained that there were children who were always resistant to learning, who found reading and writing hard work. Others were happy and fulfilled with such things. The difference could be accounted for by the contrast between those children who were sung to and read to by their mothers and fathers from birth onwards, perhaps even before birth, when the child was still in utero, and those who were not, who were neglected.

Learning, she said, began from Day One. If that learning was associated with the happiness and security of a parent's love, then the child found no impediments to learning and to the enjoyment of education. Those children whose parents were silent or indifferent had a harder slog through life.

The basis of all that was good in life was, she declared, simply love and care, which arose from a love of Christ.

Tom rose and took her hand. 'We are in perfect agreement there, at least as far as love and care of the child are concerned,' he said. 'You have probably cited the most vital thing. There's no harm in using Christ as an exemplar. We're very happy you are the headmistress here, and in charge of learning.'

Tom's and my, in some respects, mysterious, relationship deepened. I was legally adopted as his daughter at a small ceremony; I became Cang Hai Jefferies, and lived in harmony with him. To be truthful, I mean more or less in harmony with him. It was not easy to get mentally close.

Often when my new leg troubled me – it got the twitches – I would lie in his arms. This was bliss for me; but he never attempted a sexual advance.

Our activities had become formalised. Indoor sports, plays, revues, recitations, dances and baby exhibitions (the many pregnancies had yielded our first Mars-born infants) were weekly events. Training for the first Mars marathon was in progress.

A woman of French origin, Paula Gallin, produced a dark, austere play, shot through with humour, which combined video with human actors. *My Culture*, to give it its title, was reluctantly received at first, but slowly became recognised as a master work. Most of the action took place on a flat sloping plain, the tilt of which increased slowly as the play proceeded.

My Culture played a part in turning our community into the world's first modern psychologically oriented civilisation. The setting-up of the Smudge Project grew nearer to completion by the end of 2065, despite material limitations hampering its development. Dreiser kept us informed by frequent bulletins on the Ambient. But many of us sensed that the technological culture of Earth was gradually giving way to an absorption in Being and Becoming.

Being and Becoming had a very practical focus in the

maturing of our children. It was prompted by a natural anxiety regarding the happy development of the young in a confined, largely 'indoor' world. But the comparative gloom of Mars prompted introspection and, indeed, empathy. It was noted early in our exile that most of us enjoyed unusually vivid dreams of curious content. These dreams, it was understood, put us in touch with our phylogenetic past, as if seeking or possibly offering therapeutic reassurance.

Mistaken Historicism had filled the world with the idea of progress, bringing greater pressure on greater numbers of people, the rise of megacities and the loss of pleasant communication with the self. A wise man of the twentieth century, Stephen Jay Gould, said: 'Progess is a noxious, culturally embedded, nonoperational, intractable idea that must be replaced.'

We were trying to replace it – not by going back but going forward into a realisation of our true selves, our various selves, which had experience of the evolutionary chain. Exchanging technocracy for metaphysics, in Belle's words.

My true self led me to experience pregnancy. Shortly after our much delayed adoption ceremony, I went to the hospital, where I had myself injected with some of Tom Jefferies's DNA. My womb was grateful for the benevolent gravity and I delivered my beautiful daughter Alpha without pain one day in March 2067. Tom was with me at the birth. There my baby lay in my arms, red in the face after her exertions to emerge into the world, with the most exquisite little fingers you ever saw. Alpha had dark hair and eyes as blue as Earth's summer skies. And a temperament as fair.

Unfortunately the hospital permitted me no luxury of peace. Almost as soon as I was delivered I was sent back into society. That was Fangold's doing. The move upset my child for a short while, and then she recovered.

Kathi sent me a message from the science unit. It said, 'Did you succumb to Tom or to society? Why are you pretending to yourself you are an ordinary person? Better to pretend to be extraordinary. Kathi.'

It was not very kind.

Following the birth of Alpha, I – and I hope Tom too – was in a trance of happiness. His sorrow for the death of his wife was not forgotten, but he had put it behind him; he accepted her loss as one of those sorrows inescapable from our biological existence. Although I knew that one day terrestrial ships and business would return, I always hoped that day would be far off, so that our wonderful experience of finding our real selves could continue unabated.

My cloud of contentment was increased by a slogan I passed almost every day. Outside the hairdresser's salon someone had painted VIOLENCE BEGETS VIOLENCE – PEACE BEGETS PEACE. The words might have come from my heart.

Belle Rivers seemed to increase in stature. Her Becoming Individual sessions, which parents often attended with their children, as I soon did with Alpha, were perceived to contain much wisdom, which at first appeared uncomfortably to challenge the unity of the self. The significance of archetypes playing distinct roles in our unconscious was difficult for many people to grasp at first. Gradually more and more people became absorbed in the symbolic aspects of experience.

Belle said, magisterially, 'We begin to understand how health springs from our being lived, in a sense, as well as living, and from accepting that we act out traditional roles. On Mars we shall come to require new ground rules.'

During the term of my pregnancy I used to wonder about this remark. I wanted to be different. I wanted things to be different.

I discussed this point with Ben Borrow. Ben was a smooth YEA who had done his community service on Luna and was, in his own words, 'into spirituality'. However that might be, it was noticeable that he was a devoted disciple of Belle Rivers, often closeted late with her.

'The more we feel ourselves lived, the more we can live independently.'

'The melding of opposites, spirit/matter, male/female, good/evil, brings completeness.'

'Only technology can free us from technology.'

'True spirituality can only be achieved by looking back into green distance.'

These were some of Borrow's sayings. I wrote them down.

He was intent on becoming a guru; even I could see he was also something of a creep. He had a tiny little pointed beard.

Under the tutelage of his powerful mistress, Borrow started a series of teach-ins he called Sustaining Individuality. These were well attended, and often became decidedly erotic. Rivers and Borrow taught that neurophysiological processes in the mind-body, such as dreaming, promoted the integration of limbic system dramas, thus increasing awareness and encouraging cognitive and emotive areas to merge. As there are swimmers in oceans who fear the unknown creatures somewhere below, beyond their knowledge, so there were those who feared the contents of the deeper levels of mind; they gradually lost this culturally induced phobia to enjoy a blossoming of awareness.

After one of these teach-ins I had to tell Borrow that I didn't know whether or not my awareness was blossoming. How could I tell?

'Perhaps,' he said, matching finger-tip with finger-tip in front of him, 'one might say that the aware find within themselves an ability to time-travel into the remote phylogenic past, and discover there wonderful things that give savour to reason, richness to being.

'Not least of these elements is a unity with nature and instinctive life, from which a knowledge of death is absent. Consciousness is something so complex and sensuous that no artificial intelligence could possibly emulate it. Don't you think?'

'Mmm,' I said. He hurried off, still with finger-tip touching finger-tip. It was not quite the way you put your hands together in prayer. Perhaps he wanted to indicate that he was in touch with himself.

And didn't wish to be in touch with me.

Our community became locked into this physiological-biological-philosophical type of speculation. Humanity's spiritual attainments, together with their relationship with our lowly ancestral origins, produced problems of perception. If what we perceive is an interpretation of reality, rather than reality itself, then we must examine our perceptions. That much I understand. But since it's our unconscious perceptual faculties that absorb and sort out our lifelong input of information, how does our conscious mind make them comprehensible? What does it edit out? What do they edit out between them? What vital thing are we missing?

I asked this question of May Porter, who came to give a short talk about perceptual faculties.

She said, 'Ethology has shown that all animals and insects are programmed to perceive the world in specific ways. Thus each species is locked into its perceptual umwelt. Facts are filtered for survival. Non-survival-type perceptions are rejected. An earlier mystic, Aldous Huxley, cited the case of the frog, whose perceptions cause it to see only things that move, such as insects. As soon as they stop moving, the frog ceases to see them and can look elsewhere. "What on earth would a frog's philosophy be – the metaphysics of appearance and disappearance?" Huxley asks himself.

'Similarly Western humanity values only that which moves; silence and stillness are seen as negative, rather than positive, qualities.'

I was thinking of Kathi's remarks when I asked May, 'What if there was a higher consciousness on Mars that we were not trained to perceive?'

She gave a short laugh. 'There is no higher consciousness on Mars. Only us, dear.'

These and many more understandings had a behavioural effect on our community. Certainly we became more thoughtful, if by thought we include pursuing visions. It was as if by unravelling the secrets of truly living we had come up against the tantalising conundrum of life itself, and its reasons, which were beyond biology. Single people or couples or families preferred to live alone, combining with others only on special occasions, such as a new performance of *My Culture* or a Sustaining Individuality session.

Thus most people came to live as individually as limited space would permit. As a would-be utopia, it was non-authoritarian, in distinct contrast to Plato's definition of a good place.

Nor do I imply that a sense of community was lost. We still ate together once or twice a day. It happened that many a time I caught the jo-jo bus to work with Alpha in my arms and found the whole place humming and vibrating like a hive; so many people were doing pranayama yoga on their own, uttering the eternal 'Om'.

Oh, then how happy I was! For me it was the best period of our Martian existence, too sensitive, too in-dwelling to prove permanent. I clutched my dear child in my arms and thought, 'Surely, surely Mars people will never again be as united as this!'

Since all our teach-in and community sessions were videoed, beamed to Earth, and saved, we could check on our progress towards individuality. Many of us had to chuckle at our earlier selves, our naïve questions, our uncertainty.

We were moving towards a degree of serenity when I received a nasty little shock. I caught on my globe an Ambient exchange between Belle Rivers and my beloved Tom.

She was saying, '. . . on Earth. And there's a scientist by name Jon Thorgeson. He says he wants to talk to Cang Hai. He says she suggested he might give a lecture about the Omega Smudge to us plebs. Is that okay by you?'

'Just keep her out of my hair, Belle. Let Thorgeson go ahead.'

Belle's image remained. With her head on one side, she regarded Tom. Then she asked, 'Do you know of anything odd going on in the science unit?'

'No. It's true I haven't heard from Dreiser just recently. Why do you ask?'

'Oh, simply the feeling something was in the air when I was speaking to Thorgeson. Could be the oncoming marathon, I suppose.'

By the time their images faded I was worried. What did he mean by keeping me out of his hair? He was always so good and kind. He relied on me, didn't he? It was true he had become rather grumpy recently.

Perhaps it was simply that he disliked hearing Alpha cry – such a beautiful sound! I pitied him.

11

The Missing Smudge

In a rotation of jobs, I was allocated to the synthetic foods department. I preferred it to the biogas department. The smells were better. Here I helped in time to develop something which resembled a Danish pastry. We always glossed over the fact that our foods were created from everyone's manure. Nevertheless, my friends teased me about it.

One of my closest friends, Kathi Skadmorr, had adopted a teasing approach to me since I had danced naked before her and her lover. She rang me unexpectedly in serious vein and invited me on a short expedition to view what she called the 'Smudge experiment'. I was always ready to learn. Although baby Alpha was so small, I left her in the care of Paula Gallin for a few hours while I joined Kathi.

Behind the science unit, Amazonis sprawled broken-hearted under a layer of dusty colour which seemed to be sometimes pink, or rose, or sometimes orange. A swan's feather of cloud vapour overhead reflected these hues.

Kathi and I had suited up before leaving the science unit. As we walked along a netted way, where latticed posts supported overhead cables, a slight agoraphobia attacked me. I clutched Kathi's hand: she was more used to open spaces than I. Yet at the same time I found something closed about the Martian outdoors. Perhaps it was the scarcity of atmosphere; or perhaps it was the indoor feeling of dust lying everywhere, dust much older than ever dimmed the surface of a table back on Earth.

To our left, the ground rose towards the heights that

would culminate in Olympus Mons. There, I caught movement out of the side of my eye. A small boulder, dislodged by the morning heat, rolled downhill a few metres, struck another rock, and became still. Again, it was a motionless world we walked through.

The horrors got at me. Was it wise to have brought Alpha into this world? Granted that it was passion rather than wisdom which fathered babies, yet I had experienced no passion. And supposing our fragile systems broke down . . . then the dread world of the unmoving would prevail over everything . . . even over my dear baby. The past would snap back into place like the lid of a coffin.

As if she had read my thought, Kathi began talking about another kind of past, the past of a scientific obsession. She said I would see the latest produce of a line of research stretching back into the previous century.

'Dreiser is teaching me the history of particle physics. It begins before this century,' she told me. 'It's a tale of reasoning and unreasonable hopes. Last century, American physicists proposed to build a giant accelerator beneath the state of Texas. The accelerator was planned to measure many kilometres in diameter. They christened it a superconducting supercollider, SSC for short. The SSC was designed to detect what they referred to as the "Higgs particle". It would cost billions of tax-payers' money, and take an enormous chunk out of the science budget.

'This was the twentieth century's idea of Big Science.' She gave a sardonic chuckle. 'US Congress kept asking why anyone would think it legitimate to believe that so much money should go in a search for a single particle. After three billion dollars had been spent, the whole project was scrapped.'

I asked why it had been thought necessary to find this Higgs particle.

'The physicists who were searching for these basic ingredients which comprise the universe argued that finding the elusive Higgs would supply them with vital answers. It would complete their picture of the fundamental units.

They were like detectives seeking the solution of a mystery.

'The mystery remains. Hence the whole purpose of the Mars Omega Project. You might say the mystery is why we are here. The more deeply we probe nature, the clearer it becomes that these basic units have to be things without mass. There's the mystery – where does mass originate? Without mass, nothing would hold together. Our bodies would disintegrate, for instance.'

I could not help asking what the Higgs particle had to do with mass. Kathi replied that it was still unclear to her, but the physicists of the time had an idea in their heads that the highly symmetrical scheme of the universe would have that symmetry spoilt according to what they termed 'spontaneous symmetry breaking'. The Higgs was tied up with that idea.

'You see, for the pure unbroken scheme with exact symmetry, it was necessary to have all particles without mass. When Higgs enters the picture, everything changes. Most particles acquire mass. The photon is a notable exception.'

'I see. The Higgs was to be a kind of magic wand. As soon as it enters the stage, "Hey presto!" mass comes along.'

'A rhymester said it in a nutshell:

The particles were lighter far than gas.
Then Higgs weighs in, and all is mass.

'Because of this rather magical property, Higgs was christened by journalists "the God particle".'

'And the physicists of that time believed that the SSC would enable them to catch a glimpse of this God.' I found I had lost most of my fears and let go of Kathi's hand.

'According to the theory current at the time,' she said, 'there had to be a certain limited range of possibilities for the mass of the Higgs. Otherwise, there would be an inconsistency with other things which had already been established by experiment. The God particle must deign to live among its subjects, just as if it were an ordinary mortal massive particle.'

I had to ask her what she meant by that.

'In accord with Einstein's famous equation, $E=mc^2$, the Higgs particle, it was believed, would correspond to a certain energy. That energy was supposed to lie within the range of what the SSC would have been capable of. But – the SSC was never built, as I have told you.

'As luck would have it, a rival project was already at the planning stage. This was at the international research centre, CERN, in Geneva, Switzerland.

'The CERN project was greatly cheaper than the cancelled SSC would have been. It employed a tunnel already in use for an earlier experiment. The new project was the Large Hadron Collider, the LHC.'

I imagined a great tube, with a vanishing perspective into circular darkness.

'In the late twentieth century, the earlier experiment on the CERN site had yielded a great deal of information about leptons. But the energy used to produce leptons was not nearly enough to produce a Higgs. A lepton, by the way, is a member of the lightest family of subatomic particles, such as an electron or a muon. However, the clever group who constructed the LEP, as the tunnel was called, foresaw that it would be possible comparatively cheaply to modify their experiment, so that protons replaced the positrons and electrons of the original experiment.

'Protons, neutrons, and their anti-particles, belong to the family of more massive particles known as *hadrons*. Hence the terminology, the Large Hadron Collider.'

Kathi stopped. Then she spoke rather abstractedly. 'Imagine the drama of it! The world seemed to be on the brink of a great discovery. Would they be able to trace the Higgs through the LHC? The equipment was finally up and running in about 2005. A year later, it began to reach the kind of energy levels at which it seemed possible that they might actually detect the Higgs particle. This was at the lower end of the scale of theoretical possibilities for the

Higgs mass. So the fact that they found no clear candidate they could identify with the Higgs did not unduly worry the physicists.'

We stood in that unnatural place, staring at our boots. 'Do you think the day will come when we can understand everything?' I asked.

Kathi grunted. Without giving an answer, she continued with her account.

'There had never been any guarantee that the LHC could build to the energies required to find the elusive particle – unlike the potential of the scrapped SSC.'

'So more money was wasted . . .'

'Can you not understand that science – like civilisation, of which science is the backbone – is pieced slowly together from ambitions, mistakes, perceptions – from our faltering intelligences? Patient enquiry, that's it. One day, one day far ahead in time, we may understand everything. Even the workings of our own minds!'

I remembered something I had been taught as a child. 'But Karl Popper said that the mind could not understand itself.'

'With mirrors we may easily do what was once impossible, and see the back of our own heads. One step forward may be formed from a number of tiny increments. For example, the hunt for this elusive smudge has been facilitated by the seemingly trivial innovation of self-illuminating paper – ampaper – and 3D-paper. Their impact on scientific development has been incalculable.'

'So they did find the Higgs particle at some point?' I asked.

'By 2009, the entire energy range of conceivable relevance to the Higgs particle had been surveyed. No unambiguously identifiable Higgs was found. But what the physicists did find was at least as interesting.'

We had continued our walk. As we reached the crest of a small incline, Kathi said, 'More of this later. We are nearly there!'

Over the crest, the desolation was broken by tokens of

human activity. A group of suited men stood by three parked buggies. Their attention was directed towards a vast silvery tube, above which was suspended something which immediately reminded me of an immense saucepan lid. This lid evidently afforded protection against any slight aerial bombardment – any falling meteorite – for the tube below.

The men hailed us, and as we drew nearer to them I could see that this protective lid was of meshed reinforced plastic. Below it lay a large inflated bag from which cables trailed. In the background were sheds from which the sound of a generator came.

The importance of this installation was emphasised by a metal version of the UN flag, which was now raised on an extemporised flagpole.

Dreiser Hawkwood beckoned us on. His face behind its helmet appeared darker than ever. He briefly embraced Kathi, both of them clumsy in their suits, before shaking my hand in a perfunctory way. I was Kathi's guest, not his. Among the men in the background, I saw Jon Thorgeson, whose lecture I had postponed while I was pregnant.

Climbing on to a metal box, Dreiser raised himself above us to make a short speech.

'This is such a momentous day, I thought we might hold a small ceremony. It's to mark the occasion when, at last, the bag is completely filled. It has been a slow process. As you will know, we have had to avoid the possibility of setting up currents in the superfluid. But from this moment onwards, we are able to begin in earnest our search for the Omega Smudge.'

Pausing, he reached up to stroke his moustache but had to make do with stroking his visor instead.

'Jon and I were having an argument, although out here is not the best place for it. We were arguing about something hard to define – "consciousness". Jon's hard-line view is that consciousness emanates from the interaction of brute computation, quantum coherence, quantum entanglement, if you like, and quantum state reduction – those factors which produce a CPS, a sure indicator of *mind*. Many people – and our quantputers – would agree with him. He claims that science is "nearly there" – and will arrive there before long, in these areographic wastes. Is that a fair description of your position, Jon?'

Thorgeson said, 'Approximately.'

'Kathi and I take a more radical view. We see that, indeed, there are still some minor issues to be sorted out from the details of the particle physics, primarily the Smudge parameters. They will determine all the present unknowns. However, we radicals – I prefer the term visionaries – argue that something *profound* is still missing.'

'Yes,' said Kathi. 'And we believe that magneto-gravitic fields will turn out to be part of the missing story of that profundity.'

Dreiser continued briefly in this vein, before embarking on a different topic.

'You'll all have made use of the Ng-Robinson Plot? Let's just have a thought for that vital minor innovation! It was named after its inventors, Ng being a Singaporean and Robinson British. This was East meeting West – very fruitfully. The Plot has given us a wonderful method of displaying vast quantities of quantputer-generated information. At the time when it was first employed, supercomputers were already giving place to our QPs, or quantputers, to use their full name – much faster and more versatile machines. The computer read off the mass of a particle along one axis, its lifetime along another, and the q-factor along a third, all colour-coded according to the various quantum numbers possessed by the particle in question – charge, spin, parity, etc.

'And one of the crucial features Ng-Robinson introduced is a key intensity factor which indicates the probability of the detection being a reliable one. A very sharp bright image indicates firm identification of a particle, while a fuzzy one implies there may be some considerable uncertainty as to the suggested identification of an actual particle.

'The essentials of so many lines of research, which

in earlier times would have presented great difficulties, become immediately transparent. The Ng-Robinson Plot has proved extremely valuable in experimental particle physics, because a lot of that activity consists of sniffing out tiny subtle effects from enormous amounts of almost entirely irrelevant information!

'What they expected for the Higgs would have been one sharp, bright, and very *white* spot. That's according to the conventions used in this system of colour-coding. It should have stood out clearly from a background of variously coloured spots in other places in the generally dark background of the N-R Plot. These other spots would indicate the complex array of particles of different kinds generated by the experiment. Show the vidslide, Euclid.'

At this point, an android stepped forward to project a replica of the plot. It sparkled before the small audience with its dark pointillism. It could have been mistaken for a glimpse of another universe.

Dreiser asked, 'What did they see in place of a spot? They saw a *smudge*. Just a smudge. It arose around about the right place, pretty precisely where the particle physicists had come to expect that something would be found – which would be consistent with all the other junk observed earlier. But there was no clear-cut Higgs particle – merely a great big Higgs smudge!

'And the ultimate descendant of that smudge is what we hope to capture – one day, starting from now!'

We all clapped. Even Euclid clapped.

Somehow I felt depressed.

Even when I had my babe back in my arms, a feeling of my insignificance in the scheme of things persisted. To arrange for Jon Thorgeson to come at last and give his lecture on the Omega Smudge was a welcome diversion.

Paula Gallin helped me in the early stages. She found a small lecture hall we could use. Lectures made in person had proved more vital than lectures delivered over the Ambient – though I had no suspicion regarding the way this one was going to turn out. While I had forgotten about Jon in my preoccupation with dear Alpha, he had not forgotten his promise.

'Ah, my little honeypot!' was his greeting. I made no retort because it was pleasant to see his young-old face light up at sight of me. He was followed into the ante-room by a porter trundling a large man-size crate. Once it was set down, and was stood upright, Jon thumped it.

'There's someone in here who can see what we are doing. Give me a kiss before I let him out.'

I put up my hands defensively. 'No, I don't do that sort of thing.'

'I wish you did,' he said, with a sigh. I was angry. The truth was, he was attractive after a fashion; it was just that his manner was so pushy. In a burst of confidence, he told me that he had left a Chinese lover back on Earth. I was a physical reminder to him of this lady. He longed to get back to her. He was miserable on Mars; it was for him a prison. 'Sorry to offend you,' he said, with a hangdog look.

He turned and unlatched the box the porter had brought. 'This is my visual aid,' he said, over his shoulder. The door of the box opened. A small android stepped out from its padded interior.

'Where am I?' it asked in a lifelike way.

'On Mars, you idiot.' Turning to me, Jon said, with mock-formality, 'Cang Hai, I'd like you to meet my friend, Euclid.'

'I have met him before,' I said, although no recognition was forthcoming from the android.

I offered Euclid my hand. It did not move. Nor did its well-moulded face manage more than a twitch of smile.

'It's one of Poulsen's cast-offs,' said Jon. 'I borrowed it for the occasion. It's house-trained.'

I remembered it then as one of the machines Poulsen had complained about. The android was dressed in blue overalls, much as Thorgeson was dressed. Its hair was cut to a fashionable length, unlike Jon's which was trimmed short. Its face wore a blankly pleasant expression which changed little. Jon clapped it on the shoulder.

There was something in its extreme immobility I found disconcerting. It had no presence. It gave out no CPS. It lacked body language.

Jon turned to me with a grin. 'Kathi tells me you are a mother now! Was it a virgin birth?'

'Change the conversation. It's none of your business. You didn't come here to be insulting, I hope.'

He shrugged, dismissing the topic. 'All right, you invited me over just to talk science. And when I get in that hall, I am going to talk about the continuing search for the ultimate smudge. All miseries forgotten.'

'Let's go. The audience is waiting. How long will you talk for?'

'My lecture is designed for ten-year-olds,' said Thorgeson. 'Euclid helps to hold their interest through the technical bits.' He caught my wrist. 'Do you think the audience knows anything of the past history of particle physics?' As he spoke, he slid an arm about my waist.

'I think you can count on it,' I said, disengaging myself.

'Oh, good. Then I had better not go into all that too much. How long have I got to talk?'

'Until you lose their interest. Now come on and don't be nervous.'

He was anything but nervous with me. 'Be nice to me,' he begged. 'I only came over to see you again.'

I told him not to be silly. But I was not completely annoyed.

We went into the hall, followed by the android. The audience gave us a round of applause. I introduced Thorgeson by saying that he would explain why there were so many scientists on Mars, and that he would speak of the problems they were hoping to solve. He would touch on matters affecting us all. His artificial friend, I said, would assist him.

Tom sat in the front row and nodded approval of my

short speech – the first I had made before such a large gathering.

Thorgeson began nervously, clearing his throat and gesticulating too much.

'As our understanding of the basic units of the universe deepens, it becomes yet clearer that these units are entities that possess no mass. There is a profound mystery here. Ordinary matter obviously possesses mass, and so do the basic particles of which matter is composed – protons, neutrons, and electrons, and also their constituent quarks and kliks. For many decades, physicists have struggled with the question: where does mass come from?

'This is a serious issue. Without mass everything would disintegrate. We'd be instantly dispersed into a flash of ethereal substance – not even mist – spreading outwards with the speed of light. Not a brilliant way to get to the nearest star.'

The feeble joke earned chuckles enough from the audience for Thorgeson to relax a little.

Euclid spoke. 'So tell us, what is the purpose of the Mars Omega Smudge Project?'

Glancing at a prepared script, Thorgeson continued, 'The Omega Smudge is what has brought us here. To explain why we call this vital smudge a smudge I should remind you of some history of particle physics last century and earlier this century.

'Euclid, do you remember the names given to the six varieties of basic subnuclear entity which was postulated last century?'

Euclid: 'Down, Up, Strange, Charm, Bottom, Top.'

'He has a faultless memory,' Thorgeson said, as another chuckle ran through the listeners.

He continued for a while, describing highlights of twentieth-century particle physics, which I was able to follow mainly because of Kathi's earlier explanations.

He was saying, '. . . the superconducting supercollider or SSC that was planned to be built under Texas was a miracle that did not quite happen. It would have cost billions and

163

was designed to discover what was referred to as "the Higgs particle". I see that some of you DOPs remember the name, though, of course, not the excitement of the time.

'Here's an artist's impression of the proposed SSC entrance.' He showed a vidslide in 3D of an airy and imposing glass structure, topped by a geodesic dome.

Euclid: 'Why would anyone think that so much money should be spent in search of a single particle?'

'It's a good question, Euclid. In the end the US Congress dropped the project. But the physicists – why, they argued that finding the elusive "Higgs" would have supplied them with the answer to the question of what comprises the basic units of the universe.'

Euclid: 'Did they believe that in those days?'

'Well, maybe not quite. But they did regard the finding of the Higgs as vitally important in their scheme of things. Also, completing the SSC would have achieved other targets. They put all their eggs in one basket to get the collider funded. The argument became over-heated. Certain physicists assigned an almost religious quality to the Higgs, referring to it as "the God particle" – a good journalistic phrase . . .'

Euclid: 'Did they believe that in those days?'

Thorgeson looked nonplussed. 'No Euclid, that's where you say, "Why was the Higgs regarded as so important?"'

Amid sympathetic laughter, Euclid spoke. 'Why was the Higgs regarded as so important?'

At his ease now, Thorgeson said, 'I'm glad you asked me that, Euclid. It all has to do with the question of mass. You are aware that most particles of nature have mass, but the photon and graviton – the basic quanta of electromagnetism and gravitation respectively – are exceptions. Those quanta of which matter is mainly composed, the protons and neutrons or their constituent quarks, are massive particles. So also are the kliks and pseudo-kliks that compose the much less massive leptons, such as electrons and muons.'

As Thorgeson continued, referring to 'LEP', the 'LHC', and various particle physics notions such as 'lepton' and 'hadron', I found that I was beginning to lose the thread of much of what he was saying. Fortunately Kathi's earlier explanations were still useful to me, so I knew what some of the terms meant.

Then I heard Euclid saying, 'Could they use the LHC to trace the Higgs? Could they use the LHC to trace the Higgs? Could they use the LHC to trace the Higgs?'

Thorgeson thumped Euclid's back. 'You mean to say, "Could they use the LHC to trace the Higgs?" Well, they finally got the equipment working in about 2005 . . .'

I realised that Euclid was talking with Thorgeson's voice although, without inflection, it sounded almost like a foreign language. But Thorgeson had programmed it. It amused me to think that, although Thorgeson was a stalwart 'hard science' man where questions of the human mind were concerned – believing there was nothing more to human mentality than the functions of a very effective quantputer – he could not resist making fun of his creature now and again.

Kathi had once tried to explain this 'hard science' position to me. Apparently it is commonly held by today's scientists.

She told me that they are simply missing the point. She explained their view to be that human mentality results solely from those physical functions that underlie an ordinary quantputer. I'm not really familiar with these underlying principles, but Kathi did have a go at trying to explain them. Apparently quantputers, and their smaller brothers the quantcomps, act by a combination of brute force computation in the old twentieth-century sense, and a collection of quantum effects referred to as 'coherence', 'entanglement' and 'state reduction'. Although I was never clear about these terms, Kathi explained that mentatropy and CPS detectors ('savvyometers'!) are based on such effects.

Thorgeson was saying, 'The riddle of mass needed a solution. A Korean scientist by the name of Tar Il-Chosun came up with a brilliant conception that, in effect, increased the energy range of the LHC by a factor of about one hundred. As a result, by 2009 the LHC had surveyed the complete range of energies that could possibly be relevant to the Higgs mass. Frustratingly, there was nothing that could be clearly identified with the Higgs. Instead they found something else, as strange as it was interesting.'

Euclid: 'What was that?'

'Using the newly perfected Ng-Robinson Plot, they found a smudge, roughly where the Higgs particle should have appeared.'

Euclid: 'So they found the Higgs?'

'They just found a smudge. No particle.'

Euclid: 'So that's where the name Smudge came from . . .'

'Absolutely.'

Euclid: 'But if they found this smudge in 2009, why all this business of setting up an umpteen-billion-dollar project to look for it here on Mars?' (Spoken with that same bland pleasant expression on its face.)

'What excitement this smudge caused! Excitement and dissension in the ranks! This, by the way, was when the consortium we know as EUPACUS was being assembled. Since CERN was already involved, the Europeans agreed to invest massively in it. You can bet they're regretting that now!

'The first problem the smudge threw up was that, by its very nature, its appearance on the Plot merely indicated a probability of something being there. The Higgs smudge had a very faint intensity, meaning the probability of the existence of a particle corresponding to any particular position on the Plot was very slight. Yet, on the other hand, the smudge covered so large a region of the Plot that the overall probability that something was there approached certainty.

'More experiments needed. The smudge remained.

'With finances forthcoming, the Americans with Asian and European backing finally built the SHC, the Superconducting Hypercollider, of beloved memory. My father worked on it as a young man, in an engineering capacity. They constructed this monumental bit of Big Science not in Texas, but straddling the states of Utah and Nevada.'

He projected a vidslide of an artist's cutaway of the great tube, burrowing under desert.

'And when they got the SHC working – darned if it didn't come out with the same results as previously! Seems a lot of dough had gone down the drain for nothing, one more time! The sought-after smudge remained just a smudge ... At that, it was a smudge on an entirely theoretical construct, the Ng-Robinson Plot. No actual Higgs particle could be pin-pointed. Yet, you see, the overall probability that something was there amounted to certainty.'

Euclid: 'No actual particle could continue to produce just an unresolvable smudge on the Plot?'

'Quite right, Euclid. They had a first-class mystery on their hands. And there, just when it gets exciting, we're going to take a break for ten minutes.'

Applause broke out as I led Jon into an anteroom. We left Euclid on the platform, standing facing the audience with his customary pleasant blank expression.

Thorgeson shut the door behind us and came towards me saying, 'I'm doing all this for you, my little Asian honeypot!'

He wrapped an arm round my waist, pulled me close, and kissed my lips.

I gave a small shriek of surprise. Asian honeypot indeed! He did not release me, but showered compliments on me, saying he had adored me ever since he had set eyes on me in the science unit. I did not mind the compliments. When he started to kiss me again, and I felt the warmth of his body against me, I found myself returning them.

I rejoiced when his tongue slipped into my mouth. I was becoming quite enthusiastic when the door opened and Tom and some others came in to congratulate Thorgeson on his exposition. This was one time when I felt really mad at Tom.

Back we marched into the hall. Thorgeson seemed quite

calm. I was trembling. He had been about to grab my breasts under my clothes, and I could not decide how I would feel about that. I was furious with the situation. It was all I could do to sit there and listen to him. How should I deal with him when the lecture was over – with that Euclid looking on, too?

However, I now saw a new kind of passion in Jon – not a physical passion but an intellectual one, as he took over from Euclid and spoke of the next epoch of scientific discovery.

'Euclid and I were talking about the smudge mystery,' he said when the audience had settled down. 'I will skip some years of confusion and frustration and speak about the year 2024. That was the year when there were two breakthroughs, one experimental, one theoretical.

'The experimental breakthrough came when SHC got up to full power, far beyond anything originally planned for the unbuilt SSC, using a further innovation contributed by the Indonesian physicist, Jim Kopamtim. Lo and behold at far greater energies than were achieved previously, another smudge was found!

'So the Higgs smudge had to be rechristened the alpha-smudge, while the new one went by the name of beta-smudge.

'The theoretical breakthrough – well, I should say it came a while before the SHC observations. A brilliant young Chinese mathematician, Chin Lim Chung, achieved a completely reformulated theoretical basis for particle physics as it stood at the time. Miss Chin introduced some highly sophisticated new mathematical ideas. She showed how a permanent smudge could indeed come about on the Ng-Robinson Plot, *but* the culprit could not possibly be a particle in any ordinary sense.

'It was a new kind of entity entirely. So from henceforth it was simply referred to as a *smudge*.

'Soon after the SHC announcement, Chin Lim Chung, working in conjunction with our own Dreiser Hawkwood, figured out that the alpha and beta smudges had to belong to a whole sequence of smudges, at higher and higher energies. It was clear that until this sequence was known as a whole, there was going to be no solution to the mystery of mass.

'Mother Teresa! It was as though we had discovered a row of galaxies on our doorstep!' As if he could not stop himself, he added, 'The remarkable Miss Chin is still alive and working. I happen to know her daughter.'

Something in Jon's manner, in his very body language, suggested to me that this lady must have been his Chinese lover, back on Earth.

Euclid: 'You cannot forever go on building bigger and bigger machines. So why did not the physicists just give up on the mystery?'

'Well, we don't give up easily.' He shot me a glance as he said this. 'It was hoped that once the gamma-smudge was found, then the mystery of mass could be resolved after all.'

Euclid. 'So they built an even bigger super-duper collider, did they? Where this time? Siberia?'

'On the Moon.'

He showed a vidslide of a gleaming section of tube crawling across the Mare Imbrium.

'A collider that formed a ring completely round the lunar surface. Alas for ambition! The Luna project turned out to be a total failure, at least with regard to finding the gamma-smudge. It did produce some data, relatively minor but useful. But no new smudge.'

Euclid: 'A costly mistake, wasn't it? Why did it fail?'

'The bill all merged into Lunar expenses, when the Moon was the flavour of the year, in the late 2030s. After a host of teething troubles, the Luna Collider appeared to do more or less what it was intended to do.

'I guess the final disaster rested with nature herself. She just didn't come up with a smudge – not even with the fantastic energy range available to a collider of that size.'

Euclid: 'Why didn't that kill off the whole idea? But you

are about to tell us that after that disaster, funding was found to start all over again *here* – on Mars?'

'Politics came into it. The fact that Mars was a UN protectorate made it tempting. Also, there is the precept that even pure science, however expensive it may seem, pays off in the unforeseen end. Consider the case of genetically mutated crops, and how they have contributed to human longevity. Some people are willing to pay for ever-widening horizons, for freeing the human mind from old shibboleths.

'And there were two further chunks of scientific progress to encourage them – and another different kind of development which had been brewing away for some while earlier.'

Euclid: 'They were?'

'Even last century, a number of theoreticians had realised that the enigma of mass could not be resolved at the energy levels relevant to the Higgs. Why? Well, the very concept of mass is all tied up with gravitation. Gravitation . . . Let me give you an analogy, Euclid.

'Another long-standing "mystery" in particle physics is the mystery of electrical charge. It's a mystery of a sort let's say, although a good number of physicists would claim they understand why electric charge comes about.

'The trouble is that although there are good reasons why electric charge always comes in whole-number multiples of one basic charge – which is one twelfth of the charge of an electron – there's no real understanding why the basic charge has the particular value it happens to have.

'I should say there was a time, late last century, when this basic value was believed to be one third of the electron's charge. Before that it was held to be the electron's charge itself. But the one-third value is the quark charge, and it was still thought that quarks were fundamental. Only after Henry M'Bokoko's theory of leptons and pseudo-leptons was it realised there were yet more elementary entities. Things called kliks and pseudo-kliks underlay these particles in the same way quarks underlie the hadrons.

'These kliks, pseudo-kliks and quarks, taken together, gave rise to the basic one-twelfth charge that we know today. A diagram will make that clear.'

He flashed a vidslide in the air. It hung before the audience, a skeletal Rubik's cube in three dimensions.

'Now, there are certain fundamental "natural units" for the universe – the units Nature herself uses to measure things in the universe. Sometimes these are called Planck units, after the German physicist who formulated them in the early years of last century.

'You see how one finding builds on the previous one. That's part of the fascination which keeps scientists working. In terms of these units, the basic value of the electric charge turns out to be the number 0.007, or thereabouts. This number has never been properly explained. So we don't, even yet, properly understand electric charge. There is, indeed, still a charge mystery. End of analogy!'

Euclid, unblinkingly: 'So what follows?'

'The point about the mass mystery – a point made by a few physicists even as long ago as last century – was that no one would seriously attempt to find a fundamental solution to the charge mystery without bringing the electric field into consideration. Electric charge is the source of the electric field. In the same way, so the argument went, it made little sense trying to solve the mystery of mass without bringing in the gravitational field. Mass is, of course, the source of the gravitational field.

'And yet, you see, the original hopes of resolving the mystery of mass in terms of finding the Higgs particle made absolutely no reference to gravitation.'

Euclid: 'What do you make of all this?'

'It was really a whole bag of wishful thinking. You see, Euclid, finding the Higgs particle was considered just about within the capabilities of the physicists of the time. So, if a solution to the mystery of mass could be found that way – why, then it would have been pretty well within their grasp.

'But if the issue of the role of gravity had to be seriously faced – there would not have been a hope in Hell of their finding an answer to the origin of mass experimentally. They were looking for God with a candle!

'The energy required would have been what we call the Planck energy – which is larger than the Higgs energy by a factor of at least – well, if we said a few thousand million million, we wouldn't be far out.

'Put it this way. Even a collider the length of the Earth's orbit would not have been enough.' His young-old face broke into a broad grin at the thought of it.

Euclid: 'Yet you tell us that they still did not give up. Why is that?'

'As I told you, it was all wishful thinking. They believed that finding the Higgs would be enough. Anyhow, science often proceeds by being over-optimistic. It's a way in which things do eventually get done. Eventually.

'So although the mass mystery remains unsolved, we now think our project here could well be close to doing so.'

Euclid: 'More over-optimism?'

'No, this time the case is pretty convincing. The thing is that we are now really facing up to the Planck energy problem.'

Euclid: 'I may be only an android, but as far as I know our experiment does not involve a collider of anything like that length. Or any collider at all.'

Jon released a 3D projection of something like a dark matrix motorway into the lecture room. He let it hang there as he spoke. On that infinite road, smudges shot off endlessly into distance. A cloud of other coloured spots sped after them.

'We're looking at a VR projection of a succession of different smudges, alpha-, beta-, gamma-, delta-smudges. Artist's impression only, of course. You're right, we have no collider on Mars. I've said there were a couple of encouraging breakthroughs. Those breakthroughs make our Mars project possible.

'First breakthrough. The realisation that there was no point in working through this whole gamut of smudges, at greater and greater energy levels, the list continuing for ever.'

He switched off the projection. The scatter of smudges died in their tracks.

The Icelandic physicist, Iki Bengtsoen, showed that when Einstein's theory of gravitation – already confirmed to an unprecedented degree of accuracy – was appropriately incorporated into the Chin-Hawkwood smudge theory, it became obvious that the energies of all the different smudges, alpha, beta, gamma and so on, did not just increase indefinitely, sans limit, but converged on the Planck energy limit.

'You see what this implies? All would be resolved if just a single experiment could be devised to explore the "ultimate" smudge, that limiting smudge, where all the lower energy smudges are supposed to converge. It's this putative ultimate smudge we call the *Omega Smudge*.'

Euclid. 'So we have got to it at last.' He maintained an expression of goodwill. 'But maybe you can explain how an experiment out here, on Mars, can be of particular use in finding this Flying Dutchman of a smudge – supposing it to exist at all.'

'That's where our other breakthrough comes in. Harrison Rosewall argued convincingly that a completely different kind of detector could be used to find this Omega Smudge, supposing it to exist at all.

'This involves the phenomenon known as "hidden symmetry".'

Euclid: 'And what might that be?'

Jon stood gazing at the low ceiling, as if seeking inspiration. Then he said, 'Every part of the explanation takes us deeper. These facts should have been part of everyone's education, rather than learning about past wars and histories of ancient nations. Well, I don't want to go into details, Euclid, but a hidden symmetry is a sort of theoretical symmetry which is dual in a certain sense, to a more manifest symmetry than might exist in theory. The idea goes back to some hypotheses popular late last century, although at that time the correct context for the hidden-symmetry idea was not found.

'What was important for Rosewall's scheme was that there can be things called monopoles associated with hidden-symmetry fields.

'A magnetic monopole would be a particle that has only a magnetic north pole or south pole assigned to it. As you know, an ordinary ferroperm magnet has a north pole at one end and a south pole at the other. Neither north nor south poles exist singly.

'But the great twentieth-century physicist, Paul Dirac, showed that the charge values had to be integer multiples of *something*. If you could find even a single example of a separate north or south pole, then – as we have since discovered to be the case – all electric charges would have to come in whole-number multiples of a basic charge.

'So, a number of years later, experimenters set to work to find such magnetic monopoles. If just one was found, then a major part of the mystery of electric charge would be solved. One group of experimenters even argued that the most likely place to find these things would be inside *oysters*. Of which, as we know, there's a considerable shortage on Mars.'

Euclid: 'Any luck?'

'No. No one has ever found a magnetic monopole, even to this day. But, in Rosewall's case, the hidden symmetry refers to a dual on the gravitational field. Rosewall made an impressive case that a hidden-symmetry gravitational monopole – known as a HIGMO – *ought* actually to exist. In fact there is a solution to the Einstein gravitational equations – found in the early 1960s, I believe – which describes the classical version of this monopole.

'This was Rosewall's brainwave. He realised that if you built a large ring-shaped tube, filled with an appropriate superfluid – argon 36 is what we use, under reduced pressure – then whenever a HIGMO passed through the ring, it would be detectable – just barely detectable – as a kind of "glitch" appearing in the superfluid.'

A voice from the audience asked, 'Why argon 36 and not 40?'

'Proton and neutron numbers are equal in argon 36, which underlies the reason for its remarkable superfluidity under reduced pressure. A technical advantage is the low pressure of the Martian atmosphere. Fortunately, argon 36 is not radioactive. Okay?'

At this point, he projected a vidslide of a scene I recognised. There lay the massive inflated tube, protected by its lid. There stood Dreiser, delivering his little speech. I had been a part of that historic scene!

'Obviously, this is a large-scale but delicate experiment. No other disturbances of any kind must affect the superfluid in the tube. You have to do the best you can to shield the superfluid from external vibrations, because any significant outside activity is liable to ruin the experiment.

'No place on Earth is going to be remotely quiet enough for such an experiment. Never mind human activity, the magma under Earth's crust is itself active, like a giant tummy rumbling. Earth is an excitable planet.'

Euclid: 'What about Luna?'

'The Moon proved no longer possible. Too much tourist activity and mining was already taking place. Maybe forty years ago the Moon could still have been used, but not now, certainly not since they began building the transcore subway.

'But Mars . . . Mars is ideal for the Omega Smudge experiment. No moving tectonic plates, vulcanism dead . . . That is, it's ideal provided that human activity is kept down to present levels.'

Euclid: 'No terraforming?'

Thorgeson laughed. 'The UN did a trade-off. No terraforming for a few years. The hidden agenda was that this would give a breathing space for the Omega Smudge experiment. The gun at our heads is that we have to get results.'

At this there were rumblings from the audience, and an angry voice called, 'So how long is "a few years"? Tell us!'

After a moment's pause, Thorgeson said, 'There was to be a stand-off of thirty years – four years from now – before they began to bombard the Martian surface with CFC gases, to start the warming-up process. This was the deal pushed through by Thomas Gunther.'

This statement provoked angry interjections from the audience. Thorgeson calmed things down with a wave of his hand.

'Obviously the collapse of EUPACUS has altered all such arrangements.

'The experiment we're now getting under way involves only a relatively small ring, sixty kilometres in diameter. Will we discover any HIGMOs? That depends on the HIGMO density in the universe, of which there are only estimates so far. We need results. Otherwise – who knows – the terraformers take over, the CFC gases rain down . . .'

'Get on with it, then!' came a shout from the audience, followed by roars of support.

Thorgeson said, 'The terrestrial economy is still in meltdown. Don't worry.

'Our present experiment is basically a pilot project, partly to test out how we work in adverse conditions. Maybe we can manage with this. If not, we hope to build a superfluid ring around the entire planet.'

'Another way of ruining Mars!' yelled a voice.

'We need to solve the problem at last. With the planet ringed, the answer to the vexed question of mass will finally be answered. Maybe Mars was formed precisely to enable us to find that solution.'

'Victorianism!' came a cry from a now restive audience.

Thorgeson answered this cry directly. 'Okay, tell me what else is Mars good for? You invited me here. Listen to what I have to say. I'll take sensible questions afterwards. Till then, keep quiet, please.'

As if to back him up, Euclid spoke. 'Say why it is so important to solve the mystery of mass. If a few physicists satisfy their curiosity in this respect, what good does that do ordinary people?'

'It is always difficult to justify curiosity-driven research in terms of its ultimate benefit to society. We can't tell ahead of time. Nevertheless the effect of such research, which seems entirely abstract to the lay person, can be tremendous. An obvious example is Alan Turing's analysis of theoretical computing machines done in the 1930s. It changed the world in which we live. We are on Mars because of it.'

Euclid: 'You must have some idea as to the value of this immensely costly research in areas other than particle physics.'

'Smudge research will have an important impact on other areas of physics and astrophysics. After all, it is concerned with the deepest issues of the very building bricks of the universe, the particles of which we are all composed, and their constituent elements.

'A full understanding of mass may lead to matrix-drives that will carry us to the heart of our galaxy.

'It's concerned, too, with gravitation and with the nature of matrix and time. It relates in a vital way to the understanding of the big bang origin of the universe, and thus to deep philosophical questions. The whole mystery of where the universe comes from and of what the universe is composed – this is what smudge research ultimately involves.'

The same angry voice from the audience now interposed to say, 'Self-justification is no justification.'

I saw anger in Thorgeson's eyes, but he answered in a controlled manner one could not but admire.

'You might ask how any of this really affects society, although the matter remains of great interest to any intelligent person. Well, society might also be deeply affected for a different type of reason. This relates to a third breakthrough, which occurred at about the same time, having to do with the very nature of the human mind – or the *soul*, as some unscientific people put it.

'In the early years of this century, the development of electronic into quantum computers encouraged the already widely held view that *mind* was just something that developed when sufficient powerful and effective computations took place. Chess, finally even the oriental game of Go, succumbed to the brutal but speedy computations of these devices.

'Yet no matter how effective these machines were, it was always obvious that they possessed no minds. They couldn't even be called intelligent in any ordinary sense of that word. Something essential was missing.

'With the development of the quantputer about 2023, distinct new physical features were incorporated, using basic quantum-mechanical principles. We have evidence that the human brain itself operates using these same principles. Thus, it is likely that we have in a quantputer all the essentials of human mentality. As yet, we are still short of knowing all the needed physical parameters.

'In 2039, definitive experiments carried out in France established that there is a CPS, a clear physical signal, emanating from conscious entities alone, and not from non-conscious entities like our present-day quantputers.'

Thorgeson paused to let this sink in before adding, with some emphasis, 'We have to improve the quantputer. When we have all the physical parameters – which the smudge should supply – then we shall be able to construct a quantputer that will actually emit a CPS. In other words, it will have consciousness.'

The audience remained unsettled, with voices still calling that Mars was not a laboratory.

John Homer Bateson rose from his seat and spoke, arms folded protectively across his chest. 'Professor Thorgeson, I am embarrassed to admit that I lost the thread of your involved argument when you began talking about mind. Whatever mind is. Have you not strayed from your proper subject? And is this not the way of physicists – to usurp ground properly the territory of philosophers?'

'I have not moved from my original topic,' Thorgeson said quietly. But another quiet voice in the audience, that of Crispin Barcunda, said, 'At least on Mars we have escaped the powers of the GenEng Institute, busy sculpting Megarich personalities and dupes and living rump steaks. While you guys here stay away from the biological sciences and stick to physics—'

'What's your question, Crispin?' I asked, insulted by his connecting dupes with living rump steaks.

'Is not the most pressing matter that now confronts us the possible connection between mind and your proposed smudge ring?'

'That's what we hope to find out,' Thorgeson said.

Other voices started calling. I told them to be silent and allow the lecture to continue.

At this point, Ben Borrow stood up, raising his hand to be seen. 'As a philosopher, I must ask what is to be gained by this search for the Omega Smudge? Is it not *that* which, by your own admission, has brought us to this wretched planet and caused the complete disruption of our lives?'

I answered before Thorgeson could.

'Why should you talk about the disruption of our lives? Why not the extension of our lives? Aren't we privileged to be here? Can't we by will power adapt our attitudes to enjoy our unique position?'

He looked startled by my attack, but rallied smartly, saying, 'We are of the Earth and belong there. It's the breast and source of our life and our happiness, Cang Hai.'

'Happiness? Is happiness all you want? What a pathetic thing! Hasn't the cult of the quest for happiness been a major cause of misery in the Western world for almost two centuries?'

'I didn't say—'

But I would not let him continue. 'The quest for scientific truth – is that not a far nobler thing than mere self-gratification? Please sit down and allow the lecture to continue.'

Thorgeson shot me a grateful look – although he was soon to teach me a horrid lesson in self-gratification. He came boldly to the front of the dais, to stand with hands on hips, confronting his hecklers.

'Look, everything in the universe depends on the fundamental laws that govern particles. All of chemistry, all of biology, all of engineering, every human – and inhuman – action – all of them ultimately depend on the laws of particle physics. Can't you understand that?'

The audience continued to be noisy. Thorgeson pressed on.

'Most of those laws are already known. The one major thing we do not yet know is where mass comes from. Once we know the Omega Smudge parameters – which will be fixed as soon as we have sufficient HIGMO data, then we will basically know *everything* – at least in principle. Isn't that important enough to put a bit of money into, just in itself? It's philistinism to ask for further justification.'

'Not if you're stuck here for years,' called someone from the audience, provoking laughter. Thorgeson spoke determinedly over it.

'It happens that some people in the early days of setting up the Mars experiment thought there was another justification for it. These people believed that there has to be *more* to the human mind than what they refer to as "just quantputing". They reckoned that finding HIGMOs would lead us to a "mysterious something" which would provide a better understanding of human consciousness. Maybe I should use the term "soul" again here.' He gave a brief contemptuous laugh. 'There are still some people – even some important people on the project, who shall be nameless – who continue to pursue this sort of notion. A load of nonsense in my opinion.'

He spoke more calmly now, and retired behind his podium to talk rather airily.

'There's no such thing as "soul". It's a medieval concept. Our brains are just very elaborate quantputers. Maybe we do still have to tune a few parameters a bit better, but that's basically all there is to it. Even Euclid would have a mind if he had been constructed with greater sophistication and better tuned parameters. But you can see he has a long way to go – haven't you, Euclid?'

Euclid: 'But I think I have a mind. A different kind of mind, perhaps. Maybe after a few more years, research will detect . . .'

'The only kind of minds *so far* we have direct reason to believe in are possessed by humans and animals, since they alone give the clear physical signal which shows up positively in the French experiment.'

Euclid: 'You are being anthropocentric and trying to prove you are better than I.'

'I am better than you, Euclid. I can switch you off.'

'Well, what has all this to do with smudges?'

'The mind is a product of the brain, our physical brains, so that mind depends on the physics of our brains. We need to know that physics just a little better. As we shall do when the Omega Smudge reveals all. Shall we soon be able to reproduce mind artificially? Smudge is clearly central to these questions.

'Here I need to retire to relax my throat for five minutes. I shall return to answer your questions.'

He motioned me to follow him, and he, I and Euclid trooped off the platform to general applause.

His performance had converted me from mistrust to admiration. 'A brilliant exposition,' I said, as we went into the rest room. 'You must have enlarged the understanding of—'

'Those fools out there!' he exclaimed. As he spoke, he turned the lock in the door behind his back. 'What did they understand? It was all gobbledy-gook to them. They show no inclination to learn. I'm not going back. I came over here to see you, you minx, and now I'm going to have you!' As he spoke, he was tearing off his overall. His face entirely altered from one of philosophical contemplation to a mask of lust and determination, its lines working angrily.

Never had I seen a man change so rapidly. I dreaded to think what thoughts he had been storing up in his mind during his long disquisition.

'Look, Jon, let's just talk—'

'You're going to be my payment—'

He tore from his pants the instrument with which he intended to rape me. I regarded it with interest. It differed from a dog's pizzle, mainly in having a padded bulb at the top for comfort during the penetration. This must have been, I thought, an evolutionary development tending towards producing better relationships between the sexes. Nevertheless, although I admired the design, I could not conceive of having it in my body.

Or not without a lot of consideration.

Making some absurd compliments about it, I took hold of the thing and began to stroke it. Thorgeson's 'No, no, no,' turned quickly to 'Oh oh oh,' as I hastened my strokes. I moved aside as he ejaculated on the floor.

All the while this embarrassing episode was taking place, Euclid stood there, smiling his blank smile. I ran past him, unlocked the door, and rushed into the passage.

Testimony of Tom Jefferies

12

The Watchtower of the Universe

The Martian marathon was organised by a group of young scientists working on Operation Smudge. They had set an ingenious 6-kilometre course through the domes, parts of which involved them leaping from the roofs of four-storey buildings, equipped with wings to provide semi-flight in the light gravity.

The marathon was regarded as an excuse for fun. Beza and Dayo had teamed up to provide a little razmataz music. Over 700 young people, men and women, together with a smattering of oldsters, were entered in the race.

Many appeared in fancy dress. The Maria Augusta dragon was present, with several small offspring. A bespectacled and bewigged Flat Mars Society showed up. Many little and large green men, complete with antennae, were running alongside green semi-naked goddesses, jostled by other bizarre life forms.

Everyone not in the race turned out to watch. The music played. It proved an exciting occasion. First prize was a multi-legged dragon trophy, created in stone and painted by our sculptor, Benazir Bahudur, with less elaborate versions for runners who came second and third.

The winner was the particle physicist Jimmy Gonzales Dust. He finished in 1,154 seconds. He was young and good-looking, with a rather cheeky air about him; he was very quick with his answers. At a modest banquet held in his honour, he was reported to have made a remarkable speech. Feeling somewhat dizzy, I did not attend.

Jimmy said that he had once believed that the process of terraforming the planet should have been undertaken from the start of our tenure of Mars. There could be no ethical objection to such work, since there was no life on Mars that would suffer in the process.

He went on to say that the duration of life on Earth was finite. The Sun in senescence would expand until it consumed Earth and the inner planets. Long before that, Earth would have become untenable as an abode of life and the human race would have had to move on or perish.

He claimed that other ports of call – the phrase was Jimmy's – awaited. In particular, he pointed out, it was common knowledge that the satellites of Jupiter had much to offer. Whereas the hop from Earth to Mars was a mere 0.5 astronomical units on average, a much greater leap was required to reach those Jovian satellites – a leap of 3.5 AUs. Once humanity grew away from the corruption that dogged great enterprises to devise a better mode of propulsion than the chemical fuel presently used – or not being actually used, he added, to laughter – this leap would be less formidable and would prove to be nothing compared with that leap that would surely have to be made one day, the leap to the stars themselves.

Such a leap, he continued, would be undertaken within a century. Meanwhile a great engineering project, such as that which would be required to endow Mars with a breathable atmosphere at tolerable atmospheric pressure and within acceptable temperature tolerances, would attract the populations of Earth. It would provide the inspiration to look outward and to grasp that factor which, apparently, many found insurmountable – namely that, with labour equivalent to the labour which had gone to make Earth habitable for multitudes of species, many varieties of bodies could be provided with pleasant dwelling places.

Eventually, like a flock of migratory birds, terrestrial species would have to leave an exhausted Earth and fly elsewhere. Their first resting points could well be on those moons of Jupiter, Ganymede and Callisto in particular. They would have the vast water resources of Europa to draw upon, and their extraordinary celestial scenery to marvel at. Thus technology would help to achieve the apotheosis of humanity.

At this point, someone interrupted the speech, shouting, 'This is all political rhetoric!'

It is never wise to barrack a popular young hero. The banqueters booed, while Jimmy said, smilingly, 'That certainly wasn't a politic remark,' and continued with his talk.

However, he said, his ambition to see Mars terraformed – often referred to as a first step towards humanity's becoming a star-dwelling race – had been based on a mistaken assumption, about which he wished to enlighten his audience, he hoped without alarming them.

Certainly, he had some disturbing news.

'For many years, people believed Mars to be inhabited,' he said. 'The quasi-scientific opinions of Percival Lovell, author of *Mars as an Abode of Life*, encouraged interest in the idea, which had been founded on the erroneous assumption that Mars was a more ancient planet than Earth. Improved astronomical equipment, and visits by probes, had swept all such speculation away. Finally, with manned landings, the point had been conceded. There was no life on Mars.

'Millions of years earlier, some archebacteria developed. Conditions deteriorated. They died out. Since then, everyone believed, Mars had been destitute of life. Destitute for millions of years.'

Jimmy paused, to confront the seriousness of what he was about to say.

'That is not the case. In fact, for millions of years there has been life on this planet. You will know of the white tongues which surround our laboratories. They are neither vegetable nor mineral. Nor are they independent objects. We have reason to believe they are the sensory perceptors of an enormous – animal? Being, let's call it.

185

'You will be aware of the M-gravitic anomaly associated with the Tharsis Shield. That anomaly is caused by a being so large it is visible even through terrestrial telescopes. We know it as Olympus Mons.

'Olympus Mons is not a geological object. Olympus Mons is a sentient being of unique kind.'

Immediately chaos erupted in the hall. Shouts of 'It can't be!' mingled with cries of 'I told you so!' When calm was restored, Jimmy resumed, smiling rather a guilty smile, pleased by the shock he had engendered.

'My fellow scientists in this room will confirm what I say. This immense being, some seven hundred kilometres across, is a master of camouflage. Or else it's a huge kind of barnacle. Its shell resembles the surrounding terrain, much as a chameleon takes on the colour of its background. Its time-sense must be very different from ours, since it has sat where it is now, without moving, for many centuries.

'Under its protective shell is organic life.'

He gave a nervous laugh.

'Terraforming would harm it. We are, ladies and gentlemen, sharing this planet with an amazingly large barnacle!'

The learned John Homer Bateson, leaning nearby against a pillar, hands in his robe, said, 'An amazingly large barnacle! The mind is inclined to boggle somewhat. Well, well . . . Was it not Isocrates who called man the measure of all things? Such Ptolemaic thinking needs revision. Clearly it is this mollusc that is the measure of all things.'

Others present pressed forward with anxious questions.

Jimmy sought to give some reassurance.

'We can only speculate as to where the being came from, or where it might be going. Is it friend or enemy? We can't tell as yet.'

'You mad scientists!' Crispin Barcunda was heard to exclaim. 'What might this thing do if disturbed – if, say, we had started the terraforming process, with attendant atmospheric and chthonic upheavals?'

Jimmy spread his hands. 'Olympus has its exteroceptors trained on us. All we can say is that it has, as yet, made no hostile move.'

Even the special performance of *Mine? Theirs?*, revised once again by Paula Gallin, was ill attended after this disconcerting news.

Speculation concerning Olympus, as it became known, continued on all levels. Much discussion concerned whether it might be regarded as malevolent or benevolent. Did this strange being consider that it owned Mars, in which case it might well regard humans as parasitic intruders? Or was it merely some unexpected variety of celestial jellyfish, without intention?

More alarm was caused when Jimmy Dust and his fellow scientists revealed that they had secured as a specimen one of the white tongues – had, in fact, hacked it off. Its complex cellular organisation had convinced them that, whatever Olympus was, it enjoyed sensory perception. Some reassurance was afforded by the fact that it had not retaliated against this attack on its exteroceptors. But perhaps it was merely biding its time.

I did not at this juncture realise how unwell I was. However, I had sufficient energy to call Dreiser Hawkwood on the Ambient. I demanded to know why the news that Olympus Mons was a living entity had been released to us in such a casual manner, by Jimmy Dust, the marathon winner. I asked if some kind of dangerous joke was being played on us. I raved on. I even said it had been firmly established that there was no life on Mars.

Dreiser listened patiently. He then said, 'We chose to make the announcement as informally as possible, hoping not to alarm people. You will find the strategy is largely successful. People will cluck like hens and then get on with their day-to-day business. And you, Tom, I trust, will regain your customary good humour.'

It was the meek answer that increases wrath. 'You told

me when we spoke about Olympus that it was in no sense alive.'

'I never said that.'

'When we were preparing to address the assembly over a year ago, did you or did you not tell me there was no life on Mars?'

'No. I may have said we had found no life on Mars. Olympus was so big that it escaped our notice . . .' He chuckled. 'I may have said we should expect Martian life to be very different from life Downstairs. So it proves.'

'You're trying to tell me that this monstrous thing has just flopped out of the skies from space, or from another universe?'

'I might try to tell you many things, Tom, if you were fit to listen. I merely tell you this for now – that Olympus is entirely indigenous to Mars.'

When I asked how it was that he had made this discovery, rather late in our second year of isolation on Mars, Dreiser replied that a study of satellite photographs had convinced him there was some movement in the region.

'To whom did you first communicate this knowledge?'

He hesitated. 'Tom, there are two things you should know. Firstly, we owe this perception – a perception I will admit I resisted at first – to the young genius you turned up, Kathi Skadmorr. What a clever young woman she is, what a quick brain!'

'Okay, Dreiser. And the second thing?'

'This object that Kathi insists on calling the "Watchtower of the Universe" is definitely on the move. And it's moving in our direction, slow but sure. More news later. Goodbye.'

He signed off. I felt mortified that I had spoken so ill advisedly, and that the conversation had been recorded.

I went to lie down.

The physicists proposed sending an investigative expedition to Olympus. They were told to wait. Caution was to be the order of the day. Olympus might have a slower time sense than biological beings and could be planning a counterattack, so any close approach might imperil human lives.

I held private discussions with Jimmy Dust and his scientific colleagues, including the young man who maintained that cephalopods possessed intelligence.

'Human nature being what it is, the wish to believe in something bigger than themselves comes naturally to people,' one of the women said. 'But we need to discourage the idea already circulating in some quarters that Olympus is a god. As far as our limited knowledge goes, it's just a huge lump of rather inert organic material.'

'Yet we call it Olympus – traditionally the home of the gods.'

'That's just a semantic quibble. Our guess is that this being is of low intelligence, being rupicolous.'

'Eh? What's rupicolous?'

'Means it lives off rocks. Not a bright thing to do.'

'How so? At least there's a generous supply of rock around right here . . .'

The discussion broke up without coming to any conclusion.

Adminex invited Hawkwood to come to the Hindenburg Hall and address an assembled crowd on the subject of Olympus. In particular we wished him to clarify its nature.

He agreed as long as his talk took the form of an interview. If I would ask the questions. I agreed. When we had both prepared for the talk, an assembly was called.

Since the occasion was so important, children were permitted to be present. In they streamed, carrying their tammies – tammies that had been fed and cosseted before their entry.

Dreiser arrived in style. He was prompt. He came with a retinue of four, the wispy Poulsen, another scientist, a blonde personal assistant whom we had met, as Cang Hai reminded me, in Dreiser's office, and a fourth member whom I hardly recognised at first. Gone were her thick and curly chestnut locks. Her hair was now black, straight, and cut short. It was Kathi Skadmorr. When she shook my hand and smiled, I knew that smile.

The retinue settled themselves in the front seats, while Dreiser and I sat under the great photograph of the flaming zeppelin, in the dazzle of Suung Saybin's lighting.

Dreiser began by saying that he wished to inform everyone of the little he knew concerning the nature of the life form called Olympus. He reminded us that Olympus had maintained its present existence for far longer than terrestrial telescopes had been around to be trained on Mars. It was an object, a life form, of immense antiquity, almost as ancient as the rocks to which it clung.

To remind us of its size, he zapped before the audience a 3D vidslide showing Olympus in profile, with a dawn light on its higher reaches, while its tall serrated skirts remained in a dusky red twilight. Its vast span covered 600 kilometres of ground.

'There it is, waiting for we know not what, amid ancient cratered topography over three billion years old.'

A shot of Earth's Mount Everest was superimposed over Olympus. It showed as the merest pimple below the central caldera.

'As you see,' said Dreiser, 'Olympus is unusually large for a volcano. For a life form it defies the imagination.'

An uneasy hush fell on the audience.

I remarked that Mars had previously been ruled out as an abode of life.

But this, Dreiser argued, was merely a reference to the many studies that had been conducted of soil and rock samples, of the analysis of the atmosphere, and of drillings made down into the crust. None had revealed any evidence for Martian life of any kind – even when allowances were made for the fact that life here might be completely different from life on Earth.

It was still difficult, I said, not to think of Olympus as simply an extraordinarily large volcano among other Martian volcanoes, admittedly of smaller size, such as

Elysium, Arsia and Pavonis. Or were they also the carapaces of living beings?

He thought not. 'Reproduction is a basic evolutionary function. Nevertheless it seems that Olympus has not spawned. Maybe it is a hermaphrodite. Maybe it simply lacks a partner.'

We would come to what it resembled later, Dreiser said. He wished to state that he had no quarrel with all the previous research centring on the quest for life. Those conclusions were definitive. Olympus was unique.

At this juncture, Dreiser said, he believed that the spotlight should shine on his associate, who had first brought the movements of Olympus to scientific notice. Those movements were so unprecedented that at first they were not credited. In introducing Kathi Skadmorr, he knew she was already celebrated as the YEA who had courageously gone down into the throat of the Valles Marineris and found considerable underground reservoirs of water.

Kathi now came to the dais and spoke without preamble, almost before the clapping had finished. 'I'm campaigning to call Olympus Mons by a more vital name. It was christened in ignorance, long ago. I propose rechristening it, in the light of our new-found knowledge, Chimborazo, which means the "Watchtower of the Universe". So far my campaign has only one member, but I'm still hoping.

'We don't as yet know what we have here. Okay, Chimborazo moves, but whole mountains have been known to move. So movement does not necessarily mean life. Here's where we detected movement.'

She zapped a vidslide taken from the satcam, showing the tumbled regolith on Chimborazo's westerly side, and continued to speak.

'The broken regolith shows where our friend upped stumps and began to move. We secured one of those elusive white tongues you will all have seen. They are in fact inorganic, but with organic nerves and feelers lacing them. It seems not all tongues are identical, and that they serve different functions.

191

'Our hypothesis at present is that the tongues, more scientifically termed exteroceptors and proprioceptors, were once digestive organs, and that they have been modified over the eons. Not only do they provide nourishment to Chimborazo: they also function as rudimentary detectors. Thus, you see, they provide evidence that Chimborazo is not only a massive life form: it is also a life form with some kind of intelligence.

'Now I will hand over to Tom and Dreiser again.' She did not leave the dais, but took a seat next to me.

After thanking Kathi, I asked Dreiser where this monstrous thing had come from? From outer space? The Oort Cloud?

Not at all. 'Olympus Mons,' said Dreiser, then hesitated. 'Very well then, Chimboranzo—'

Kathi immediately interrupted, saying, 'It's Chimborazo, Dreiser!'

He gave a grunt and grinned at her. 'Chimborazo is entirely indigenous. Nor is there anything uncanny about it. Our belief is that it is the result of a curious form of evolution – curious, that is, from the point of view of one accustomed to thinking in terrestrial terms. Curious – but by no means irrational.'

But if this life form actually evolved on Mars, as Dreiser claimed, there would surely be evidence of other life in the atmosphere, I said. Not only in the atmosphere, but in the rocks and regolith. 'Evolution', after all, implied 'natural selection', so there must have been other forms of life with which this monstrous Olympus organism had been in competition. I remarked that it would be silly to turn our backs on Darwin's findings, since natural selection was now a well-established principle.

Dreiser had adopted a slouching posture, as if scarcely interested in the topic we were discussing. Now he sat up and looked at me with a direct stare.

'I am not disputing those principles, Tom. Far from it. But it is all too easy to fall into the way of thinking that how natural selection has operated in the main on Earth is its only method. Conditions here are vastly different from those Downstairs. Which is not to say that Darwin's perceptions do not still apply.'

Of course conditions differed, I agreed. But I could not see how his Olympus could have extinguished all other life forms on the planet, simply by sitting there like a great lump, all in one place.

'For some while we thought exactly as you do. I have to say it is a limited point of view. Mounting evidence that Olympus is a living thing has made us change our opinions, our rather parochial earthly opinions. In fact, evolution on Earth itself has not been entirely "Nature red in tooth and claw". I could name many examples of cooperation between species that have led to vital evolutionary advantage. I stress that: cooperation, not competition.'

I supposed he was thinking of man and his long relationship with the dog.

'Unfortunately we did not bring our loyal friend the dog here with us, more's the pity. We will certainly need him when we travel towards the stars to face unforeseen challenges. We did bring all the bacteria in our stomachs, without which we could not survive. That's a handy example of a symbiotic relationship.'

What could that have to do, I asked, with his Olympian organism wiping out the rest of Martian life?

'That is not my argument. Not at all. There are many examples where symbiosis has played a vital role in evolution. Let's take lichens. Two differing organisms got together, a fungus and an alga, to form the unbeatable lichen, the hardiest of terrestrial life forms. Lichens are the first to move in after a volcanic eruption has wiped a mountainside clean. Even we, resourceful humankind, depend on our bacteria, just as swarming microlife depends on us.'

We had found no lichen-like organisms on Mars, I argued, and asked where that left us.

'Hang on. I'm not finished. I have some even more apposite examples of cooperation. There were times in the evolution of life on Earth when symbiotic relations have been absolutely vital.

'Take the eukaryotic cell. This is the kind of cell of which all ordinary plants and all animals are composed. It's a cell that contains a distinct nucleus within which chromosomes carry genetic material. It has long been established that the first eukaryotic cells came about by the union of two other more primitive types of organism, the earlier prokaryotic cell and a kind of spirochete. The development of all multicellular plants and animals – and humans – stems from this union.

'Incidentally, on the subject of life, you might ask yourself how likely – what are the odds – of such a coincidence happening elsewhere in our galaxy. Long odds, I'd say.'

Although I was in agreement with this statement, I got Dreiser back on track again by asking what all this had to do with Olympus's extinction of the rest of Martian life.

'No, no, you have the wrong picture in your head still, Tom. That's not what happened here, as we envisage it. There was no extinction.'

He paused before continuing, perhaps considering how to explain most clearly.

'With the very different conditions on Mars, the balance of advantage in evolutionary processes was also different. Even on Earth, two types of evolutionary pressure have been important. We have become accustomed to considering the idea of competition as being the more important. This may be because Darwin's splendid perceptions were launched in 1859 into a highly competitive capitalist society.

'In the competition scenario, the different species battle it out, and the "fittest" are, on the whole, the ones that survive. But the cooperative element in evolution has sometimes proved important – vital, you might say – as we've seen in the instances of symbiotic development I have already mentioned.

'On Earth, competitive aspects of evolution have rather dominated the cooperative elements in our consideration. Our enforced social competitiveness has led us in that direction. We tend to think that the competitive element predominates, although in fact the entire terrestrial biomass works in unconscious cooperative ways to create a favourable environment for itself.

'These cooperative processes stem from the early days when life first crept from sea to the land. Initially both land and atmosphere were hostile to life of any kind, and various symbiotic relationships had to be adopted. Otherwise life could not have survived. But gradually, as conditions on Earth became more favourable, competitive elements began to assert themselves. We now see – or think we see – the competitive elements dominating the cooperative elements.'

Somewhere in the audience, a tammy began to chirp and was hushed. I asked Hawkwood if evolution had taken a different course on Mars.

'Possibilities for life here differ considerably from Earth, as we have said. Conditions have never been other than harsh. Now they weigh heavily against life. We have low atmospheric pressure, almost zero oxygen content, abnormally dry conditions. But basic natural laws always applied.

'In the case of evolution, cooperation had a distinct edge over competition. In the early days of Mars's history, conditions more closely resembled Earth's. But gradually oxygen became bonded into the rocks while water vapour leaked away. As conditions became more and more adverse, cooperation among the indigenous life forms won out over competition.

'The enormous diversity of life forms, such as we find on Earth, never had a chance to develop here. Evolution on Mars was forced into a combining together of life. All forms eventually huddled together for protection against adverse Martian conditions. It was the ultimate Martian strategy.'

They huddled together, I suggested, under what we have always thought was a volcano, Olympus Mons. Why should they have chosen that particular shape?

'A cone shape is economical of material. And since the life forms were not going to be particularly mobile, they chose a defence readily adopted by countless of Earth's creatures – they opted for camouflage. Camouflage against what we can't tell; nor, I suppose, could they. But their instincts are readily understandable. In fact, the shell is just that, a shell made from keratin and clay – very tough and durable.'

It would keep heat in, I suggested.

'Yes, and fairly large meteorites out.'

A child's voice from the audience asked, 'What are the people like under the shell, Dreiser?'

'They aren't people in our sense of the word,' Dreiser replied. 'The use of keratin as a binder in the shell suggests hair, nails, horns, hooves, feathers . . .'

At the words 'hooves, feathers . . .' a frisson ran through the audience like the rustling of great wings.

Dreiser continued. 'Olympus Mons – sorry, Kathi, Chimborazo – has grown gradually into the vast volcano shape we know today. The creatures under it must be still surviving, perhaps even thriving, since Olympus is now in a growth phase. It extends very slowly, we think upwards. But our surveys indicate an expansion of something like 1.1 centimetres every other decade.'

So how did it feed?

'Its exteroceptors suck nourishment and moisture from the rocks.

'As you have heard from Kathi here, Chimborazo is executing a slow horizontal movement. It advances at the rate of a few metres every Martian year.'

At the exclamations from his audience, Dreiser looked gravely ahead of him. He spoke next with emphasis.

'This advance began only when these domes and the science unit were established. Chimborazo is probably attracted by a heat source.'

'You mean it's advancing on us?' cried a nervous voice from the floor.

'Although its forward movement is much faster than its growth rate, it is still no speedster by terrestrial standards. A snail runs like a cheetah by comparison. We're all quite safe. It will take nearly a million years to drag itself here at present rate of progress.'

'I'm packing my bags now,' came a voice from the floor amid general laughter.

Vouchsafing the remark a wintery smile, Dreiser continued, 'We monitored the horizontal movement first. You may imagine our incredulity. We did not immediately realise we were dealing with a living thing – undoubtedly the biggest living thing within the solar system.

'We did not connect it at first with those white exteroceptors, which flick so quickly out of sight. They are the creature's sensors, and of complex function. Not eyes exactly. But they appear to be sensitive to electromagnetic signals of various wavelengths. The multitude of them together is probably used to build up a picture of sorts. They retract at any unexpected signal, which caused us problems in getting a clear picture of them to start with.'

A subdued voice asked a question from the audience. Dreiser needed it repeated: 'I can't believe what you're telling us. How can that enormous thing possibly be alive?'

Kathi answered sharply. 'You must improve your perceptions. If it can think, Chimborazo is probably asking itself how a small feeble bipedal thing like you could possibly be alive – not to mention intelligent.'

The questioner sank back in her chair.

'You can perhaps imagine our shock when we discovered that Chimborazo was advancing towards our research unit. Nothing can stop its approach,' Kathi said. 'Unless we make some sort of conscious appeal to it . . .'

I asked if Dreiser thought that Olympus had a mind anything like ours.

'The balance of opinion is that it has a mind radically different from ours. So Kathi has half persuaded us. A

197

mind compounded of a multitude of little minds. Thought may be greatly slowed down by comparison with our time-scales.

'Yes, I have to say it may well have awareness, intelligence. We have detected a fluttery CPS – the clear physical signal that is the signature of mind. It may tick over slowly by our standards, but speed of thought isn't everything.'

'Now you're being anthropomorphic!' said a voice from the floor.

'It is one of the functions of intelligence to respond discriminatingly to the events that come within its scope. Which is what Olympus seems to be doing. Its response to mankind's arrival here is to move towards us. Whether this can be construed as hostile or friendly, or merely as a reaction to a heat source, we have yet to decide. It has decided!'

He paused for thought. 'It may well have consciousness. Consciousness is not necessarily the gift solely of earthly beings such as ourselves.

'In our discussions here, I have noticed the frequency with which ancient authorities are appealed to, from Aristotle and Plato onwards – to Count Basie, I may say. This is because our consciousness has a collective element. "No voice is ever lost," if I may take my turn at quoting. Our consciousness has been enriched by the minds of those good men who lived in the past. Perhaps you may regard this as a mental evolutionary principle of cooperation in action.

'Consciousness is unlike any other phenomenon, compounded of many elements and apparent contradictions along the quantum-mechanical level. In the close quarters engendered by its shell, the huddled creatures of Olympus would probably have developed a form of consciousness.

'I will also venture the suggestion that here in our cramped quarters we could be developing a new step forward in human consciousness, represented by the word "utopian". A thinking alike for the common good . . .

'If that is so – and I hope it may be so – it will mean the

fading away of individualism. This is what has happened with our friend Chimborazo, if I guess correctly. It has become a single creature consisting of the symbiotic union of all indigenous Martian life.'

Came a shout from the audience. 'What gives you the idea that this weird mind is good?'

Dreiser responded thoughtfully. 'I repeat that individualism had no chance on Mars. To survive, this entity evolved a collective mind. It has therefore learned control . . . But we can only speculate upon all this. With awe. With reverence.'

Here Kathi chipped in to say, 'It may seem to us slow and ponderous, but why should we not believe it to be superior to our own fragmented minds?'

After the talk, Helen Panorios came up to Dreiser and asked, timidly, why Olympus had camouflaged itself as a volcano.

'Olympus lies among other volcanoes. So it can become pretty well lost in the crowd.'

'Yes, sir, but what has it camouflaged itself against?'

Dreiser regarded her steadily before replying. 'We can only suppose – although this is terrestrial thinking – that it feared some great and terrible predator.'

'Space-born?'

'Very probably space-born. Matrix-born . . .'

From this occasion onwards, Dreiser and I spent more time together, discussing this extraordinary phenomenon. Sometimes he would call in Kathi Skadmorr. Sometimes I called in Youssef Choihosla, who professed an empathy with Olympus.

One of the first questions I asked Dreiser was, 'Are you now going to abandon your search for the Omega Smudge?'

He stroked his moustache as if it was his pet, gave me an old-fashioned look, and replied with a question, 'Are you going to abandon your plans for a utopian society?'

So we understood each other. Ordinary work had to continue.

But it continued under the shadow of that enormous life form that unceasingly inched its way towards us. Despite warnings to the contrary, the four of us drove out one calm day to inspect Olympus at close quarters. Crossing the parched terrain, we began to climb, bumping over parallel fracture lines. Kathi, in the rear seat with Choihosla, seemed particularly nervous, and clutched Choihosla's large hand.

When I jokingly made some remark to her about her nervousness, she replied, 'You might do well to be nervous, Tom. We are crossing Chimborazo's holy ground. Can't you feel that?'

The terrain became steeper and more broken. Dreiser drove slowly. The exteroceptors were all about us. They seemed thicker here, more reluctant to slide back into the frozen regolith. The buggy dropped to a mere crawl. Dreiser flicked his headlights on and off to clear the track. 'God, for a gun!' he muttered. We were all tense. No one spoke.

We surmounted a bluff, and there the rim of it was, protruding above ground level like a cliff. We stopped. 'Do we get out?' I asked. But Kathi was already climbing from the vehicle. She walked slowly towards Chimborazo.

I got out and followed. Dreiser and Choihosla followed me. Suited up, we could hear no external sound.

Even near to, Olympus closely resembled a natural feature, its flanks being terraced in a roughly concentric pattern. There were imitations of flowlines, channels and levees, as well as lines of craters that might or might not be imitations of the real things. We could by no means see all of its 700-kilometre diameter. Even the caldera was hardly visible, though a small cloud of steam hovered above it. Whether as a volcano or a living organism, it seemed impossible to comprehend.

In its presence I felt the hair at the back of my neck prickle. I simply stood and stared, trying to come to terms with it. Dreiser and Choihosla were busy with instruments, noting with satisfaction that there was no radiation reading, receiving a CPS.

'Of course there's a CPS,' said Kathi. 'Do you really need instruments to tell you that? How's the back of your neck, for instance?'

Braver than we were, she climbed up on to the shell and lay flat upon it, her little rump in the air. It was as if – but I brushed aside the thought – she desired sexual intercourse with it.

After a while, she returned and joined us. 'You can feel a vibration,' she said. She returned to the buggy and sat, arms folded across her chest, head down.

Cang Hai's Account

13

Jealousy at the Oort Crowd

At this period, I used to like to go with my baby daughter to a small café on P. Lowell called the Oort Crowd. The talk there was all about Chimborazo. The threat from outside seemed to have drawn people together and the café was more crowded than ever.

My Ambient was choked with messages from Thorgeson, which alternated between apologies, supplications, abuse and endearments. I preferred café life, as did Alpha.

Although I did not wish to be impolite, I eventually sent Thorgeson a message: 'Go to hell, you and your ventriloquist's dummy!' At the same time, I found some sheets on the Ambient network and tried to gain a better understanding of particle physics. I was making little progress, and called Kathi, asking if I might see her.

'I'm busy, Cang Hai, sorry. We have problems.'

Trying to keep the disappointment from my voice, I asked her what the problems were.

'Oh, you wouldn't understand. There's some trouble with the smudge ring. Stray vortices in the superfluid. We're getting spurious effects. Sorry, must go. Meeting coming up. Love to Alpha.' And she was gone.

Possibly this was what my Other in Chengdu had warned me about. I had been walking up a mountain with a king – or at least a man with a crown on his head. The air was so pure. We listened to bird song. Another man came along. He too had something on his head. Or perhaps it was a mask. I wanted him to join us. He smiled beautifully, before starting to run at a great pace up the mountain ahead of us. Then I saw a lake.

The manager of the Oort Crowd was Bevis Paskin Peters. He had taken over a department of the old Marvelos travel bureau. He ran the café very casually, being a part-time dress designer – the planet's first. Peters was rather a heavy man, with a sullen set to his features that disappeared when he smiled at you. In those moments, he looked amazingly handsome.

However, Peters was not the reason I went to the Oort Crowd. Nor was Peters often there, leaving the running of the café to an assistant, a fair-haired wisp of a lad. I went because Alpha loved to watch the cephalopods. The front wall of the café consisted of a thin aquarium in which the little cephalopods lived, jetting their way about the tank like comets.

A YEA marine biologist had become so attached to his pets that he had brought two pairs with him to Mars. Convinced of their intelligence, he had built them a computer-operated maze. The maze, built from multi-coloured perspex, occupied the tank. Its passageways and dead ends altered automatically every day. The cephalopods multiplied and had to be culled, so the Oort often had real calamari on the menu. Ten of the creatures lived in the tank, and seemed to take pleasure in threading their way about the maze.

Alpha sat contentedly for hours, watching. Her particular admiration was for the way in which the squid changed body colour as they glided through the coloured passageways.

We were there one day – I was chatting to some other mothers – when in came Peters with a dark-skinned man I did not know, together with the famous Paula Gallin.

She scooped up Alpha, who knew her well, and kissed her passionately, calling endearments and making Alpha give her beautiful chuckle. The two men, meanwhile, were putting a cassette into a player at the rear of the bar.

Then Paula demanded the attention of the café's clientele.

'I just want you all to take a look at a piece of film. A sneak preview of my next production, okay? It won't take a minute. Okay, guys.'

The mirror behind the bar opaqued and there were figures moving and talking. They were in a long hall, filmed in longshot. All was movement. A man and a woman were talking in the crowd, talking and quarrelling. In the main, they avoided each other's gaze, shooting angry glances now and then. As they continued walking but their voices grew louder, the crowd about them froze into immobility.

The man said, 'Look, all I do I do for you.'

'You don't. You do it for yourself,' said the woman.

'You're the selfish one. Why are you always attacking me?'

'I don't attack you, you liar. I was just asking you why—'

'You were distinctly interrogating me,' he said, breaking into her sentence. 'You're always on at me.'

'I simply had a small suggestion to make, but you would not listen. You never listen.'

'I've already heard what you have to say.' He was red in the face now.

'I do everything for you. What do you do for me?'

His manner changed entirely. 'I do nothing for you, do I?' He appeared completely crestfallen. The woman turned her head angrily away.

The film cut, the mirror returned.

Paula laughed with a rich kind of gurgle. 'Okay, folks, now which of those two characters do you think was in the wrong, or was most wrong?'

We gave our opinions, the few of us sitting in the café. Some thought the man was feeling guilty about a misdemeanour. Others thought the woman was a nagger. Most of the speakers took sides. I said that they had got themselves into the kind of situation where both parties were wrong; they needed to stop quarrelling and try to find agreement, if necessary calling in a third party.

'Gee, you're an enlightened bunch,' said Paula, joshingly. 'Now tell me what you make of the woman's last remark, "I do everything for you; what do you do for me?"'

So we chewed it over, we café-goers, while Paula cooed over Alpha. We were more or less in agreement that the woman's statement was destructive in itself. We disagreed about whether it was made more awful by being the truth or a vicious lie. Nor could we agree about the man's response: was it a sullen repudiation of her remark or a wretched admission of the truth?

'That's enough,' Paula said, sharply. 'Thanks. Bevis, Vance . . .'

What we did not realise was that the mirror behind the bar was a two-way mirror. Later, we saw an edited version of ourselves in Paula's new filmplay, *Mine? Theirs?* Since we never knew what the filmed pair were quarrelling about, our judgements seemed facile. It was one of Paula's rather unpleasant tricks.

Perhaps that habit of hers caused the tragedy that was to follow – a tragedy that for a while eclipsed our preoccupation with Chimborazo.

Paula had a beautiful and strong face with marked features – a forceful jaw, in particular, and a beaky nose; her features were very unlike my rather ambiguous ones. Although she often took and discarded lovers, her real interests, or so it seemed to me, were directed elsewhere. Her predatory and creative mind wished to ingest the experiences of other people, and by so doing widen her own dimensions. Perhaps she had a driving need to resolve her own tensions.

Her clothes were designed by Bevis Paskin Peters. She rejected the customary unisex Now overalls, so Peters became the planet's first popular costume designer. He evolved a classical line imaginatively in keeping with the shortage of materials. The other man in Paula's ménage à trois was called Vance Aylsha. He was a technician and rather a genius, according to report. He also looked after the little cephalopods in the café aquarium.

At times Paula could be large and florid. At other periods she appeared smaller, perhaps when she was actually working in her studio and unconscious of her own persona. I cannot say I liked her much. She was bigger than I, and unpredictable.

Nevertheless I was quite frequently in her company because she adored – or at least was fascinated by the growth experience of – Alpha. She would cease her work, towards which she was otherwise obsessive, to play for two hours at a stretch with Alpha. There was nothing Alpha liked better.

Nor was there much I liked better than to see these two intellects, the mature and the awakening, meeting in quizzes and tricks and mock deceptions and sheer nonsenses. I was aware of the antiquity of these games and that awareness added to my happiness.

How starkly the lovely energies of the three of us, the warmth of our bodies, contrasted with the frozen world outside, making it more thrilling to be there!

It was not all plain sailing; with such an outgoing character, arguments were always springing up. I had made some remark in praise of Tom Jefferies, whereupon Paula said, cuttingly, 'You should stay away from that creep.'

When I protested that Tom was a courageous and altruistic man, Paula gave this reply.

'Not at all. He's a creep. Of course he loves his plan. He wants us all to conform to it. He wants us all to be better people. That's because he doesn't like us much. Maybe he's scared of us – no, not of you, Cang Hai, but you're another sexless little thing, aren't you?'

'I'm certainly not sexless. Nor is Tom.'

'But you don't have sex, do you?' She laughed. 'You need awakening. Come to bed with me and I'll show you what you're missing.'

Although I did not take up her offer, it was from lack of courage rather than from virtue. I saw why her two current men lusted for her.

I saw how her interest, as expressed in her plays, was in

people rather than theories of behaviour. She liked chaos. It answered a dangerous element in her make-up.

At the time of which I am speaking, Paula Gallin was working on *Mine? Theirs?* She spent her days cutting, editing, morphing, swearing. I was witness to her outbreaks of anger against her male friends, whom she found necessary even as they broke her concentration. Creativity was by now better understood and better respected, but I went to the Ambient stand to look at the words of an old savant, Doctor Storr, whose work on the dynamics of creation remained of value.

Doctor Storr says that a child who has a parent who ill treats him but on whom he is nevertheless dependent will regularly deny the 'bad' aspects of the parent and repress his own hatred, perhaps by developing some symptom such as nail-biting or hair-pulling. These activities show the displacement of repressed aggression and its turning against the self.

'It seems likely, however,' the doctor continues, 'that there is another way of dealing with incompatibles and opposites within the mind, provided one is sufficiently robust to stand the tension; and this is the way adopted by creative people. One characteristic of creative people is just this ability to tolerate dissonance. They see problems that others do not see; and do not attempt to deny their existence. Ultimately the problem may be solved, and a new whole made out of what was previously incompatible, but it is the creative person's tolerance of the discomfort of dissonance that makes the new solution possible.

'The process is easy to see in the case of scientific discovery. Something very similar may be going on in the case of the production of works of art. I have discussed the quest for identity characteristic of at least some creative artists, and suggested that, if this is a particular need for such people, as it seems to be, it is connected with an attempt to reconcile incompatibles or opposites in the mind. This is, of course, intimately connected with the problem of identity; for identity, or rather the sense of one's own identity, is a sense of unity, consistency and wholeness.

'One cannot have a sense of one's continuous being if one is always conscious of two or more souls warring within one breast. In the case of Tolstoy, the ascetic and the sensualist were never reconciled; but one aspect of his creative existence was certainly an attempt to bring this about.'

I was surprised. For the first time I saw that the doctor's statement, true as far as it went, did not encompass the contrasts and conflicts built into the mind by blind evolutionary development – the phylogenetic, as opposed to the ontogenetic, brain.

To employ the doctor's rather poetic phraseology, there would always be the two souls warring within one breast; this was what gave to *Homo sapiens sapiens* our restless drive to develop further; it was part of the general creativity we were attempting to harness. We were now developing into a phylogenetic-conscious society, accepting and coming to terms with our inbuilt contradictions, revealing the 'natural' human.

Paula's drama on which she was working, *Mine? Theirs?*, was precisely about the interplay between the two kinds of conflict, the ancient generic and the personal.

I considered these intellectual ideas but, even when practising my pranayama, I taunted myself with the thought of what it would be like to be in bed with Paula, with her dark tempestuous body against mine. These images crept in upon my meditation . . .

At this juncture Vance Alysha and Bevis Paskin Peters were the two rivals for Paula's love. Both were men of spirit and worked on the computer simulations necessary for episodes in Paula's drama. Alysha was Caribbean; he had been a star on television in his native Jamaica, and remained proud of it. Peters had won a prize for paranimation at the age of six; he was vain and had a quick temper. And he was said to dress privately in his own flamboyant women's costumes.

An argument arose between the two men over the interpretation of a turn in Paula's narrative: was a certain character's decision to retreat into the wilds a brave or a cowardly act? This developed into a quarrel over which of them best satisfied Paula's sexual needs. Happily, Alpha and I were not present.

They fell on the floor, wrestling with and punching each other. Peters seized on a length of computer cable and wrapped it round Alysha's neck. Paula entered the workshop at this point and screamed for Peters to stop. He did not stop. Although Alysha struggled, he was choked to death.

Mars City had no police as such. Paula called for the guards – those men who maintained the integrity of our structures. They hauled Peters away, unresisting. Since there was nothing like a prison on Mars, they shut Peters in their office, where he sat and wept, overcome by what he had done.

The guards summoned Tom. Tom and Guenz called our legal forum together to discuss the case. It assembled under the blow-up of the incandescent Hindenburg.

We were silent, rather sullen this time. Everyone was miserable in their own way. I sat at the rear with other onlookers, holding Alpha, next to a grim Paula. She shed no tear, but her face was ashen. I put a comforting arm round her waist, but she shrugged it off.

Thinking back to that time, I am surprised that we had faced no such crisis before. There had been animosities and quarrels, certainly, but all had been settled peaceably. Without the aggravation of money or those inhibitions of marriage so wrapped up in old-fashioned notions of property, the levels of discontent had been considerably lowered.

Jarvis Feneloni was one who spoke up for Peters's execution. Since the sallow-complexioned young man had attempted to leave Mars with his brother – nothing more had ever been heard of Abel and his ship – he had gained something of a reputation by being unruly. 'We have no doubt the man is guilty. He confesses to the crime. We have nowhere to imprison him. In any case, the traditional punishment for murder is death. Why muck about? We must execute Peters. Let's discuss how that should be done.'

'His confession lessens the case against him, while his remorse is his own punishment,' Tom responded. 'How exactly do you suggest we should kill him? By the methods he used on Alysha? By throwing him out on the Martian surface? By cutting off his head or his oxygen? We have no more right to kill than he. All methods of deliberate killing are distasteful to civilised men.'

'Well, I'm not civilised! We must set an example, take strong measures. This is our first case of murder, particularly the murder of a—' He stopped himself. We guessed what he was about to say. Instead Feneloni finished lamely, 'Particularly the murder of one so young. We must set an example, so that it does not happen again. And we must build a prison.'

Tom replied that he agreed an example must be set. But they had to set that example for themselves. If a family has a boy who misbehaves, punishment will probably make him worse; the family must seek to discover what makes him misbehave and remedy it. They will in all probability find that they themselves are in some way at fault. Far from punishing Peters, the assembly should try to see what provoked him to violence.

'Sex, of course,' said Feneloni, with a laugh. 'Look no further. It's sex. Why are your sympathies with the murderer, not his victim?'

Guenz responded, eyes twinkling. 'I fear, Jarvis, that sympathy with Peters's victim can do the victim little good.'

'Okay then, try to discover what motives Peters had, other than sexual jealousy. Then we hang him. Both phases of the operation to be done in public.'

Tom said that could not be permitted, else all would be implicated in a second death. Peters must submit to a private course of mentatropy.

Then, said Jarvis, legislation had to be drawn up. Were they to deal with crimes of passion as a special subject, subject to special measures?

Interruptions from the floor continued for many minutes. 'We want no deaths here!' Choihosla shouted.

Someone claimed that freedom could not be legislated for. He was answered by another voice that said that they were not free, were indeed isolated far from their home ground, but had founded a contented society; fulfilment need not depend on freedom at all.

At this, there was uproar. A woman claimed that their 'happy society' was breaking up. It had been at its best one of de Tocqueville's 'voluntary associations', viable only while everyone subscribed.

But like de Tocqueville's, another voice replied, it depended on hierarchy. Perhaps all this time, they'd been living under the wrong hierarchy. Laughter followed this remark, and the temperature cooled.

So soon after the disgrace of Dayo, no one in the court dared suggest there was a racial element in Alysha's murder. Perhaps there wasn't, although such suspicions circulated on the Ambient. But who could prove a negative? Better to sweep the whole notion under the carpet.

Bill Abramson rose to suggest that they had paid too much attention to building a good society and not enough to lobbying Earth to rescue them and restore them to their own planet. What if the subterranean fossil water gave out? It was to their credit that a sort of mediating structure had been established, permitting them to live orderly lives; but perhaps they forgot on what an uncompromising basis that order was built. For himself, with a family at home in Israel, he prayed every night that Earth would send ships.

'Pray there'll be no more murders,' called a voice from the rear.

Paula and I had been listening in silence to all this. She

211

now rose, and brought the debate back to the subject, saying in a quiet voice, 'You lay no blame on me, the cause of the men's quarrel. But I also must share the guilt. I liked to have the men vying for me with each other. It satisfied my egotism – and other senses as well. I'm greedy for life, as Peters is and Alysha was. But frankly I'd rather be hanged than have some fool shrink prying into my past life. My past is my property as much as my breath.'

Tom asked if Paula was trying to alienate the forum's sympathy. 'You might think differently about hanging if you were actually on trial for such a hideous crime. A course of mentatropy must be Peters's sentence. It can but have a better effect on him than a hanging . . .'

A vote was taken on what Peters's punishment should be. The audience was four to one against his execution.

Jarvis Feneloni bowed to Tom, who declared the court adjourned. Jarvis's manner throughout had been courteous. But I caught a look of hatred as he made his salutation to Tom. He had ambitions for himself as well as for justice, and did not like to be bested in argument.

As usual, the debate was filmed. No one gave a thought to how it would be received on Earth.

14

'Public Hangman Wanted'

Tom was unwell after the Peters debate. He became with-drawn and easily irritated. His answers were brief. I wanted to take him up into the Lushan Mountains in China, to fresh air and solitude. It was the first time I had longed for Earth, with its sensuous landscapes.

When I said this to him, he told me – quite politely – to go away.

I took to painting the mountains in watercolour, to amuse myself as well as Alpha. I talked to her about the mountains, the mists in early morning, and the beautiful clouds, the temples looking out over precipices. All this, as it later transpired, was a mistake; it planted a seed of longing in her mind.

My counterpart in Chengdu sent me a beautiful sexual fantasy, in which a ship somehow enfolded me. We flew through the blue air and I was its engine.

One day we received a message on our Ambient terminal, as did everyone else on Mars. The harsh voice of Jarvis Feneloni spoke:

Friends,

We have amused ourselves too long with the foolish utopian schemes of our elders. By beaming all our debates to Earth, the terrestrials become sedated. They see no reason to hurry and rescue us. Our broadcasts must cease forthwith.

I am not alone in being bored by VR representations of beaches, seas and palm trees. I want the real thing again. I can't live without my home and family.

If we broadcast once more, it should be only to

213

send strongly worded demands to terrestrial powers to come and get us out of this dump.

Otherwise, I predict mayhem here.

Feneloni

'I must speak to everyone,' Tom said.

'You are not well,' said Guenz. 'If I may, I will address them. I believe I am a fluent speaker.'

He did so. Tom seemed relieved to have the duty taken from him. Guenz said that there were times when everyone was tired of the hardships they endured.

Nevertheless, those hardships were endured communally. It was that which made them bearable, even ennobling.

But the hardships were an essential. There was an old Latin saying he remembered from his university days, *Sine efflictione nulla salus* – 'Without suffering, no salvation.' They were reaching towards salvation, in an unprecedented attempt to build what he might call, to use an old Chinese term 'a spiritual civilisation'.

'All of us are a part of this challenging task. The weaker-minded among us are fortunate in being able to enjoy VR simulations of an easier life, of palm trees and golden beaches. For the rest of us, our unreal reality is enough, and the building of a just society reward enough.

'I will tell you something I believe with all my heart. That when the ships finally return here, and those of us who wish to leave go back to Earth, we shall never forget this momentous time, this brave time, when we struggled with ourselves to create a better way of social existence – and triumphed. And we shall never again find such happiness as we have here, so far from the Sun.'

There was some applause for what many regarded as a final peroration. But, delighted by his success as an orator, Guenz puffed out his cheeks until their capillaries began to resemble an imaginary map of the planet, and started again.

'Some of us don't dream hard enough. Some of us think

214

they don't need a utopia. But it's inevitable. It has already been born—'

From the front row, Jarvis Feneloni rose to interrupt. 'And is already threatened by that monstrous barnacle—'

From the rear of the hall a violin sounded. Guenz's rhetoric and Feneloni's interruption alike were swept away on a torrent of Baza's music.

Many were the suggestions of how punishment should be meted out, both in the present case of Peters and in any possible future cases. For a while the idea of penitential suits was popular; stocks were suggested, but the humiliation of a wrongdoer, it was decided, only increased his animus against society.

Confinement with civilised treatment won the day, the malefactor to meet with a mentatropist every day, and with a number of ordinary people once a week for conversation, topics to be confined to everyday events and not directed against the prisoner.

Those who protested that such treatment was too lenient and would encourage crime were reminded that the abolition of public hangings had met with similar outcry. The civilised decision that had been reached was one on which all could pride themselves.

After this debate, Bill Abramson circulated a message on the Ambient. He appeared, saying, 'The case of Peters, with his mild punishment, gratifies our liberal instincts but represents a case of cognitive dissonance, the disjunction between reality and one's ideas. Such is usually the case with utopianists.

'Since we are not free of terrestrial vices, we must adhere to terrestrial laws in these matters. Peters committed murder. His pretence of penitence is immaterial. Murderers were traditionally put to death. Peters should be put to death.

'Despite the collapse of financial infrastructures on our home planet, it cannot be long before ships arrive here to return us to our families. Nevertheless, let us suppose we have to remain here for another year. Or even, if we suppose ships set out now, half a year. In that time, I calculate that something like five hundred extra mouths will have to be fed. That is the result of our unchecked population growth, and unchecked promiscuity. But our food output cannot very greatly increase. So at some point in the future we shall face starvation, or else possibly our precious reservoir of water will dry up.

'Those who increase their numbers promiscuously are a threat to our small community. I propose that they also should be punished – if not with death, then with a jail sentence and isolation in prison. To my mind, a prison is more urgently needed than utopia.

'Thank you for listening to me. I require no cheap abuse in return, but will gladly receive constructive suggestions.'

The Adminex made an immediate response. They built a gallows on Bova Boulevard and appended to it a large notice: PUBLIC HANGMAN WANTED.

Downstairs, on Earth, a queue for the job would have formed. But in our small enlightened community, no one wished to be branded a hangman. So Bill Abramson was answered.

A committee of three interviewed the senior mentatropists, the Willa-Vera Composite. The Composite marched into the meeting loaded down with equipment. Mendanadum was in white, White was in lilac. They proceeded to demonstrate how every area of the brain had been precisely mapped, and how mind-body connections had been established over recent decades. In consequence, nanoneurosurgery was proving its worth.

With the aid of the quantcomp, the mentatropist could despatch 'remotes' to explore the entire structure of the brain and nervous system. Vera spoke enthusiastically of the 'wired neurons' that served this purpose.

'These synthetic neurons send back a receivable signal,

and can be programmed to trigger the release of chemicals that store memory. We guide the wired neurons to reach the appropriate synapse. We don't really expect you to comprehend the science behind our science – which may seem like magic to the uninformed – but Willa and I assure you that our work is a mingling of technical ability and sheer artistry.

'Indeed, we are somewhat taken aback that you find it necessary to question our abilities. You have received our CVs, after all.'

The Composite was engaged for the task of remedying Bevis Paskin Peters.

Nevertheless, the mentatropy of Peters, conducted by the Willa-Vera Composite, was a slow business, continuing over many months.

I was permitted to be present at their first session.

The remotes travelled slowly forward, downward. Neurons glowed and died on the monitor like small security lights as they ventured onward, probing various cytoarchitectonic areas. To the remotes, every neuron marking a local circuit was like a single star, while about them macroscopic systems resembled entire galaxies, dense with suns and dark matter.

Something that resembled light flickered away from their progress.

The remotes journeyed through the hemispheres of the cerebrum, some diverting to the diencephalon, a collection of nuclei below the hemispheres, into the thalamus and hypothalamus. Other remotes entered regions of the limbic system and putamen. Still others toured in the cerebral cortex, the blanketing mantle of the cerebrum, a massive and complex constellation of synaptic activity, by one system of measurement a mere 3 millimetres thick.

It was these latter remotes that detected an area of disturbed neurotransmitters. They moved into the region and began to activate the groupings involved. Here they entered the large-scale quantum coherences that are essential to the generation of consciousness.

On the screens where the neuroscientists, Willa and Vera, watched, pictures and actions became evident. The skill of the women lay in interpreting the pictures as the remotes fired adjacent synapses.

'Slightly viridian,' said Willa.

'Needs fewer fibres,' said Vera. They had their own slang for what they did. 'We're getting coherency.'

Specific tightly interconnected groups of neurons acted coherently as a single unit. The validity of these groupings was sustained by a coherent quantum-mechanical process, like that of a superconductor or superfluid.

With tuning, the fibres sank back to form a huge black anatomy, its head hardly visible. Screaming cream things wavered in the background. A pudding cowered in a puddle.

Home life of Bevis Paskin Peters, aged three. Perception, as someone had said, was all. The sun was square and permeated by fish.

The Composite caught a signal from a remote homing in on the amygdala. They checked its programme. Here, deep in the limbic brain, wavered a primitive recollection. It had remained there, undiminished by time, since electrical resistance diminishes to zero in the HTC structures located there, much like the similar high temperature superconductors in our electrical cables.

Although a good theoretical understanding of ordinary superconductivity had been established halfway through the previous century, a proper understanding of HTCs had to wait until the early years of the twenty-first. This understanding had been put to important use in the new brain sciences. The neuron probe began to participate in the collective quantum state, showing a blur on the mentatropy screen which refined itself into an interpretable picture.

Pressures created an oval viewing like a squeezed lemon. Again a monster male, shouting and raving in deeper than viridian, the waves of anger misshaping it. The monster loomed over a limp white worm. Pale in pink the helpless something fluttered what might have been a hand.

The two separate remote fleets activated their groupings. The effects of quantum entanglement began to manifest themselves. The patient's anciently stored pain became now.

A door of jelly slammed and wiped the oval all away.

'He resents us,' murmured Willa. 'We'll rest him and try again.'

It took expertise, but Willa-Vera interpreted the code to recognise in the white worm the being that would later grow to become the huge black body, the parent.

'Father dominant,' muttered Vera. 'Son wishing to be father?'

I could contain myself no longer but said I hardly understood what was going on.

'Basically, it's fairly simple,' said the fragile Willa Mendanadum, standing on tiptoe in her eagerness to explain. 'Our remotes are travelling in areas where the effects of quantum state-reduction first become important. That's where a quantum superposition actually becomes one of the classical alternatives. In fact, it appears that the entire phenomenon of consciousness is activated only when certain such quantum-coherent states begin to resolve into these classical alternatives.'

'But I don't know what you mean by classical alternatives!' I wailed.

'Oh, that's simple too,' Vera White said, with a knowing smile at her partner. 'Imagine the nebulous borderline between the quantum and classical levels of physical activity, right? This has to do with the measurement problem of quantum mechanics: why is it that when we measure a quantum system we get one answer or another – the classical alternatives – instead of a quantum superposition of alternatives, which are an inherent part of the quantum-mechanical description of nature?'

I shook my head, feeling foolish.

'Well, you see, when an observer steps in, the rules

change. The standard quantum-mechanical procedures are interfered with! So what effect does the observer have? Why, quantum state-reduction comes in, and one thing or another happens, as Willa has said.'

She turned to her little partner. 'Ready for another probe? Try coordinates between D60 and – let's open E75.'

They peered into their spec-monitors. Behind them, paralysed but aware, strapped on the couch while the picoprobes toured his brain, lay Peters, screaming without sound.

Mentatropy, which would eventually hunt down his terrors and weaknesses and eradicate them, was not an easy option.

Neuroscience was a subject of popular satire; but, no other workable system of remedy presenting itself, since nobody was prepared to turn themselves into hangman or jailer, the mentatropists continued their work.

So gradually the dispute regarding the treatment of criminals died down, as other matters arose to be considered.

Signals were still being sent to Earth Control, the technical centre, and to the UN, both on roughly Feneloni's suggested lines. The response was evasive. The ramifications of EUPACUS's collapse had bitten deep into the socio-political structure of the planet. Until the recession was over, all matrix operations had been suspended. So we were told.

Now an extra body of advisers congregated about Tom, who continued to be unwell. Supporters included Val Kissorian and Sharon Singh, the woman who had found the rock crystal. I must confess I was jealous of the way in which Tom so clearly doted on her. Sharon was an amiable but shallow personality.

Of the new questions arising, the most pressing concerned the education of children.

Following the murder of Alysha, the Oort Crowd closed

down and the cephalopods disappeared. I ceased to associate with Paula Gallin, who was not much to be seen.

A crowd of us used to go to the Captain Nemo to sit around and talk in the evenings, while sipping coffdrinks.

Generally the talk was about Chimborazo. When I could bear Kathi's silence no longer, I called her on my Ambient.

'So what's new, Kathi? Why don't I hear from you? Are we not friends any more?'

'Friends for ever, Cang Hai – however long that may be,' she said in her best sarcastic tone. 'Just to prove it, I will tell you a secret. Don't go spreading it around, eh?'

'What is it? Are you in love with someone else?'

'Yes, with that great alien intellect on our doorstep, ninny! You know what? We have discovered that it is accelerating towards us!'

'What?' I was shocked.

'It's making much faster progress, babe! It's accelerating at such a rate that it could even collide with the science unit in a year or two . . .'

'Kathi! What does this mean? How awful!'

'And I'm luring it on!' She screamed with laughter and closed down. Her face sank into oblivion.

I managed to keep quiet about Kathi's news, although I wondered if Tom had been told. I sat in the Nemo with Alpha on my knee as if nothing had happened.

One day Belle Rivers appeared, accompanied by Crispin Barcunda, carrying several pages downloaded from her Ambient which she spread before us. Belle was her usual majestic self, rock crystal beads jangling down to the waist of her long dress. Crispin was diminished beside her, lightly though he carried his age. We noticed with what old-fashioned courtesy he behaved towards Belle. He sported a long, floppy white moustache and his eyes at least were full of life as he smiled at the company.

'Crispin and I have become firm friends,' Belle said, cocking her head to one side. 'Between us we encompass much experience of dealing with difficult people. I wish to get away from the concept of good and bad persons, and to speak of difficult people. I know the difficult ones as children, Crispin as adults, when he was Governor of the Seychelles. We have a plan for decreasing the difficulties experienced by difficult people, which we wish to present to you.'

'We have to talk about this plan,' said Crispin. 'Maybe it will never get further than talk, since it requires many years for its fruition and we may not have that long.'

'Well, now, it all sounds very mysterious,' said Tom, in rather grumpy fashion.

'On the contrary, Tom,' said the old man, laughing. 'Like all good radical plans for mankind's happiness, it contains nothing that most sensible people don't already know.'

Belle began to talk. She said that her educational regime was now running smoothly. It included, as yet informally, the education of parents in the pleasure of being parents, of reading to and listening to their progeny. The Becoming Individual classes she had established received a good response from the children. She had been interested to perceive – here she shot a stern glance at Tom – how most children had what she called 'a religious sense of life'.

'No one denies that,' Tom interrupted. 'It's the divine aspect of things, Belle – what you have called the phylogenic aspect of things. Your charges have but recently evolved from the molecular state of being. Of course they are full of wonder. I'm delighted you give it expression.'

She nodded and continued. She loved her children and was concerned that the best possible teaching might not help them prevail in the rough and tumble of terrestrial life (assuming they ever returned to Earth, as she personally did not intend to do). There had been much discussion about punishment for crime; the right conclusion had been reached – that care and consultation were more effective than punishment. She wanted Crispin to talk for a moment about the bad situation on Earth.

222

15

Java Joe's Story

Crispin Barcunda spoke. 'As Governor of the Seychelles, I was plagued by petty crime. Muggings, theft, aggression against tourists, hot-rodding, break-ins and murder, which sprang from these sometimes rather petty incidents. And we had drug barons and their victims. Often the crimes were drug- or alcohol-related.

'In short, the Seychelles was a paradigm in small of the rest of the world. Except it was a tropical paradise . . .

'Only I didn't see it as a paradise, I can tell you. Fast as we locked the little buggers up, others sprang to take their place. Our prisons were pretty savage places, sordid, old-fashioned, with frequent floggings of delinquents for deterrent effect.

'Only we know floggings don't deter. They just keep the middle classes happy. Of the little buggers they make big buggers with a grudge against society. I will tell you how we changed all that.

'It says a great deal for the human race that goodness survives even in the worst places of confinement. Among faces that bear the expressions of rats and snakes, cold, merciless, vindictive, you meet faces that beam decency and kindness.

'Such a good face belonged to a prisoner called Java Joe. Maybe he had another name, but I never heard it. Just an ordinary black man who happened to be released from a jail sentence on the day I made a very popular speech. I had addressed my audience in Victoria town square by our famous clock tower, exhorting *them* to value themselves and turn from crime. I had called them, I blush to say, the noblest creatures of the universe.

223

'As I was resting up from this hypocrisy, this ex-prisoner, Java Joe, was shown into my presence. He was perfectly polite. He even made himself obsequious. Yet he carried himself with pride. He had come, he said, especially from Crome Island to hear me speak. I asked him if prison had reformed him.

'His answer was simple. Delivered without reproach, it was simply, "Hell's for punishment, not reformation, isn't it?"'

Crispin tugged the ends of his moustache in order to contain a smile.

'Java Joe had come to me with a suggestion, he said. He told me he had read a remarkable old book when he was held in solitary confinement in prison. Java Joe emphasised that he was not a fussy man, but the state of what he called "the bogs" in the prison was a disgrace, planned and intended to humiliate all who had to use them. He repeated this latter phrase. This made a passage in this old book he was able to read all the more impressive.

'"What was the book?" I asked him.

'Joe was uncertain whether it was a history or a fiction. Maybe he did not understand the difference between the two types of writing, which is little enough, I grant you. Part of the book concerned the building of an ideal house, called Crome.

'The architect of Crome, Joe told me, was concerned with the proper placing of his privies. By which he meant, in plain English, sir, begging my pardon, the bogs. And here Java Joe began to quote verbatim from the book: "His guiding principle in arranging the sanitation of a house was to secure that the greatest possible distance should separate the privy from the sewage arrangements. Hence it followed inevitably that the privies were to be placed at the top of the house, being connected by vertical shafts with pits or channels in the ground."

'Java Joe eyed me closely to make sure I understood this elaborate language from the ancient book. Seeing I appeared to do so, he continued to quote: "It must not be thought that Sir Ferdinando (the architect, sir, you see) was moved only by material and merely sanitary considerations; for the placing of his privies in an exalted position he had also certain excellent spiritual reasons. For, he argues, the necessities of nature are so base and brutish that in obeying them we are apt to forget that we are the noblest creatures of the universe." '

' "Are you trying to be satirical at my expense?" I roared. But plainly he was not. He explained that to counteract these degrading effects, the author of the strange book advised that the privies in every house should be nearest to heaven, that there should be windows opening on heaven, that the chamber should be comfortable and that there should be a supply of good books and comics on hand to testify to the nobilty of the human soul.

' "Why vex me with this recitation?" I demanded. "Is it not more appropriate that the privies in our prisons should be down in the bowels of the earth?"

'Java Joe explained to me that he had thought much about this wonderful place, Crome, while passing his motions. He saw it all as a metaphor – although he did not know that particular word. From this vision of the good house his suggestion had evolved. Here he paused, searching my face with that good-natured gaze of his. I prompted him to go on.

' "Us shits," he said, "should be kept separate as far as possible from the sewers of your prisons. We've never been far from their stink in all our lives. We should be placed in a good place with a view of heaven. Then we might be able to stop being shits." '

Crispin looked about him to see what effect his story was having before he went on. 'Was there anything in what Java Joe said? Maybe there was more sense than in all the rhetoric of my speech in the town square. I decided to act.

'We had an empty island or two in the Seychelles group. To the north was Booby Island, a pleasant place with a small stream on it. What was to be lost? I had it renamed

Crome Island and shipped a hundred of my criminals there, to live in daylight rather than darkness.

'What a howl went up from the respectable middle classes! That men should enjoy themselves in pleasant conditions was no punishment for crime. This experiment would kill the tourist trade. It would cost too much. And so on . . .'

'Let's get to the end of the tale, Crispin,' said Tom, with some impatience. 'Obviously the experiment wasn't a failure, or you would not be telling us about it.'

Crispin nodded cordially, saying merely, 'We can learn from failure as well as success.'

'Come on then, Crispin,' said Sharon. 'Tell us what happened to your criminals. I bet they all swam away to freedom!'

'They were marooned on an island round which fierce currents ran, and could not escape, my dear. They dug themselves latrines, they built a communal cookhouse, they built houses. All using just local materials. They fished and grew maize. They sat about and smoked and talked. They were prisoners – but they were also men. They regained their self-respect. A supply ship protected by armed guards called once a week at Crome Island, but no one escaped.

'And after their sentence was served, very very few reoffended. They had done what I could not manage to do, and reformed themselves.'

'What about Java Joe?' I asked.

Crispin chuckled. 'He went to live voluntarily on the island; the convicts christened him King Crome.'

At this juncture Paula Gallin came and sat down at a nearby table, escorted by Ben Borrow. They were deep in conversation but, after they had ordered two sunglows, began taking an interest in our discussion, which certainly was not private.

'We hope,' said Belle, 'to follow that example Crispin has offered. Earth is a planet full of prisons. It must never happen here. At one time, in a brief period of enlightenment, the British government permitted me to teach reading and writing to prisoners. The majority of people in prison, I found, were young bewildered men. They were ignorant and brutalised, two elements the penal system encouraged. Many had been brought up without a family. They had mostly been "in care". They were truants from school, fly boys. Most of them hid deep misery under a hard shell.

'In a word, the prisons – not only the one in which I worked – were filled by the products of poverty, unemployment, underprivilege and depression. The politicians were locking up the victims of sociopolitical crimes.'

'Excuse me, you surely go too far there,' said Hal Kissorian. 'We are mistaken in expecting politicians to remedy matters that are beyond political scope. That there are the rich and successful and the poor and unsuccessful, and every shade in between, is surely a natural and ineradicable phenomenon.'

I saw he glanced at Sharon for approval of his little speech. She gave him an encouraging wink.

Belle became so stern that her beads shook. 'There is the case of nurture as well as genetic inheritance. Prison and punishment do not reconcile these unfortunate and malevolent youths with society. Quite the reverse. They leave prison only to reoffend more expertly. Of course I am speaking only of the reformable majority. A different case can perhaps be made for the mad and the really dangerous.

'It is when we come to consider the state of affairs beyond the prison walls that we see how unenlightened we have become. Judges are now constrained by their governments to deliver fixed sentences of a number of years for various crimes. Mandatory sentencing deprives the judges of administering justice according to the facts of the case. Thus both sides of the law become machine-like. Quantputers might as well take over, as no doubt they shortly will.

'How did mandatory sentencing become the rule? Firstly,

because it speeded up the legal process, much as the banishing of juries has done. Then, later, it simplified the introduction of computerisation, to cut costs.

'All this because of the rise in crime. More and more people become imprisoned, and in consequence more violent and skilled in violence. Of course, the real crimemongers escape the law, as seems to be the case with the swindlers within EUPACUS. Our isolation here lasts so long because, to my mind, the law cannot indict the culprits.

'Most governments attempt to solve the increasing crime rate by building more prisons. They can't adopt Crispin's scheme of marooning them on a desert island to create their own society—'

'As we are marooned here—' Kissorian interjected.

'—so they continue to build prisons whose one objective is to maintain security, not to re-educate or train the inmates in various trades. So I'll come to my point at last.

'All that is being done is worse than useless. Criminals are the activists of unjust societies. Our Dayo's relatively innocent scam with his musical composition was a case in point; he strove merely to become equal, no more than that, in what he feels is a society unjustly prejudiced gainst his kind. Behind every young thug there are several depressed people, usually women, living out their short lives, battered and afraid and probably slow-witted. Undernourished certainly. And certainly harmless, within the meaning of the word. Hopeless, too. The cure for crime is not punishment but its reverse, love, caritas . . .

'We need a revolution that no politician would countenance – fundamental changes in society, with really good education for our children from the earliest age onwards. With a rebuilding of family life and the arts and pleasures of citizenship. Community work was a good start towards a caring society, but it did not go far enough.

'The civilised countries must increase taxes and invest extra revenues in rebuilding slums and lives, and listening to those who have had no say. In a very few years, I guarantee, the exorbitant cost of crime prevention would

228

be diminished. A better and happier and more equable culture would result. And it would be found to be self-sustaining.'

Sharon clapped her pretty hands. 'It's wonderful. I can see it already.'

But Kissorian asked, 'What happens to the abortion issue in this happier world of yours?'

It was Crispin who answered. 'An unwanted child tends to retain his unwanted feeling all his life. Of course, that may turn him into a philosopher. It's more likely he will turn to rape or arson or become the driving force of a security company, wielding a big stick.'

'So you're pro-abortion?'

Belle said quietly, 'For reasons I hope we've made clear, we're pro-life. Which means at this stage of existence that we reserve the right of women to control their own bodies and to abort if they are driven to take such a grave step.'

'Then say it,' interposed Grenz Kanli. 'You're pro-abortion.'

'We're pro-abortion. Yes,' said Belle, adding, 'until both men and women learn to control their sexual urges.'

I saw Sharon returning Kissorian's glance. She gave a sly smile. There, I thought, was another kind of happiness that could not be legislated for. I could not help liking her a little – and envying her at the same time.

Turning from her companion, Ben, Paula at the next table entered the discussion. Belle's remark about people curbing their sexual urges had made her restless.

'Haven't you people forgotten about mothers?' she asked. 'You know, the people who actually bring forth babies from their goddamn wombs into the world? Since it's a result of sexual activity, I suppose you've forgotten about mothers.'

'We've not—' Belle began, but Paula overrode her.

'You don't need all this bureaucracy if you honour mothers as they should be honoured, treat them properly, favour them in society. Start thinking about actual people rather than legislation.'

'We are thinking about people. We're thinking about children,' said Belle, sharply. 'If you have nothing better to contribute to the discussion, I'd advise you to keep silent.'

'Yes, yes, yes ... If anyone doesn't think your way, they'd better shut up. That's your way of thinking, isn't it?'

'I was thinking,' said Belle, coldly, 'more of your recent abortion. That is a pretty clear indication of your precious regard for motherhood.'

Paula looked absolutely astounded. Belle turned her back on her and asked me, 'How's Alpha getting on, my dear?'

I could not answer. Paula rose and marched out of the café. As she went she clicked her fingers. Ben Borrow stood up, gave us an apologetic glance, and followed Paula.

Only afterwards, when I talked to Kissorian and Sharon about this spat, did I understand the emotions that provoked it. The reason was simple. Belle stepped out of her normal rather magisterial role because she was jealous. Ben Borrow had been her protégé. She was furious to see that he had taken up with Paula. He had said nothing. His mere presence was enough to irritate Belle.

I reflected on my ineptness at reading motives.

After more discussion, and more coffdrink, Belle calmed down enough to return to the conversation.

She said, 'For some centuries, the civilised nations, so-called, have had health-care services. Time and again, those services failed, in the main through underfunding. The essence of our scheme involves continuity – that an underprivileged child should have a helper to whom he can always turn, who indeed meets up with him over a cup of something once a week.'

'We call this the C&S system, and it can run throughout life if necessary,' said Crispin. 'C&S – Care and Share. Always someone there to share problems and talk to.'

Kissorian laughed. 'Isn't that what husbands and wives do, for heaven's sake? Your C&S is a kind of sexless marriage, isn't it?'

'No, it's sexless parenting,' Crispin said sharply.

'I had as difficult a childhood as you can imagine, and I could never have tolerated any stranger's shoulder to cry on.'

'Just stop and think about that, Kissorian,' Belle said. 'Suppose there had been not strangers but a steady friend, always there to turn to . . .'

'I'd have stolen his wallet!'

'But with our C&S system in operation, your childhood would not have been so difficult, and so you would not have felt that compensatory need to steal a wallet. You can't be glad you had such a difficult childhood?'

He smiled, directing half of that gleam towards Sharon. 'Oh yes, I can. Now that it's over. Because it is an integral part of my life, it formed my character, and I learned from it.'

Silence fell while we digested what had been said.

At length Tom spoke. 'You have some concrete proposals, Belle and Crispin. They're certainly sane and benevolent in intention, although how any terrestrial politicians can be strong enough, enlightened enough—'

Belle interrupted. 'We have a singular advantage here, Tom. No politicians!'

'At least, not in the accepted sense,' added Crispin, with a smile.

'We enter this plan into our constitution here, and enact it as far as is possible – in the hope that Earth may take it up later. Example sometimes wins converts.' Belle turned her regard suddenly on me. 'And what does our silent and watchful Miss Cang Hai make of all this?'

I saw in her expression ambition and hostility, which were quickly wiped away by a mask of patience; the confusion of human senses is such I remained unsure whether I had read her correctly, or was projecting my own misgivings.

'It's benevolent but cumbersome to operate,' I told her. 'Who would you find willing to take on these burdens of assisting the young, perhaps often in opposition to the natural parents?'

'People are surprisingly willing to assist when they see a worthwhile enterprise. Their lives would also be enriched.' She added firmly, 'For a civilised society, there is no other way.'

I paused, wondering if I cared to contradict this forceful woman. 'There is another way. The way of medicine. Simple supervision of a child's hormone levels – oestrogen, testosterone, serotonin – is better than many a sermon.'

As if the thought had just occurred to her, Sharon said, leaping in, 'And what if all this well-meaning stuff did not work? What if the kids still offended?'

Without hesitation, Belle Rivers said, 'They would be beaten before witnesses. Where kindness fails, punishment must be available.'

Sharon screamed with laughter, displaying the inside of her mouth like a tulip suddenly opening.

'Would that do them good?'

Crispin said, 'At least it relieves the frustrated feelings of the teachers . . .'

'So be it,' Tom said. 'Let's take it to the forum of the people and try to gain support for your plan. We'll see what our friend Feneloni has to say to it.'

All this while, the days and weeks and months of our lives were eroding away. As we entered on the third year of our isolation on Mars, I had to speak to Tom about the news of Olympus's accelerated progress towards the science unit.

'I know,' said Tom. 'Dreiser told me.' He sat there with his head in his hands and said not another word.

16

Life is Like This and This . . .

My head was extremely bad. I did not attend the discussion when Belle Rivers stood beneath the blazing Hindenburg and argued her case for continuous education. As expected, it was opposed by Feneloni. Cang Hai and Guenz and the others reported the essence of the meeting.

After Belle and Crispin had outlined their plan, there was general applause. Several people rose and affirmed that the upbringing and care of children held the secret of a better society. One of the scientists quoted Socrates as saying that only the considered life was really worth living, and that consideration had to be nurtured in the young to sustain them throughout life.

Feneloni thought differently. The whole Rivers scheme was unworkable, in his opinion, and deserved to be unworkable. It was against human experience. It was wet nursing of the worst order. He became vehement. All living things had to find their own way in life. They succeeded or they failed. Rivers's plan, in trying to guarantee there were no failures, guaranteed there would be no successes.

Was she not aware, he asked, of the tragic sense of life? All of the world's great dramas hinged upon error or failure in an otherwise noble or noble-minded person. He cited Sophocles ('already mentioned'), Shakespeare and Ibsen as masters of this art form, which purged us with pity. Tragedy was an integral part of human society, tragedy was necessary, tragedy increased our understanding.

233

And at this point, someone laughed. It was the murderer, Peters, under mentatropy, who to many remained an outcast.

Others idly joined in the laughter. Feneloni looked confused and sat down, muttering that people who took him for a fool would soon find they were wrong.

It was agreed that the 'Rivers plan' should be implemented, and allowed to run for a test period. The universe was too young for an emphasis to be laid on tragedy.

Volunteers were called for. They would be vetted and asked for their qualifications.

As usual, the proceedings were recorded, and the decisions arrived at entered on our computers.

My state of mind was low. Although we seemed to be making progress, I feared some malignant force from within might burst like a cancer into the open and render our plans and hopes useless. Outside, beyond our spicules, beyond our community of 6,000 biological entities, was the great indifferent matrix, a confusion of particles inimical to humanity.

And there was Olympus, monstrous and enigmatic. It was never far from our thoughts. Like life itself, it seemed imponderable, its laboured progress somehow a paradigm of the approach of illness.

It was in this glum mood I looked in on the C of E, the Committee of Evil, holding its weekly meeting. The rather comical title had been dreamed up by Suung Saybin, but the purpose was serious enough: to try and determine the nature and cause of evil, with a view to its regulation. 'Perhaps the humour lies in the fact that they haven't a hope,' I thought to myself. Maybe the committee was just another way in which people kept themselves amused.

Suung Saybin remained as chair and Elsa Lamont, she of the orthogonal figures and an Adminex official, as secretary. Otherwise, members of the panel changed from month to month. As I entered, John Homer Bateson rose to his feet.

'The previous speaker wastes our time,' he declared. 'We cannot eradicate evil by religion, or even control it, as history shows. All history is a demonstration of the workings of evil. Like Thomas Hardy's Immanent Will, "it weaves unconsciously as heretofore, eternal artistries of circumstance". Nor will reason work. Reason is frequently the ally of wrong-doing.

'Here we are, stuck on this little dried-up orange of a planet, and we plan to banish this monster? Why, we're in its clutches! What are the component parts, the limbs, the testicles, of evil? Greed, ambition, aggression, fear, power . . . All these elements were integral to the very nature of EUPACUS, the conglomerate that dumped us here.

'What impossibly naïve view do you have of the nations that stranded us? The United States is by no means the worst of them. But it seeks to extend its empire into space – apologies, matrix. All the grand designs we may have about exploring this matrix mean nothing to the absconding financiers who backed matrix exploration. All this talk of utopia – it means nothing, absolutely nothing, to the greedy men in power. Power, money, greed – if you kicked out the present set of slimebags, why, more slimebags would fill the breach.

'I'll tell you a story. It's really a parable, but you'd distrust that term.'

'You have five minutes, John,' interposed Suung Saybin.

Ignoring her, Bateson continued, 'A man was stranded alone on a planet that was otherwise uninhabited. He lived the blameless life of a hermit, befriending bats, rats, slugs, spiders – anything that amused him. That way, you attain sainthood, don't you? One day, a vessel came down from space – pardon me, from the matrix – to rescue him. A grand sparkling ship, from which emerged a man in a golden space suit with long wavy blond hair and a manly tan, bearing a large picnic hamper.

'"I'm your saviour," he exclaimed, embracing the hermit.

'The hermit got a good grip on the man's throat and strangled him. Now he owned the spaceship. And the picnic basket.

'What, I ask you, were his motives? Hatred of intrusion on his privacy, hunger, envy of the golden suit, aversion to this intruder's display of hubris, greed to possess the ship, ambition to enjoy power himself? Or all these things? Or had solitude driven him mad?

'You cannot resolve these questions – and I have offered you a simple textbook case. The promptings to evil are in all of us. Evil is not a single entity, but a many-splendoured thing. You're wasting your time here if you think otherwise.'

I crept from the room.

Being unable to take lunch, I went to a remote upper gallery in search of solitude. Fond though I was of Cang Hai, I hoped to avoid her endless chatter. But there I happened upon my adopted daughter, sitting with her child playing at her feet. Alpha ran to me. I hugged her and kissed her cheeks. Cang Hai, meanwhile, picked up her sheets and assumed a pose whereby I was to take it she had been studying them.

'I'm surprised to see you up here, Tom. How are you?'

'Fine. And you?'

'Trying to learn some science. I'm trying to understand about superfluids. Apparently they are called Bose-Einstein condensates.'

Alpha said, 'Mummy looks out the window.'

'Yes. I believe that's what Dreiser's ring contains.'

'I said, Mummy looks out of the window most of the time!' screamed Alpha.

'You can certainly learn science there,' I said. Under the endless panoply of stars, dark matter and particles, the Martian landscape rolled its dunescape away into the distance, unvarious, unchanging, and baked or frozen by turns. The thought came, What harm in trying to turn it into a garden?

'Is something troubling you?' I asked.

'No.' Then, 'I try to study here, alone with Alpha. I'm glad, always glad, to see you.' Then, 'Those lustful hounds I had to work with in Manchuria . . . No . . . Only the ambiguities of this research.' She tapped her 3D sheets. 'Even light behaving like both waves and particles. It's hard to grasp!'

'We're subject to the dissolution of absolutes. Our life here is a bit ambiguous . . . Perhaps that's why we question everything. But that's not what's wrong?'

After a pause, during which she took her child on to her knee: 'I told you about Jon Thorgeson. He stays in my mind, making me unhappy. Or my behaviour does.'

'He was impertinent.'

'I don't mean that. I mean . . . he wanted me. He was not unpleasant, physically. Why didn't I – you know, let him get on with it? Why does that sort of thing not attract me? Is it that I'm . . . ? Well, I don't know. It's absurd to be a puzzle to yourself, isn't it?'

'Mumma, let's play, please, please, Mumma,' said the child, looking into Cang Hai's face.

Whatever her failings, Cang Hai, a cloned person, possessed plenty of maternal instinct. As mother and daughter cosseted each other, I continued to gaze out at the world we had inherited – we, who must find a reason for this Martian testing ground, we, the creatures who had only recently learned to walk upright, who had harnessed fire not much more than a million years ago, who had emerged from various forgotten creatures – and who must be the forerunners of myriads more various peoples – oh yes, it was apparent why sex so dominated our thoughts . . . But there my reverie was broken by the child's laughter.

I thought, as I turned back to this nervous, perceptive little person I loved – ah, but not one quarter as much as I had loved my Antonia! – how the Martian landscape was to me, as Charles Darwin had the phrase in one of his letters, not a landscape but 'a most strange assemblage of ideas'.

I said, 'It doesn't have to be either/or, daughter. We have moved into a mode of both/and understanding.'

'I mean,' she said boldly, 'am I a saint, a prude, or a lesbian?'

'Don't force a decision. You are young. Be clear that you consist of your confused self. But in the case of that impositioning Thorgeson, you evaded a case of rape as any woman might have done, had she a cool enough head.'

'And a warm enough hand!' Suddenly, she laughed, and squeezed Alpha. 'Had I not done so, I would be pregnant now. But no man is going to terraform me until I say so.'

Why did her words make me happy? Were they designed to do so? Weren't the human mind and human courage great things? I kissed her and her daughter.

That afternoon we underwent one of our periodic discussions regarding money. Certainly one element distinguishing the texture of Martian life from life Downstairs was that we carried no credit cards. Some people wanted to bring the credit system back, saying it made them feel more like functioning humans. Against that, our economists on Adminex argued that where there was no ownership of property it was impossible to fix prices.

We had an electronic points system up and running. It worked through the Ambient. The unit was called a credit. To launch the system, our 'bank' – once a cash till in the Marvelos offices – allocated everyone a hypothetical 1,000 credits, somewhat like the dummy money we were given at the start of a game of Monopoly. These credits could be drawn on at any time.

On the whole, prices of what few things there were to acquire for personal use remained trifling. A cup of coffdrink, for instance, was two credits, moonglow and sunglow were three. In practice it made the system hardly worth bothering with. So the money element withered away. We found we could get along happily without it.

No one drew wages or paid taxes.

A reckoning will come when – if ever! – the rockets

return from Downstairs. But, after all, we own the planet, thanks to the UN constitution, and so can sort the matter out without too much friction.

One evening, Cang Hai was on her way to see a dupe friend of hers living above the We Mend Everything post, in the recesses of the old cadre building. The lane was deserted. Of a sudden, a door ahead of her was flung open and three masked men rushed out. Cang Hai had barely turned to run before they slammed into her, seized her and dragged her into a bare room, a store of some kind.

She heard the door being locked as they tied her to a chair. A bright light was shone into her eyes. She could scarcely make out the outline of her attackers for its dazzle.

She heard their breathing and was afraid.

'Right, girl, don't be frightened. We only want to talk to you,' said a voice that Cang Hai recognised as Feneloni's. 'We are not planning to do anything unpleasant, as we could easily do, such as raping you or pulling off that artificial leg of yours.' Someone behind the light chuckled.

'The time to talk was during the forum,' she said, but could hardly bring the words out from her trembling lips.

'Now then, just you listen to us. We've had enough yacking from your lot. You and your pal Jefferies. This shit about the Rivers plan and utopia has got to stop. It's nothing but a time-waster. How are you going to improve people – people stuck on Mars? It's crap! We're going to die here if we just sit around yakking.'

'Let me have a go at her. She's a tasty little dish,' said one of the hidden men.

'In a minute,' said Feneloni. 'She's a wimp, doesn't much like sex. Maybe you could teach her.' They laughed. She begged them not to touch her. Feneloni replied, 'Look, we're trying to scare some sense into you. Get real! Stop all this pissing about. Stop beaming these stupid sessions of yours back to Earth, as if everything here was okay. It's not okay. My brother's ship was lost, worse luck, or he'd have done something about us being stuck here.

'We need to get back to real life. We should be staging scenes of riot, carnage, starvation. We have to force the hand of the UN. Get a ship up here, get us out of this mess. You understand that?'

'Yes,' she said. 'Yes, of course. But—'

'So you go back to Jefferies and tell him to keep his namby-pamby mouth shut from now on, or you're going to suffer damage, you and your kid. You understand?'

'Let's have a little fun with her,' said one of the men. 'So she takes us seriously . . .'

'Don't think about it,' Feneloni ordered.

The door burst open. Two security guards ran in, armed with torches and truncheons. The store had been designed as a dry goods warehouse and was covered by functioning security cameras, a factor Feneloni had disregarded. Directly he saw the men he shouted to the others to follow and rushed the intruders. The guards kicked his legs from under him and pinned him to the floor as he fell. The other two men burst out of the door and ran for it down the passageway.

Once Feneloni was tied up, the security men went over to Cang Hai and released her from the chair. She collapsed with shock. They phoned me. I arrived and helped her back to our quarters. After a shower she fell asleep, to wake in the morning recovered, at least in part.

Now the question arose of what to do with Feneloni. I went to see him. He was being held in his quarters on Tharsis Street, and looked as sullen as one might expect.

I asked him what he had to say for himself.

'You're the talker.'

I stood looking at him, saying nothing, trying to master my anger.

Finally he burst out in a torrent of words, saying that he had intended no harm, but could not get a proper hearing for his view, which everyone shared, that everyone hated my guts, that he was only acting on behalf of all, who wished to get back to normal life on Earth and not waste their time on 'this miserable stone'. All he wanted was a decent life again . . .

'So is your idea of a decent life to capture and threaten an innocent woman – to threaten to rape her and tear off her leg? You're a coward and a brute, Feneloni, no less a coward and a brute because you do this on Mars rather than Earth. Isn't it to guard against your kind that we try to set up decent rules to live by under our difficult conditions?'

'Look, we were only scaring the girl.'

'And were you in control of the situation? Violence of any kind releases baser instincts. Right now I'd like to beat your brains out, but we've tried to set up laws against that kind of thing. What the hell are we going to do about you? A course of mentatropy?'

He hunched his shoulders and hung his head.

I waited. 'Well?'

After a long silence, he said, 'Not mentatropy . . . I'm not the brute you take me for. There's plenty worse than me. I don't have your powers of speech. That doesn't mean I don't suffer. Why should we be ruled over by those with better powers of speech?'

I had no wish to talk with him, but forced myself to answer.

'In every society so far there have been top dogs and underdogs. The question is how we here can make the gulf between them as narrow and as flexible as possible. Would you rather be ruled by those who have – as you put it – "better powers of speech", or those who have the greater brute strength?'

He stared at the ground. After a pause he said, in a low voice, 'It's a stupid question. All men are supposed to be equal, but if they aren't heard then they aren't equal.'

'You were heard and dismissed. I could give you an example of a man with great powers of speech – the academic called John Homer Bateson, who is laughed off whenever he addresses the audience. We know that all men are not equal, although it befits a government of any kind to attempt to behave as if they were.'

'But you're trying to establish your little government here, instead of busting a bracket to get us back to Earth.'

'Don't be ridiculous, man. What leverage have we with Earth in its present state? Nothing's going to get us home until the repercussions of the EUPACUS disaster clear up. Meanwhile we must do our best to live like humans.'

The alternatives were clear enough to me. Not to Feneloni. He said that all our committees and forums were a waste of time.

'I'm not entering into a debate with you, Feneloni. Not only am I determined to establish a fair society, but I expect the intellectual exercise involved to protect us from violence and unrest.

'Any scum determined to promote violence and unrest must be isolated, as if they had an infectious disease.'

'No such thing as justice,' he muttered, and hung his head again.

I waited. I was curious about the way his mind worked; I knew there was good in him.

After a silence, he said, 'It's all right for you. Some of us have families back on Earth. Kids.'

I gave him no reply, only wishing I could claim as much.

Feneloni looked up angrily. 'Why don't you speak, since you're so good at it?'

'You cannot be allowed to attack a young woman and go unpunished. Tomorrow we will hold a court to decide what that punishment should be. Probably a course of mentatropy. You will be allowed to speak in your defence.'

Turning on my heel, I left him. Afterwards I wished I had said that to be eloquent was not necessarily a virtue; but it implied orderly thought and, perhaps more than that, wide experience and knowledge. But such, of course, was the reward of privilege, if only genetic privilege. My own troubled boyhood came back to me.

We made no attempt to track down Feneloni's associates, hoping that without a leader they would not reoffend.

So it proved. Nevertheless we knew they were there, ready for violence should the opportunity arise.

Cang Hai was nervous after her experience.

'Tom, this is the second time I've been threatened with rape! What is it about me . . . ?'

We talked it over and over. Ben Borrow came and let her talk it out of her system, as far as that was possible.

One evening, she said to me, 'We know there are such men on Earth. Why should we be surprised to find them here, except that you and I are such innocents?'

It surprised me that she should think me an innocent, but I made no comment on that. 'They will submit to the rules of society as long as it suits them.'

'I don't know. Perhaps there's an undercurrent of violence here we are blind to. Just as you and I are blind to the great amount of busy sexual activity going on. How is it that we enjoy debate more than sexual intercourse? Are we exceptions to the rule?'

I was stung by what she had said; I had assumed that my sexually active life had faded away during my period of mourning for my dead wife. As for Cang Hai, she clearly needed indoctrination into the pleasures of sex. That night, when the domes lay under their usual suspirations that passed for silence, and Laputa and Swift slid across the sky outside, I undressed and went to Cang Hai's bed.

She sat up angrily. She told me she did not wish me to try and prove anything. That was not love.

'Don't be silly. Let me in! We may as well have some pleasure.'

'Go away! I'm having a period. You're too old. I'm not prepared for anything like this. Why didn't you warn me? You're taking advantage of me.' She kicked out at my legs.

Having been sent away, I lay in the dark in my own bed,

wakeful, listening to the great machine that gave us life, breathing, breathing.

What had her real motives been, what mine?

How badly the human race needed a period of quiet, for reflection, and to become acquainted with its deepest motives . . .

After only brief discussion, we decided that Feneloni should be confined to the store room to which he had taken Cang Hai. The door should be strengthened. He should speak to no one, although he would be permitted the statutory one conversation with visitors. He should have three meals a day. A television monitor would be permitted, on which he could follow the events of the day in the domes. He should be incarcerated for two weeks, and then questioned again, to be set free if he had come to any better conclusion about himself.

If not, then mentatropy was to be applied.

In order to hasten Cang Hai's return to her normal state of equilibrium, and to allow me some relief from the burdens of organisation, which seemed to be exacting a toll on my health, the two of us sat in on some of Alpha's nursery classes.

Their Social Skills class began with a song:

> Folk of many creeds and nations
> Travelled in realms of thought,
> Made their computations,
> Forged from steel and flame
> Ships of no earthly sort –
>   Leaving earthly port –
> So strangers to Red Planet came.

The song ran though several verses. The children sang lustily, with enjoyment. It was noticeable that the girls concentrated on the music. Some of the boys were secretly prodding each other and making faces.

Afterwards I asked Alpha what she thought of the song, which sounded rather laboured to my ears.

'We like it,' Alpha said. 'It's a good song, about us.'

'What do you like about it?'

'"Ships of no earthly sort" – that's really hot. What does it mean, do you suppose?'

The teacher, the sculptor Benazir Bahudur, kept the two sexes in the same classroom but segregated. 'It's a difference in the genes,' she explained. 'The boys have more difficulty in learning social skills, as you know. The girls are more intuitive. We think the boys need the girls in the room, to be given a glimpse of an alternative way of behaving. You will see the difference when we get to the games. But first we have a Natural History Slot. Are you ready, kids?'

Benazir was a slightly built woman. Her leisurely movements suggested a certain weariness, but when the full regard of her deep-set eyes was turned on you, an impression of drive and energy was received.

A screen lit on the wall. Insect noises could be heard. A brilliant landscape was revealed, the landscape of East Africa. The viewpoint moved rapidly towards a fine stand of trees.

'They're acacia trees,' said Benazir.

Young saplings grew here, as well as mature trees with their corded bark. Benazir gave the children an explanation of what trees were and how they had developed. As she was explaining how grazing animals threatened the very existence of trees of all kinds, the viewpoint snuggled into the shade of a particular tree as if it would nest there. The children were silent, wondering.

A branch served as a highway for ants. The creatures were busy patrolling the whole tree. The camera followed them down to the ground and up to the fragrant blossoms of the acacia.

'I'm glad we don't have those little things up here, miss,' said one of the girls.

'Ants are clever little creatures,' Benazir replied. 'They

have good social organisation. They guard the acacias from enemies – from herbivores and other insects. In return, the trees give them shelter. You wouldn't want to climb that tree, would you? Why is that?'

'Because you'd get stung/attacked/bitten/eaten alive,' came gleeful answers from various parts of the room.

A thoughtful-looking boy asked, 'What about the tree having sex? How can bees get to the flowers if they are attacked by these creepy little things?'

Benazir explained that the young acacia flowers, which smell very sweet, put out a chemical signal to keep the soldier ants away, so allowing the bees to pollinate them.

'What do the flowers smell like, exactly?' the boy asked.

Cang Hai and I debated privately if such glimpses of life on Earth would not start the children wondering about what they were missing. When we put this point to Benazir, she said that her charges had to be prepared for their return to Earth. She fed them with these shots of knowledge before they went out to play.

The children's games had been cleverly adapted to encourage the boys without discouraging the girls. Skipping and counting games were played 'outside', on the Astroturf. The differences between the temperaments of boys and girls became clear when Alpha volunteered to tell everyone a story.

Her story was about a little mummy animal (evidently a mole), who lived with her tiny family under the Astroturf. She told her children to behave and, if they were good, they would get extra cups of tealem, their favourite drink. They all went to bed in little plastic beakers and slept well till morning. The End.

Scornfully, a boy called Morry took up Alpha's tale. The mummy animal was going off to get some groceries. She popped her head up above the ground just as the machine that trimmed the Astroturf was whizzing along. Zummmm! It cut off her head, which went flying with a trail of blood like a comet into someone's shoe!

246

'Oh no, it didn't at all!' shrieked Alpha angrily.

'Well, let's see how likely these events really are,' said Benazir, smiling at both sides.

'Her head did not come off,' said Alpha firmly. 'More likely it was Morry's head.'

Unable to sustain verbal argument, Morry stuck his tongue out at her.

Benazir said nothing more, but began to dance in front of her pupils. Her steps were slow, teasingly cautious, her hand gestures elaborate, as if they said, 'Look, dear children, life is like this and this, and so much to be enjoyed that no quarrels are required . . .'

As Cang Hai and I walked back to our apartment, we discussed what kind of future citizens of utopia these children would make. We decided that the anti-social phase the children were going through would not be sustained; and we hoped the element of fantasy and imagination would remain. We realised how important were the skills of mothers, fathers and teachers.

Back in our apartment, I was forced to lie down. I slept for a while.

17

The Birth Room

Despite recurring dizzy spells – and advice from Cang Hai and Guenz and others to consult a doctor – I continued to work steadily with the team to finalise our utopian plans.

Guenz protested that it was useless work if Olympus could rouse up and destroy our little settlement at any time. Mary Fangold replied that it was not reasonable to sit about waiting for a disaster that might never happen. She used a phrase we had heard several times before – almost the motto of the Mars colony – 'You gotta keep on keeping on'.

Dreiser Hawkwood and Charles Bondi set up a secure Ambient group with Kathi Skadmorr, Youssef Choihosla and me. We discussed, at Dreiser's direction, the question of whether Earth should be informed of Olympus's movements.

We studied the latest comsat photographs. 'As you can see,' Dreiser said, 'its rate of progress is increasing, even though it is crossing rough territory.'

'It has withdrawn its exteroceptors from around this unit,' Kathi remarked. 'One deduction is that it requires them elsewhere to act as under-regolith paddles. Hence the abrupt acceleration.'

Bondi was busy measuring. 'Using the churned regolith as the base line, Chimborazo has covered ninety-five or ninety-six metres in the last Earth year. This is an extraordinary rate of acceleration. If it could maintain this acceleration rate – pretty ridiculous, in my opinion – its prow would strike the unit – let's see, well, hmm, it still has nearly three hundred kilometres to go, so . . . well, we would have plenty of time – four years at the very least, even on that reckoning.'

'Four years!' I echoed.

Interrupting, Choihosla asked if Chimborazo left excreta behind on its trail.

'Don't be silly,' Kathi exclaimed. 'It is a self-contained unit, can't waste anything. It'll have excreta-eaters in under that shell.'

'The point of my question is – do we inform Downstairs or not? I'd like your answer, Tom,' said Dreiser. 'This doesn't have to go to Adminex. We five must say yea or nay.'

'They probably have the Darwin fixed on Mars,' I said. 'So they'll see this thing's hoof marks.'

'Maybe they have not maintained their telescope since the breakdown,' Dreiser said. 'Or, if they have, they may not be too quick to evaluate the implications of the tumbled regolith. What I mean to say is, they may just reckon we triggered a landslide of some magnitude.'

'We should inform Downstairs that "the volcano" has shifted,' said Kathi. 'No other comment. We certainly don't inform them that we think Chimborazo has life, never mind intelligence. Otherwise they'd probably nuke the place – xenophobia being what it is.'

So that was agreed on, after more discussion.

Bondi said, wryly, 'You can't predict what they'll do down there. They may simply conclude we've gone mad.'

'They probably think that already,' I said.

A thousand questions poured through my mind that night, sometimes merging with phantasmagoric strands of dream. My mind was like a rat in a maze, being both rat and maze.

At the 'X' hour of night, I climbed from my bed and walked about the limited confines of my room. The question arose in my consciousness: Why was it that, in all the infinitude of matrix, mankind built itself these tiny hutches in which to exist?

I longed to talk with someone. I longed to have Antonia again by my side, to enjoy her company and her counsel. As tears began to roll down my cheeks – I could not check them, though she had been gone now for three years – my Ambient sounded its soft horn.

The face of Kathi Skadmorr floated in the globe.

'I knew you were awake, Tom. I had to speak to you. The universe is cold tonight.'

'One can be lonely, locked in a crowd.' It was as if we exchanged passwords.

'However we may aspire to loneliness, we can't be as lonely as . . . you know, that pet of ours out there. Its very being preys on my mind. It's a case for weeping.'

Guiltily, I wiped away my tears. 'Kathi, it's an immense vegetable thing. Despite its CPS, we don't know that it has anything paralleling our form of intelligence. How do we know it didn't grow silently in vegetable state – a sort of fungus, well nigh immune to external influence.'

She was silent, sitting with downcast eyes. 'You appreciate the curious parallel between it and us. We live as it does, under a dome . . .' Seeing she was thinking something out, I said nothing. I liked her face and her sensibility in my globe. For once, she was not being prickly; that too I liked. We certainly were parked in a lonely part of the universe.

Looking up smartly, she said, 'Tom, I admire you and your gallant attempt to make us all better people. Of course it won't work. I am an example of why it won't work – I was born with an obstinate temper.'

'No, no. Something may have made you obstinate. You're . . . you're just the sort of person we need in utopia. Someone who can think and . . . feel . . .'

As if I had not spoken, she said – she was looking into a dark corner of her room – 'Oh, Chimborazo is conscious right enough. I feel it. I felt it when we were there, right by it. I feel it now.'

'We got a CPS, certainly. But . . . I fear that if there is a mentality at work under its shell, then human understanding has to change. It must change.' I stared down at the digits on my watch, ever flickering the seconds of life away. 'If there is life on Earth's neighbour, then the universe must be a great hive of wildly diverse life. As if intelligence was the natural aim and purpose of the universe.'

'Yes, if consciousness is not simply a local anomaly. But that is too anthropocentric, isn't it? I came on such ideas too recently to know. Me with my Abo background.' Some of her old scorn sounded in her voice. And then, as if in contradiction, her thought took off. She said about this thing on our doorstep that perhaps in its solitude, in its stony centuries of meditation under its camouflaging shell, it had come to comprehend universals that had never even impinged on human skulls. The human race had always been driven by a few imperatives – hunger, sex, power – and lived by diversity; maybe – just maybe – the unity of this huge thing was proof of a vastly greater strength of understanding . . .'

She sighed. 'Beau's here with me, Tom. He's sleeping. He does not feel Chimborazo's presence as I do. Oh, we're so limited . . . Maybe its unity is proof of a greater understanding. Something gained through the chilly expanses of time – what we comprehend as time, anyway – until it has reached perfect knowledge and wisdom. Does that sound like wishful thinking?' She laughed at herself.

'Suppose it was like that, Kathi. Would we be able to converse with it? Communicate? Or would its understandings put it for ever beyond our conceptual reach? "What we comprehend as time" – there's an example . . . So it's to us a kind of god – totally without interest in anything outside itself.'

'I wouldn't be too sure of that . . .'

She put her hands to her cheeks in a gesture I had seen her use before. 'It's that time of night when imaginations run away with themselves. Could be it's just a freak mollusc, stranded on a failed planet that long since yielded up its essence . . . Tom, go to sleep! I wish I were there to talk to you, closely . . .'

Her face faded and was gone.

I could not sleep. The conversation lingered in my mind. My head ached; I felt stifled.

I staggered out of my chamber in search of company, and barged without knocking into Choihosla's apartment.

Youssef Choihosla was kneeling on a small mat, his forehead to the floor. A dim lamp stood nearby.

I halted in the doorway. Choihosla looked up with a brow of thunder. He began a stream of abuse, biting it off when he recognised me.

'Tom? You look ghastly! Come in, come in. What's up? It's "X" hour.'

He rose as I entered. I said, 'You were in the midst of prayer. I'm sorry to break in.'

'Allah is great. He will forgive an interruption. Come and sit down.'

I sat weakly and he brought his great bulk close and also sat, hands on knees. I spoke of my confusion of mind, brought about by the thought of the unknown life form not far away from us. He confessed that his prayer – 'largely wordless' – had been seeking reassurance for the same reason.

We talked for a long while, merely speculating.

My curiosity got the better of me. I saw an electronic gadget with a small screen, at present blank, lying on the floor by Choihosla's prayer mat, and asked him what it was.

He hesitated, then picked it up and presented it to me for my inspection.

Pressing a button, I set golden bodies in motion on the screen, while figures jerked across the lower section of it.

This was a Muslim ephemeris. It calculated the positions, not only of the Sun, the Moon, Earth and Mars, but also of Mecca, throughout the year. It enabled Choihosla to pray towards the holy city when the revolutions of Earth brought Mecca to a point facing towards Amazonis, where our structures were situated. Choihosla explained that it was considered poor theology to pray when Mecca was on the other side of Earth's globe, facing away from Mars.

'Well, it's ingenious,' I remarked. He hefted the little calculator in the palm of his hand. 'You buy these ephemerises for a few cents in the bazaars,' he said, offhandedly. 'Of course, it's a Western invention . . .'

Seeing the puzzlement in my eyes, he said, 'You wonder about my faith – maybe how I persist in it? Don't you need something bigger than yourself in life?'

I pointed in what I imagined to be the direction of Olympus Mons.

'It's out there,' I said.

Monstrous things apart, we came to realise nothing could be achieved without decent living conditions. The thinness of the atmosphere of Mars rendered us susceptible to meteoritic bombardment, as we had been well aware. We now set about extending our quarters by excavation, creating a new subterranean level where the apartments had rooms larger than those in our previous quarters. These apartments had balconies and galleries; the bricks we fabricated were glazed in various colours, while genetically altered plants – in particular creepers – were planted and flourished under artificial light. Rooms were decorated in various bright colours and afforded better opportunities for solitude.

I found a glowing message waiting on my Ambient. When I punched Receive, Charles Bondi's voice came to me, full of controlled anger: 'Jefferies, what are you people doing over there? Why do you think our research unit was positioned on Mars? It was because we required complete silence and no vibrations, wasn't it? Our foundation represents the whole reason for habitation on this planet. Your drillings are threatening our search for the Omega Smudge. We're getting strange readings. I have to tell you that all drillings and excavations must cease at once. Immediately. Please acknowledge that this has been done.'

I froze his face. Studying it, I did not see the aggression implied by his words.

My reply was brief. 'Charles, I am sorry we upset your solitude. But so far your researches have produced nothing. Meanwhile we have to live. This is why our spicules were sited at a distance from your foundation. We shall be finished within a few days. I have no intention of failing to complete what will be new much required living quarters, and I invite you to inspect them when you have recovered from your annoyance.'

He sent a one-word reply, 'Luddite!' Then we heard no more of the matter. While marvelling at scientific arrogance, I saw its necessity and urged the workers to press on as speedily as possible, to get the vibration over and done with.

As the plans for our utopia came nearer to realisation, so discussions on the employment and containment of power became more urgent. In what sort of context would an autocratic temperament like Bondi's be content? How could the admirable restlessness of enquiry be satisfied by a utopian calm? How could our utopia maintain both stability and change? These were some of the questions that confronted us.

We debated the nature of power and the striving for power. Eventually it was Choihosla who suggested that we should question our concept of power itself.

He began by asking us a riddle. Who is it who holds most power of life and death over another?

Answers from the floor included an executioner, an army sergeant in the heat of battle, a murderer, the chief of a savage tribe, the launcher of nuclear missiles, and (mischievously) a scientist.

Choihosla shook his head. 'The answer is – a mother over her newborn child. Bear that in mind while I speak to you.'

He said he realised his proposals would be anathema to all whose brains had been, as he put it, 'dissolved by the Western way of life'. But a little thought was needed on the matter and that thought must be directed to overturning accepted ideas of power as an opportunity for gain.

The various presidents, monarchs and dictators who wielded power Downstairs were not to be emulated Upstairs. All of them sought to accumulate wealth for themselves. The citizens under them also sought to accumulate wealth for themselves. We, fortunately, had no wealth. Nevertheless we would need a leader, a man or a woman, to whom all questions of justice could eventually be referred. He suggested this person should assume the title of Prime Architect. The title was neutral as regards gender, and it correctly implied that something constructive was going on.

But the conception of power as a force that enabled an individual to gain more than was his or her due had to be discarded. Power had to derive from the determination to achieve and maintain a well-organised society. Since this determination would be reinforced by the hope – however illusory – of achieving the perfectability of humanity, it would follow that the powerless would not be harmed by power, any more than a child is harmed by the mother's power over him. Indeed, the linkages of power, from officials to parents, to children, to pets, would share by example the unifying hope of a general well-being. Both child and mother benefit by the maternal wielding of power.

At this point, Cang Hai said, 'You are trying to bring back Confucianism!'

'Not so,' replied Choihosla. 'Confucianism was too rigid and limited, although it contained many enlightened ideas. But these days we hear much about "human rights" and too little about human responsibilities. In our utopia, responsibility carries with it satisfaction and a better chance for benevolence.'

'So what is your revised nature of power to be?' someone asked.

'No, no.' He shook his heavy head, as if regretting he had spoken in the first place. 'How can I say? I don't seek to change the nature of power – that's ridiculous. Only our attitude to power. Power in itself is a neutral thing; it's the use of it that must be changed from malevolent to benevolent. By thought, by empathy. I am sure it can be done. Then power will provide a chance to increase everyone's well-being. Given a society already positive in aspect, that will be the greatest satisfaction. Both Prime Architect and citizen will benefit by what I might call a maternal wielding of power.'

He was a big clumsy man. He looked oddly humble as he finished speaking and folded his massive arms across his chest.

After a meditative silence all round, Crispin said, quietly, 'You are wanting human nature to change.'

'But not all human nature,' Choihosla replied. 'Some of us already hold the concept of power-as-greed in contempt. And I think you are one of them, Mr Barcunda!'

While the excavations for our extension were in progress, I was busier than ever. Fortunately, our secretary, the silent Elsa Lamont, arranged my appointments and saw that I kept them. She and Suung Saybin dealt personally with all those applying for rooms in the new building.

Unexpectedly, one evening, working late at night when we should both of us have been relaxing, Elsa turned to me and said, 'In my love affairs, I have always been the one who was loved.'

I was startled, since I had not associated the rather drab-looking Elsa with affairs of the heart or the body. For me, she was just an ex-commercial artist with a head for figures.

'Why are the figures I paint faceless? Tom, I realise I am not capable of deep love. It's unfair to my partners, isn't it?'

Since my eyebrows were already raised, I could only think to ask, 'What has prompted this reflection, Elsa?'

She had been thinking about Choihosla's redefinition of power. Mothers loved deeply, yes, she said. But perhaps for those who were unable to love deeply, power was the next best thing. Perhaps power was a kind of corruption of the reproductive process.

'I can see that the need to be free to reproduce can lead to all kinds of power struggle . . .' I began.

Elsa repeated the words slowly, as if they were a mantra, ' "I can see that the need to be free to reproduce can lead to all kinds of power struggle . . ." That's true throughout nature, isn't it? We have to hope that we can unite to prove Choihosla's statement holds some truth.' Then without pause, she added, 'A delegation of women has booked a forum in Hindenburg Hall tomorrow, 10 p.m. They wish to talk about better ways – more congenial ways, I suppose – of giving birth. Can you be there?'

'Um . . . you're not trying to tell me you're pregnant, are you, Elsa?'

Perhaps a pallid smile crossed her face. 'Certainly not,' she said. 'If only I were pregnant with the truth . . .'

She turned back to her work. And then said, 'Could be I prefer detachment, rather than letting go and returning the love of my lovers. Does that give me more power?'

It sounded like a weakness to me, but I cautiously treated her question as rhetorical.

Prompt at ten next morning, a delegation of women met under the giant Hindenburg mural.

The Greek woman, Helen Panorios, spoke on behalf of the group. She placed her hands on her hips and stood without gesture as she spoke.

'We make a demand that may at first seem strange to most of you. Please hear us out. We women require a special apartment in the new extension. It need not be too large, as long as it is properly equipped. We wish to call it the Birth Room, and for no men ever to be allowed inside it. It will be sacred to the processes of birth.'

She was interrupted by Mary Fangold, the hospital personnel manager. 'Excuse me. Of course I have heard this notion circulating. It is a ridiculous duplication of work that our hospital's maternity branch already carries out effectively. We have a splendid record of natal care. Mothers are up and out a day after parturition, without complications. I oppose this so-called "Birth Room" on the grounds that it is unreasonable and a slur against the reputation of our hospital.'

Helen Panorios barely moved a muscle.

'It is your cooperation, not your opposition we hope for, Mary. You condemn your system by your own words. You see, the hospital still carries out production-line methods – mothers in one day, out the next. Just as if we were machines, and babies to be turned out like – like so many hats. It's all so old-fashioned and against nature.'

Another woman joined in in support. 'We have spent so much time talking about the upbringing and education of our children without looking at the vital matter of their first few hours in this world. This period is when the bonding process between mother and child must take place.

'The bustle of our hospital is not conducive to that process, and may indeed be in part the cause of negligent mothers and disruptive children. The Birth Room will change all that.'

Crispin asked, 'Is this a way of cutting out the fathers?'

'Not at all,' said Helen. 'But there is always, rightly, a mystery about birth. Men should not be witnesses to it. Oh, I know that sounds like a retrograde step. It has been the fashion for men to be present at bornings, and indeed often enough male doctors have supervised the delivery. But fashions change. We wish to try something different.

'In fact, the Birth Room is an old forgotten idea. It's a place for female consolation for the rigours of childbearing. Women will be able to come and go in the Room. They can rest there whether pregnant or not. Female midwives will attend the accouchement. More importantly, mothers will be able to stay there after the birth, to be idle, to suckle their child, to chat with other women. No men at all.

'No men until a week after the birth. Women must have their province. Somehow, in our struggle for equality we have lost some of the desirable privileges we once enjoyed in previous times.

'You must allow us to regain this small privilege. You will soon discover that large advantages in behaviour flow from it.'

'And what are husbands supposed to do?' I asked.

Helen's solemn face broke into a smile. 'Oh, husbands will do what they always do. Enjoy their clubs and one another's company, hobnob, have their own private places. Look, let us try out the Birth Room idea for a year. We are confident it will work well and serve the whole community.'

A Birth Room was built in the subterranean extension, despite male complaints. There women, and not only the pregnant ones, met to socialise. Men were totally excluded. After giving birth, woman and baby remained together in peace, warmth and subdued light for at least a week, or longer if they felt it necessary. When they emerged, to present the husband with his new child, a little ceremony called Reunion developed, with company, cakes and kisses. The cakes were synthetic, the kisses real enough.

The Birth Room soon became an accepted part of social life, and a respected feature of the comforts of the new extension.

18

The Debate on Sex and Marriage

Weeks turned into months, and months into another year. There were many who, despite the misfortune of their confinement on Mars, regarded our society as a fair and just one. I, on the other hand, came to see utopia as a condition of becoming, a glow in the distance, a journey for which human limitations precluded an end. Yet there were comforting indications of improvement in our lot.

Kissorian and Sharon were among the first to take advantage of the greater scope for solitude afforded by the subterranean extensions. Their marriage was celebrated to the joy of many (and the envy of some), and they retired for a while from public life.

At the same time, the men who worked on the Smudge Project were experiencing new difficulties. One of the positive results of the recognition of Chimborazo as a life form was a closer union between scientists and non-scientists. Most of the gallant 6,000 realised that ours was one of the great scientific ages, and took pride in sharing its news. So we all felt involved when Dreiser announced that there was a minor glitch in the superfluid. At last, a signal had been received that was interpreted as the passage of a HIGMO through the ring.

Dreiser said that the Mars operation was coming to fruition as planned.

'When we have found just two more HIGMOs, or even one more, we shall finally have an approach towards an estimate of the crucial parameters of the Omega Smudge.'

'How long do we have to wait?' someone asked.

'Depends. We must be patient. Even ten or fifteen more

HIGMOs will begin to give us fairly accurate values for these parameters. Various controversial issues will be settled once and for all, among other important things.' He glanced sidelong at Kathi Skadmorr, as if saying 'Don't rock the boat', when her face now came up on the Ambient.

'We should just say there are some minor anomalies about the glitch detected in the superfluid,' she said. 'Maybe we have a signal representing a HIGMO passing through the ring, maybe not. Some of us have a few worries about that. So we are waiting for the second HIGMO. As Dreiser says, we must be patient.'

But a second HIGMO was indicated only two days later.

'Well, it does seem a little fishy,' said Dreiser. 'The ring has only been in full working order for a year. I'm talking terrestrial years now, as though we were no more aware than our androids that we are on another planet.' He gave a dry chuckle. 'A year till we get a signal, then a second so soon.'

'Can't they come in groups?' I asked.

He seemed to ignore the question, muttering to someone beyond lens range. Turning to face his audience again, he said, 'There's something particularly odd about the signature of this second glitch. It's not the form we expected. You see, there's a gradual oscillatory build-up instead of the anticipated almost clean "step-function" you'd expect from a HIGMO. You have to appreciate that the first glitch took us unawares. Full details of its profile were not obtained.

'We'll keep you posted.'

So we had to get on with our lives. The betterment of conditions brought about by the development of Lower Ground, as we called it, improved everyone's morale. But, as with many improvements, these would not guarantee lasting contentment. I had taken a liking to Dayo Obantuji, the anxious young Nigerian, who showed great interest in our circumstances. We often discussed the developments of

Lower Ground. Having abandoned musical composition, Dayo proved adept at devising decorative tile patterns, bursting with life and colour, to adorn the main corridor.

But I said to him, 'If we look back to the metropolises of the nineteenth century, we see filthy cities. In New York and Paris and London, filth and grit and stench were permanent features of life. These cities – London in particular – were coal-oriented. There was coal everywhere, coal dumped down chutes in the street, coal dragged upstairs, coal spilt and burned in a million grates, grimy smoke, cinders and ash strewn here and there.

'The exudations of coal mingled with the droppings of the horses that dragged the coal carts through the streets and pulled all kinds of carriages and cabs. The whole place was a microclimate of filth. The twentieth century saw vast improvements. Coal was banished, smokeless zones were introduced. The noisome fogs of London became a thing of the past. Electric heating developed into central heating and air-conditioning. Solar-heating panels replaced chimneys. Animals disappeared from the streets, to be replaced by automobiles, which – at least until they multiplied beyond tolerance and were banished from our cities – brought a decided improvement to urban life.

'And was the new comfort and ease of the home, reinforced by vacuum-cleaners and other devices that made homes more hygienic, considered utopian? Not at all. The improvements came in gradually and, once there, were taken for granted.'

'I wish they could have been taken for granted where I came from,' said Dayo. 'Our governments never had the interests of the people at heart.'

'To greater or lesser extent,' I said, 'that is the characteristic of all governments. It happened that in Western countries an educated population had a strong enough voice to regulate or become government. That educated class also accumulated the capital to invest in sustained improvement, which has in itself promoted more improvement, often in unanticipated spheres.

'To give an instance of the sort of thing I'm thinking of, back in the 1930s, in the fairly early days of motoring, an ordinary family found that a small car was within its price range; they could buy what was called, in those bygone days, "the freedom of the road".

'Crude though methods of contraception were in those days, the family then had a choice: another baby or a Baby Austin? Another mouth to feed or a T-model Ford? By opting for the car, they lowered population growth rates, which improved family living standards and encouraged the liberation of women.'

Dayo looked moody. 'In Nigeria it is scarcely possible to speak of the liberation of women. Yet when I think how intelligent my mother was – far more clever than my father . . .' Looking at the floor, he added, 'I wish I was dead when I think how I behaved to her – learned behaviour, of course . . . Now she's gone and it's too late to make amends.'

Because I was afflicted by a migraine, Belle Rivers and Crispin Barcunda conducted the debate on sex and marriage. The motion was opposed by John Homer Bateson and Beau Stephens.

Bateson began in his most flowery manner: 'To look back over the history of matrimony is to recoil from the cruelty of it. Love between a man and a woman hardly enters into the picture. It all comes down to a question of property and dowry and enslavement, either and most probably of the woman by the man, or of the man by the woman. As a woman by name Greer or Green said last century, "For a woman to effect any amelioration in her condition, she must refuse to marry."

'I would say too for a man to attain the detachment that wisdom brings, he also must refuse to marry. He must quell the lust to possess, which lies at the base of this question. The woman, until recently, was legally bound to give up everything, her freedom, even her name, while the man was supposed to give up his freedom of choice and to apply

263

himself, sooner or later, to the expense of the rearing of the children he conceived on his wife.

'Thus, while the word "wedding" may cause some excitement in some breasts, somewhat like the word "mealtime", the excitement is evanescent as the true nature of marriage dawns on the wedded pair. They must then contrive somehow to love their demanding offspring, who, it is fair to say, are most unlikely to requite that love by reciprocal affection or gratitude.

'We have already made what to my mind is overdue provision for children here – not to mention their careless addition to our population. Let them go – as the saying used to be – "on the parish", into the care of Belle Rivers and her professional carers. Let there continue to be the usual conjunction of overheated bodies, men with women, women with women, and men with men. But let us not consider the continuance on Mars of matrimony in any shape or form. We are imprisoned enough as it is.'

Bateson sat down and Crispin took the stand. 'The genial Oliver Goldsmith remarked that a man who married and brought up his family did more service to the community than he who remained single and complained about the growing population. The outburst of misogyny we have just heard takes no account of love. I know it's a word that covers a multitude of sins as well as virtues, but if we weigh love against its opposite, hatred, then we see how easily love wins.

'True, marriage once involved property. That's history. In any case, Upstairs here we have no property beyond our persons. Now we marry to make public our commitment to each other, and to ensure, as far as that is possible, the stability of our lives for the enhancement of our children's most tender years.

'If we do not want children, then we need not marry, but must take precautions until lust gives out and we forsake our partner for another.

'How satisfactory that is, I leave you to judge, but it would be folly to legislate against it. Is free love a prescription for contentment? I remind you of the old joke I heard in the Seychelles long ago. "Remember, no matter how pretty the next girl is who comes along, somewhere in her background there's a guy who got sick of her shit and nonsense."' He showed his gold tooth in a wide grin, before adding, 'And that goes for the other sex as well, ladies . . .

'I can tell you now that I believe, on the other hand, that there is something ennobling about marriage and constancy, and that those qualities should be encouraged in our constitution. So convinced of their virtue am I that I'm proud to say Belle and I – despite some difference in our ages – intend to marry soon.' He burst out laughing with joy, gesturing gallantly towards Belle.

Belle immediately rose to her feet. She was seen to blush. 'Oh, that was meant to be a secret!' she cried, between tears and laughter herself. He put his arms round her and they clung together.

I wished that Kissorian and Sharon could have been present, but we had not seen them for a while. 'After this display, we're bound to win,' Cang Hai whispered to me.

But Beau Stephens now rose, frowning. 'Friends, this is a disgraceful spectacle, carefully rehearsed, no doubt, to persuade us to vote with our hearts instead of our heads. If these two rather ageing people are emotionally involved with each other, it is better it should be kept secret than acted out before us in this embarrassing charade.

'The case against marriage is that it is out-of-date and has become merely an opportunity for display and sentiment. Present-day ethics are against the whole idea. After the party's over, and the gifts mauled about and complained of, before the confetti's trampled into the mud of the pavement, most couples get divorced, only to indulge in legal wrangles that may continue for some years.

'That's when we see that marriage is simply about property and lust. It shows no care for any children. It's dishonest – another bad old custom that must go, if only to impoverish the lawyers.

'You seem fond of quoting, so I'll give you a quote from Nietzsche, whose *Also Sprach Zarathustra* I read in my university days. As far as I recall, Nietzsche takes a spiritual view. He says that you should first be mature enough to face the challenge of marriage, so that marriage can enable you both to grow. You should have children who will profit by your spirituality, to become greater than you are. He calls marriage the will of two people to create a someone who is more than those who created it.

'This is a rigorous view of marriage, I know, but, as a child of divorced parents who hated each other, I took stock of Nietzsche's words. The gross side of marriage has killed it as an institution.

'What we propose should be written into our constitution is that marriage is forbidden. No more marriages. Instead, an unbreakable contract to produce and rear children. Demanding, yes, but with it will come benefits and support from the state.

'This unbreakable contract may be signed and sealed by any two people determined to devote themselves to creating the brilliant and loving kind of child Belle Rivers thinks can be produced by an impractical rank on rank of shrinks. The new contract cannot be broken by divorce. Divorce is also forbidden. So it will be respected by one and all. Outside of that contract, free love can prevail, much as it does now – but with severe penalties for any couple producing unwanted babies.'

Stephens sat down in a dense silence as the forum chewed over what he had said.

Crispin slowly rose to his feet. 'Beau has been talking about breeding, not marriage. Just because his – or rather, Nietzsche's – ideas are admirable in their way, that doesn't make them practical. They're too extreme. We could not tolerate being locked for ever into a twosome that had proved to have lost its original inspiration, or to have found no other inspiration. To grow as Beau suggests, we must be free. We offer no such draconian answer as Beau proposes, to a question that has defeated wiser heads than ours.' He sighed, and continued more slowly.

'But we do know that a marriage is as good as the society in which it flourishes – or fails . . . It may be that when our just society is fully established the ancient ways of getting married – and of getting divorced where necessary – will prove to be adequate. How adequate they are must depend not on laws, which can be broken, but on the people who try to abide by them.

'Marriage remains a lawful and honourable custom. We must just try to love better, and for that we shall have the assistance of our improved society.'

He sat down, looking rather dejected. There was a moment's silence. Then a wave of applause broke out.

At this period, I felt dizzy and sick and little able to carry on with my work. I seemed to hear curious sounds, somewhat between the bleat of a goat and the cry of a gull. Even the presence of other people became burdensome.

There was an upper gallery, little frequented, which I sought out, and where I could sit in peace, gazing out at the Martian lithosphere. From this viewpoint, looking westward, I could see the sparsely fractured plain, where the fractures ran in parallel, as if ruled with a ruler. These lines had been there – at least by human standards – for ever! Time had frozen them. Only the play or withdrawal of the Sun's light changed. At one time of day, I caught from this vantage point the glint of the Sun on a section of the ring of the Smudge Project.

Visiting the gallery on the day following the marriage debate, I found someone already present. The discovery was the more unwelcome because the man lounging there was John Homer Bateson, who had displayed such misanthropy in his speech.

It was too late to turn back. Bateson acknowledged my presence with a nod. He began to speak without preliminaries, perhaps fearing I might bring up the topic of the recent debate.

'I take it that you do not subscribe to this popular notion

that Olympus Mons is a living thing? Why is it that poor suffering humanity cannot bear to think itself alone in the universe, but must be continually inventing alternative life forms, from gods to cartoon characters?

'Make no mistake, Jefferies, however industriously you busy yourself with schemes for a just society, which can never come about, constituting as it does merely another Judeo-Christian illusion, we are all going to die here on Mars.'

I reminded him that we were looking for a new and better way to live – on which score I remained optimistic.

He sighed at such a vulgar display of hope. 'You speak like that, yet I can see you're sick. I'm sorry – but you have merely to gaze from this window to perceive that this is a dead planet, a planet of death, and that we live suspended in a kind of limbo, severed from everything that makes existence meaningful.'

'This is a planet of life, as we have discovered – where life has survived against tremendous odds, just as we intend to do.'

He pulled his nose, indicating doubt. 'You refer, I assume, to Olympus? You can forget that – a piece of impossible science invented by impossible scientists enamoured of a young Aborigine woman.'

'Ships will be returning here soon,' I responded. 'The busy world of terrestrial necessity will break in on us. Then we shall regard this period – of exile, if you like – as a time of respite, when we were able to consider our lives and our destinies. Isn't that why we DOPs and YEAs came here? An unconsidered life is a wasted life.'

'Oh, please!' He gave a dry chuckle. 'You'll be telling me next that an unconsidered universe is a wasted universe.'

'That may indeed prove to be the case.' I felt I had scored a point, but he ignored it in pursuit of his gloomy thought.

'I fear that our destiny is to die here. Not that it matters greatly. But why can we not accept our fate with Senecan dignity? Why do we have to follow the scientists and imagine that that extinct volcano somewhere out there, out in that airless there, is a chunk of life, of consciousness, even?'

'Why, there is evidence—'

'My dear Jefferies, there's always evidence. I beg you not to afflict me with evidence! There's evidence for Atlantis and for Noah's flood and for fairies and for unidentified flying objects, and for a thousand impossibilities ... Are not these absurd beliefs merely unwitting admissions that our own consciousness is so circumscribed we desire to extend it through other means? Weren't the gods of the original Greek Olympus one such example, cooked up, as it were, to explain the inexplicable? I suspect that the universe, and the universes surrounding it, are really very simply comprehended, had we wit enough to manage the task.'

'We have wit enough. Our ascendancy over past centuries shows it.'

'You think so? What a comfortable lack of humility you do exhibit, Jefferies! I know you seek to do good, but heaven preserve us from those who mean well. Charles Darwin, a sensible man, admitted that the minds of mankind had evolved – if I recall his words correctly – from a mind as low as that of the lowest animal.'

Attempting a laugh, I said, 'The operative word there is evolved. The sum is continually ever greater than its parts. Give us credit, we are trying to exceed our limitations and to comprehend the universe. We'll get there one day.'

'I do not share your optimism. We have made no progress in our understanding of that curious continuity that we term life and death since – well, let's say, to be specific, because specificity is generally conceded to be desirable – since the Venerable Bede wrote his *Ecclesiastical History* some time in the seventh century. I trust you are familiar with this work?'

'No. I've not heard of the book.'

'The news has been slow to reach you, n'est ce pas? Let me quote, from my all too fallible memory, the Venerable

Bede's reflections on those grand questions we have been discussing. He says something to this effect. "When compared with the stretch of time unknown to us, O king, the present life of men on Earth is like the flight of a solitary sparrow through the hall where you and your companions sit in winter. Entering by one high window and leaving by another, while it is inside the hastening bird is safe from the wintery storm. But this brief moment of calm is over in a moment. It returns to the winter whence it came, vanishing for ever from your sight. Such too is man's life. Of what follows, of what went before, we are utterly ignorant."'

Sighing, I told Bateson I must return to my work.

As I walked away, he called to me, so that I turned back.

'You know what the temperature is out there, Jefferies?' He indicated the surface of Mars with a pale fluttering hand. 'I understand it's round about minus 76 degrees Celsius. Even colder than a dead body in its earthly grave! Nothing mankind could do would warm that ground up to comfortable temperate zone temperatures, eh? Do you imagine any great work of art, any musical composition, was ever created at minus 76 Celsius?'

'We must set a precedent, John,' I told him.

I left him alone on the upper gallery, gazing at the bleached landscape outside.

19

The R&A Hospital

On the following day, when I was resting, Dayo came to visit me again. He tried to persuade me to see what 'the computer people', as he called them, were doing. I could not resist his blandishments for ever, and got myself up.

Going with him to the control room, I found that Dayo was popular there too. He had been learning to work on the big quantputer with the mainly American contingent who staffed the machines. The striking patterns on his tiles for the Lower Ground had been devised using it.

The mainframe had originally been programmed to handle the running of the Martian outpost – its humidity, atmospheric pressure, chemical contents, temperature levels and so forth. Now all these factors were being handled by a single rejigged laptop quantputer.

I was astonished, but the bearded Steve Rollins, the man in charge of the programme under Arnold Poulsen, explained they had evolved a formula whereby interrelated factors could all be grouped under one easily computable formula. Our survival and comfort were being controlled by the laptop. The change-over had taken place at the 'X' hour, during a night some five months previously. No one had noticed a shade of difference, while the big mainframe had been freed for more ambitious things.

And what things! I had wondered why the control staff took so little interest in our forums and the utopian society. Here was the answer: they had been otherwise engaged.

At Dayo's prompting, Steve showed me the programme they were running. He spoke in an easy drawl.

'You may think this is unorthodox use of equipment,'

Steve said, stroking his whiskers with a gesture he had and grinning at me. 'But as that great old musician, Count Basie, said, "You just gotta keep on keeping on". If you regard science as a duel with nature, you must never drop your guard. Stuck here on this Ayers Rock in the sky, we must keep on keeping on or we stagnate. Guess you know that.'

'Guess I do.'

'As a kid I used to play a game called Sim Galaxy on my old computer. It produced simulations of real phenomena, from people to planetary systems. If you kept at it long enough, fighting entropy and natural disasters, it was possible to get to rule over a populated galaxy.'

Steve said that his team had adapted a more modest version of the game, into which they had fed all the quantputer records, sedulously kept, of every person and event on Mars. The simulation had become more and more accurate as the programme was refined. Every detail of our Mars habitation, every detail of each person in the habitation, was precisely represented in the simulation. They called the programme Sim White Mars.

We watched on a widescreen monitor. There people lived and moved and had their being. Our small Martian world was totally emulated; the one item missing was Olympus, a being as yet incomputable.

I fought against the suspicion that this was not a true emulation but a trick, until Steve mentioned casually that they were using a new modified quantputer that computed faster, fuzzier, than the old conventional quantputer – certainly than any of the quantcomps people carry around with them.

The scale of the thing made me feel dizzy. Dayo was immediately at hand, fetching me a stool.

In full colour, recognisable people went about their business, around the settlement and in the laboratory. They seemed to move in real time.

The scene flipped to a schoolroom, where Belle Rivers was talking with a jeuwu class of ten children. Steve moved a pointer on to Belle, touched a key, and at once a scroll of characteristics came up: Belle's birth date and place, her entire CV and many other details. They flashed on the screen and were gone at another touch of a key.

'We call these simulated objects and people emulations, they are so precise,' said Steve. 'To them, their world is perfectly real. They sure think and act like real.'

'But they are mere electronic images. They can't be said to think.'

Steve laughed. 'Guess they don't realise they're just a sequence of numbers and colours in a computer, if that's what you mean.' He added, in lower key, 'How often do we realise we're also just a sequence in another key?'

I said nothing.

The people on screen were now gathering in the main thoroughfare. This was recognisably the day the third marathon was held. There were the runners, many with false wings attached to them. There were the officials who ran the race. There were the crowds.

A whistle blew and the runners started forward, struggling for space, so closely were they packed, even as they had done weeks previously.

'All this takes real heavy puting power, even using the quantputer,' Steve said. 'That's why we are running some weeks behind real time. We're working on that problem.' The runners began to trot, jostling closely for position. 'I guess we'll catch up eventually.'

'Want to bet on who will win?' Dayo asked mischievously.

'You see this is a kind of rerun of the marathon,' Steve said. 'And now, I just tap on a couple of keys . . .'

He did so. The screen was filled with phantom creatures, grey skeletons with strange pumping spindles instead of legs, naked domes for heads, their teeth large and bared. The inhuman things pressed onwards, soundless, joyless . . . The Race of Death, I thought.

'We got the X-ray stuff off the hospital,' Steve said. 'It's spare diagnostic equipment . . .'

273

The skeletons streamed on, with ghostly grey buildings as background, racing through their silent transparent world.

Steve tapped his keyboard once more and the world on the screen became again the one we recognised as ours.

With a flash of humour, he said, 'You have your utopia, Tom. This is our baby. How do you like it?'

'But in the wrong hands . . .' I began. A feeling of nausea silenced me.

Dayo took my arm. 'I want you to watch yourself as an emulation, Tom. Please, Steve . . .'

Steve touched a couple of keys on his keyboard. The scene changed. An office block along the marathon course came into focus. Moving through the window, the emulation picked out a man and two women, standing close together, watching the runners pass their building. I recognised Cang Hai, Mary Fangold and myself.

My emulation clutched his head and went to the back of the room to sit on a sofa. Cang Hai came over to it and stood there in silence, looking down at its – my – bowed head. After a moment, I stirred myself, smiled weakly at Cang Hai, rose, and returned to the window to watch the runners.

'I don't remember doing that,' I said.

'The CV, Steve,' Dayo prompted.

The key. My details, my birth date and place, my CV. Momentarily my skeletal self was there, grey, drained of all but emptiness, long bony fingers clutching at my ostrich egg of skull. Then: 'Diagnosis: Suffers from untreated brain tumour'. Only later did it occur to me that had I died then, my emulation would have continued to live, at least for a while.

I found Steve gazing at me and stroking his beard. 'You better get yourself looked after, chum,' was all he said.

The old R&A hospital was greatly enlarged in order to cope with its new general functions. Entry was through an airlock, the hospital atmosphere being self-contained against external emergencies and slightly richer in oxygen than in the domes in order to promote feelings of well-being. Extensive new wards had been built and a nanotechnology centre added, where cell repair machines were housed.

I must confess to feeling nervous as I entered the doors. I was greeted warmly by the hospital personnel manager, Mary Fangold.

As we shook hands, her dark blue eyes scrutinised me with more than professional interest.

'You're in good hands here, Tom Jefferies,' she said. 'We are all admirers of your utopian vision, which is carried out in our hospital as far as is possible. I hope to take care of you personally. We are treating only a few persistent sore-throat and eye cases at present.

'We regard those who are ill and enter here less as patients than as teachers who bring with them an opportunity for us to study and repair illness. Our progress is less towards health than towards rationality, which brings health.'

When I remarked that, despite her kind sentiments, the old, the ageing, would become a burden, she denied it. No, she said, the burdens of old age had been greatly exaggerated in former times. The old and experienced, the DOPs, cost very little. On Earth, many of them had savings that they gradually released after retirement on travel and suchlike. Thus they contributed to society and the economy. Their demands were much fewer than were those of the young.

I asked her if she was keen to return to Earth, to practise there.

She smiled, almost pityingly. Not at all, was her answer. 'The elements in the formula have been reduced here to a manageable level.'

She was determined to remain on Mars in her interesting experimental situation, free of many diseases which plagued Earth, helping to bring about a utopian phase of human life. For her money, we could remain cut off for good! Were not working and learning the great pleasures for anyone of rational intelligence?

She and a nurse conducted me to a ward-lounge, where we sat over coffdrink gazing out of windows that showed simulated views of beach, palm trees and blue ocean, where windsurfers rode the breakers.

Continuing her discourse, Mary said that it was the young who were expensive. Child benefits, constant supervision and education, health care, the devastations of drink and drugs, and – at least on Earth – crime, all formed major items in any nation's financial regimen of expenditure. Contrary to the general consensus that children were a blessing, she maintained they were rather a curse; not only were they an expense, but they forced their parents to participate in a second childhood while rearing them. She regarded this as an irrational waste of years of young adulthood.

'It's true,' I answered, 'that most crime on Earth is committed by the young. Whereas, if I recall the statistic correctly, the over-seventies account for only 1.3 per cent of all arrests.'

'Yes. Mainly for dangerous driving, the occupational hazard of the age! Happily, we do not have that problem on Mars.'

We laughed together. But her laughter was rather abstracted. She began thinking aloud. Belle Rivers's jeuwu did not carry matters far enough. Although Mary had nothing against children per se, she would like to see them removed from their parents at birth, to be reared in institutions where every care would be lavished on them; protected from the amateurishness and eccentricity – if not downright indifference – of their parents, they would grow up much more reasonably. She repeated this phrase in a thoughtful manner. Much more reasonably . . .

Knowing that Mary Fangold had been disappointed by the establishment of the Birth Room, I asked her how she regarded the matter now.

'As a rational person, I accept the Birth Room as an

experiment. I do not oppose the Birth Room. Indeed, I permit my midwives to go there when summoned. However, its function is undoubtedly divisive. The division between the sexes is increased. The role of the father is curtailed.'

'Do you not think that the important mother-baby bond is strengthened by the Birth Room procedures? Are we not right to encourage birthing to become a ceremony? The role of the father is enhanced by the celebration when he is again united with his wife?'

'Ah, now, there you should say husband rather than father. Men favour the husbandly role above that of a father. I will speak plainly to you. The one reason why I did not oppose the Birth Room is that the new mother is given a week's freedom from the importunings of the male. You perhaps would not credit how many men insist on sexual union again, immediately after their wives have delivered, when their vaginas are still in a tender state. The regulations of the Birth Room protect them from that humiliating pain.'

'You must see the worst of human nature in hospital.'

'The worst and the best. We see lust, yes, and fear – and courage. The spectrum of human nature.' After a pause, she added, 'We still have women who prefer to come here to hospital to give birth, and have their husbands with them.'

'But increasingly fewer as time goes by, I imagine?'

'We shall see about that.' Her lips tightened and she turned to summon a nurse.

After a while, Mary said she had a vision of what life could be. For her, Olympus the Living Being (as she phrased it) was an inspiration. Its age must surely be a guarantee of its wisdom, its eons of isolation a promoter of thought. I questioned that. 'Eons of isolation? I would think they might as easily promote madness. Could you endure being alone for long?'

Her glance was humorous and questioning. 'You're really alone, Tom, aren't you? What may be good for the vast living being may not be so good for you . . .'

She would like to see a society where the young were supported financially until their eighteenth birthday, in order to 'find themselves', as she put it. Only then would they be put to work for the good of the society that had nourished them.

At the other end of the scale the compulsory retirement of men and women at the age of seventy-five would be abolished. Molecular technology had reached a point where the curse of Alzheimer's disease had been banished and both sexes lived healthily well into their early hundreds – barring accidents. It was expected that the class known as the Megarich would live for two centuries. Meditech, she said, had accomplished much of recent decades, although the time when humans lived for 500 years – an opportunity to learn true wisdom, she said – was still far in the future. Say twenty years ahead, given the peace they enjoyed on Mars. Longevity would become inheritable.

When I asked her what pleasure there would be in a lifespan of 500 years, Mary regarded me curiously.

'You tease me, Tom! You of all people, to ask that! Why, given five centuries, you would be able fully to enjoy and appreciate your own intelligence, with which you are naturally endowed. Growing out of the baser emotions, you would achieve true rationality and experience the pleasures of untroubled intellect. You would live to see the perfection of the world to which you had contributed so much. You'd become, would you not, an authority on it?'

I asked playfully, 'The baser emotions? Which are they?'

As she leaned towards me to fit a light harness on my head, I caught a breath of her perfume. It surprised me.

'I don't mean love, if that's what you imply. Love can be ennobling. You pay too little heed to your emotional needs, Tom, do you understand?' Her deep blue eyes looked into mine.

While this discussion was taking place, the nurse was busy securing a cable to my wrist, making sure that it fitted comfortably where a tiny needle entered a vein. The other end of the cable ran to a computer console where a technician sat, his back to me. It in turn was linked with the nanotank.

'What is happening in surgical advance,' Mary was saying, 'is essentially in line with your reforming principles. The technology has developed because of a gradual change in public attitudes. Notably, the dissociation of the acceptance of pain from surgery, which began with the discovery of ether anaesthesia halfway through the nineteenth century. You, similarly, wish to separate the association of aggression from society, if I understand you aright.'

Before I could agree or disagree Mary rushed on to say that, as we talked, the computer was analysing the findings of the nanobots that had penetrated my system to check on the concentration of salts, sugars and ATP in the renegade cells of my brain – to, in short, perform a biopsy. The quantputer would order them to redirect the energies of malignant cells, or else to eliminate them.

'So the words pain and knife no longer—' I began. But a curious light was streaming in from I knew not where. I could not trace its source. Perhaps it was a flower, temporarily obscuring my view, as if I were a bee entering it for honey, for pollen, burrowing, burrowing, among the white waves of petals, endless white waves, festive but somehow deadly. With them, a dull scent, an unreal buzzing, the two of them interfused.

As if new senses had roused themselves . . . In the middle of them, a dull orange-tinted stain that moved, weeping through puny mouths as it sucked its way onward. But the holy rollers were pressing forward, extinguishing it to the sound of – sound of what? Trumpets? Honey? Geraniums? It was so fast I could not tell.

Then the light and sound were gone, only the endlessness of white waves remaining, churning over in a great ocean of confused thought. Antonia's face? Her nearness? Mary's lips, eyes? A sense of great loss . . .

'—spring to mind,' I finished. I felt as weak as if I had

been away on a long swim. I could hardly focus on those violet-coloured eyes looking into mine.

'It's all over,' said Mary Fangold, kindly, stroking my hand. 'The nanobots have removed your tumour. Now you will be well again. But you must rest awhile. I have a neat little ward waiting for you, next to my apartment.'

She came to me quietly at the first hour of the night, when the sigh of air circulation fell to a whisper. Her lips had been reddened. Her hair lay about her shoulders. Her pale breasts showed through a semi-transparent nightdress. She stood by my bedside, asking if I slept, knowing well the answer.

'Time for a little physiotherapy,' she murmured.

I sat up. 'Come in with me, Mary.'

Slipping her garment from her body, she stood there naked. I kissed the bush of dark hair on her mons veneris, and pulled her into the bed. There we were in joy, all night, our limbs interlocked, hers and mine. At times it seemed to us that we were back on the great fecund Earth, rolling on its course with its ever changing mantle of blue skies and cloud and its restless oceans.

I remained in hospital for a week, indifferent to what was happening elsewhere. Every night, at the first hour, Mary came to me. We sated ourselves with each other. By day she was again the rational, professional person I had known until then, until the revelation of her lovely body.

During my recuperation period, Cang Hai visited me, accompanied by her precocious child, Alpha. And many other visitors, Youssef Choihosla among them.

On one visit, finding that I looked perfectly well, Cang Hai ventured to ask me why it was that my late wife had not undergone nanosurgery for her cancer. I was mortified to feel that I had ceased, or almost ceased, to mourn the death of Antonia.

'My distrust of religion springs in part from this. Antonia was a Christian Scientist all her life. She was brought up in her parents' creed. She held that her cancer could be healed by prayer. Nothing would persuade her other-wise.

'I could not force her,' I said. 'She had every right to her beliefs, however fatal.'

A tear trickled from under the neat epicanthic fold of Cang Hai's eye. 'You surely can't believe that still, Tom.' But I believed I caught her thinking, even as she wiped the tear away, that some good had come from my dear wife's death, whereby I had sublimated grief by striving to change society.

Little Alpha liked to be told stories of bikers and their gang warfare in the days before I was born. In the under-privileged part of the world where my boyhood had been spent, it was sometimes possible to obtain a magazine entitled *Biker Wars*, which I had greatly relished at the time.

As I was telling the child one such story, we were interrupted by a tiny cry, something between the bleat of a goat and the shrill of a gull.

''Scuse me, unkie,' said the child. 'My little Yah-Yah needs attention.'

She brought forth from the basket she was carrying what appeared to be a small cage. It contained a kind of big-eyed red animal. Alpha showed it to me when she had attended to its needs. So I had my first close look at a tammy.

'Crispin gave it to me,' she said, with pride.

The men and women in the fire prevention force had been rendered virtually unemployed by the success of the Sim White Mars operation. Rather than remain idle they had cannibalised some of their equipment, making an improved version of a toy that had enjoyed a vogue on Earth many decades previously.

In Alpha's cage was a small VR pet. It was born and it grew, constantly needing feeding, cleaning and loving care from the child who owned it. If neglected, the pet could die or 'escape' from its cage. In adolescence, it became rather rebellious and needed tactful handling. Con-veniently, at this age a pet of the opposite sex entered the cage. With some guidance from the small owner, the two pets could mate and eventually bring forth another generation of pet.

Time inside the VR cage had been speeded up. The lifespan of a pet was rarely more than twenty-eight days. The far-sighted leader of the fire prevention team had designed the computer pets as a learning toy. When I eventually spoke to this lady, she said, 'Belle Rivers recognises that the children need love. She is less ready to recognise that children also need to give love, to own love-objects, something other than human, to help in developing their own personalities. Kids with tammies will grow up into caring adults – and have fun meanwhile.'

It was far-sighted, but not far-sighted enough. Every kid wanted a tammy. The domes were maddened by the moans, howls and chirps of a wide range of the VR pets. Concerts and plays were ruined by the incessant demands of the toys in the audience. Eventually, tammies had to be banned from such occasions, although this meant that children excluded themselves, lest their charges perished . . . I hated imposing bans, but the government of behaviour was an inescapable part of civilised society.

Tammies next became banned at mealtimes, so that children might associate properly with adults. Adminex had in mind here a passage from Thomas More's *Utopia*, in which he says, 'During meals, the elders engage in decent conversation with the young, omitting topics sad and unpleasant. They do not monopolise the conversation for they freely hear what the young have to say. The young are encouraged to talk in order to give proof of the talents which show themselves more easily during meals.'

This was not always successful. The elders sometimes grew tired of childish prattle. The atmosphere was always soothed by music – not Beza's music, but something much more anaemic, suited to our austere diet.

20

A Collective Mind

I managed to drag myself away from the raptures of Mary Fangold and her delicious physiotherapy. Although I was back in the busy world, finding a juster society slowly developing, act by act, I wished to give Mary a present.

Seeking out Sharon Singh, I asked to see her collection of rock crystal pieces. She displayed them for me, meanwhile gazing up at my face from under her dark fringe of hair. Among the many shapes, I chose one that, in its finely detailed folds, closely resembled a vagina.

Giving it to me, Sharon said, 'Isn't it curious that the cold pressures of Mars should create such a hot little thing?'

She gave a tinkling laugh.

Olympus – now more frequently referred to as Chimborazo; Kathi Skadmorr had won that argument – had taken hold of people's imaginations. Discussion groups met regularly to chew over the riddle. It was a subject for argument in public and across the Ambient.

Most Ambient users found it hard to accept that Chimborazo could be conscious. They were daunted by the thought of that great solitary intellect sitting permanently upon a planet that had become hostile to life. What was it waiting for? was a frequently asked question.

Certainly not a bombardment by CFC gas, was one answer.

The parallel between Chimborazo's shelter for collaborating species and our own situation in the domes was quickly seized on. Fondness replaced fear as a response to its existence.

Dreiser's remark about a stack of thoughts 23 kilometres high kept returning to me. Also there was the speculation about what one might encounter if one prized up the protective shell and looked – went? was drawn? – inside.

I believe that Hawkwood's interview was a great persuasive force in the establishment of our utopian constitution.

One interesting theory I heard discussed on my return to society was that Chimborazo's power of consciousness was far greater than we had suspected. Its attention had become directed across the gulfs of matrix to where it sensed other minor flames of consciousness. It had kept the minds of terrestrials busied with ambitions to visit Mars in order to lure them to provide it with company.

These were speculations without much ground in fact. However, when I contacted Dreiser and Kathi, I found that they too were in the midst of a welter of troubled speculation. Their new findings presented us with new problems. I moved Adminex to call a meeting in Hindenburg Hall at once.

A whole phalanx of scientists attended. The meeting was crowded. Children were welcomed. Their tammies had to be left behind.

Dreiser began speaking without preamble. 'We have a confusion of opinions here. You have every right to hear them. In some cases they amount to serious disputes between us.

'The fact is that, over the last week, we have observed no less than twenty-seven glitches in the superfluid of the ring. The interpretation of these phenomena is unclear as yet. When examined closely, the build-up to these glitches has a curious and complicated structure. Most of us have therefore reached the conclusion that the glitches are not caused by HIGMOs after all.

'The question then is: What does cause them?

'I am going to ask Jon Thorgeson to give his point of view.'

Thorgeson rose. As when he had spoken in public before, he began nervously but soon got into his stride.

'I don't really expect you non-scientists to understand all the nuances of the situation. Maybe you've heard before that there is something going wrong in the ring. There may be stray vortices in the superfluid which lead to spurious effects. I believe that to be the case. It is the obvious explanation.

'Before we go any further, or develop any crazy ideas, we have to turn off the refrigeration units so that the superfluid can return to its normal fluid state. Okay, so then we examine the tube thoroughly and clean it. That is a meticulous job. Then we switch the refrigeration on again, turning it up very very slowly, so that no vortices can develop.

'It's just lousy luck that this procedure will take about a year. By that time the ships will be back, I don't doubt – and their vibrations would spoil everything. We have to take that chance.

'To be honest, I have a suspicion that the irresponsible excavations of your Lower Ground may be the cause of everything . . .'

He sat down and folded his arms across his chest.

While he was talking I noticed Kathi shaking her head in mute disagreement, but it was Charles Bondi who spoke next, in flat denial of the last speaker.

'I'm sorry, but that's all arrant nonsense. Vortices in the superfluid are well understood. They would produce quite different effects from the patterns we have observed. You need only simple calculations to see that it is so.

'Besides which, we have no spare year to play around in. We must find a solution for today. Leo Anstruther made the plea for White Mars, but somehow he was ruled out as Administrator of the UN Department for the Preservation of Mars. When the ships return they will probably be obsessed once more with the idea of terraforming Mars. It makes our situation an urgent one.'

A YEA technician rose and said, 'We don't want to let a plea of urgency destroy understanding. I'd say we should haul off and wait to see what comes next. I mean, what the ring comes up with. Seems we have run out of HIGMOs this week. We should keep watch on next week.'

Georges Souto spoke next. 'I'm largely in agreement with the last speaker. For one thing, we don't know what exactly is going on Downstairs. Maybe they've turned their back on the whole notion of matrix travel. Maybe they're never coming back. Think of that!'

That the audience was thinking of it was apparent from the general exclamation that went up at Souto's words.

Souto continued. 'It could be that the conventional hypothesis that HIGMOs were distributed randomly and uniformly throughout the universe is just plain wrong. Our findings imply that the distribution of HIGMO encounters with the ring may be extremely clumped. The explanation for seeing all these HIGMOs together in such a short space of time is simply that we're passing through a HIGMO shower, okay?'

Even as he spread wide his hands in explanation, someone shouted out that he was talking nonsense.

Suung Saybin spoke from the audience. 'Could all these glitches that you're worrying about be caused by one and the same HIGMO being trapped in Mars's gravitational field, so that it oscillates back and forth in the ring?'

'That's not possible,' Souto answered and was echoed by several other voices.

'All right, smartarses, it was just a suggestion,' said Saybin tartly.

Dreiser said, 'Just to make it clear, I can show you what we actually saw in our screens.'

A large 3vid hung in the air above the dais, as Dreiser projected it. The image was as severe as a text-book diagram. It showed, against the fuzzy grey background, a colourless blur that wavered before shooting up a step halfway along, then continuing on a straight horizontal course.

'The phase is the vertical,' Dreiser explained. 'The horizontal is time. In this case, it's something like 0.5 of a nanosecond from one side of the screen to the other. The step up is 4π. As you see, the signal is not at all clear. But the step function makes it plain that something passed through the ring from above to below. Otherwise the step would have been down by the same 4π. The oscillation before the step becomes more complex throughout our series of glitches.'

A silence fell over the proceedings.

The image faded from overhead.

Kathi spoke quietly from her seat, without getting up. 'So you're all off track. Forget the HIGMO question. The glitches are being caused by Chimborazo itself.'

Laughter came from some scientists as well as the audience.

'Chimborazo is causing the glitches,' repeated Kathi, as if the statement was made more understandable by being recast.

This time the laughter was more mocking.

'Let's hear what the lady's case is,' Dreiser interjected. 'Give her a chance. What's on your mind, Kathi?'

She flashed him a grateful look before standing to say, 'Arnold Poulsen is experimenting to see whether his 16-hertz sound oscillations will cause people to be more conciliatory towards each other. As yet, he has nothing conclusive.

'Over the last few months, however, I have become convinced that we are experiencing a genuine improvement in personal relations. I notice the difference even in myself.' At this there was brief laughter.

'I've become equally convinced that this has nothing to do with Arnold's experiment. Or, for that matter – sorry, Tom – with the utopia effect. No, it's Chimborazo working on us, the Watchtower of the Universe.' She paused to let this sink in, confronting her audience with arms akimbo.

'We know there is a powerful consciousness in that being. We get a CPS, and this has now been confirmed on an ordinary savvyometer, which we modified to accommodate an extremely low frequency range. Our rapidly advancing friend has plenty of awareness right enough!'

She paused as we all took a deep breath at that.

'We know too – or we think we do – that Chimborazo is a symbiotic and epiphytic being; all its component life forms have learned to cooperate rather than compete. That strong cohesive influence appears to work satisfactorily.

'I do not think it would be at all surprising if this "influence", whatever it is, has had its effect on our own human conscious behaviour. We know that quantum effects can hold over great distances. Quantum entanglements between photons have been observed to stretch over a hundred thousand kilometres at least. Probably there is no limit.'

'Sounds to me like fifteenth-century mysticism,' remarked Thorgeson. '*The Will of God.*'

'Well,' Kathi said challengingly, in something like her old style, 'so what does that prove? Not all fifteenth-century mystics were fools!'

Dreiser, ignoring this exchange, said to Kathi. 'You talk about your Chimborazo – if I'm forced to use that label – having a powerful consciousness. Would you care to clarify that for us?'

Several of the men sitting behind him showed signs of discontent. They evidently did not like the respect Dreiser – the great Dreiser Hawkwood – paid this newcomer.

Once he had given Kathi the floor, she went happily on.

'Well, we still aren't sure about consciousness. It's a riddle awaiting solution. The CPS device is simply a passive detector, much as a geiger counter used to register radioactivity. It does not in any way alter consciousness. It registers the presence of consciousness by the effect of consciousness on a quantum state-reduction phenomenon – let's say on some coherent quantum superposition involving a large number of calcium ions.

'What we do know is that consciousness in an entity can detectably affect the reduction of a quantum state, and can be affected by it. That's how a mentatrope works, after all. The quantum superposition in a mentatrope is influenced by the presence of consciousness as well as influencing consciousness. So it's not at all unreasonable that consciousness might affect the quantum coherence in our superfluid ring.'

Willa Mendanadum spoke from the audience. 'Excuse me, Kathi, but a mentatrope contains no superfluid. The quantum superposition is between different calcium ion displacements. It's much the same as the superpositions of electron displacements in a quantputer.'

'I'm aware of that,' Kathi replied. 'But no quantputer gives a reading on a mentatrope. The organisation of calcium ions in a mentatrope is of a completely different character from that in a quantputer – much more like the superfluid in our ring, where the total mass involved begins to be significant.'

Willa was adamant. Her slight figure seemed to vibrate with scorn. 'Sorry, Kathi, I know you're bidding fair to be a guru and all that, but there is absolutely no evidence of any similarity between this ring and a mentatrope. The scale's completely different, for one thing. The geometry is different. The materials are different. The purposes are different.'

'But—'

'Let me finish, please. I must make the point that there is absolutely no evidence that the proximity of a conscious human being has any effect whatsoever on the functioning of the ring. In fact, as I understand it, the argon 36 in the ring's superfluid is geared specifically to detect the monopole gravitational effects of a HIGMO – not of a brainwave!'

Kathi seemed unmoved. She said, 'We don't know what the appropriate quantum superposition parameters are for Chimborazo. Chimborazo is built on an entirely different scale from us humans. Very possibly it has the ability to tune its own internal mental activities so as to relate specifically to the ring.'

'Absurd!' exclaimed Jimmy Gonzales Dust from the back row of boffins.

She turned to him, saying mildly, 'Absurd, is it? For an

289

alien intellect twenty-five kilometres high? How dare we presume to suggest its limitations?'

'But you are speculating wildly,' Jimmy protested.

'I'd say that at this juncture, a little wild speculation is in order,' Dreiser said. 'Continue, Kathi.'

'My speculation is based on fact, by the way,' Kathi said, with something of her old tartness in her voice. I remembered her fondness for correcting those who were basically on her side. What her relationship was with Dreiser was difficult to guess. 'We know that a mentatrope works, but not why. The discovery of the Reynaud-Damien effect was an accident. The implication was that consciousness has a subtle influence on the reduction of a quantum state.'

'I don't accept that, Kathi,' Jimmy said, cutting in. 'However, one result of the French guys' researches was the development of a CPS detector.'

Her eyes flashed irritation, but she said with disarming mildness, 'And the CPS detector led to the development of the mentatrope for psychiatric purposes. Thanks for your contribution, Jimmy. At least we do know that a mentatrope has something in common with the ring. In each case the important element is a quantum state-reduction phenomenon. I've looked into the history of the subject. You people, like Jimmy here, are too sunk in ring-technology to remember where it all comes from.'

Jimmy broke in indignantly. 'We all know about quantum state-reduction. That was sorted out early this century with the definitive Walter Heitelman experiment.'

Kathi studied him for a moment, gave a brief nod, smiled, and said, changing tack, 'And there were some ideas put forth last century, suggesting various possible connections between consciousness and quantum state-reduction. They all petered out because of lack of experimental confirmation, in most cases because of a direct conflict with observation. But the general idea itself still remains, at least in principle. There were heated discussions in the scientific literature, most of it forgotten.

'I'd say that if you put these ideas together – bearing

in mind that the glitches in the ring are indeed state-reduction effects – there's a plausible case for a connection between the ring glitches we've recorded and Chimborazo's consciousness.'

Thorgeson gave a curt laugh. 'You'll be telling us next that the ring will reveal "a soul".'

'Souls are even harder to define than consciousness. But, after all – why not?'

Clapping his hands, Dreiser interposed. 'The next obvious move is to perform a mentatropic examination of the ring. I agree with Kathi that these glitches we've been observing imply that the Watcher of the Universe has already transferred some "consciousness effects" to the ring. We must find out if that is the case.

'And, by the way, this notion that the ring is "pregnant" or "getting ready to conceive" is just a silly joke – which Jimmy probably started!

'We do not yet understand the powers of Chimborazo. We have discussed this endlessly, and think the life form is probably benign and even defensive. Its collective mind may be immensely powerful. Maybe it could wipe out all our minds with one blast of directed thought; but shelled animals are generally pacific, if terrestrial examples are anything to go by.' He paused to let this sink in.

'One explanation for its camouflage may be that it long ago sensed other consciousnesses on Earth – even across the great matrix distances separating the two planets – and was fearful. Despite its great bulk, it concealed itself as best it could.'

Someone in the audience asked what Dreiser would do if it was found that the ring was acquiring elements of consciousness.

He stroked his little moustache thoughtfully before answering. 'If that does turn out to be the case, we'll have to rethink the whole Smudge experiment. To turn off the refrigeration would be tantamount to murder. Or, let's say, abortion . . . It might also be dangerous with Chimborazo towering above us! It's a dilemma . . .

'The ring would no longer be a viable tool in the search for the Omega Smudge. The UN authorities, supposing they still exist, would not be happy about that. On the other hand, we would stand on the brink of another great discovery. We would be on the way to understanding what consciousness is all about – what causes it, sustains it . . .'

Kathi had a word to add. 'Just to respond to Charles Bondi's earlier remark. Of course, if the ring were to be kept going, there could never be any terraforming permitted . . .'

My thoughts were so overwhelmed by speculation that I could not sleep. I was walking down East Spider (late Dyson Street) in dim-out, when the unexpected happened. Two masked men jumped from the shadows, armed with either pick helves or baseball bats or similar weapons.

'This is for you, you bloody titox, for ruining religion and normal human life!' one shouted as they pitched into me. I managed to strike one of them in the face. The other caught me a blow across the base of my skull. I fell.

I seemed to fall for ever.

When I roused, I was in the hospital again, being wheeled along a corridor. I tried to speak but could not.

Cang Hai and Alpha were waiting for me. Alpha was sitting on the floor, watching her mother bounce a ball again and again against the wall. I saw how Cang was still something of a child, using the excuse of her daughter to play childishly. She stopped the bouncing rather guiltily, scooped Alpha up in her arms, and approached me.

'My dear little daughter,' I tried to say.

'You need rest, Tom, dear. You'll be okay and we'll be here.'

Mary Fangold came briskly along, said hello to Alpha and directed my carriage into a small room, talking meanwhile, ignoring Cang Hai. The room became full of tiny specks of light, towards which I seemed to float.

With an effort I roused, to see Cang Hai close by. A spark of anger showed in her eyes. She said, determinedly and loudly, 'Anyhow, as I was saying, my Other in Chengdu told me of a dream. An orchestra was playing—'

'Perhaps we'd better leave Mr Jefferies alone just now,' said Mary, sweetly. 'He needs quiet. He will be fully restored in a day or so.'

'I'll go soon enough, thank you. You could use that symphony orchestra as a symbol of cooperative evolution. Many men and women, all with differing lives and problems, and many different instruments – they manage to sublimate their individualities to make beautiful harmony. But in this dream, they were playing in a field and eating a meal at the same time. Don't ask me how.'

'Would you like a shower, Mr Jefferies?' Mary asked. I gestured to her to let Cang Hai rattle on for a moment.

'And you see, Tom, I thought about the first ever restaurant – no doubt it was outdoors – which opened in China centuries ago. It was a cooperative act making for happiness. You had to trust strangers enough to eat with them. And you had to eat food cooked by a cook who maybe you couldn't see, trusting that it was not poisoned . . . Wasn't that restaurant a huge step forward in social evolution . . . ?'

'Really, thank you, I think we've had enough of your dreams, dear,' said Mary Fangold.

'Who's this rude lady, Mumma?' Alpha asked.

'Nobody really, my chick,' said Cang Hai and marched indignantly from the room.

I managed to say goodbye after she had gone. My head was clearing. Mary looked sternly down at me and said, 'You're delivered into my care again, Tom!' She suppressed a joyous laugh, pressing her fingers to her lips. 'I hope all this irrational chatter did not disturb you. Your adopted daughter seems to have the notion that she is in touch with someone in – where was it? Chengdu?'

'I too have my doubts about her phantom friend. But it makes her rather lonely life happier.'

Wheeling me forward, she tapped my name into the registry. 'Mmm, same ward as before . . .'

She gave me a winning smile. 'There I have to disagree with you. We must try to banish the irrational from our lives. You have fallen victim to the irrational. We need so much to be governed by reason. Most of your gallant efforts are directed towards that end.'

She wagged her finger at me. 'You really mustn't make private exceptions. That's not the right route to a perfect world.

'But there, it's not for me to lecture you!'

The attack on me had shattered a vertebra at the top of my spine. The nanobots replaced it with an artificially grown bone-substitute. But a nerve had been damaged that, it appeared, was beyond repair, at least within the limited resources of our hospital.

I stayed for ten days, in that ward I had so recently left, to enjoy once more Mary's pleasant brand of physiotherapy. I lived for those hours when we were in bed together.

Perhaps all ideas of utopia were based on that sort of closeness. In the dark I thought of George Orwell's dystopia, *Nineteen Eighty-Four*. Orwell set forth there his idea of utopia: a shabby room, in which he could be alone with a girl . . .

Mary looked seriously at me. 'When your assailants are captured, I have drugs in my pharmaceutical armoury that will ensure they never do anything thuggish again . . .' She nodded reassuringly. 'As we agree, we want no prisons here. As my captive, you naturally want me to keep you happy.'

'Passionately I want it,' I said. We kissed then, passionately.

I practised walking with my arm on a nurse's arm. My balance was always to be uncertain; from then on, I found it convenient to walk with a stick.

I rested one further day in hospital. As I was leaving its doors, Mary bid me farewell. 'Go and continue your excellent work, my dear Tom. Do not trouble your mind by seeking revenge on those who attacked you. Their reason failed them. They must fear a rational society; but their kind are already becoming obsolete.'

'I'm not so sure of that, Mary. What kind are we?'

Laughing, she clucked in a motherly way and squeezed my arm. She was her professional self, and on duty.

Suddenly she embraced me. 'I love you, Tom! Forgive me. You're our prophet! We shall soon live,' she said, 'into an epoch of pure reason.'

I thought, as I hobbled back to Cang Hai with my stick, of that wonderful satire of Jonathan Swift's, popularly known as *Gulliver's Travels*, and of the fourth book where Gulliver journeys among the cold, uninteresting, indifferent children of reason, the Houyhnhnms.

If our carefully planned new way of life bred such a species, we would be entering on chilly and sunless territory.

Where would Mary's love be in those days?

Yet would not that rather bloodless life of reason be better than the world of the bludgeon, the old unregenerate world, continually ravaged by war and its degradations in one region or another? My father, whose altruism I had inherited, had left his home country to serve as a doctor in the eastern Adriatic, among the poor in the coastal town of Splon. There he set up a clinic. In that clinic, he treated all alike, Catholic, Orthodox or Protestant.

My father believed that the West, with its spirit of enquiry, was moving towards an age of reason, however faltering was its progress.

In Splon I passed many years of my boyhood, unaffected by the poverty surrounding us, ranging free in the mountains behind the town. My elder sister, Patricia, was my great friend and ally, a big-hearted girl with an insatiable curiosity about nature. We used to swim through the currents of our stretch of sea to gain a small island called Isplan. Here Pat and I used to pretend to be shipwrecked, as if in prodromoic rehearsal for being stranded on another planet.

Civil war broke out in the country when I was nine years old, in 2024. My father and mother refused to leave with other foreign nationals. They were blind to danger, seeing it as their duty to stay and serve the innocent people of Splon. However, they sent Pat away to safety, to live with an aunt. For a while, I missed her greatly.

Civil war is a cancer. The innocent people of Splon took sides and began to kill and torture each other. Their pretext was that they were being treated unfairly and demanded only social justice, but behind this veneer of reasonable argument, calculated to dull their consciences and win them sympathy abroad, lay a mindless cruelty, a wish to destroy those whose religious beliefs they did not share.

They set about destroying not merely the vulnerable living bodies of their former neighbours, the new enemies, but their enemies' homes as well, together with anything of historic or aesthetic worth.

The bridge over the River Splo was one of the few examples of local architecture worthy of preservation. Built by the Ottomans five centuries earlier, it had featured on the holiday brochures distributed by the tourist office. People came from all over the world to enjoy the graceful parabola of Splon's old bridge.

As tanks gathered in the mountains behind the town, as an ancient warship appeared offshore, as mortars and artillery were dug in along the road to town, that famous Splo Bridge was available for target practice. It fell soon, its rubble and dust cascading into the Splo.

The enemy made no attempt to enter the town. Their soldiers loitered smoking and boozing some metres down the road. They laid cowardly siege to Splon, setting about destroying it, not for any strategic purpose but merely because they had hatred and shells to spare.

Anyone trying to escape from Splon was liable to capture. As prisoners, they suffered barbaric torture. Women were raped and mutilated. Children were raped and used as target practice.

Occasionally, one such captive, broken, was allowed to crawl back to Splon to give a report on these barbarities, in order that the fear and tension of the starving inhabitants might be increased. Often such survivors died in my father's little surgery, beyond his aid.

The great organisations of the Western world stood back and watched dismayed at the slaughter on their TV screens. In truth they were puzzled as to how to quell civil war, where the will to fight and die was so strong and the reason for the struggle so hard to comprehend.

During that year of siege we lived for the most part in cellars. Sanitation was improvised. Food was scarce. I would venture out with my friend Milos under cover of darkness to fish off the harbour wall. More than once hidden snipers fired at us, so that we had to crawl to safety.

Starvation came early to Splon, followed by disease. To bury the dead in the rocky soil, exposed to snipers on all sides, was not easy – a hasty business at best. I spent some days away from the town, lying in long grass, trying to kill a rabbit with a stone from a catapult. Once, when I returned, triumphant, with a dead animal for the pot, it was to find my mother dying of cholera. My sorrow and guilt haunt me still.

I can never forget my father's cries of misery and remorse. He howled like a dog over mother's dead body.

Exhaustion set in among the struggling factions. The war finally petered out. Days came when no shells were fired at us.

A party of the enemy arrived in a truck, waving white flags, to announce an armistice. The leader of the party was a smartly uniformed captain, wearing incongruous white gloves. Quite a young man, but already bemedalled.

It was the chance our men had waited for. They rushed the truck. They set upon the soldiers with rifles and knives and bayonets, and carved up the party, all but the captain, into bloody pieces. They rubbed the face of one man into the broken glass from the vehicle's windscreen. They set fire to the truck. I stood in the broken street, watching the massacre, enjoying it, thrilling to the screams of those about to die. It was like a movie, like one of my Biker stories.

The captain was dragged into a burned-out factory down the road. He was stripped of his gloves and his uniform, made naked. Some of Splon's women were allowed – or encouraged – to hack off his testicles and penis and ram them into his mouth. They beat him to death with iron bars.

I was curious to see what was going on in the burned-out factory. A man stopped me from entering. Other boys got in. They told me about the atrocity afterwards.

Next day, a Red Cross truck rolled into town. My father and I were evacuated. My father had lost his will to live, dying in his sleep some weeks later. That was in a hospital in the German city of Mannheim.

While I was laid low in hospital these past memories returned vividly to mind. I was forced to relive them as I had rarely done before. In fear of the horrors of that awful period, I recognised my strong desire for a better ordered society, and for a time and place where reason reigned secure.

Mary and I sat up in bed. She listened sympathetically as I told my tale. Tears, pure and clear, escaped from her eyes and ran down her cheeks.

Perhaps the riddle of Olympus had brought on my horrors. The mood under that vast carapace could be one of regret, rage even, at the way the life forms had had to imprison themselves in order to survive as the old free life died. A billion years of rage and regret . . . ?

Several visitors came while I was recovering. They included Benazir Bahudur, the silent teacher of children.

She said, 'Until you recover fully your ability to move,

dear Tom, I will dance for you to remind you of movement.'

She danced a dance very similar to the one I had watched once before. In her long skirt, with her bare arms, she performed her dance of step and gesture, as supple and subtle as deep water. Life is like this and this. There is so much to be enjoyed . . .

It was beautiful and immensely touching. 'You manage to dance without music,' I said.

'Oh, I hear the music very clearly. It comes through my feet, not my ears.'

Another welcome visitor was Kathi Skadmorr. She slouched in wearing her Now overalls and perched on the end of the bed, smiling. 'So this is where utopias end – in a hospital bed!'

'Some begin here. You do a lot of thinking. I was thinking of dystopias. Presumably you think about quantum physics and consciousness all the time . . .'

She frowned. 'Don't be silly, Tom. I also think a lot about sex, although I never perform it. In fact, I spend much time sitting in the lotus position staring at a blank white wall. That's something I learned from you lot. It seems to help. And I also recall "I saw a new heaven and a new Earth: for the first heaven and the first Earth were passed away." Isn't that what you Christians say?'

'I'm not a Christian, Kathi, and doubt whether the guy who wrote those words was either.'

She leaned forward. 'Of course I am fascinated by scientific theory – but only because I would like to get beyond it. The blank white wall is a marvellous thing. It looks at me. It asks me why I exist. It asks me what my conscious mind is doing. Why it's doing it. It asks if there are whole subjects the scientists of our day cannot touch. Maybe daren't touch.'

I asked her if she meant the paranormal.

'Oh, the way you use that label. Tom, dearest, my hero, your adopted daughter whom you so neglect – she has inexplicable, paranormal, experiences all the time.

They're part of her normal life. Nobody can account for them. We need to reconceptualise our thought, as you have reconceptualised society. Stop clinging to frigid reason.

'Chimborazo is a million times stranger than Cang Hai's world, yet we think we can account for it within science, can accommodate it within our perceptual *Umwelt*. Yet all the time it's performing miracles. Turning a sack of superfluid into a conscious entity . . . That's a miracle worthy of Jesus Christ. Yet Dreiser doesn't turn a hair of his moustache . . .

'Anyhow, I must be going. I just called to bring you this little present.' From a pocket of her overalls she produced a photocube. In it a complex coil slowly revolved, its strands studded with seedlike dots. I held it up to the light and asked her what it was.

'They've analysed one of the exteroceptors they hacked off Chimborazo. This is just an enlarged snippet of its version of a DNA structure. You see how greatly it is more complex than human DNA? Four strands needed to hold its inheritance. The doubled double helix.'

When I was up and about I went to see Choihosla again, this time taking the trouble to knock at his door. We talked these matters over. I even ventured to speculate whether mankind was experiencing a million years of regret that it had achieved consciousness, with the burdens that accompanied it.

'We all suffer on occasions from the dark soul of the night,' he said.

'You mean the dark night of the soul, Youssef.'

'No, no. Look outside! I mean the dark soul of the night.'

Was it the old quirky sage, George Bernard Shaw, who had said that utopia had been achieved only on paper? Perhaps it had been achieved too in Steve Rollins's simulation. The people in his quantputer went about their business without feeling, without any sense of tomorrow, being subject to Steve's team's supervision. Not a sparrow fell without proper computation.

An enviable state?

It was time to get to work again.

I called the advisers of Adminex to me. The date was the first day of Month Ten, 2071.

'Hello!' Dayo said, seeing me with my stick for the first time. 'What's happened to you?'

'The human condition,' I told him.

It was necessary to set about drawing up a constitution for our community. We needed to have the best possible way of life memorialised and, as far as might be, made clear to all.

The Adminex meeting was well attended. Clearly the external threat – if threat it was – from Chimborazo had served to excite our intelligence, if not to unite us. Only once before had so many people attended our forums, when Dreiser had addressed us. They gathered under the doomed Hindenburg and sat there quietly. By now, I thought with affection, I knew all of their faces and most of their names, these creatures of a human Olympus.

A late arrival at our discussion was Arnold Poulsen, who came by jo-jo car. It was a long while since I had seen him; he so rarely entered our forums. He sat now, his hands clasped between his knees, his long pale hair straggling about his face, saying nothing, contributing nothing but his presence.

Because I had been away I knew that things had moved on, and I anticipated argument and opposition. But even Feneloni seemed to have undergone a change of mind.

Speaking slowly, he said, 'I must put aside my reservations regarding your creation of a better and just society. I felt the wisdom of your judgement while I was shut away, and it seems to have had its bearing on my change of mind. While it's true I long to get back to Earth, that's no reason to create difficulties here. I can't exactly bring myself to back you, but I won't oppose you.'

301

We shook hands. Our listeners applauded briefly.

Crispin Barcunda was present with Belle Rivers. She was looking younger and dressing differently, although she still strung herself about with rock crystal beads. It was noticeable how affectionately she and Crispin regarded each other.

'Well, well, Tom Jefferies, you will turn us yet into a pack of coenobitic monks,' Crispin said, in his usual jocular fashion. 'But your declaration of utopia, or whatever you call it, must not be padded out with your prejudices. If you recall the passage I quoted, to the benefit of everyone, from the good Alfred Wallace's *Malay Archipelago*, he states that a natural sense of justice seems to be inherent in every man.

'That may not be quite the case. Perhaps it was stated merely in the fire of Victorian optimism – a fire that has long since burned itself out. However, Belle and I believe that a natural sense of religion is inherent in every man. Sometimes it's unrealised until trouble comes. Then people start believing all over again in the power of prayer.

'The little nondenominational church we set up has been well attended ever since we learned about Olympus – Chimborazo, I mean – and its movements.

'We are well aware that you are against religion and the concept of God. However, our teaching experience convinces us that religion is an evolutionary instinct, and should be allowed in your utopia – to which we are otherwise prepared to subscribe. We need you, as chief law-giver, to realise there must be laws that go against your wishes, as there will be some laws contrary to everyone's wishes. Otherwise there will be no reality, and the laws will fail.'

Belle now turned the power of her regard on me and reinforced what Crispin had said. 'Tom, our children need guidance on religion, as they do on sex and other matters. It's useless to deny something exists just because you don't like it, as we once denied there was life on Mars because it made us feel a bit safer. You have seen and heard the kids with their tammies – a nuisance to us maybe, but seemingly necessary to them. You must listen too to the squeaks of the godly.

'If we are to live rational lives, then we must accept that there are certain existential matters beyond our understanding – for the present at least, and maybe always and for ever.

'It is certainly no perversion to feel a reverence for life, for the miracle of it, for the world and for the universe. Doesn't the discovery of Chimborazo increase our wonder? Into such reverence the idea of God slips easily. Our minds are not quantputers. They work in contradictory ways at one and the same time. It's for this reason we sometimes seem at odds with ourselves.'

While listening intently I nevertheless noticed at this moment a fleeting smile on the face of Poulsen, who had sat motionless, not shifting his position, making no comment.

Belle was continuing. 'Those most vehement against established religion are often proved to be those most attracted to its comforts. We exist at the heart of a complexity for which any human laws we promulgate must seem flimsy, even transitory.

'There was a time when it was bold to take up an anti-religious stance. That time is past. Now we see that religion has played an integral role in our evolution. It has been a worldwide phenomenon for many centuries, and—'

At which point Dayo broke in, sawing the air with one hand, saying, 'Look, Missis Belle, slavery too was a worldwide phenomenon for many centuries. It still exists Downstairs! Millions of people were snatched from West Africa to serve the white races in the New World – twenty-five million people snatched from East Africa by Islamic traders in one century alone. I have the figures!

'Slavery isn't done away with yet. Always it's the rich and powerful against the poor and powerless! That doesn't mean to say we don't need to banish slavery – or religion. Or that these terrible things are good, just because they're old, does it? Antiquity is no excuse. We're trying to reform these horrible blemishes on existence.'

Dayo received a round of applause. A look of delight filled his face. He could not stop beaming.

Belle gave Dayo a nod and a tigerish smile, while seeming to continue her monologue uninterruptedly.

'Life for all generations, more particularly in the dim and distant past, has been filled with injustice, fear, injury, illness and death. God is a consolation, a mediator, a judge, a stern father, a supreme power, ordering what seems like disorder. For many, God – or the gods – are a daily necessity, an extra dimension.

'We like, in our Christian inheritance, to think that God made us in His image. It's more certain that we made Him in our image.

'And where does that image live? Beyond matrix, beyond time, beyond space-time. Was it intuition that dreamed up such a place, which scientists now believe might exist?'

'You make,' I replied, 'religion sound like a unitary matter. In its many sects, in fact, it has proved divisive throughout Earth's history, a perennial cause of war and bloodshed.'

'But we are creating Mars's history now,' said Crispin, smiling and allowing a glimpse of his gold tooth, while Belle, scowling radiantly, said, 'Tom, let me quote a phrase Oliver Cromwell once used: "I beseech you, in the bowels of Christ, think it possible you may be mistaken!"'

I let myself be persuaded by their eloquence. 'As long as you don't start sacrificing goats,' I said.

'Heavens,' Crispin said. 'Just show me a Martian goat!'

The discussion then turned to other subjects, on which agreement was reached with unique ease, and – with everyone's assistance – Adminex accordingly drew up and put on record our laws.

As Arnold Poulsen was about to depart as silently as he had come, I caught his sleeve and asked him what he made of the debate.

'Despite wide divergence of opinion, you were agreeable together, and so able to come to an agreeable conclusion. Did you not find that a little unexpected?' He brushed his hair back from his forehead and scrutinised me narrowly.

'Arnold, you are being oblique. What are you saying?'

'From my childhood,' he said, in his high voice, 'I recall a phrase expressing unanimity: "Their hearts beat as one". Perhaps you agree that seemed to be the state of affairs here just now. Even Feneloni was amenable to a point . . .'

'Supposing it to be so, what follows?'

He paused, clutching his mouth in a momentary gesture, as if to prevent what it would say. 'Tom, we have difficulties enough here, Upstairs. You have difficulties enough, trying to resolve the ambiguities of human conduct by sweet reason.'

'Well?'

Smiling, he sat down again and, with a gesture, invited me to sit by him as the hall was clearing. He then proceeded to remind me of the extract from Wallace's *Malay Archipelago* that Crispin Barcunda – 'very usefully', as Poulsen put it – had read to the company. Poulsen had thought about the passage for a long while. Why should a community of people, those islanders characterised by Wallace as 'savages', live freely without all the quarrels that afflicted the Western world? Without, indeed, the struggle for existence? Such utopianism could not be achieved by intellect and reason alone.

Was there an underlying physical reason for the unity of these so-called savages? Arnold said he had set his quantputer to analysing the known factors. Results indicated that the communities Wallace referred to were small, in size not unlike our stranded Martian community. It was not impossible to suppose – and here, he said, he had consulted the hospital authorities, including Mary Fangold – that one effect of isolation and proximity was that heartbeats synchronised, just as women sleeping in dormitories all menstruated at the same time of the month.

On Mars we presented a case of all hearts beating as one.

305

The result of which was an unconscious sense of unity, even unanimity.

Poulsen had established a small research group within the scientific community. Kathi had referred to it. To be brief, the group had decided that an oscillating wave of some kind might serve as a sort of drumbeat to assist synchronisation. In the end, adapting some of Mary Fangold's spare equipment, they had produced and broadcast a soundwave below audibility levels. That is to say, they had filled the domes with an infrasound drumbeat below a frequency of 16 hertz.

'You tried this experiment without consulting anyone?' I demanded.

'We consulted each other.' He spoke in the light, rather amused tone into which he frequently slipped. 'We knew there would be protests from the generality, as there always are when anything new is introduced.'

'But what was the result of your experiment?'

Arnold Poulsen laid a thin hand on my shoulder, saying, 'Oh, we've been running the beat for six days now. You saw the benevolent results in our discussion. All hearts beat as one. Science has delivered your utopia to you, Tom . . . The human mind has been set free.'

I didn't believe him. Nor did I argue with him.

Later, when I was lying with Mary, I told her of what Poulsen claimed to have done, for his pride in scientific ingenuity had irritated me. 'To claim that an oscillating wave brought about our utopia, instead of our own endeavours – why, you might as well claim that God did it . . .'

She was silent. Then she said, almost in a whisper, 'I don't want to sound unreasonable, but perhaps all those things conspired together . . .'

I kissed her lips: it was a better course than argument.

Further Memoir by Cang Hai

21

Utopia

Dear Tom has been dead now for twenty years. He died at the youthful age of sixty-seven. I zeep these words in what would be midway through 2102 by the old calendar.

A statue to Tom stands at the entrance of the Strangers Hall of Aeropolis in Amazonis Planitia. It depicts him in an absurdly triumphalist pose. I never saw him stand like that. Tom Jefferies was a modest man. He regarded himself as ordinary.

But perhaps the legend below his name is correct:

Prime Architect of Mars –
2015–2082
The Man Who Made Utopia Part of Our Real World.

Did Tom love me? I know he loved Mary Fangold. They never married. Marriage had gone out of fashion. But they were In Liaison as the new rationalism has it.

Do I miss him? Probably I do. I did not remain on Mars. In my old age I have decided to move further out, to lighter gravities.

My daughter Alpha went to seek out those Lushan Mountains I painted for her when she was a child. But I find I am an independent animal, as long as I retain contact with my Other. So our lives unfold.

On the occasion when Tom's just society was announced and its constitution read aloud, everyone was in a mood for rejoicing. We truly knew we had made a human advance.

Our proceedings, together with the celebrations that followed, were recorded as usual and, as usual, broadcast to Earth.

One incident of that day is vividly recalled. I had not seen my friends, Hal Kissorian and Sharon Singh, for some while – not, in fact, since their marriage – and longed for their company to make my happiness complete.

I rang their bell and was admitted. Both of them greeted me warmly. They were scantily dressed. As they embraced me, I smelt sweet and heavy odours about the room. We talked about all that was happening – or rather, I talked. I talked about Chimborazo and about the wonderful sense of social completeness we had managed to build. They regarded me with fixed smiles on their faces. I belatedly realised that the topics held little interest for them.

On the wall behind the sofa on which they sat was a hand-painted mural. I recognised a blue-skinned Krishna with his flute. Krishna was plump, his figure rather rounded in a girlish way, his eyes large and sparkling. Around him lounged pink ladies in diaphanous gowns, holding flower buds or tweaking one of the god's oily locks scarcely contained by his crown. They all gazed with lascivious approval at his immense mauve erection.

'Well, that enough of my affairs,' I said. 'What have you two been doing?'

Both Kissorian and Sharon burst into joyous laughter. 'Shall we show you?' asked Sharon.

I came away with that curious mixture of shame and envy that people of the mind feel for people of the flesh.

It was then I decided I was a solitary person. With a numb heart, it is easy to behave like a true utopian.

By the fifth year after the collapse of EUPACUS our society had settled on an even keel. All our various disciplines had taken root and were beginning to blossom. The Birth Room was a thriving institution. We had found room for diverse personalities to live together peacefully.

At that time, I visited the Birth Room frequently. I

miss it now such things do not exist. I went not only for companionship but to enjoy the transformation in women's personalities from their personae among men when they entered there. They became simpler and more direct, perhaps I should say unguarded, when they escaped from male regard.

Many were the arguments there about a possible return to Downstairs. By no means all women wanted it. Life Upstairs, although austere, was far less abrasive than it had been on Earth. Certainly child-rearing was easier, while the new generation of children seemed brighter and more companionable, despite their tammies.

Received wisdom was traded.

'Earth has decided to leave us here.'

'Let Downstairs get on with its affairs while we get on with ours.'

'They've forgotten all about us.'

Such remarks, often heard, were made with varying tones of optimism or gloom.

Olympus was moving steadily nearer. Observation showed, alarmingly, that its rate of progression was ever increasing. Various attempts to communicate with it failed. Willa and Vera, the mentatropists, had driven to the site, where they picked up a CPS, followed by a scrambled signal. The signal was intensively studied, but years passed before it was understood.

It was in that fifth year of our exile that Meteor Watch reported an object approaching Mars at a considerable velocity. Everyone was alarmed. But the speed of the object decreased. Eventually, a capsule shot from it, extruded a helichute, and landed a few kilometres north of the domes. An expedition set out immediately to investigate it.

The capsule bore a large symbol, TUIS, painted on its side. When transported into the domes and opened up, it was found to contain various medical supplies, scientific equipment, and a veritable store of foodstuffs, many of the names of which we had all but forgotten.

The supplies were accompanied by a plaque that read, 'With the Admiration of the Terrestrial Utopian International Society'. We wondered at the title, which indicated that the times were changing Downstairs.

Early in our sixth year, which is to say six terrestrial years on the calendar to which we clung, notching up days like Crusoe on his island, the outer rim of Chimborazo appeared over the horizon, to be clearly viewed from both domes and science unit. Its leading edge seemed now to be approaching at a rate that was hard to credit – at least 500 metres a day. It was easy to imagine its paddles beating furiously through the underlying regolith. However, the speed of movement did not represent the motion of Chimborazo as a whole. Chimborazo's scope encompassed more and more of the Martian surface, tumbling in our direction – a terrifying wave of regolith ploughed up before its prow.

Willa-Vera announced they would soon decode the signals they had recorded: Chimborazo's 'voice' fluctuated up and down the electromagnetic spectrum, and might be comprehended more as music than actual speech. They would have everything interpreted in a year or possibly two.

Their well-publicised conviction was that, after many centuries of meditation, this towering mentality – a mentality dwarfing Everest – had become a virtual god in wisdom. Once its mode of communication was understood, Chimborazo's immaterialism and transcendent qualities would set humankind upon a fresher and more vital path than could at present be visualised.

We would then move forward into 'an ultimate reality'.

I would certainly welcome a reality beyond my present day-to-day life . . .

It was six years and 100 Martian days since the economic collapse that had swept EUPACUS away, carrying the terrestrial infrastructure with it. A manned ship arrived within Mars matrix and went into orbit about the planet. The visitor appeared enormous, resembling, some said, St

Paul's Cathedral turned upside-down. We marvelled at it as if we were peasants.

Another age had dawned in the history of matrixflight. This strange object proved to be a ship powered by nuclear fusion. The epoch of wasteful chemical rockets was dead.

'What – what kind of rocket is that, for God's sake?' exclaimed a young YEA.

It was John Homer Bateson who replied, and even he sounded impressed, 'I would suggest that rockets are now as obsolete as the bathysphere.'

'What in hell is a bathysphere?' was the response.

A ferry floated down from this new marvel. Witnesses remarked that in the gentleness of its descent it was like a giant metal leaf. Our isolation was now ended . . .

Much jubilation broke out in the domes. Of a sudden, the prospect of green meadows, golden beaches and blue oceans became almost overwhelmingly desirable. We looked eagerly to see the faces of our rescuers from Downstairs.

Three unsmiling men confronted us. Marching into the domes, they announced that the Premier of the UK had taken over the assets of the failed EUPACUS consortium. They were the legal inheritors of all EUPACUS property. A EUPACUS ship had been stolen five years previously; its pilot, one Abel Feneloni, together with his accomplices on the ship, had been arrested. The ship was badly damaged when crash-landing in the north of Canada.

In his defence, continued the newcomers, Feneloni had claimed he was sent in the stolen ship under direct orders from the so-called government of Mars. A considerable stack of dollars was therefore owed by Mars to the government of the UK. Until this outstanding bill was paid, no free flights back to Earth were going to be allowed.

So we were quickly given the opportunity to relearn the value of money, and that some people lived by it.

Tom stepped forward. 'We do not use money here.'

'Then you do not use our ship.'

The three terrestrials were invited to a consultation

meeting. They refused, saying there was no necessity for consultation. All they required was settlement of an unpaid debt. They were clumsy in their spacesuits and we easily overpowered them.

To our disgust we found they wore guns under their suits. These were the first guns ever seen on Mars, our White Mars. We imprisoned them, took over their ship and signalled the UN on Earth.

We stressed that guns were not permitted on Mars; their importation therefore constituted an illegal act. Nor did we accept responsibility for the actions of Abel Feneloni; we regarded him as an outlaw. The UK had no entitlement to try and extract monies from us for Feneloni's crimes.

To ameliorate this confrontational tone, we declared that we possessed a discovery beyond price that, as utopians, we were prepared to share with everyone.

Clearly, much had changed on Earth during our absence. The United Koreas had become a great power, but were at odds with the UN – and with the rest of the planet. The response we received was favourable to us. The matter of the stolen ship remained to be resolved. Meanwhile our three captives had to be convinced that they were in the wrong and released, pending trial; and as many people as wished to return to Earth were immediately to embark on the waiting ship. They would be welcome Downstairs.

It was done. Many of our people crowded aboard the great orbiting ship – in particular, those who had children.

I wept when saying farewell to my friends.

I cannot tell here the histories of those who returned Downstairs. Some adjusted to the hectic heavy-gravity globe. Some became happy and settled. Some struggled in a world grown unfamiliar – and, of those, some prospered while others sank into failure.

Sharon Singh and Hal Kissorian parted company. Perhaps their involvement with each other had been too intense to endure. Kissorian became a great utopianist, and held a responsible position in government in Greater Scandinavia. Sharon Singh emigrated to Mercury and joined the FAD rebels in the Fighters Against Dictatorship struggle for Mercurian utopia.

The fact remains that when our Martians stepped out from the rescue ship into the dazzling draughty light of their mother planet, they were greeted like heroes. Receptions were held for them in many of the world's great cities. Several of them found themselves to be famous, their faces well known, even their speeches memorised.

Dreiser Hawkwood was the star of this select group. TUIS, the Terrestrial Utopian International Society, which had sent provisions to Mars, had gained power in several places, and in some countries had become the de facto government. They saw to it that Dreiser's achievements were widely recognised.

The explanation for this widespread acceptance was not far to seek. Leo Anstruther had become the founder of TUIS. Against the interdictions of many powers, his society had recorded all our transmissions from Mars and beamed them via satellite round the world. At that time, the world – humbled, uncertain – had been in the mood to listen, watch and learn.

Ramifications of the EUPACUS collapse had brought the capitalist system into disrepute and, in some cases, had demolished it entirely. The tentacles of corruption had reached out to involve famous figures in both East and West. Complex legal proceedings were still grinding through the law courts of California, Germany, China, Japan, Indonesia and elsewhere.

Climate, that unacknowledged legislator in the history of mankind, was a contributory cause of the marked change in political thinking. The overheating of the globe had brought hazardous weather and great oceanic turbulences. New York, London and Amsterdam, together with many another low-lying city, had been invaded by ocean. These cities were now practically deserted, crumbling under the force of the tides. Climatic change had ruined many an economy and revived others, the United Koreas among them.

Into this unsettled situation the possibility of building a free and just society had infiltrated. The example of the Martian exiles proved more attractive than we could have imagined.

Planet Earth, we found, was now largely a Han planet. Which is to say that modes of Chinese Pacific thought prevailed, as more confrontational Western modes of thought had dominated in the previous century.

Yearning for a better life had always been latent in society. Now came a renaissance. One of its effects was the establishment of Huochuans in many global centres. Huochuan was a Chinese word for cargo vessel; the name caught on for travelling institutes, which drifted from city to city with a freight of learning and wisdom. One whole section of a Huochuan was devoted to a huiyan, literally 'minds that perceive both past and future', now applied to life-story-storage systems.

As nationality came to play a less active role in human affairs, the concept of age-grouping, with activities suitable for each age, became predominant. Divisions such as YEAS and DOPS were influential in this shift in thinking. It proved to be the thirty-something group that received most benefit from Huochuan teaching.

Huochuans promoted a system of two-way communications. Those whose lives had taken a wrong turning could receive consultation and/or counselling. A method developed whereby long-bygone conversations could be recalled verbatim and improved. Anyone had opportunities to reconsider their lives and alter career or direction if insight demanded it.

In payment the beneficiary contributed to the huiyan by depositing a vid, document or disk, recording their inward and outward lives. In this way, the Huochuans accumulated a grand compendium of the experiences of generations in a kind of psychic genetic inheritance. For the first time in human history, attention was paid to the individual life – to all individual lives – 'this odd diversity of pain and joy', as an old folk song has it.

Such huiyan records served as a style of general entertainment/enlightenment (called tuokongs), much in the way of some serious TV programmes of the twentieth century.

With the proliferation of genetically altered vegetables and fruits, the eating of meat became a thing of the past in many regions. Domesticated animals became a rarity, although cats, dogs and songbirds were almost venerated, as were the semi-domesticated reindeer of far northern lands. Here and there, gates of zoo cages were flung open and their occupants set free.

People lived differently. They thought differently. Their cities were now contained; they kept in contact with one another by Ambient, much as ships at sea had once kept in touch by radio satellite. The old system of M-roads fell into decay. Beyond city walls, the wilderness was allowed to return. There, as on Mars, a degree of solitude could be enjoyed.

'The Utopians!' It became a magical word. While a percentage of those returning from Mars fell prey to terrestrial diseases, the virus of utopian thinking spread. I am told that, in the great hall of the Unified World (as the reconstituted United Nationalities is called) stands a row of bronze busts of those of us who made history. There in effigy is Dreiser Hawkwood, there is Tom Jefferies, of course, and Kathi Skadmoor and Arnold Poulsen. And I am there too!

If future generations enquire why I, my humble little self, should stand there with the great, there is a reason. For I it was who went out with Kathi and Dreiser to confront Chimborazo when it gave birth.

The inspiration to do this came to me in a waking dream from my earthly Other. I was walking somewhere in a kind of desert called Crapout – though how I knew its name I have no idea – with another person, maybe

315

male, maybe female, when a strange manifestation filled the sky.

It appeared like the cloud of an explosion, very alarmingly. I sheltered my companion in my arms, and was unafraid. A noise of trumpets sounded when, from the great threatening cloud, something beautiful appeared. I can't describe it. Not an angel, no. More like a – well, a winged octopus, a pretty winged octopus, trailing streamers. It seemed to glance down at me with much kindness, so that I woke crying.

I gathered my courage and called Kathi. She spoke to Dreiser. We suited up and went out on the surface. Chimborazo was immense; the furrow of regolith it ploughed before itself was close to the science unit. The Smudge ring was covered in a layer of grit.

Chimborazo towered over us, ridged and immeasurable. A fearful wind blew. I remember the date. It was the second day of Month One of the year 2072.

Then came the noise, a call of some kind, like bugles and cellos combined.

The three of us stood our ground. The mighty thing reared up. We had a glimpse of pronged exteroceptors and a kind of mucus curtain. From the curtain shot a pale stalk, perhaps like an elephant's trunk, withered in appearance, with a mouth and labia, moist, at its end. This strange protrusion penetrated the ring.

Again the trumpet note of triumph. I gripped Kathi's hand. Liquid surged. Dreiser said faintly, 'Amniotic fluid!'

The enormous creature seemed to back away and settle down. It became motionless.

On the churned regolith lay a thing resembling a small boulder. I went forward and lifted it with ease. It was comparatively light. As I carried it in my arms into the science unit, the thing began to open up.

After billions of years, Chimborazo had managed to reproduce itself, pumping both male and female cells into the receptive fluid . . .

*   *   *

316

So the great yearning for utopia spread on Earth. It brought about revolution first of all in Europe, that fertile ground of so many past upheavals. Was it Chimborazo's influence that made us unite as one, as never before? Be that as it may, we must believe we achieved utopia of our own volition. We must believe in free will and the strength of will.

Now my daughter Alpha lives far away from me, while I myself am even further from Earth than Mars is. She has a man and a child, so her life is fruitful and, I suppose, happy. I will never see her again, or embrace her, or kiss her little daughter.

At least it is a consolation to know she will enjoy the promises of what to me is the inaccessible future.

Note

By Beta Greenway, Daughter of Alpha Jefferies

I am a Jovian. I live a life of pattern. My actions are premeditated. I am pleased to contribute to this report.

Since the Jovian moons carried little or no emotional freight for human beings, they were not treated with the scruples Mars had once enjoyed.

Monitor probes, accompanied by a freighter, arrived by the turn of the century at what Galileo Galilei originally termed 'the Medician stars', our four sizeable moons. A base was established on Ganymede while the other satellites, in particular Io and Europa, were surveyed by machinonauts.

Ganymede was made habitable by bioengineered plant-insect stock. These ephemeral life forms had been despatched in unmanned probes, to soft-land here and prepare it for human life. They clothed it in their corpses before we arrived. Such advances were not possible in the early days of Mars landings.

Our first ugly prefabricated buildings have long since been devoured and regurgitated to form our spinlifters.

Life is pleasant here. I find much scientific research to keep me occupied, and am compiling an Amb entitled *Pluto As an Abode of Life*. Although the sun is distant, we enjoy the brilliant spectacle of Jupiter in our skies, together with the swarming variety of other moons to inspire us and tempt our thoughts ever outwards, into further and better transformations of human life.

The quest for knowledge continues.

Indeed, such work continues beyond the solar system, beyond the Oort Cloud. There, beneath the light of stars, a Cheeth-Rosewall is coming into operation. This Chheeth-Rosewall is immeasurably larger than the failed miniature HIGMO detector constructed on Mars a century ago.

The ring has a diameter of about the same extent as one of Saturn's outer rings, with a cross-section of just a few millimetres. The volume of superfluid is therefore not too large. However, we expect to detect a HIGMO at last.

HIGMO density is a good deal less than anticipated. However, the research has acquired vital importance: as generally agreed, it will yield important truths about the nature of *consciousness* – as well as solving the riddle of mass.

Once we can control these things, we shall be able to project our minds across the universe. And what we shall there encounter, who can say?

I have no communication with the person who was my mother. She lives on Iapetus, out by Saturn. But I will zeep this note to her for her mother's record of ancient times. Frankly, the thought of womb-birth amuses me. How clumsy and inefficient it was, and how inconvenient for womankind! We do not have families.

Our Jovian generations are now all of extra-uterine extraction, apart from the subbermans. E-u techniques have enabled us to combine pseuplant life into our genes; when our lungs breathe out, our foliagics breathe in; what the foliagics emit, we breathe in.

Thus we are almost entirely independent of atmosphere suits for long periods. We are a mathematical people. By the end of their first year, infants can calculate the orbits of most matrix bodies we observe orbiting about us.

Having trained Chimborazo to spawn, we now have small Chimbos with us everywhere. We benefit from their acute diagnostic powers. Indeed, it can be claimed that human and Chimbos form a symbiotic species.

Together, we and Chimbos are planning to voyage out into the universe, far beyond the heliopause. We hope to call it to account. Because we are utopians, we can do this. One can proudly say that the human race, risen from lowly and irrational forms, with a mind, in Darwin's words, once as low as that of the lowest animal, has at last become REASONABLE.

Appendix by Dr Laurence Lustgarten

The United Nationalities Charter for the Settlement of Mars

The peoples of the Earth, represented through the United Nationalities, do hereby make provision for the human settlement of our sister planet, Mars, consistent with respect for its equal status with the nations of Earth within the solar system.

The United Nationalities, recognising the fragility of the Martian environment and acutely conscious of our present ignorance of the capability of its ecosystem to sustain physical incursion and change, hereby agrees:

Art. I: All nations comprising the United Nationalities do individually and collectively disclaim any territorial rights of ownership or control over any portion of the planet Mars or its airspace. Equally they bind themselves to reject any such claims that may in future be asserted by any political entity on the planet Earth.

Art. II: Mars shall be governed by the United Nationalities as a trusteeship, held in trust for the entire population of Earth. It shall be treated as a single entity, and never sub-divided and subject to different regimes. The environment of Mars shall be regarded as sacrosanct; any large-scale projects that threaten its individual character shall be prohibited, at least until such time as the entire globe has been scientifically explored and studied.

Art. III: In light of the severe limitations on its ability to sustain the intrusion of an alien civilisation, human settlement of Mars shall be strictly limited in numbers and subject to qualifications by the United Nationalities. While it is accepted that member states may select exclusively their own nationals for their share of any settlement quota, they shall observe the principles of non-discrimination on grounds of race, colour, sex and religious or political opinion in their selection.

Art. IV: All questions of economic or other relations with the settlement established on Mars shall be conducted with the delegates of the United Nationalities, who shall be ever mindful of their trusteeship obligations.

Art.V: Mars shall be used for peaceful purposes only. All activities of a military nature, such as the establishment of bases or fortifications, or the testing of any type of weapons, are absolutely prohibited. Serious scientific projects that find the Martian environment advantageous to their researches are not prohibited.

Art VI: The disposal of waste products generated on Earth, of any kind, is absolutely prohibited. The exiling of criminal elements from Earth to Mars is also prohibited.

Art. VII: The United Nationalities shall appoint observers whose function is to ensure compliance with the foregoing provisions. The observers shall enjoy full freedom of access at all times to any installation or structure established on Mars.

How It All Began

APIUM: Association for the Protection and Integrity of an Unspoilt Mars

Plans are already afoot to send human beings to Mars. Behind these exciting possibilities lies a less worthy objective: an assumption that the Red Planet can be turned into something resembling a colony, an inferior Earth. This operation would extend prevailing dystopian tendencies into the next century.

Planets are environments with their own integrity. Any vast engineering schemes would be invasive. The end result could only be to turn Mars into a dreary suburb, imitating the less attractive features of terrestrial cities. A military-industrial complex would probably rule over it.

APIUM stands for humanity's right to walk on Mars, and is against its rape and ruination. Mars must become a UN protectorate, and be treated as a 'planet for science', much as the Antarctic has been preserved – at least to a great extent – as unspoilt white wilderness. We are for a WHITE MARS!

Mars should remain as a kind of Ayers Rock in the sky. It must be made visitable to ordinary men and women (the travel costs to be met by community service at home). Its solitudes will be preserved for silence and meditation and honeymooning. From Mars, traditionally the God of War, a myth of peace will spread back to Earth, supplanting the myth of energy/power/exploitation that has so darkened the twentieth century.

APIUM believes that great good will come to both planets if we have the courage to sustain a WHITE MARS.

Brian W. Aldiss
President, APIUM
Pamphlet distributed January 1997
Green College, Oxford, England

323